The
Streets of Winter

The
Streets of Winter

Stephen Henighan

thistledown press

National Library of Canada Cataloguing in Publication

Henighan, Stephen, 1960–
The streets of winter / Stephen Henighan.

ISBN 1-894345-76-2

I. Title.

PS8565.E5818S87 2004 C813'.54 C2004-900130-2

Cover photograph by Al Francekevich/CORBIS/MagmaPhoto.com
Cover and book design by J. Forrie
Typeset by Thistledown Press

Thistledown Press Ltd.
633 Main Street
Saskatoon, Saskatchewan, S7H 0J8
www.thistledown.sk.ca

Thistledown Press gratefully acknowledges the financial assistance of the Canada Council for the Arts, the Saskatchewan Arts Board, and the Government of Canada through the Book Publishing Industry Development Program for its publishing program.

The
Streets of Winter

There are as many moralities as there are relationships; there is not even such a thing as a city, only changing settings for self-preserving compulsions. But if I myself am the intersecting point of labyrinthine human relationships, this city is a far larger maze . . . I can easily match the city's dense networks with my own.

—George Konrád: *The City-Builder*

Rien ne saurait être plus différent de moi, que moi-même.
[Nothing could be more different from me than myself.]
—André Gide: *Les faux-monnayeurs*

The Basement (1)

THE VOICES OF THE CITY FRIGHTENED HIM. In the village his father came around with money and food when he had it, or the fathers of his brothers and sisters came around, and on days when the fathers failed to come his uncle and auntie lived just down the road. Here, when he fought with the bastard who had moved in with his mother, there was nowhere to go.

He had to get inside. If the beasts saw him ambling down Sherbrooke Street, they'd hassle for him for sure. The last time he'd been out this late, old Beauchamp had clubbed him with his baton. I know your game, Rollie, he said, and next time I'll bust you.

He stuck close to the sides of the buildings. He was beginning to give up on finding a place when, a couple of blocks shy of Westmount, he pulled on the front door of a three-storey brick apartment building and felt it open. Inside he found a dark corridor tiled with glinting marble. He followed the corridor to the back of the ground floor, where broad steps led down into the basement. It was dank and cold down there, but the brick walls insulated him from the sounds of the traffic. He snuggled into a corner, zipped his jacket up to his neck and murmured to himself in his auntie's patois.

When he woke in the morning, a huge old white man with bristly crewcut hair stood gazing at him, one big hand resting on the banister of the staircase.

One

Marcel-Teddy-André-Marcel

HE WAS AN ACCOUNTANT, HE WAS THIRTY YEARS OLD; NO ONE WAS going to treat him like a delivery boy. He lingered in the outer office, fixing himself a second coffee. Abitbol yelled at him to get moving. Marcel picked up the contract, went down the stairs to the parking lot and climbed into his Honda.

He cut through the shaded avenues, turned onto Côte Ste-Catherine and rode the contour-line of the street around the back of the Mountain to the Rubinsteins' office in Côte St-Luc. He hated driving through Outremont. Yesterday he had made a sharp left turn to avoid their old street.

It had taken them barely six months to fall behind on the mortgage. The high interest rates doomed them. In the end he let Abitbol buy him out. Now they lived in an assembly-line duplex, which they rented from Abitbol, just off the Laurentian Autoroute in Ville St-Laurent. The front door was too narrow to admit Maryse's oak wardrobe. The large windows looked out on other, identical bungalows. Maryse packed her art collection in cardboard containers in a spare room of her parents' Outremont home. She gave out her telephone number but met her girlfriends in cafés on Avenue Bernard or Rue St-Denis. Two weeks after the move Marcel was unfaithful to her for the first time since their wedding: an hour of hurried, clawing sex with a nineteen-year-old waitress from Chicoutimi. Pleading a cold, he wore a T-shirt to bed for the next two nights.

He parked in front of the Rubinsteins' office. When the deal closed, in two days' time, he would return to this office to witness Abitbol's signature. The thought of someone else being bought out by his brother-in-law made him climb the stairs with triumphant rage. For years he had planned to re-take his chartered accountancy exams and move on to a job in a company where he would be his own man. How far away those memories seemed!

He opened the office door without knocking and found Ruthie sitting at a bare desk. The old farts had gone out for coffee. "They could be gone for hours," she said.

"I'll wait." Marcel sat down. "My instructions are to deliver the contract to the two Mr. Rubinsteins personally."

Ruthie looked at him over the fat paperback she was pinching between soft, beringed fingers. She shook her spray of curly hair and shut her book. "You work for Mr. Abitbol?"

Marcel straightened his back. "I am his partner."

"Then how come he gives you instructions?" she asked, teasing a curl in the crook of a long white finger.

"The instructions don't come from Abitbol. They come from a law that says some contracts must be delivered in person."

"I'm going to be a lawyer."

She was staring him in the eyes. "Oh yes?" he said. "Which law school do you study at?"

"That's the problem." She twisted a ring. "I could do it at McGill. That's where I did my B.A. But if I go to McGill I'll probably stay in Quebec and then I have to work in *French*."

"I speak French."

"You're lucky." She shrugged her shoulders.

"I mean French is my first language. I only learned English because I went to an English school."

"No way! But you're supposed to be Jewish. My great-uncles said they were selling to a Jewish family."

"We are Jewish but we speak French."

"Oh, you're Sephardic. Well, that's still Jewish, I guess . . . " She looked down to open a drawer and slide her paperback inside. "For a moment I thought you were French-Canadian. French Canadians really bug me. I don't know what it is about them."

My wife is French-Canadian. He remained silent, studying the girl's face. Ruthie wore a bright blue blouse with padded shoulders; he could make out the layer of foundation covering her cheeks. He wondered why, locked away all day in this vault of an office, she bothered to make herself up.

Her levity fading, she said that the smart choice would be for her to attend law school in Ontario, pass the bar there and settle in Toronto. Most of her McGill friends had taken "the one-way ticket down the 401" to Toronto as soon as they had graduated. But she couldn't leave; her family had lived in Montreal since her grandparents had got off the boat from the *shtetl.*

"It can be difficult to leave your family," he said. The dust motes floating in the air enveloped them in a speckled cloud that silenced conversation. Ruthie folded her hands on the desk in a way that covered her rings.

He tried to meet her eyes, but found his glance veering away in the direction of a photograph of one of the old farts, decades ago, in the company of a woman with dark curls.

"So those are all my terrible problems." Ruthie laughed. "But my real problem is this job. It sounded perfect when my dad told me about it: I could take a year off, help my great-uncles sell up and retire to Florida, get some work experience and figure out what I wanted to do with my life. I thought I'd spend the whole year partying."

"And it hasn't been like that?"

"No." Her bright eyes speared him. Was he pursuing or being pursued? The telephone rang. As she turned to answer it, the fabric of her blouse snagged in a horizontal crease across her right breast.

He caught her wrist. "Tomorrow night you must have dinner with me."

The phone rang again. She struggled until an unruly smile broke over her face. "Okay, bully, you win."

He released his grip and allowed her to answer the phone.

CR CR CR

Over the phone they told him to look for a three-storey brick building on the north side of Sherbrooke Street. He spotted it right away, dominating the corner where a sidestreet rolled downhill from between the leaf-buffered townhouses higher up the slope. Two small balconies, barely large enough to accommodate a deck chair each, poked out from the third floor. Below each balcony was an entrance fronted by grey concrete steps. The entrances housed heavy oak-framed double doors fitted with translucent glass panels. Inscribed in eroded copper script on the lozenge of glass above the door nearest the corner were the words *The Victoria*; the second door was *The Waterloo*.

Teddy crossed the street, opened the Waterloo door and followed the long hall into the building. The apartment was at the back of the ground floor, next to the staircase that twined up to the second floor and down into the basement. The floors were parquet, the twelve-foot ceilings were supported by pillars of stripped, varnished wood, the mantlepiece of the boarded-up fireplace flared towards the ceiling in whitewashed curlicues. The apartment was huge; the rent was a pittance. The students, pleased that he liked it, led him back out onto Sherbrooke Street and into the Victoria side of the building. They knocked on the door of a ground-floor apartment, stepped inside and said: "This is our new tenant. We can move out now, eh?"

A huge dull-eyed man in his sixties offered Teddy a leaden hand to shake. The concierge wore a white tank-topped T-shirt; he had a moth-eaten grey crewcut. Spikes of silver stubble glinted in the warthog folds of his jowls. "Pleased to meet you."

"No kids. No more students," a peeved voice said.

Teddy saw two balding men in their seventies seated at a table in the middle of the room. Tongues of white hair framed the men's small ears. They peered at him through thick-lensed glasses. The old man on the right glared at the students from beneath heavy brows. "You don't move out until you find someone responsible."

"Are you implying that I'm not responsible?" Teddy took a step forward.

The old men looked nonplussed. "Buddy," the man on the right said, "you got a job? For me, responsible is a guy with a job."

"This lad's okay," the concierge said. "I can tell a good lad from a bad one. You've been a cadet, eh?"

"Jesus," Teddy said, "can't you tell the difference between a punk haircut and a crewcut?"

"You can trust a cadet to keep his quarters clean and pay on time."

"Joe," the old man on the right said, "if you don't learn to say no, this building's gonna go to hell. Every shiftless nigger in N.D.G. will move in here."

"He's too young," the old man on the left said, his head bobbing. "No more students. No young punks."

"That's not fair, Mr. Rubinstein!" one of the students said. "We always pay on time."

"I don't know your case. If you're like most of them, you spend your money on drugs and girls."

"I don't spend my money on drugs and girls," Teddy said. "I have money right here." He took out his wallet and peeled off three-hundred-fifty dollars. "First month's rent," he said, setting the money on the table in front of the two Mr. Rubinsteins.

"Yeah?" the Mr. Rubinstein on the right said. "And where's the second month gonna come from?"

"My family has been in Canada for more than two centuries," Teddy said, "and nobody has ever defaulted on his rent." He took a step forward across the parquet floor into a hostile silence. "The second month's rent comes from here." He unzipped the pocket of the leather jacket that clutched his shoulders and failed to reach to his waist. He counted off a pile of fifty-dollar bills. "Let's make it second month's and third month's rent together, okay?"

"What part of town are you from, lad?" Joe asked.

"I'm not from Montreal. I'm from Ottawa. But I've been down in the States for a few years. I decided it was time to come home."

"What part of Ottawa are you from?" the righthand Mr. Rubinstein asked.

"Rockcliffe. Have you heard of it?"

"I heard of it."

As the two Mr. Rubinsteins stared at the money, Teddy wondered if he had gone too far. He was surprised by his own qualms. He didn't usually care if he offended people. The tightness in his shoulders increased. He longed to shrug off the leather jacket. "You've got three months' rent. There's more where that came from. What else would you like?"

"Okay, Joe," the righthand Mr. Rubinstein said. "You can give this guy a lease."

෬ ෬ ෬

Maman and Papa, railing at him for not returning to live in Ville Lasalle after months in a foreign country, had detained André for most of the afternoon, and now he was late. He entered Parc Lafontaine to find the demonstrators already gathering. All the way from Angrignon, observing the dark-skinned foreigners thronging the Métro platforms, he had felt that Montreal was no longer his. His city had abandoned him. And his body had betrayed him. At thirty-nine, after months of French food, the weight on his hips had spilled forward to ring his stomach in a paunch. His hair had receded in front on the right and the left, marooning one maddeningly flimsy strand, like a strip from a shredded pennant, in the middle of his forehead. He had grown a beard to offset his receding hairline; it had emerged tainted with grey.

Stepping out of the Métro at the Mont-Royal station, he had passed the crowd lining up at the automatic teller of the Caisse Populaire Desjardins, the garish Jean-Coutu pharmacy, the forbidding block-long stone façade of Notre-Dame-du-Très-Saint-Sacrement. He wished he could show the bored, insolent Parisians the unique institutions his people had built. Perhaps that would rock their complacent condescension. How he had hated being a foreigner! After a few weeks in Paris he had been longing to reimmerse himself in the intuitive rush of Québécois history. 1988! It was hard to believe that the 1960s and 1970s were over, that Félix Leclerc and René Lévesque, his homeland's poetry and its politics, were dead. Lévesque had died shortly after André's arrival in France, Leclerc just before his return. He had stared at their photographs on the cover of *Paris Match*. Pacing the alleys of St-Germain-des-Prés, he had pined for the ramparts of Quebec City. He had longed for Raymond and Lysiane and Marie-Christine, wishing they could talk for hours, as they had in the old days, with a case of Labatt's Blue, a twist of pot and a Beau Dommage LP on the stereo.

Yet coming back to Montreal, he found himself changed. He had decided not to phone François; this gave him time alone to think. Paris had been his first experience of a city where French was the only language, its dominance unquestioned. The precariousness of Quebec's French face leapt out at him upon his return, the constant intrusion of English demoralizing him as never before. He had raged against this colonization since his teens, but now, for the first time, he wondered whether French could survive in Quebec. The shock had brought him back out onto the street, drawing him to this demonstration at a time when he had thought his preoccupations were turning inward. Bill 101, the safeguard of his language, was being challenged before the Supreme Court of Canada. The Anglos wanted to make it illegal for Quebec to protect its culture. As fed-up and introverted as he felt, he could not sit still for that.

The protesters in the park were handing out signs. He took a long-handled placard on which *LA LOI 101 C'EST TOI ET MOI* was stencilled in blue letters on white bristol board. In private André was shy; it had taken him years to get used to teaching, to learn to deflect the scorn of teenagers. But swathed in a crowd or family he could overcome any inhibition. Twenty years ago, in this same park, he had hurled Pepsi Cola bottles at the reviewing stand where the Outremont snob Pierre Elliott Trudeau had surveyed the St-Jean-Baptiste Day festivities. The other dignitaries on the platform had dived for cover at the first smack of shattering glass, but Trudeau's chipped, mongrel features had stared out over the mob in unflinching hatred. Once Raymond had thrown the first bottle, André felt a barrier crumble inside him. He reached forward, picked up a Pepsi bottle and threw it. The air sang with glass. The police charged, their truncheons thrashing. He saw Raymond's slight figure collapse between two beefy cops. Raymond caught himself and struggled to his feet. The truncheons brought him down again. Blood gummed his long black hair; his tie curled over the shoulder of his jacket. André gripped another bottle and hurled with all his might. He saw a dignitary in a baggy suit drop to his knees and crawl towards the edge of the platform. Two cops bore down on him. He twisted away, shoving through the screaming crowd. He had lost sight of Lysiane. Marie-Christine, backed up against the trunk of a tree, was pushing her splay-fingered hand into a cop's gaunt face. A second cop grabbed her long hair and slugged her on the shoulder with his truncheon. The barricades set up to hold back the crowd toppled over. The crack of snapping boards cut through the confusion of screams and insults and tinkling fragments of glass. He cocked his final bottle. A cop tackled him around the legs. The world swung downwards as he threw. His last glimpse of the reviewing stand, before the tarmac wheeled up and smacked him in the teeth, was of Trudeau's angry, inscrutable glare defying the bottles to strike him. The next day Trudeau was elected Prime Minister of Canada. His sour, unQuébécois features and chanting monk's voice haunted every television screen for the next sixteen years. Betraying his own race, he swindled Quebec out of its independence. André could not help thinking, each time that face materialized before him, that had he aimed his final Pepsi bottle with greater care, history might have been different.

ଔ ଔ ଔ

Slowing the Honda to a crawl near the street corner in Côte St-Luc, he wondered whether he would recognize her. He pulled in against the curb, remembering the night he and his brother-in-law had got drunk together, one of the rare moments when Abitbol had relaxed his authority. They had talked about women. Abitbol, nineteen years his senior and married to Marcel's sister Véronique, had approached the topic with rheumy nostalgia. Women were creatures of his youth, ornaments of his first hard, adventurous years in Montreal.

—I like women with big tits, Marcel said, hoping to provoke an indiscretion.

—You only care about material things! Abitbol said. —Making love to a woman is an immersion in spirituality. It's not just conquest.—

But Abitbol was far from indifferent to conquest. Having arrived in Canada as a young hairdresser, he had turned himself into a property developer. Marcel had never mastered all the details of his rise—although he recalled the later stages and had been reared on exemplary, half-mythologized anecdotes that Abitbol dished out to encourage or intimidate him—yet he knew that if Abitbol had remained a faithful husband it was not because he had disdained the urge for conquest. That was a need he and Abitbol shared.

He spotted Ruthie waving at him from a bus stop shelter. She looked leggy and wide-hipped in a very short pleated skirt. As she slid into the front passenger seat, he became aware of a penetrating scent. The fact of her having perfumed herself excited him. "Is it all right if we eat in the Plateau?" he asked, swinging the Honda through a U-turn.

"Where's that?"

Marcel squeezed the brakes. "You don't know where the Plateau Mont-Royal is? How long have you lived in Montreal?"

"All my life. Now stop being mean to me."

He tried to imagine Maryse's reaction to such a profession of ignorance: it would confirm all her most ferocious allegations of Anglo boorishness.

When he had begun to go out with other women, he had trained himself to banish Maryse from his mind. One disastrous evening her presence had grown so overwhelming that he had been unable to get an erection with a hotel receptionist he had met in a bar on Rue Crescent. The humiliation had scared him away from other women for months. With the next woman guilt was no longer a problem. It was a stage he had overcome. Maryse hung on the periphery of his consciousness, benign and innocuous as an icon of a religion to which he still belonged without continuing to practise it. He was Maryse's husband in the same way that he was a Jew: he felt a passionate devotion to the basic tenets of his commitment, but his secular existence had become so cluttered that he no longer complied with all rituals of his faith. Driving down the divided four-lane Boulevard St-Joseph, the stone faces of the large old houses frowning down from either side with the solemnity of carven bishops, he thought of Maryse busying herself with her evening activities: flipping through an art dealer's catalogue, chatting with her *copines* on the telephone, catching up on episodes of one of the three *téléromans* that she videotaped. The vision filled him with warmth. As he turned the Honda onto Rue St-Denis, he reached across and touched Ruthie's elbow. "Here. We are in the Plateau."

"Oh," she said. "The French Part. I've been here before. I didn't know it was anything special." Marcel followed her gaze as it combed over wrought-iron spiral staircases, crowded sidewalks, limestone walk-ups whose ground floors had been converted into shiny boutiques. "This place used to be a dump," she said. "My grandparents lived around here when they were penniless immigrants . . . " She stretched her long legs. "Has Mr. Abitbol bought out people here, too?"

He was unable to reply. He parked in a narrow sidestreet, bought a bottle of Italian white wine in a Haitian *dépanneur* and led Ruthie to a small Vietnamese restaurant. She ordered in English. The waiter, a gaunt Vietnamese youth, responded in French; Marcel translated. "You don't speak French?" he asked, as they sipped their wine.

"I took French in school. I don't see why I have to speak it when I go out. I mean, I grew up here."

She talked about her great-uncles. The two old men had been born in Kiev and brought to Montreal as children. They had started their careers working in their father's scrapyard. As adults they had bought a delicatessen on Boulevard St-Laurent ("St. Lawrence," Ruthie called it). For a few years, after marrying and having their families, the brothers had gone their separate ways. In middle age, both widowed, they had begun to work together again, pooling their holdings in a single company. Over seventy now, they had despaired of their children moving home to Montreal and decided to sell everything, buy a house in Florida and funnel the bulk of their savings to their descendants, now scattered through suburban

Toronto, before the sum could be eroded by death duties and inheritance tax.

"They're incredible guys," Ruthie said. "They speak so many languages—Russian and Ukrainian and Yiddish and German and English—"

"Everything except French," Marcel said. "Every language except the language of the city where they live."

"You didn't have to speak French when they came here." She swallowed a mouthful of wine. "Anyway it's sad. I always thought my cousins would take over the business . . . Are you going to be there tomorrow when they sign the contract?"

Marcel nodded. "I'm witnessing Abitbol's signature."

She asked for a fill-up. He poured her a few drops of wine; she motioned to him to continue pouring. In spite of himself, he felt a twinge of guilt. His other flings had been with Québécois or immigrant women: Ruthie was his first Jew. He had known few Ashkenazis. He thought of them as arrogant and frivolous: they did not take their religion as seriously as they should. Véronique and Abitbol might criticize him for his slipshod observance of the *Chabat*, yet when he stared into Ruthie's eyes he felt assailed by religious qualms. Was it right to act this way with a Jewish girl? Rather than trying to seduce her, shouldn't he be persuading her to settle down with a nice Jewish boy? Or—the thought jabbed him—did she take him for the Jewish boy with whom she might settle down?

She brushed her fingers across his hip as they stepped onto the street. He leaned over her, his hand hovering close to her body. A red light stopped them at the corner. Ruthie teetered slowly backwards until he had no choice but to enclose her in his arms. Her laughing, long-limbed weight shivered against him without dispelling his misgivings. "Drive me somewhere," she whispered.

"Where?"

"I don't know. Wherever you usually drive girls."

The four lanes of traffic roared past them through the taillight-pricked blackness. The cafés had set out their sidewalk tables. The spring's first influx of idlers had taken possession of Rue St-Denis: thin students with black clothes, white faces and short dark hair, greying hirsute bohemians, women sporting scarves and extravagant leather handbags. He spotted two women who reminded him of Maryse's Outremont girlfriends. "Let's go," he said, curling his arm around Ruthie's waist.

"You're in a hurry." Ruthie stretched, aimed a kiss at his face and landed it on his throat. "And you're tall."

He kissed her on the cheek and bundled her into the Honda. As he sat down behind the steering wheel, he kissed her mouth. Ruthie broke away, toyed with the radio and regarded him with an off-kilter smile. "So where are we going?"

"A chalet in the Laurentians. It's not far."

"It's yours?"

He manoeuvred along the narrow streets where the stone triplexes stood in unbroken walls, each one soldered to its neighbours. "Mine and Abitbol's."

"But you don't live there? It's just where you take girls when you want to fool around?"

"Abitbol doesn't fool around. He's a very religious man."

"What about you? Are you religious?"

"What the hell are you trying to do, Ruthie?" He heard a thickness in his voice: the shadow of a French accent that invaded his English in moments of strong emotion. The failing gnawed at him, compounding his anger.

"You're buying out my family," Ruthie said. "I want to know who you are. My great-uncles said you were Jewish, but you're not like us. You're really different—"

Marcel drove along the elevated highway, concentrating on the sliding pattern of red taillight blips fleeing before his low beams. He turned north off the Metropolitan, cruising onto the Laurentian Autoroute. Five minutes later, as the highway curved past the nook of Ville St-Laurent where he and Maryse were living, he could not prevent himself from glancing out the window into the darkness.

"Look," Ruthie said. "I know you're married."

He braked the Honda. "Why don't I just drive you home?"

"No, I'm thrilled. You're my first married man. This is part of my education!" Her words tumbled out so quickly that he couldn't tell whether she was eager or upset. "Please," she said, touching his shoulder. "I want to see your chalet. But could you answer one question for me? One tiny little question? You promise not to get mad?"

He grunted a promise.

"What do you tell your wife on the nights you don't come home?"

He gripped the steering wheel, cursing himself as a fool. "Abitbol owns two apartment buildings in Lennoxville. I go out there every month to collect the rent. Sometimes I make trips to supervise repairs and maintenance. Or, if there is a difficult tenant, I negotiate with him. Sometimes I stay overnight."

"So that's what we're doing! Negotiating!" Her fingers rattled the cassette collection in the plastic box between the front seats. She put on a Peter Gabriel album and mouthed the words of the song under her breath. Her fingers spider-walked down the front of his shirt. He intercepted her as she reached his navel.

"Spoilsport." She turned down the volume on the stereo. "Does your wife know about the others . . . about *us*? She must, eh. Women know these things."

"I don't know what women know."

"Aren't you afraid she'll leave you?"

He felt her staring at him. He looked straight ahead over the steering wheel. "No. We both risked a lot when we got married. We can't go back on it. And—"

"And you don't throw it in her face so she can keep pretending everything's okay . . . I know the type. It's sicko when people live that way."

"That is how we choose to live. It is best for us both." The highway was beginning to climb. A knot of tension had bunched in Marcel's stomach. His other women had been poor and dazzled by his wallet full of hundred-dollar bills; two had been immigrants who had never seen the Laurentians; with all of them he had spoken French. He had realized too late that in English he would remain at a disadvantage to a brash, self-confident girl like Ruthie. In French he could dispatch a feeling with a single well-turned phrase. English did not permit such elegant summations: emotions were hauled out and worried at like lumps of impure meat. Ruthie was not the first of his women to guess that he was married; but none of the others had used that fact to make him feel inferior to her.

He guided the Honda down the exit ramp. The cassette ended. Neither of them spoke as he drove through the small Laurentian village and up the hill into the trees. The chalet stood on a rocky spur. A grove of spruce and poplar insulated the one-acre lot. They climbed out of the car and picked their way across the damp grass. Crickets trilled in the bushes.

Ruthie shivered. "If you'd told me we were going up north I would have worn slacks." Her voice sounded small in the high, chill silence of the hills. The unwanted rush of fraternal protectiveness returned.

He unlocked the front door and snapped on the lights. "This is really nice!" Ruthie said. He watched her gaze riding the polished grain of the woodwork. He felt relieved, vindicated, relaxed—yet not at all sexy. One more barbed query would finish him as a lover. He snared Ruthie's wrist, pulling her away from the well-stocked bar. "What do you want?" she said.

What, what? If only he knew! He smothered the question by gripping her in his arms.

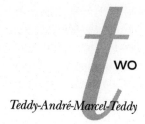

two

Teddy-André-Marcel-Teddy

THE RECEPTIONIST LED HIM DOWN A CARPETED CORRIDOR WHERE polished doors lined the woodstain-coloured walls. The doors hung ajar; each glimpse into an office revealed a man in a blue suit sitting at a desk. They entered the barren room at the end of the corridor. The white-tiled floor and bare cinder-block walls amplified the din of half a dozen young men sorting manila envelopes and tossing them into shopping carts. The foreman sat in a tiny office in the back.

He looked sixty, with slack grey cheeks and streaky black-grey hair. The small office had compressed his square body. He wore an ancient Timex wristwatch of the kind Teddy had received as a present on his sixth birthday. He left Teddy's extended hand hanging in the air. "What part of town you from, Teddy?"

"I'm from Ottawa—"

"That godawful boring place! I was there in 1955." He glanced at a file embossed with the logo of the employment agency that had set up the interview. "So where are you living in Montreal?"

"On Sherbrooke Street in Notre-Dame-de-Grâce."

"You're from N.D.G.? You know you need to be bilingual for this job."

—A great emphasis was being placed on bilingualism when I was growing up in Ottawa in the 1970s.— As soon as he began to speak, Teddy could see the grating effect his "international" French was having on the man.

—*Tu parles comme un livre.* Who'd you take yourself for?— The foreman shrugged out a grunt. "Even if you are bilingual I can't hire you. An M.A. in political science—Jesus Christ, you should be one of those guys wearing suits down the hall there!"

"I've applied for jobs like—"

"And you haven't been able to place yourself? You got a problem?" He closed the file with his square hands. "It was totally stupid of the agency to send you here. I'm gonna give that gal hell. I know guys like you. You'll stay two weeks, then you'll go to some suit job because you think you look more debonair carrying a goddamn briefcase."

"You don't know guys like me!" Teddy said, as he stamped out of the office.

Since he had returned to Canada, everyone felt they knew him; everyone slotted him into a category. He was a cadet because he had short hair, he was incapable of speaking French because he lived in N.D.G., or he was a snob because he spoke French in a certain way. Man, he thought, in California I was just *me*! He had expected to find in Montreal a wide-open bilingual city whose residents shuttled contentedly from English to French. He had discovered instead a fractured wheel of a metropolis, with the tree-shaggy Mountain at its core pushing the neighbourhoods out and away from the centre, until each district flaunted its own accent and idiom, its own version of English or French, that indelibly marked people from a few blocks away as foreigners. What hope did he have of fitting in? Real immigrants—the ones who came from Italy, Greece, Portugal, China, Vietnam, Haiti, Jamaica or Morocco—created their own village-like neighbourhoods; but Teddy, being neither ethnic nor a lifelong Montrealer, was looking for a Canadian city. A place where he could get back in touch with everything he had forgotten in the States. It had to happen soon. The three months' rent he had thrown onto the table in front of the two Mr. Rubinsteins had left him almost broke. Not that there wasn't more money available—the sleek windowed envelopes that he received monthly must still be piling up on the kitchen counter of Zach and Marian's house in Berkeley. But he had promised himself not to stoop to that level. He would live on the money he earned. He would try out a normal Canadian life.

As he climbed the steps of the Waterloo side of the building, a young woman came out the door. She had a round-faced Mediterranean look softened by a curve of dark, glossy hair falling over her forehead. She caught Teddy's eye with an expression of subdued ferocity. Brushing past him, she uttered a murmur too soft to be a greeting. It was the second time this had happened. After taking a desultory glance at his mailbox, Teddy turned around to watch her depart. She disappeared down the sidestreet in the direction of the Vendôme Métro station.

"You'd better not be planning on staying here long," a voice behind him said, "'cause this building's going downhill."

Teddy had met Mrs. McNulty the day he moved in. She was a stiff-backed woman whose heavy black shoes lent her an air of martial authority. Her permed red hair, greying at the tips, enclosed a face masked and hardened by thick-framed glasses that looked one size too large. She and her son Paddy had lived in the Waterloo for twenty-one years. "This used to be a decent place to live. Those Rubinsteins don't put a cent into keeping it up. And now they've hired Joe as concierge. They hired him because he was supposed to be a handyman. But you watch and see if he does a lick of work." She glanced over her shoulder. "He's got a bad heart," she whispered. "They invalided him out of the Armed Forces. My late husband was in the Forces. I know these things."

Teddy had difficulty concentrating on what Mrs. McNulty was saying. The sight of the woman on the steps had staved open a cavern of loneliness in him. This was his country, but he knew no one. In this whole enormous half-continent, from St. John's to Victoria to Ellesmere, no one paused to wonder what he might be doing, no one knew or cared that he was in Montreal. For a moment he could hardly breathe.

"Something wrong? You're not on drugs, are you?"

"I'm not on drugs. I'm just mad. I had this job interview with an old bastard who didn't take me seriously."

"My Paddy can't get a good job either. He's had the same low-life job since he dropped out of Cégep." She followed him towards the door of his apartment. "You see what old Joe's done? He's gone and built them a clubhouse."

"Built who a clubhouse?" Teddy pulled his keys out of the serrated slantways opening of his chest pocket.

Mrs. McNulty gazed down into the gloom where the stairs descended into the unlighted basement. "That black boy. The one that lives down there with his buddies. Rubinsteins told Joe to get rid of them. Joe made a deal with them instead. They do the cleaning and he lets them live in the basement for free. Joe doesn't want to do any work 'cause he's afraid about his bad heart. If his heart's so frigging bad, how come he can spend two days building them a clubhouse?"

"Is that who that is? They're right below me. They keep me awake at night."

"You call the cops if they keep you awake. They got no right to be there. They don't do a lick of cleaning. They're crooks. They shoplift and they steal. That's how they make their living. Mrs. Austin across the hall from me—she's from Jamaica and even she thinks they should be locked up."

"Thanks for telling me." Teddy unlocked the door, stepping into his apartment, where the roar of the Sherbrooke Street traffic dimmed. He continued to breathe in short heaves that set off a strumming in his temples. He stumbled into the bedroom. As a result of a visit last weekend to a garage-sale up the hill, he had graduated from a sleeping bag on a blanket to a mattress strewn with rumpled sheets. He twisted out of the leather jacket, letting it clank to the floor. Why did he want to be a fucking punk anyway? He had transformed himself on a whim, after getting high at a party in North Berkeley during his last weekend in the States. He had let a woman he hardly knew cut off his shoulder-length hair at three o'clock in the morning, as they sat straddling the diving board of a swimming pool. His glossy locks, floating on the unreal light-wrinkled water, had glowed with a stole-like density deepened by the cross-pollination of hash and magic mushrooms. On Monday he had gone to an alternative hairdresser and had the sloppy punk haircut rounded off. He had bought a black leather jacket and two Elvis Costello cassettes. It felt important to complete this transformation before moving back to Canada.

Kicking the jacket into the corner, he unbuckled his belt and fell on his knees on the mattress. He thought about the woman who had sat behind him on the diving board, her thighs clamped to his buttocks, her bra-free nipples fretting at his back as she slid her fingers close to his scalp to snip off his hair. Once he was shorn he had twisted around and kissed her on the mouth; their dangling feet bumped against each other. They scrambled off the diving board. When he suggested that they find an unoccupied room in the free-for-all of the mansion, she shook her head. "I don't feel like fucking anybody tonight. And besides, no man has ever given me as much pleasure as I can give myself." Teddy unzipped his jeans, liberating his swollen penis. Eyes closed, he summoned up that woman, whose name he had never learned, saying "fuck." Even if she had refused to do it; even if she had said it, then walked away. To fend off the rush of despair that threatened to shrivel his lust, he thought about the woman he had passed on the steps. Remembering the gyration of her hips, he began to pull and thrust. Imagining a single woman was never enough; it was the rage to penetrate a merging of bodies, a triumphant conglomeration of all the women he had failed to possess, that excited him. He pumped and rolled until his breath creaked, then tried to hold the pitch the way he sometimes could with a woman. But as always when alone, he came too fast: ejaculation without climax. He stumbled to the bathroom with cupped, gummy hands and leaned over the sink to wash. He had slicked the front tail of his shirt. He unbuttoned the shirt, tossed it into the corner on top of the leather jacket and collapsed on his back on the mattress. Dull light filtered in the window from the shaft in the middle of the building. Let me tell you, baby, he thought, struggling to reconfigure the face of the woman on the diving board, women have given me a lot more pleasure than I've ever given myself.

He lay back, feeling relieved, headachey, worthless; a vein throbbed in his ankle. He could have made it last longer by lying on his back. He masturbated on his knees when he hated himself. He felt knocked out, the way he had begun to feel in recent months the morning after smoking pot. He had cut back on pot as a result, but how to cut back on masturbation? It lay in wait for him every sentient moment. He wondered why the novels about men's lives that he had continued to read for amusement while studying for his M.A. never mentioned this subject. He could think of one novel, set in Montreal, that included a masturbation contest among a group of adolescent boys. But the scene was played for laughs; private masturbation was a more mournful matter.

The drumming in his temples subsided into the vicegrip of a headache. He had barely had a serious girlfriend during his years in Berkeley. His sheltered Rockcliffe upbringing had ill-prepared him for studying with the progressive upper class of the United States, where everyone had been sexually active since the age of thirteen and by eighteen could claim twenty or thirty partners. His Berkeley classmates had survived the collapse of long-term relationships and months of therapy. He had nothing to offer these women who snickered on learning that he was Canadian. Had the American women been a cultural mismatch, or was he simply a loner, a weirdo, a sexual failure? This was part of what he had come home to find out. Yet he was not meeting anyone. He had been plagued by solitude since infancy. His childhood, unfurling in long silences broken when the wind in the trees made the branches clatter overhead on the tiny, wooded lot behind the house, had felt like a fantasy. His grandmother read six newspapers a day, four in English and two in French. From the time he began to live with her, she urged him to read the newspapers also. He must inform himself on the business of the nation. "You will always be provided for," she said. "Your actions must have a goal beyond self- interest."

His grandmother had a cleaning lady and maid, Madame Dubois, who stayed from nine to five and, dressed in a frilly uniform, sometimes remained in the evening to serve at dinners. His grandmother's dinners featured not only illustrious relics from her own generation who had drinks with members of the Privy Council, but people who were younger than Teddy's parents had been: New Ottawa Men and Women. The women piled their plaited hair on top of their heads, the men cultivated sideburns. They spoke of the extension of bilingualism, the consolidation of a unified federal state, the Third World and the need to implement the Third Option of diluting U.S. influence by expanding trade with Europe. They were on first-name terms with the cabinet ministers responsible for these portfolios. Contacts and flare, more than money, determined who was important. Money, though it helped, must not be flaunted. Their cabinet minister neighbours drove Buicks and Oldsmobiles when not on government business, scorning limousines as a sign of Torontonian vulgarity. The boys he studied with at Ashbury understood these rules, and they understood the rules that prevailed when Ashbury boys were invited by Elmwood girls to their Christmas dances. Teddy had grown up too alone to enjoy these events. He remained aloof, or else he met a girl and took her far too seriously; he could

not strike the right social note. The excited voices in which
other boys told him about girls they had met over the summer
at Gatineau Hills lakes girdled with sumptuous cottages left him
feeling thwarted. If he went back there now he would find
Ashbury boys married to Elmwood girls. His former school-
mates would lead him through the dance of "Do you know so-
and-so?" and "Do you know he's working for management
consulting firm X. or cabinet minister Y.?" and "Did you know
his brother who went to Harvard . . . Oxford . . . the
Sorbonne?" and "Did you ever visit their cottage in the
Gatineau . . . in the Rideau Lakes? No? *I* did!" They would all
have more answers and more contacts than he did. The only
original information he would be able to offer concerned his
own fate, which remained undecided. No one, he was
confident, had heard a whisper about him since his last trip
back to Ottawa, during his third year at Berkeley, for his
grandmother's funeral. His only remaining connection with
that world was his address book, which contained the phone
numbers of his grandmother's eminent friends. They were all
ancient, but some of them must know people in Montreal.

He listened to the grind of the traffic. A warble of voices
fluttered up from the basement. He could lie here half-naked
all night and nothing would happen: no one would call or come
to the door. No one would notice he was alive.

Unless he got to his feet and made somebody notice.

ೞ ೞ ೞ

Darkness fell and the streetlights came on. The cross on the
Mountain glared to life overhead. Marching in front of him,
André recognized a former Member of National Assembly who
had joined an ultra-orthodox splinter group. There were gaunt
Marxist-Leninists, three old men propping up a banner that
announced them to be conservative Catholic nationalists, and
a gaggle of rowdy guys with long grey hair whom he half-
recognized from *manifs* twenty years earlier. Behind the aging

radicals came a pot-bellied union contingent, a group of feminists and a dozen Latin American refugees whose banners, blotched with spelling mistakes, made no mention of the threat to Bill 101 or the French language. Patrol cars had parked diagonally at the intersections; bored cops redirected traffic. André remembered when the sight of cops had made the crowds surge forward in anger, snarling at the traitors who had sold their bodies and brains in return for a uniform, a truncheon, a gun. In those days every *manif* had been a celebration of joyous fraternal intimacy. Everywhere he turned there had been brown eyes, long hair glinting almost black in the sunlight, sharp cheekbones and square Norman or Breton jaws. A people had been on the march! Lysiane, Raymond and Marie-Christine had been his friends *and* his family.

He had met them in a school basement: two or three hundred people crammed together in the gloom, every seat occupied, more people packed in on the floor, cigarette smoke permeating every fold of flesh and fabric. He arrived late and sat cross-legged in the aisle listening to an exiled Haitian professor give a galvanizing speech about Frantz Fanon and the colonized francophone peoples of the Americas. The pounding of hands shook the basement. André clapped until his palms stung. A high-pitched voice shouted: —*Nous sommes les nègres blancs de l'Amérique!*—

The applause roared up again. He kept his eyes fixed on the thin guy with the glossy goatee who had uttered the cry. When the crowd began to disperse, he dived towards him. — Thank you for speaking the truth!— Raymond took his arm and introduced him to his gang. He had arranged to meet them all in a café a few nights later. Over the weeks, under the pungent scent of Raymond's Gitanes, the informal gatherings had been pared to a core group of four. Raymond, already a sociology student at the Université de Montréal, was the instigator of their cousinly comradeship. The son of an impoverished notary who worked out of a one-room office in the family apartment half a dozen blocks east of Parc Lafontaine, he had grown up engulfed in words and bitterness. His revolutionary expositions left them raging and breathless. The reason they had all lived in awe of him, André perceived now, was that Raymond had been decolonized in infancy: he had been raised in a household where his father worked in the French language. Lysiane and Marie-Christine, neighbours from Rue Fabre, were like André: their fathers worked with hammers and drills and bowed their heads before the commands of Anglo foremen, while their mothers rode herd on flocks of children.

Marie-Christine was dimpled and round-jawed. Her smooth cheeks jammed his heart to a halt when she leaned close to let him light her cigarette. André tried to think of ways to tell her that he loved her. He schemed to get her alone: to walk her home from a café or the Paul-Sauvé Arena. Then she and Raymond came in the door of a basement café arm-in-arm and necked in the corner of the table. Raymond worked the sleeve of Marie-Christine's blouse back over her plump shoulder. He slipped his hand under her blouse. André stumbled out into the street in an anguished daze. He watched Raymond and Marie-Christine turn the corner and disappear. For the next week he stayed at home in Lasalle.

The press of the crowd in the Carré St-Louis had given him the courage to fling his arm around Lysiane. The jet of the fountain stuttered up behind Pierre Bourgault's bantam frame as he declaimed on the platform; green summer leaves obscured the gables of the Victorian houses. Driven into each other's arms by the need to restore symmetry to their fractured foursome, they had been dreading this moment for days. Over the next few weeks he and Lysiane made love on spare mattresses in apartments whose tenants were away at work or school. He fell in love with her slender, hard-hipped body and her cascade of dark hair. With her, he felt tough-minded and adult. Her personality asserted itself, while Marie-Christine's feelings remained veiled by enigmatic smiles and oblique remarks. And Marie-Christine's eternal impulse to comfort men, wonderfully warm though it might be, would in the end rack him with guilt. Or so he told himself, watching Marie-Christine's fingers stroking Raymond's hair. Lysiane made a better partner for a politically active man. She possessed the stamina for long meetings, late nights, endless poster-plastering odysseys; she accepted the political necessity of his evenings in remote apartments. Marie-Christine refused to condone similar behaviour in Raymond. They married while Raymond was still working on his unfinishable thesis on class formation during the urbanization of Quebec in the 1940s. Their marriage lasted four years. Marie-Christine, Raymond told him later, had made no effort to overcome petit-bourgeois fetishes. —She wants a house and children, he whispered. —You're lucky, André. Lysiane understands.—

Lysiane's understanding was fitful and eternally changing. Despite her rowdy personality, she squashed her resentments deep inside her until they gushed out in torrents of unpredictable activity. He was stunned when she announced that she had registered at Hautes Études Commerciales. It was her turn to trail in late, case studies popping from her lips when he grumbled about supper. He complained about her absences; she accused him of crushing her career. Her pursuit of freedom for women yielded to praise of the free market. She was striking back, now that he was older and more vulnerable, at the thoughtlessness that had led him to neglect her. When he argued against her business school slogans she retorted that times had changed: his brain had ossified, he would end up as reactionary as Papa.

From insults they moved on to more insidious ways of wounding each other. They embellished their accounts of their evenings out by mentioning in passing members of the opposite sex. How infantile they had been! Their war of nerves went on for months. By the time they separated, bitterness had been displaced by sheer exhaustion. He wished they had split up five years earlier when they had both been young enough to start again. Even though, in his own way, he had started again, on a path Lysiane would not have suspected, he could not forgive her. He continued to be gripped by bouts of rage: moments when, if Lysiane had materialized before him, he might have struck her.

On Rue St-Denis the boutiques and cafés lighted up the sidewalks into glistening tunnels. Ahead of him, the marchers swung right onto the red-cobbled Avenue Duluth. He saw feminists and environmentalists, pushed together by a bottleneck farther up the street, eyeing each other. Most of the Latin Americans had disappeared.

Two cars were lodged across Avenue Duluth. The crowd shuffled around as the police gestured to the driver of an Audi to back up. The former Member of National Assembly slipped into a Vietnamese *dépanneur* and emerged clutching a pack of Export A. Early diners, like the inmates of so many aquariums, stared out at the marchers through the glass fronts of the restaurants. Car horns honked. André was turning away when a hand touched his shoulder.

—André? a woman's voice said. —*C'est vraiment toi?*—

He caught himself and looked.

Marie-Christine.

᯽ ᯽ ᯽

They undressed facing each other. Ruthie stood with her back to the window. The moonlight froze her shoulders, pitching the front of her body into shadows that made Marcel catch his breath. He stepped forward, closing his hands over her hips. Once they were between the sheets his hesitations dissolved; he scrambled to keep up with her. Each of his women was a tempo, a beat to which he briefly danced, skipping away before the movements could be dulled by habit. Ruthie's energy left him feeling cuffed about, wrung out and laid still like one more sheet draped across her body.

"That was nice," she said. Her finger traced the line of his hip. "You had a good rhythm at the end."

Her assessment prodded at him, swelling to a throbbing, headache-sized irritation by the time the blaze of morning sunlight awoke him to the realization that he had missed his meeting. He was sleeping in another man's bed: a bed that belonged to Abitbol. Mesmerized by the light guttering over Ruthie's exposed right breast, he lay still for a long time before flinging the covers off her body. She refused to stir. He gave up and stumbled into the bathroom. When he returned the bedside clock read twenty-five to ten. Abitbol would slaughter him.

Ruthie remained comatose. He courted an impulse to drive away without her. The sprawled white crescent of her body detained him. He bent over to wake her with sucking kisses on the earlobes. When the kisses failed to elicit a reaction, he stroked her shoulder blades. By the time she uttered a drowsy giggle, his tongue was feeling out the curve of her spine bump by bump; his fingers crawled between her thighs. Ruthie sighed. He couldn't stand it any longer. He hauled her legs off the bed, swivelled himself around behind her, dragged her staggering and drowsily giggling to her feet, then folded her over the bed once more, her legs spread. He thrust into her from behind. He felt the exquisite silky fretting of the hair at the base of his stomach and the hair scrawling out of the crack of her ass matting and meshing and catching. He lunged and gasped. The blood piping through his legs reversed its course, beating down into the soles of his feet. Pressing her into the mattress, he thrust until he lost control of himself.

They lay in the morning sunlight, baking together, he thought, like two rolls of unleavened yeast.

Ruthie dislodged herself from his embrace and walked into the bathroom. The shower came on. He rolled over onto his back. When she returned, she began to dress without looking at him. "Next time," she said, fastening her skirt, "you might consider letting a girl wake up before you start fucking her."

"Ruthie—"

"Let's go. I'm late for work."

They dressed and went, leaving the bed unmade. The detail nagged at him as he accelerated along the passing lane of the autoroute. He must return to the cottage to change the sheets before Véronique and Abitbol came up for the weekend. The conifers striding up the steep Laurentian slopes deflected the bright morning sunlight; the hub of hills and trees shrank to a glaring ball of light in the middle of his brain. He rolled down his window, imagining he was inhaling the distant scent of pine needles.

Ruthie's fingers rooted among his tapes. She slid a Bryan Ferry cassette into the stereo. "I'm sorry I got mad at you. Don't worry about me being late. I'll just take the day off."

"We've missed the meeting. We won't be there to witness the signatures." He leaned forward over the steering wheel, squeezing down on the accelerator.

Ruthie laid a hand on his elbow. "Relax. They'll find someone else."

"That's not the point." He couldn't continue. She challenged him too much. She would ridicule him if he confessed his fear of Abitbol.

He drove in silence. The cassette ended. The hills dwindled to fields scarred by housing developments. He opened the glove compartment and dipped into his cache of Mars bars, gesturing to Ruthie to help herself.

She shook her head. "How can you eat sugar this early in the morning?"

Another strike against him. He must have been out of his mind to expect anything but disdain from an Ashkenazi. Abitbol would laugh his head off. Look at how the Ashkenazis treated the Sephardics in Israel, he would say; it was the same story everywhere. Marcel chewed his Mars bar in despondent rage. "Where do you live in Côte St-Luc?" he asked, as they crossed Rivière-des-Prairies and returned to the city.

"Actually, I live in Hampstead. But you can drop me in Côte St-Luc. I'll get a bus. There's no reason for you to schlep over to Hampstead. I wouldn't wish that on anyone!"

Before he could thank her she unleashed a satirical monologue on the nouveau-riche horrors of her neighbourhood. "Everybody in Hampstead's so busy earning money they forgot to learn about taste. We build our houses too big for our lots so we can take a good look at the neighbours' interior decorating. We have electric-blue street signs and the only five-way stop in North America because the streets have to be safe for our children! . . . Sad to say, my parents are among the afflicted. They grew up really poor on Drolet Street, my dad bucked the Jewish quota at McGill and became a chemical engineer and now they have tons of money and they just love it!"

Her words kindled a confused warmth in Marcel. Growing up in Outremont, he had felt alienated from the Hasidic Jewish boys with their sidelocks, who lived nearby, and excluded by the affluent English-speaking Jews from the western part of the city. Their own way of life, Véronique and Abitbol had given him to understand, represented a healthy balance of spiritual and material imperatives. He did not know how to react to Ruthie's pillorying of her parents. She was confirming all his harshest prejudices against Ashkenazis; but he would never speak of *his* family with this kind of disrespect.

By the time they reached Côte St-Luc he was laughing out loud. He gave Ruthie a long goodbye kiss. She lingered in the front seat, her dark eyes searching his face. "I'm late," he said. "I must go."

Ten minutes later he was pulling into the yard behind Abitbol's office. The burly sons of the Greek who owned the furniture store on the ground floor were unloading coffee tables from a delivery van. Ignoring their greetings, he dashed up the back stairs.

Sylvie grimaced as he opened the door. —Pierre's inside.— He negotiated the clutter of the outer office, stopping to straighten his hair before the mirror hanging above the unplugged coffee pot. Sylvie said: —You haven't shaved . . . He's angry, Marcel.—

Marcel stared at the brown-stained wooden door on which Abitbol had mounted his black plastic plaque: *Maître Pierre Levine Abitbol, Avocat.* He pushed his way into the office, hoping his abrupt entry would short-circuit Abitbol's tirade.

—Get out! Abitbol said. —Knock before you enter my office!—

Marcel backed off, closed the door and knocked. There was no reply. He stood staring at Abitbol's plaque. He knocked again. The third time he knocked, Abitbol said: —*Entrez.*—

Marcel stepped into the stuffy office. Bookshelves jammed with boxed files rose from floor to ceiling along each wall. Paired portraits of Golda Meir and King Hassan II hung against the whitewashed plaster. The yellowing, fly-specked blind had been lowered over the single grated window. Trusting no one, Abitbol hoarded every file of importance in his office.

—Sit down, you irresponsible little shit.—

Abitbol lowered himself onto the lip of his desk. Marcel noticed that his broad body was growing bulkier, acquiring a gristly heaviness that suggested less an accumulation of fat than a thickening of his bones. The deep seams stitching across his forehead in uneven horizontal lines anchored the clipped tumult of his wiry hair. He wore black dress slacks, a matching jacket, an open-necked white shirt revealing the top of a coarse cotton T-shirt. His face, soaked with a jaundiced pallor, looked neither light nor dark. His French retained the heavy Moroccan accent that Marcel had jettisoned in youth.

—I won't tax you with an account of all the trouble you've caused me. That would be cruel, and I am not a cruel man.

I'm merely an ordinary man who is trying to earn a living for his family and support his aged mother in the old country. Who is trying to make a place for his children. Who is trying to be a good husband and a good Jew . . . Why must you make it so difficult for me, Marcel?—

His right hand seized Marcel's ear, snaring a lock of hair. Abitbol twisted his wrist. Marcel heard a squeak break from the bottom of his throat. His ear was flaming.

—Your pain is nothing compared with the pain I feel at the spectacle of your immorality. It is nothing compared with the pangs of hunger you would have experienced if we hadn't rescued you from the *mellah*, brought you to Canada, opened our home to you, raised you as one of our own children.— Abitbol released him. —And what did we ask in return? Only that you become a responsible adult, a good example for our children. You chose to marry outside your faith. Well, did we try to stop you? Has anyone ever tried to stop you from doing as you wished? Do you even know what it feels like to *need* money, to *need* to prove that you are a better man than everyone thinks you are?—

—Yes, I do!— He leaned forward in the chair, suppressing the urge to jump to his feet. —How do you think I felt when you took away my house? You think that because I was an orphan you can control me forever. You watch out: I'll pass my exams and go to work for a big accounting firm and you'll never see me again!—

—No, Marcel. You need your family. You have too much freedom. In Morocco our faith was strong, we were so close that we all drew the same breath . . . —

Marcel slumped in his chair. It was the old refrain: *les liens qu'on avait au Maroc.* All emotions had been attenuated, all intimacy dulled, since they had crossed the Atlantic. Véronique and Abitbol returned to this theme incessantly; Louis and Madeleine must know the lecture by heart. Marcel waited in silence for his chance to counter-attack. Devastating tirades and

long silences: properly timed they were the two keys to intimi-
dation. He had learned to manipulate them by watching
Abitbol.

The telephone on Abitbol's desk shrilled. —No calls, Sylvie,
he called through the closed door.

—It's Maryse.—

Marcel reached around Abitbol's body to pick up the
receiver. —*Allô, chérie.*—

—What are you doing? Why haven't you come home?—

—I'm sorry, I just got back. The business in Lennoxville took
forever. The tenant who refuses to pay wasn't in last night, then
the plumber we got to do the work downstairs overcharged us
and the concierge, who was too stupid to see we were being
robbed, signed for the work. I had to go around to the
plumber's office this morning and argue with him. I've been
running myself ragged, Maryse.—

Abitbol swore in Judeo-Arabic.

—What about me? Don't I matter to you?—

—*Chérie*, it is for you that I work so hard.—

—I'm sorry, Marcel.— He still caught his breath in wonder
each time she made a concession to him. More than money,
what he *needed*, as Abitbol would say, was Maryse's approval. The
realization of her importance to him broke over him in the
wake of each infidelity, sluicing away the residue of his most
recent conquest.

He longed to be with her.

—I'm sorry to bother you at the office, but I'm not myself
out here in this desert.—

—It's only temporary, Maryse. The harder I work the sooner
we can move back to Outremont.—

—I know, she said in her fluting, *pointu* voice. —I just need
to hear you say it.—

—I'll come home after lunch, he said. He hung up.

—You lie very well, Abitbol said, tugging at the front of his
black trousers. —Lying! Of all the talents to be blessed with,

Marcel!— He waved him back into the chair. He prowled before the ranked dog-eared files. —Your marriage is a stain on our family. If you hadn't married outside your faith— —

—My marriage is my business.—

—It is clear, Abitbol said, continuing to pace, that a man who ignores his faith becomes incapable of maintaining moral standards. If you studied Torah— —

—I don't have time to study Torah. I'm too busy trying to make money so my wife doesn't die of boredom in Ville St-Laurent.—

—Do you really care about your wife?— Abitbol fixed him with a hard, hostile glare. —If you are interested in making money, I have a proposition for you. A proposition regarding the Victoria-Waterloo . . . but I doubt that money will solve your problems.— Abitbol pulled out his padded armchair and sat down behind his desk. —Your problem, Marcel, is that you don't know who you are. You don't appreciate what it means to be a Jew in Morocco.—

—I hardly remember Morocco.— He thrashed in the small, hard chair. His recollections of the *mellah* swarmed up in a buzz of voices and a gale of musty, sugary scents—*tajine* cooking at smokey stalls, effluent from leather workshops, mint tea and camel dung—wafting through the chilly shadow of narrow streets enclosed by the overhanging second and third storeys of closely packed buildings. His visual memories remained blurry by comparison with his pungent recall of voices, smells and tastes: they hadn't realized until he arrived in Canada that he needed glasses.

He met Abitbol's eyes. —Tell me how I can make money from the Victoria-Waterloo.—

ଓଽ ଓଽ ଓଽ

Teddy stepped out of his apartment to find the West Indians gathered in the hall. A bald older man stood flexing the brim of a Montreal Expos baseball cap in his hands. The homeless boy for whom Joe had built a clubhouse—Mrs. McNulty had discovered his name was Rollie—loitered at the top of the basement stairs. Tall and emaciated, he kept his distance from the others. His chapped hands gripped the banister. The older man was bombarding him with questions. Rollie stood thin as a teetering ladder, saying nothing. As Teddy started past them, the older man reached out to halt him. His bald head gave off a mahogany shimmer. Holding out his baseball cap upside down, he said: "It's my birthday, mon. What you buy me for my birthday?"

Two young men sitting on the stairs burst out laughing.

"I don't know you," Teddy said. "I don't give birthday presents to people I don't know."

"Sure you do, mon. You give me money. It's my birthday and I got no money to buy myself a present." Flashing a bright grin spoiled by missing teeth, he pushed forward the baseball cap until it brushed Teddy's chest. "My name's Family Man. Everybody's my family."

"Look, I'm unemployed right now." The baseball cap gave the front of his shirt another soft swat. "If I give you money for no reason you're not going to respect me and you're not going to respect yourself. Right?"

"Right, mon," Family Man said with a mock-grave nod.

"You hear what he say?" one of the young guys said. "We gotta respect we!"

They laughed. Teddy headed down the corridor, his discomfort accentuated by his destination: his first Westmount party.

That afternoon, sweeping behind the refrigerator, he had threshed the enumeration sheet from the last provincial election into the middle of the floor. He stared at the list, wondering which of the names belonged to the dark woman he had passed on the steps. Mrs. McNulty was listed as *homemaker* and her son Paddy as *clerk*. Other Victoria-Waterloo tenants' occupations were: *labourer, sailor, security guard, student.* On the back of the sheet was the list for the next building east, one block closer to Westmount: *airline pilot, engineer, lawyer, consultant.*

The mood changed the moment he started up the hill. The houses were built of red brick and surrounded by trees. As he climbed higher, the red brick gave way to grey stone and the houses bulged with arches, turrets, embrasures. Each house was a private castle, the mountainside a heaped assemblage of much of the wealth accumulated during Canada's first three centuries, when few profits were made without goods passing through Montreal on their way back to Europe. Despite himself, Teddy felt a soothing familiarity. Westmount was a grander, higher, less cramped Rockcliffe; he realized to his discomfort that part of what he had been seeking in returning to this country was insulation—insulation from Californian brashness, from the convulsions of the world; insulation, even, from the rougher-edged aspects of this city. Peace, order and good government, he thought, in recollection of high school history classes.

He drew back his shoulders as he prepared to ring the Thornbridges' doorbell. He wished he had mustered the courage not to exchange his black leather for a corduroy jacket that transformed his punky gristle into a crisply conservative haircut.

A dark-skinned young woman wearing a uniform answered the door. Teddy addressed the older, taller woman standing behind her. "Mrs. Thornbridge? I'm Teddy. My grandmother's friend Mr. Sharp called you from Ottawa—?"

"Do come in. I'm sure my husband knows who you are." She shrilled an indecipherable pet name over her shoulder. Her voice sounded almost British; the Persian carpets muffled her sibilance. Her husband arrived at a robust clip, rings glinting on his fingers, and subjected Teddy's hand to a metallic clasp. He provided his wife with a summary of Teddy's pedigree. "Now

I remember," Mrs. Thornbridge said. "It completely slipped my mind. Were you studying in California?"

"Yes. Political science at Berkeley."

"That will be useful." Her watery eyes blinked towards concentration as she led him inside. "Our daughter came back here after her M.B.A. at Harvard. Our son, on the other hand, got fed up with all the separatist fuss and went out to Hong Kong to work in merchant banking. Now it looks as though there's no future there either, so he's thinking of moving to Australia. So many problems everywhere, I'm afraid."

The hall opened into a vast living room. Wide-winged coffee tables sat decked with plates of snacks. Guests wearing bright blazers, tweed jackets, Ralph Lauren sweaters, trim dress slacks and Swiss watches—when had he last seen a whole room of people whose watches were equipped with hands rather than digits?—circled each other in a circumspect shuffle. One body moved faster than the rest. He glimpsed a face that for half a second seemed to belong to the Mediterranean-looking woman from the Waterloo. But only her eyes were darkly hooded; this woman's cheeks and chin were of a northern European pallor. Her kinky dark hair slid on her shoulders as she hurried away from a man whose mouth was stretching open. The woman's gaze paused on him, holding for a second, before she pushed her way through a door that led to a balcony.

Mrs. Thornbridge waved at the opposite wall of the room, where paintings hung as thick as postage stamps on the pages of an old collector's album. Teddy recognized well-known artists: Riopelle, Colville, McEwen. Vivid abstracts glared alongside the firm strokes of morose realism. "Eclectic," he murmured, appraising shelves of Book-of-the-Month Club main selections and a set of kidney-shaped leather couches and chairs.

The doorbell rang. "I must fly!" Mrs. Thornbridge said. "Enjoy."

He glanced towards the back door where the dark-eyed woman had disappeared. He edged in the direction of the snacks. Having eaten only a turkey-on-bagel sandwich from a delicatessen for supper, he was starving. He had hoped to find food at the party, but the munificence of the Thornbridges' catering exceeded his expectations. He glanced again at the balcony door, then slipped between the coffee tables, sampling the food. The array of tastes delighted him. There were celery sticks, carrot sticks, sliced apples, sectioned pears, peeled oranges, mild dips, tangy dips . . .

"Hello, David. What have you been up to since I saw you last?"

"Building up my Pacific Rim export markets. How about you?"

"I was just talking to my son, who's involved in the free trade negotiations—"

"Oh, is he? What do you think of this free trade idea?"

. . . Canadian cheddar cheese, pale Swiss cheese, Gruyère, Brie, Camembert, Stilton, halvah, Russian caviar . . .

"Nine and seven? They're practically the same age as ours. Aren't they demanding at that age?"

"They certainly are. And to make matters worse, ours are both Gifted Children—"

"Really? So are ours!"

The man whose mouth had been stretched open crossed the room towards the back door. He looked about forty, brawnily built but subsiding into fat. His eyes were filmed with an imperviousness that Teddy recognized from Rockcliffe Park and Ashbury College. His movements oddly languid in such a self-assured-looking figure, the man opened the balcony door on the dark night, then closed the door behind him.

"That's right, Jack, I'm going to take the plunge. What do you think? Should I run as a Grit or a Tory?"

"A Liberal if you can find an anglophone riding, a Tory if you end up in a francophone riding. In fact, I might know of an opening coming up for a Liberal in the West Island. You know old Scotty . . . ?"

. . . Château red wine, California white wine, champagne, fruit punch, apple juice, tonic water, Seven-Up, Canada Dry, Perrier, Evian . . .

"I'm finally going to a woman gynecologist. I have suffered so long at the hands of men gynecologists."

"'Suffered' is the operative word!"

"The last one commented on my abstemious habits by asking me, 'What are you? A nun?'"

"That's terrible. That's none of his business."

. . . tuna sandwiches, liver pâté sandwiches, Ritz crackers, pretzels, salted almonds, curried almonds, water biscuits, whole wheat thins, cheesies . . .

"Scotty from the board? Sure, his summer place in the Townships is just around the lake from mine."

"He's president of the riding association out there. He can help you stickhandle around the dinosaurs who'll label you a parachute candidate. You get in touch with Scotty—"

"That man over there is the Thornbridges' art investment consultant. He says that the market for Paterson Ewen—"

"I said, 'Yes, I'm the first Presbyterian nun.' I mean, I wouldn't say something like that to my worst enemy!"

"You should be proud of being abstemious these days."

The back door opened and the man returned to the living room. His mouth had grown thin. A moment later the woman reappeared in the same rush of movement that had carried her out the door. She glanced around. Seeing the man pouring himself a drink near the entrance hall, she turned in the opposite direction. She's coming towards me, Teddy thought. He couldn't stop watching her face.

"But culture isn't on the table! What are you afraid of? Do you think we'll end up with Wal-Mart stores, private medical care, a huge gap between rich and poor . . . ?"

"David, David . . . "

" . . . born-again Christian politicians, a common currency, Sunday shopping, Californian shopgirls who shout, 'Have a great day!' when you pay for your groceries? Come on! It's just a trade deal."

"That? That's Monsieur LePape. He works for Power Corporation. And that's Monsieur Beaudiscours. He's a vice-president of Lavalin."

"Funny—we never used to see French Canadians at these parties."

"Or anywhere else in Westmount."

. . . chocolate chip cookies, brownies, date squares, cheese cake, carrot cake, mocha cake, chocolate éclairs . . .

"In this op-ed piece I'm writing for the *Financial Post*—"

"Capri? No, we prefer Sardinia. At least for a *short* holiday. When you have Gifted Children—"

"I argue that free trade—"

"You look like you're having an even worse time than I am." Teddy wiped his lips. "I—"

"If a woman ate three chocolate éclairs in a row they'd say she was bulimic. But if a man does it, he's got a great appetite." Her laugh resounded with a gutsy loudness. Averting her gaze as he swung around to face her, she turned to the table for a drink. She poured herself a glass of the Château red, downed it in two quick swallows, then filled the glass again. Teddy was about to leave when she said: "You can't fool me. You were eating a chocolate éclair when I went outside and you were eating another one when I came back in. That's two anyhow, and I figure you probably ate a third one while I was out there telling Graham what a goddamn *jerk* he is."

"I'm glad you noticed," Teddy said. "I noticed you, too."

Her next sentence shrivelled as she stared at him over her drink. This time their eyes met. Her heavy-lidded Mediterranean look accentuated her intensity. Her pale cheeks were pouched. Teddy wondered how the contradictions of her face would resolve themselves as she aged. He realized that he had never before asked himself this question about a woman. A chill crept through his guts, making him wish he could call back his forwardness.

"I like a man who admits he's looking at you," she said. "These Westmount jerks will stare at your ass every time you turn your back, but butter wouldn't melt in their mouths." Her laughter rang out again. "Maybe I've offended you. Are you a Westmount jerk?"

"No, I'm a Rockcliffe jerk."

"Is that in Ottawa? That's probably worse."

"It is worse. I hate it. But it's me."

"So you hate yourself. Nobody should hate himself." She finished her glass of wine. He noticed the silver rings on her fingers; they were engraved with runic-looking inscriptions. "Except jerks like Graham. They should all learn to hate themselves! But they never will." She glanced in the direction of the entrance hall, where Graham had been joined by Mrs. Thornbridge, who, Teddy saw, was directing a frown in *his* direction. "I'm going back onto the balcony," the woman said, touching his forearm. "If you want to talk you can come with me."

She lifted a bottle from the table. Teddy watched her leave, realizing that he didn't know her name.

*t*hree

André-Marcel-Teddy-André

SETTING ASIDE HIS PLACARD, HE KISSED MARIE-CHRISTINE ON BOTH cheeks. The gaslight-style lamps were kind to her: he hoped they were being equally kind to him. Marie-Christine's cheeks had become soft pads, her eyes nestling darkly above them. She had grown her hair long; the tousled grey overlaying her black locks lent her a distinguished air. Dressed in a thigh-length South American sweater, she looked slimmer than she had at twenty.

—As committed as ever, she said, knocking his placard. — You looked so ferocious I almost didn't come after you.—

—This march is screwed up.— Over the heads of the feminists he saw a cop's uniformed arm paddle the air. The Audi backed up, tail-lights glowing, and turned off the red cobbles of the avenue onto the pitted tarmac of a sidestreet.

—André, she said, shaking his arm. —It's been eight years!—

The second car backed around a corner. The cops waved and the marchers trudged forward like children returning to school.

Realizing that the colour scheme of his placard matched that of a nearby souvlaki house, he propped up the poster against the wall. —I've had enough.—

—I have to get to the store before it closes, Marie-Christine said. —Will you walk with me?—

Eight years, he thought, falling into step with her. Their foursome had dissolved after the referendum; life had turned thin and flat. When the Parti Québécois government had asked the people to support a sovereign Quebec, their dream had glittered on the brink of realization. Then it had vanished. But in 1980, the last time he and Lysiane and Raymond and Marie-Christine had got together, it was not evident that their dream was finished. For two weeks after the defeat of the referendum they had done nothing but go to parties. Raymond and Marie-Christine had been divorced long enough by then that they could once again get drunk together, each accompanied by new lovers. The parties had turned into bittersweet wakes for their youth. They were all thirty or thirty-one years old. The tension that had been mounting in them crested and broke. They stayed up all night; they sobbed and crooned folk songs. And yet in the midst of so many tears, so much hugging and dancing and storytelling, they had failed to grasp the significance of this moment. They had seen the referendum defeat as a temporary setback. They had plastered their refrigerators with decals that read *Oui . . . à la prochaine.* But there would be no next time. They flung themselves into the post-referendum parties as eternal students, carefree young activists, and when they sobered up two weeks later they were middle-aged. Their lives had lost the only common focus they had possessed. André's diligent little sister Céline and her friends took over the university classrooms. His political friendships became either strained or desperate as splits developed between orthodox and pragmatic tendencies. The crowds at meetings dwindled; groups folded; organizing a *manif* became a way of exposing yourself to humiliation. Lysiane grew impatient with his staying out late; her business studies pulled her into another orbit. His attempts to explain his feelings had degenerated into ventings of rage. After Lysiane moved out, his students became his only audience. A few weeks later the evening dusk began to draw him to Parc Lafontaine.

He lost touch with Raymond and Marie-Christine. His joyous extended family disintegrated. Now and then he heard rumours that this person or that one had strayed into vegetarianism, feminism, gay-rights activism, astrology, insanity, biker warfare or big business. But he could not remember having heard about Marie-Christine.

He gripped her arm. —What have you been doing for the last eight years?—

—André! You expect me to give you an instant *compte rendu?*—

Why did this always happen when he met old friends? As they turned onto Boulevard St-Laurent, walking downhill past immigrant women carrying bags of groceries and skinny young people wearing tight black slacks and bleached white-blond hair, he wondered whether it wouldn't have been better to keep his memories intact. What could be gained by learning the mundane details of Marie-Christine's present? He stared down the rickety funnel of the street. It was the first time he had set foot on St-Laurent since his return. Many of the old Eastern European delicatessens had closed; the buildings housing them had been refurbished as trendy clothing shops and bars with neon-tangled façades.

In the health food store, he watched Marie-Christine fill plastic bags with grains and powders. She scooped nuts out of a bushel, flipped through a book on sugar-free cooking and one on *le rebirthing*. She topped up her basket with unrecognizable snacks. At the check-out, he was startled to see a bill for thirty-five dollars appear on the cash register.

—I could buy a week's groceries for that money.—

—This is a week's groceries.—

—No wonder you look so slim.—

—It has been a great pleasure to see you again, André.— Her formal diction, reinforced by a fixed smile, condemned his teasing as impropriety. He sensed her preparing to leave. Over her shoulder, he glimpsed the red-splashed white façade of La Main, his favourite smoked meat house. During his entire stay in France he had not tasted a Montreal smoked meat sandwich. —I'm going to eat a smoked meat. Will you come with me?—

—I'm a vegetarian.— She swung her shopping bag in her right hand. —All right. But I can't stay long.—

શ શ શ

— . . . Suddenly we were living in an independent country— —

—You were going to tell me about the Victoria-Waterloo.—

—That's what I'm doing. You must wait for meaning to reveal itself.— Abitbol looked cheerful. —You're like me when I was growing up in the Sahara and thought I was one more Arab like the rest. Only after we moved to Fes, where there was a *mellah* and synagogues and Jewish schools, did I realize who I was. I learned that I was Jewish and I learned to hate the French. We sneered at the French, Arabs and Jews alike, as we caroused in our night clubs. In 1956 I heard the crowds shouting, *'Hia l'Malik! Hia l'Malik!'* I was seventeen. Independence made my father nervous. He tried to persuade me to go to Israel. I laughed. My life was full of joy, I was taking courses to become a hairdresser, I went to a party every night of the week except the *Chabat.* There were always girls to dance with— —

The aftertaste of Ruthie's hair invaded Marcel's nostrils. A nagging erection punctuated his boredom, making him shift in his seat.

— . . . who cared if their legs were covered down to their ankles? They wore bright yellow robes and held themselves against you without blushing. When the government brought in laws guaranteeing Jewish property rights, my father became suspicious: why should they make laws about Jews' rights unless they were planning to abuse them? Our friends began to leave.

I kept going to parties. We made a lot of noise at these parties and sometimes the neighbours called the police. The police would come in and check everyone's papers, then tell us to go home. But one night they caught me by the arm and said, 'The rest of you leave. The Jew comes with us.' My friends started to protest. Then they shrugged their shoulders. Our whole youth fell away in those shrugs. I was alone with the thudding of my heart and the policemen's hands bending my arms behind my back.—

Marcel sat up, staring into Abitbol's eyes.

—They drove me to the police station and locked me in a cell. Two hours later five of them arrived together. Early in the morning they dropped me on the edge of the *mellah*. I was in constant pain for days afterwards. I feared I would be unable to have children.— Abitbol looked down at the stacks of paper on his desk. —My father decided that I must emigrate. But I didn't want to live in Israel or France. Sylvie, of course, was our cousin and her relatives had come to Canada . . . I knew nothing about Canada. It was *Maria Chapdelaine*: blizzards and bush and peasants who spoke with quaint accents. And it was *l'Amérique*: fast cars, Hollywood movies, easy money. And I knew they spoke French. I thought I would stay here for a year or two, get rich, then go back to Morocco and live in a mansion. Ha!— Abitbol's laugh was more pained than uproarious. But he had relinquished his invincibility. They could be equals now, as brothers-in-law should be. Yet Marcel, remembering their discussion about women, doubted this would happen. He leaned forward in the hard chair, watching the snatching movements of Abitbol's thick fingers as he picked at a thread on the cuff of his jacket.

Breaking the silence, Abitbol said: —You have no self-discipline, Marcel! I started law school five months after I arrived in Canada. I cut hair all day, I studied at night, and I never failed to observe the *Chabat*. On a visit to Fez, I met Véronique. Your parents had died a year earlier and our engagement was complicated by the problem of what to do with you: eight years old and the terror of the *mellah*, never out of trouble for a moment. We decided to look after you. That is what I call being responsible, Marcel. Véronique and I sponsored your immigration, we sent money to my mother. It was years before I could buy my first rental unit, have my first tenant . . . When are you going to start showing self-discipline? I thought that marriage would mature you— —

—Leave me alone!—

—No, Marcel.— Abitbol thrust his head forward. The yellowish hue of his cheeks burned darker. —That I will never do. You may escape everyone else, but your family will never leave you alone.—

He had been tricked. Abitbol wasn't vulnerable, he just wanted to make Marcel feel guilty. He got to his feet. —My life is my own business.—

—That is your great problem, Marcel. Now please sit down so I can tell you about the Victoria-Waterloo.—

Marcel took a step towards the door. When he looked down, his brother-in-law's thick body, stretched forward over his desk, had the warped shape of a man who had been fitted sideways on the rack. Letting his hands fall to his sides, Marcel returned to his chair.

—You'll be glad to hear that despite your negligence the Rubinstein deal went through. At first we couldn't find anybody to witness our signatures: the old bastards' secretary also forgot to come to work this morning.—

—I'm sure she was busy.—

—So now I own a large building on Sherbrooke Street. The tenants are shit: niggers, little old ladies, students, *bien-être social* bums. I don't want to do a condo conversion because I'll have to sink too much money into the place and I'll have the Régie du logement and do-gooding lawyers breathing down my neck. So I'm going for a half-conversion: a quick flip. We get the tenants out fast, spruce up the apartments, raise the rent by a couple of hundred dollars per unit, fill the building with decent tenants, then sell it.—

The accelerating rhythm of Abitbol's voice, his eyes growing small and still in his puffy face, roused Marcel from his despondency. He heard himself ask: —What are the apartments like?—

—Large. Four, five, six rooms. High ceilings. A little dark, but lots of exposed woodwork. The rents are in the low three hundred range: the premises haven't been maintained. You can kick some of the parquet floors apart with your shoes, there's a cockroach problem, the basement stinks and some of the wiring is defective. But what I like about the building is that with just a little bit of work it will look much, much better. I paid a million for it. I estimate that we'll have to sink half a million into renovations. If we can get the old tenants out and the new ones in within six months, we can put the building on the market for three million.—

—A million and a half profit in six months? You've never tried anything this big before. How are you going to avoid losing all that money in taxes?—

—I'm glad to hear you express an interest in this, Marcel, Abitbol said. —Because I want you to run it for me.—

◌ ◌ ◌

"What I hate about rich people," Janet said, "is that you never have to work for anything, you never have to do a job interview—"

"I just had a job interview where I was treated like shit."

"You see? I don't let people do that to me. I had to learn to stand up for myself."

"I can stand up for myself."

"How? By coming to a Westmount party so Mr. Thornbridge can make you a member of the board and give you a key to the men's room of the right male-bonding sports club . . . ? Isn't that why you came here, Teddy? Well, let me tell you, you've hit on the one fucking full-fledged working-class girl at this party. Are you sure you don't want to go back inside and look for somebody else to network with?"

Teddy hunched against the cold. Below the balcony, sparse lights staked out the plunging hillside of darkened treetops. The city centre, where the glow of the lights seeped upward around the silhouettes of churches and office towers, looked as distant as a landscape viewed from an airplane. The black St. Lawrence, bending around the outer reaches of the view, reminded Teddy that they were on an island. The river must be four kilometres away, yet he could feel its cold breath. "What do you think of this view?" he said. "I guess they don't have views like this in your neighbourhood."

"Fuck you, Rockcliffe boy," Janet said.

"I was just trying to see your point of view."

"Don't be condescending. I may have grown up on St-Jacques Street, but I know how the world looks from Westmount. Graham Thornbridge taught me all about that." She swigged from her bottle with a high-shouldered movement that sent a tremor through her copper-coloured dress. Teddy followed the ripple down to her knees, conscious of her awareness of his scrutiny. She offered him the bottle with a sideways look that emphasized the distrustful hoodedness of her eyes—that shadowed, lurking quality that sent his mind diving towards images of soft thighs. Breathless, he felt his brain take a moment to catch up with her words. "Graham Thornbridge? That guy in the hall is Mrs. Thornbridge's son?"

"Her nephew. The pudgy, stay-at-home mama's boy nephew who can't marry the right rich girl and isn't the go-getter all the others are. The one they're all so protective of. Did they ever hate it when he was seeing me . . . Why don't you take your drink?" Janet gestured with her chin towards the bottle that had stalled on its way to Teddy's mouth. She laughed. "You didn't realize I was breaking up with the hostess's favourite nephew? You leave this party with me, laddie, and you'll never be invited back to this palace in the sky."

Teddy drank his wine. It tasted too rich to be drunk so quickly. He stepped forward, leaning his elbows on the balcony. They stood next to each other, the steep mountainside plunging away below their feet. The scent that came off her— was it from her shampoo?—was as pungent as musky fur. The smell brought back an infant memory of a raccoon on a camping trip, when his parents were still alive. He mistrusted the image, as he did all memories of his reckless, unrecallable parents. At Berkeley he had discovered that meeting their parents enabled him to understand in an instant the contradictions of his friends' personalities: the sources of their prejudices, private wars and weaknesses for the wrong kinds of lovers. The experience had driven home the enigma he would always remain to himself. If other men were attracted to women who resembled their mothers, or women who made them feel like their fathers, what determined the attractions of a man who had not known his mother or father? He felt rudderless, lacking the essential psychological cargo his Berkeley classmates had hauled to their therapy sessions. Could any of his perceptions be *grounded?* "I didn't realize," he murmured, regretting the words as soon as he uttered them, "that we'd decided we were leaving together."

"We don't have to if you don't want to. I've left too many parties with too many jerks already in my time. That's how I got into this mess. Would you believe I slept with that spoilt little rich boy the first night . . . ? I never do that! My grandmother would be turning in her grave!"

Teddy's mind ranged back to the party in North Berkeley— God, had it been only three weeks ago? He couldn't imagine an American woman mingling sexual uninhibitedness and ancestral interdictions in the same breath like this. He leaned closer to Janet, inhaling the deep-woods scent of her hair. "I'm sorry this is so painful for you, but could you stop getting mad at *me?* I didn't do all this stuff—"

"I'm not getting mad at you—"

"How many times have you called me a jerk so far? Have I done anything to deserve that?"

She pulled the bottle from his hands, tilted it back and took slow sips, as though sucking down the alpine urban view. The bunching of her cheeks was unbearably fetching. "How old are you?"

"Twenty-five."

"Good. I like younger men. I'm twenty-eight. Graham's thirty-eight. He gets so slow and dreary . . . I need energy. I want someone who's *wild*. Are you *wild*?"

"You bet." Teddy laughed until he realized Janet was serious. "I've been downplaying my wild side. In California if you move too fast you're not *cool*."

She asked him what he had been doing in California, when he had arrived in Montreal and where he was living. He told her that his M.A. was a booby prize: a farewell ticket given to people who dropped out of the Ph.D. program. "I could see who I was going to be in ten years' time. A typical American poli sci prof. You know, the type who writes some mildly liberal opinion article in the newspaper once every three years, jets around to conferences—"

"Most people don't jet around to conferences," Janet said, meeting his eyes until he looked away. "I never go anywhere. I mean I've been to Toronto to see the trendoids and I go back to Scotland in the summers to see my relatives, but I've never lived anywhere but Montreal. It seems kind of weird to think of living in another city. I think Montreal is the best place to live." She paused in the manner of someone waiting to repel a challenge. His silence seemed to stymy her. Behind them, the murmur of the party had dimmed. "What do your parents do in Ottawa?"

"They were civil servants. Government economists. Old money, thought it was their job to run the country. My dad was a deputy minister. They died in a skiing accident in Alberta when I was five—an avalanche. I was brought up by my grandmother."

"That's why you're hard to get to know."

"I'm not hard to get to know!"

"You are!" she said, stepping towards him with a suddenness that made him flinch. The hair on her shoulders glinted. "You think that just because you answer back you're communicating. But anybody who grew up in a real family can see that you don't know anything about communication . . . Maybe it's because you're bourgeois—it makes you uptight."

"You don't know me," Teddy said, keeping his voice low. "What gives you the right to call me uptight?"

"I know you rich guys. You're always uptight."

"Then why don't you go out with some raunchy working guy with oil under his fingernails? What are you doing driving me crazy?"

"Now you're getting mad."

Thinking again about how she would look as she aged, he glimpsed a Scottish censoriousness dulling the gleam of her rounded cheeks. "Look, I'm always going to be like this. I'm always going to be angry and crazy—you'd better get used to it if you want to see me again." This time she didn't hesitate or glance at him and Teddy realized that he had not felt any hesitation either. In a rush of gratitude, he laid his hand over hers on the railing of the balcony. Her wide rings with their Celtic engravings were so cold they stung. "When you grow up where I grew up you see things. If you're sensitive"—she looked at him—"they affect you. It hurts. The first guy I kissed when I was twelve robbed nine banks and when he came out of jail he was gay. By the time I got to university the working class people were gone. I don't even know where they are any more."

"Still . . . you didn't have to go after Graham Thornbridge."

"What are you? Jealous or something?"

"Of him? Give me a break."

She squeezed his hand, then pulled away. "Come on, let's get out of here." She opened the door. The heat and the glare dazzled him. He barely had time to register the thinned-out crowd and pillaged food trays before they had crossed the living room to the entrance hall. Janet searched for her coat on the rack that had been wheeled into place in front of a Group-of-Seven-ish landscape. Teddy glanced around and could not see Graham Thornbridge. Waving at him, Mrs. Thornbridge made her way forward through the crowd.

"Leaving already? There are so many people you haven't met. There's the whole tennis crew—"

"Thank you very much, Mrs. Thornbridge. Another time. I've promised Janet I'll walk her down to the taxi stand on Sherbrooke Street."

"I see," Mrs. Thornbridge said, her angular head shifting one iota in Janet's direction. "There's nothing like a gentleman, is there, Janet?" Before Janet could reply, she shook Teddy's hand. "I wish you the best of luck in your job hunt."

The young woman in uniform opened the front door as they left.

"Fu-ck-ing *bitch*!" Janet shouted into the sepulchral street with its tombstone mansions, once the door had closed behind them. "She's the perfect lady, but she managed to call me a gold-digging slut and tell you you'll never get any help from her—"

"Don't worry about it. You don't have to see her again and I can find a job on my own."

"You can always teach English as a second language in some little language school. That's what everybody in Montreal does until they find something better."

"I didn't even know that." Teddy settled into a ginger downhill gait. He had forgotten how long and steep the trek down to Sherbrooke Street was. Janet's free-swinging stride, her hair trailing over her shoulders like black rapids, carried him along with a wondrous buoyancy. They didn't speak. It was enough to cavort downhill together across deserted intersections and corners of dormant parks, matching each other's pace and movements. When he accelerated she caught up to him with a laugh; when he dawdled she urged him on. Her smile widened. From the tumult of her eyes to her strong, rounded body he had never seen such a beautiful woman. For the first time in his life he felt that he was in the right place. He wanted to be like Janet. He wanted to feel, with her, that living anywhere other than Montreal was unnatural.

The grind of traffic returned them to the world as they hit the flat, shop-lined stretch of Sherbrooke Street. A red light at an intersection enabled him to ease himself alongside her until their hips nearly touched. He took her hand in his. She gave his palm a squeeze then, as the light changed, released him. Crossing the street, she said: "The taxi stand's over there."

"I live two blocks from here," he said.

"You said you were going to walk me to the taxi stand."

"I said that to Mrs. Thornbridge." At the end of the block he could see two taxis lined up at the corner of a pharmacy.

"I slept with Graham fucking Thornbridge the first night and I wish I hadn't," Janet said. "I'm not going to make that mistake twice. You think I'm crazy?" She was reaching into her bag, scribbling on a piece of paper. He accepted the scrap in numb misery and pushed it into his pocket. Before she could turn away, he laid his hands on her hips. His body felt deranged with desire. Staring into her eyes convinced him he could spend every instant of his existence naked and erect.

He craned forward. Their lips brushed together. She allowed him a nuzzle, the hot ghost of a purchase. Before he could press his mouth into hers, she pulled away. "Goodnight, Teddy."

He watched her go in a sliding disarray of dress, jacket and shoulder bag. "Janet!" he said, as she reached the back door of the taxi. "What am I supposed to do? What happens now?"

"Don't you know anything, Teddy? You've got my phone number. Call me!"

CR CR CR

—Why did you go to Paris?— Conversations crossed and interlaced among the low-sided, close-packed booths of the smoked meat house. At his elbow, three hefty men were discussing horse races in English that even he could recognize as accented. Behind them a solitary, swarthy man was ordering supper in French whose purity reminded André of Paris, distracting him from Marie-Christine's question.

—*J'étais tanné*. I'd been teaching the same courses for fifteen years. I thought it would renew me to listen to lectures at the Sorbonne. But the courses were infantile: classes of three hundred, full of Lebanese and Algerians frantically trying to marry French girls so they could stay in France.—

—That didn't leave many French girls for you, did it, André?—

Girls, he thought. I was in love with her . . . All that felt so far away. Could she imagine . . . ? But no: the years had hardened Marie-Christine's soft maternal air. The grey-tousled black wings of her hair veiled deep lines crawling out from the corners of her eyes. He bit off a deliciously salty mouthful of smoked meat. —You know what the problem with France is, Marie-Christine? You can never relax. Every time you open your mouth in front of them, you feel like you're taking an elocution test.— He pulled his cigarettes out of the inside pocket of his jacket and tilted the pack towards Marie-Christine.

She shook her head. —I've stopped smoking.— Conscious of her appraising gaze, he raked his fingers through his hair, sculpting the strand in the middle of his forehead. —You're not in France any more. What are you going to do until classes start?—

—Work for causes I believe in.—

—More marching? Oh, André, it's time to move on.—

—I've moved on.— He stubbed out his cigarette. He was incapable of defending himself against criticism from women. Papa had never been able to hold his own against Maman, either. He would roll home late and drunk, insult his sons in English, accuse his daughters in French of being ready to *dévergonder* with the first boy who came along . . . Then Maman would put her foot down and it would stop. He slid his cigarette pack into his jacket pocket.

—I'm very, very proud of being Québécoise, Marie-Christine said, but there are so many ways of being in touch with the world. Look at all the different cultures the immigrants bring us— —

—The immigrants! We should send half of them back to where they came from!—

Two tables away, heads turned in a pocket of silence. The men at the next booth continued to discuss the horses.

—*C'est pas possible!* Marie-Christine said, shaking head. —*Tu es con!*—

—You're like the Anglos who write for *The Gazette*. If I defend my language I am a reactionary, if I defend my culture I am a racist. Listen: every culture needs a homeland. This is our place.—

—Without immigrants, Marie-Christine said, stealing the pickle he had left untouched, we wouldn't have smoked meat sandwiches. With our birthrate, we'll disappear without immigrants.—

—We're more likely to disappear because of them.—

—I have to go. My daughter's at the neighbour's. I said I would be back in an hour.—

—The bill, please, André called to the waitress. He stared into Marie-Christine's moon-shaped face, picking out the haze of fine hair on her cheeks. Her daughter. That was the change he had sensed in her. Not so much a hardening as a purpose-fulness; her nourishing warmth, once lavished on friends

without discrimination, had been channelled towards an object.
—How old is your daughter?—

—Almost five.— She reached down to pick up her bag of
groceries.

André paid the bill at the counter. A daughter, he thought.
He asked if he could walk her home. —I want to know what
you're doing, he said, and what's happened to Raymond.—

—So you're still defining me in terms of the man I used to
be married to.—

He bowed his head. They strolled up St-Laurent for two long
blocks, then turned east.

—Raymond took over his grandfather's farm, Marie-
Christine said. —He hardly ever comes to Montreal. He's
decided the Québécois are a rural race: the city destroys us.
He's become an *habitant*. He has a crumpled hat and a grey
beard and grey chest hair poking out of the front of his shirt.
He talks about his livestock like a Beauce farmer and
pronounces his *j*'s like *h*'s.—

Raymond? He thought of the frail body that had strained
towards him over café tables: the smack of Gitanes, Raymond's
intricate intelligence elaborating theories, the tiny glistening
eyes that pinned you in place, demolishing your every objection
until you conceded that his insights cancelled out all other
perceptions, that his conclusions were the only ones
admissable. He tried to imagine Raymond attaching a milking
machine to a cow's udders. Identity *must* contain a core, an
essence that time and place could not wither.

—The last time I went to see him was two years ago, Marie-
Christine said, just after I came back from India. I was very
excited about some of the concepts I'd encounted. And he told
me I wasn't Québécoise any more because I meditated!—

Brick walk-ups fronted by wrought-iron spiral staircases
loomed over them, their mazy symmetry canting the night up
on its heels. He hesitated at the bottom of Marie-Christine's
staircase, waiting for her to break stride. When she kept going,

he followed her around and upwards. She unlocked the middle of three doors on the balcony; they climbed the steep indoor stairs to where they forked at the top. Marie-Christine knocked on the left-hand door. A thin young woman wearing skin-tight bluejeans opened the door on a cauldron of cigarette smoke. —Francine! she called, as Marie-Christine apologized for returning late. The neighbour was peering at André; Marie-Christine did not introduce him. A ruggedy, dark-haired little girl with an aloof self-possessed expression reached up and took Marie-Christine's hand. The neighbour continued to stare at him; he ducked his head before her sharp-jawed scrutiny. When the neighbour's door closed, Marie-Christine said: —You've come this far. You might as well see my apartment.—

Uma Vida Nova (1)

FROM THE AIR THE CITY WAS A LIGHT-DAPPLED PLAIN, the mound of the Mountain swelling the south end and the wide black river passing behind; from the airport bus it became a grid of highways and concrete warehouses; from the taxi it smelled ancient, the odour of old brick belying the gaudy patterns cast by white streetlights and looped neon.

A Portuguese plumber in a Paris *brasserie* with topless posters on the wall and dry couscous on the menu had given João the address of a cousin in Montreal who kept a rooming house. No promises, no guarantee that there would be a bed for him; just an address. He repeated it to the taxi driver.

The driver, a French-speaking black man, nodded. The radio blared an interview in a dancing language he did not recognize. The street ran uphill into the setting sun. The driver told him they were travelling north. They turned into a residential area in which he detected a shadow of France—walls of sagging brick, each gabled house fused to its neighbour—but as the taxi crossed a main street the French on the signs was interspersed with Greek lettering, a knotted Cyrillic chain, even a dash of Portuguese.

The taxi stopped a few blocks off the main street. He climbed out, paid the driver and looked around. The rectangular niches of front doors were recessed into the brick like plugged loopholes. He carried his suitcase across the sidewalk.

A woman of sixty answered the door. She spoke to him in sharp English. He shook his head, replying in French. She gestured with upraised palms, uncomprehending.

—*A senhora fala português?* he said.

Her hand slid down the edge of the door, coming to rest on the handle. — You're lucky, *senhor*, she said, when he had explained what he wanted. —I had one leave last week.—

She motioned to him to bring his suitcase into the hall. She was short and upright. Shuffling past her, he noticed the down of her sideburns.

—Upstairs, she said. —The room under the gable.—

The sun had set. The woman's voice, echoing off the plaster, transported him back to the village he had left at seventeen: the chilly house, Father's creaking complaints about money and thin-voiced praise of Salazar's valour, Mother propped up in bed to murmur to the crucifix on the wall, the brothers he hardly remembered long since departed for Paris, marooning him among the heaped laundry of seven older sisters who chose the clothes he wore, the food he ate, the wording of his confession.

He staggered, clutched at the balcony.

—Are you all right, *senhor?*— She studied him from the top of the stairs, her black eyebrows pulled together.

—*Sim, senhora.*— His vertigo receded. The doctor he had consulted in Lyon, baffled by his dizzy spells and occasional temporary paralysis, had suggested a long holiday. He had taken the prescription as one more reason to emigrate. — *Onde 'stá o quartinho?*—

She led him to a small room under the slant of the roof. Squiggles of caulking swam beneath the overbright light bulb. The room contained a bed, a low bedside table and a chest of drawers in which pairs of interwoven initials had been carved.

—The room costs two hundred dollars a month. The bathroom's at the end of the hall; you have the right to one shower a day. I don't cook for you and the kitchen is off limits. You can buy a smoked meat sandwich on St-Laurent. No noise after ten o'clock. No women in your room.—

João signed over two hundred dollars in traveller's cheques to cover the first month's rent. He was nearly broke. He needed to find a job.

☙ ☙ ☙

On Boulevard St-Laurent he spotted two restaurants advertizing smoked meat sandwiches. In spite of his hunger, curiosity kept him drifting up the street. He passed the fenced-in yard of a Hebrew headstone cutter, a public bath, a porno cinema. The sight of the cinema reminded him of the Rue Confort in Lyon.

The low booths of the smoked meat house were jammed so close together that the patrons seemed to be sitting elbow to elbow. A current of gnarled language surged over him: French, English, something Slavic. The waitress handed him a menu. French and English descriptions of dishes marched down the page in facing columns. The smoked meat his landlady had recommended became *viande fumée* on the French side.

—*Pis? Es-tu prêt à commander?*—

He wanted to snicker at her twanging accent, but the waitress's presumptuous use of the intimate *tu* stung him into silence. —*Une viande fumée, s'il vous plaît.*—

He tried to stress the *vous*; she gave no sign of having noticed his reproof. —*Un smoked meat*, she noted, jabbing at her pad.

Un smoked meat! In his mind's eye he saw the two columns of the menu folding over each other like Flore's crossed legs as she had perched on his stool in her short skirt asking him questions he didn't want to answer. An overwhelming urge to correct the waitress, putting her on the road to proper French, rose up in him. But he had become an immigrant again; he must learn to defer. Never criticize the country or its ways, never say anything that could be interpreted as demonstrating a lack of gratitude, never speak of your homeland other than in terms of its failings: this was the code that had sustained him in Lyon.

—*Voilà ton smoked meat*, the waitress said, returning with his sandwich. *Ce sont des paysans là-bas*, a Paris barman had warned him about Quebec. But peasants, as he knew, compensated for their quaint accents with reticence. The waitress's combination of peasant diction and urban brashness made him clench his teeth.

He demolished his sandwich and ordered a slice of chocolate cake. He patted the curve of his belly, revelling in his muscular solidity.

—The immigrants! a voice two tables over proclaimed, rising above the multilingual chatter. —We should send half of them back to where they came from!—

João lowered his head. The man who had spoken wore a greying beard and long dark hair receding in front and trailing over his collar behind. The woman sitting opposite him reminded João of the American hippie girls who used to drift through Lyon. Her face displayed the beseeching openness that told you that American girls were easy to get into bed. She responded to the man with an angry whisper.

He strained to overhear them. The couple spoke infinitely better than the waitress. As he listened to their quarrel, João grew puzzled. In France people who dressed like bohemians and spoke like books labelled themselves anti-racists; it was the workers who hated immigrants. Could the situation be the reverse in Quebec? Or would he be set upon by hostility from all sides?

He picked up his bill, paid at the counter and escaped into the street.

ଔ ଔ ଔ

Deep in the night, his eyes gummy with jet-lagged exhaustion, he was wrenched awake. A baby was bawling to be fed. He stared up at the slanted ceiling. His arms hung limp at his sides. A car ground down the street, a distant shout flicked at the darkness. No baby. He fell asleep again. Flore was sitting on the stool in her short skirt and scanty working girl's blouse. —It's yours, you're going to have to help me look after it.— Panic stirred in her eyes. He knew that she mistook his silence for an absence of emotion. He had never tried to explain to her that he sank into a shell to keep from feeling too deeply. If he cried, Father would stagger to his feet, his anger fractured by coughing. — Be a man, João! How can Professor Salazar protect our African provinces unless Portugal gives him men?— The collection of dogs lumbering at Father's heels would toss their snouts and howl. His sisters would fall upon him. Seven plump, black-haired figures emanating strange smells, they had firm damp hands and cushion-like breasts that brushed his face when they bent over him. They combed his hair, made him cross himself and disputed with Father the privilege of beating him when he was bad. They had all married late. Suppressed maternal impulses raged through the house, bursting over his head like storm-clouds. As an infant he had delighted in the attention, but around the age of eight it began to make him feel uncomfortable. His adolescence had been dominated by long tramps through the pine forests cloaking the hillsides above the village. Father, hacking and coughing, walked the same paths with his dogs, but they rarely walked together. Father accepted the snub, content to boast to the neighbours about João's independence. Everyone had taken for granted that he would leave the country to find work; perhaps he would follow his brothers to Geneva. But the year he graduated from the *liceu*, the Renault plant in Lyon seemed more promising. Neither Father nor his sisters wished to lose him. —You can come back for Christmas, they said. I'll never set foot here again, he thought, his habit of secrecy already rooted.

In Lyon, lonely and terrified, he drank with men for whom women meant neither the Blessed Virgin nor a gaggle of attentive sisters. Women were wives who were always menstruating when you wanted to fuck them: coarse, physical, gross. His first few months at the plant, before he learned to recognize boastful fantasies, he felt numbed by his workmates' sexual prowess. Desperate to shatter his innocence and solitude, he tried to pick up a proud French girl. She was a secretary in the plant's front office; they rode the same trolley-bus to work. She ridiculed him, calling him a dirty Arab. A couple of weeks later he skulked into his first movie in the Rue Confort. It became a compulsion. He would ride the trolley-bus home, lurching back and forth with the vehicle's swinging motion to preserve his erection. Hidden away in his apartment in the midst of ranks of identical buildings, each plastered with the warning *Surveillant au R.C.*, on the edge of the autoroute in the southeast section of the city, he conquered dozens of women. On nights when the barroom talk turned to women, he was any man's equal.

He lived like that for seventeen years; would still be living that way had he not met Flore. She was twenty-seven, divorced from a worker in a steel plant. She took in laundry to supplement her income as a waitress at a bar where he drank. They collided on the sidewalk one evening as she was coming off her shift. They were both drunk enough to laugh at the accident. The next time he saw her, she suggested they drink together. Her terrifying audacity in asking him first made it impossible for him to back down. He had wrestled down his loneliness by filling every minute of his life with a routine: he never missed a day at the plant, he signed up for a company evening course that would earn him qualifications as a large-engine mechanic, he drank at the Lisboa or one of the French working-class bars with the usual crowd of men, he rebuilt his car on weekends. Like Father's dogs, his cars came and went and never changed. Once he had brought a wreck up to a roadworthy standard he sold it and sank his earnings into another crippled heap. Despite years of labour, he rarely owned a car in running order. His savings grew at a rate so slow as to be negligible; his profits from each car's sale were whittled away by parts and tools as he set to work on his new obsession.

Planning his repairs kept his mind occupied; the men he drank with provided him with a social outlet. Until meeting Flore, he had never thought that the company of one particular person could matter to him. Confused by his yearning to be with her, he was careful always to take her drinking in neighbourhoods where he knew no one. They crossed the Saône into the Vieille Ville and whiled away their evenings in the more expensive cafés patronized by tourists and the bourgeoisie of the Presqu'Île. She was as easy to talk to as a man. But it wasn't the same.

—Walk me home, she said the fourth time they went drinking. —You don't even know where I live.—

Half an hour later he was taking off his shirt in a small stark room. His body sagged before him like a stranger. His tentative erection softened the moment they slid into bed. The rank, salty smell of Flore's flesh sent him spinning back to the cold tile floor of the house built into the fir-covered hillside; a cloud of handkerchiefs was descending.

Flore rolled over onto her back, folding her hands behind her head. He gave the shocks of black hair filling her armpits a long look. She turned towards him. Her wine-and-Gitanes breath overpowered the smell of their bodies. —Have you slept with many women?—

—About fifteen, he said, hoping it sounded right.

She turned over, sliding on top of him. The burning blanket of her body felt wonderful, yet the expression in her eyes told him he was doing something wrong. His tenseness, probably; she had mentioned it in the café, a moment after reaching for his hand. He shifted beneath her, stretching his arms to caress her shoulders with his fingers. She regarded him with an unrelenting gaze.

By the time they finally made love a week later, he had told her almost everything. In between they had spent two long awkward nights in the same bed. After the first night he never wished to see her again. He did not understand why he went back the second night or the third. What could he possibly need from her? She joked about his inability to get an erection. The disruptions her demands wreaked in his routine of work-bar-car enraged him. There were moments when, overwhelmed by an onrush of fury, he hated her. The rest of the time he did not know how to describe his feelings towards her. She had become part of his existence—that was all.

One hot Sunday afternoon Flore smashed the boundary between their life and the life he had led before meeting her. She slipped into the friend's garage where he kept his car, crouched down to find him flat on his back under the chassis and called out to him to come and see her that night. He grunted, continuing to unscrew bolts. By the time he slid out from under the car, the other men were laughing. That evening everyone in the bar would know.

—Why did you do that? he asked as he shut the door of her room behind him.

—I wanted to see you. I need a man like you in my bed.— She took two steps forward, thrusting her body against him.

Why me? he thought. If she had been looking for a real man his revelations of their first two nights together would have persuaded her to look elsewhere. He began to ask himself what she saw in him. It perplexed him: didn't women select the most virile, manly men available to them? The tall French girls who paraded around the centre of the city in their tight slacks and loose white blouses made him feel inadequate. Yet Flore, as French as any of them despite having grown up in the country, seemed to relish his inexperience; she liked being the knowledgeable one, the boss in bed. Disgusted with himself, he vowed to end the affair. But when his buddies at the bar teased him in tones of twisted envy, he saw that he had accomplished something they only envisaged in boozy reverie: he had snared a Frenchwoman. His workmates and acquaintances were subsiding into middle age in the company of the wives who had accompanied them from Portugal. The women had grown indistinguishable from one another, worn down into sharp-featured querulousness by endless cleaning jobs, their names nearly erased by having been addressed by every French family they worked for as "Conchita." João, meanwhile, was plundering the female riches of France.

The thought put a swagger in his stride. He stayed with Flore, even though making love with her began to make his skin crawl. Their intimacy felt like a violation. Each time he whimpered towards a climax, his head locked close to hers, he felt pathetic. In becoming at last a man who did the things men were supposed to do with women, he had been shorn of the dignity and self-reliance which had defined his manhood.

Their affair ended the day she entered his apartment without knocking. Her hands empty—he realized later it was the first time he had seen her without a purse or bag—she seated herself on the stool and folded her arms across her stomach in a white-knuckled barrier. Her skirt rode up her thighs as she crossed her legs. He asked her how she had got past the *surveillant* on the ground floor. But that was not what she wished to discuss.

It had taken him almost a year to realize that he must leave. He had thought Flore would agree to an abortion; he had hoped she would disappear from Lyon, bury herself in her village in the Auvergne. Her determination grew savage. When he moved apartment buildings, she tracked him down. The *surveillant* who called him downstairs assessed Flore's belly and scowled at João. He moved out at the end of the month, taking refuge in a room left vacant by a man who had returned to Trás-Os-Montes. Three months later, when he had moved on to another apartment building, she brought the baby to his door: a bawling deflated-inner-tube of humanity swaddled in stinking blankets. It smelled of the piles of his sisters' undergarments. Conversation ceased when he walked into the Lisboa. For all their boasting, his drinking partners were Catholic family men. João, who had lost God somewhere between the Beiras and

Lyon, tried to mine his misadventure for lusty jokes. —I'll bet there isn't a man at this table who hasn't fathered a bastard!—

His smile of invitation fell flat. Next morning at the Renault plant, hooded by his soldering mask, he began to plan his escape.

*f*our

—I'VE SET UP A NUMBERED COMPANY TO MANAGE THE BUILDING, Abitbol said. —I'll rent you an office downtown. You can borrow Sylvie two days a week. You'll continue to earn your salary. Once the conversion's finished you'll get a ten-per-cent commission on our profit.— He paused. —You'll be able to buy back your house in Outremont.—

—Buy it back from you.—

—There'll be more work in the future. As long as you act responsibly we'll all prosper.—

Blackmail, Marcel thought as he drove home. By the time he had nodded his acquiescence and asked Abitbol for the rest of the day off, he had begun to feel faint. The folder-packed walls of the inner office blocked the flow of air to his brain. Sweat plastered his hair to his forehead. He arranged to meet Abitbol on Sherbrooke Street in the morning.

Sylvie did not look up as he passed through the outer office. He shut himself into the Honda and trailed his fingers over his tape collection. Ferry? Gabriel? No, he was on his way back to Maryse. He slipped a Michel Rivard cassette into the tape player, twisted up the volume, and threaded his way through Outremont. He was still sweating. He hated Abitbol, he loved him. He had never felt closer to his brother-in-law, yet their new closeness—if that was what it was—unnerved him.

—*Libérer le trésor!* Michel Rivard sang.

Liberté. Abitbol uttered the word in a derisive tone. How could anyone who had gained so much from Canadian freedom despise the claims freedom made on a traditional way of life? And why does he take it out on me? He tries to make me live like a Moroccan! He envisaged himself hurling these complaints at Maryse in a few minutes' time. Family loyalty roared back, gutting his complicity with Maryse. He longed for her steady hands and soft breasts: she was a stranger who comforted him. Maryse took him shopping in boutiques on Avenue Laurier where before he would have felt uncomfortable setting foot; as her husband, he attended parties in Outremont houses he used to stare at as a boy, wondering what the old bourgeois families living there were like. Yet she did not always follow the twists of his psyche. He knew her world better than she knew his. He had grown up in Quebec; she had not grown up among Jews.

He turned the Honda into the housing development. The hum of the Laurentian Autoroute made him think of the unmade bed in Abitbol's chalet. He snapped the tape out of the player, parked the Honda in the down-sloping driveway and bounded up the front steps. A trembling in his calves recalled the depleting lunge of this morning's orgasm. As he opened the door and confronted Maryse, his sight was hazed by a vision of the spider's-leg hairs creeping out of the crack of Ruthie's ass.

Maryse greeted him in baggy designer bluejeans and a name-brand cotton top, a tapered paint brush in her right hand. She had spread a dropcloth over the living-room carpet and opened the windows. A water colour leaned against the top of her easel. She was four years older than he was. He admired the length and delicacy of her fingers, anomalous by contrast with her broad palms. The scrutiny of her clear artist's eyes made him feel plumbed and revealed, absolved of any need to confess.

She kissed him on the tip of the chin. —Can't Abitbol send someone else to Lennoxville?—

—I've got good news, he said. —I'll tell you about it when I've had a shower.—

As she followed him up the narrow staircase, he watched her drag her fingers over the stippled nobbles of the finish on the walls. Maryse pined for varnished wood panels, muted wallpaper, brick fireplaces. She stood in the hall, watching him undress on the bathroom tiles. Had Ruthie's lovemaking marked him? He threw away his clothes. Maryse picked them up and carried them to the wicker hamper in the laundry room. He stepped under the hot jet of the shower. His heart thumped as he soaped and scrubbed himself. Maryse, returning to the bathroom, studied him.

—I'm glad you're home.— She took his hand as he stepped out of the shower. She dried him with brisk scrubbing movements, wielding the towel as though it were one of the pads she used to wash out her paint brushes. In the bedroom, Maryse tugged the cord and the Venetian blinds clattered down.

Nothing was more exciting than making love with Maryse while another woman's imprint lingered on his skin. From the bun of light brown hair at the back of her head to the curve of her thighs and the fullness of her stomach, she conjoined cushioned loops of hair and skin. He sucked and bit her breasts until she cried out. He hurtled around the spirals of her body until dizziness overcame him.

He woke to the sound of the Iraqui children next door arguing over their badminton game. The taste of Maryse's nipples and clitoris lingered on his tongue.

—You must have been exhausted. You've been sleeping like a baby.—

He reached for his glasses and realized they were in the bathroom. His fingers bumped against the spicebox he had bought Maryse in an antique shop. She kept it on the bedside table like a trophy: proof that he was capable of showing good taste.

Resigning himself to speaking to Maryse through a blur— it didn't matter, in some ways it brought her closer—he shrugged himself up against the pillow and told her about Abitbol's plans for the Victoria-Waterloo. When he mentioned the ten-per-cent commission, she raised her head.

—Marcel! We could move back to Outremont— —

He listened in covetous silence as she murmured in her high, *pointu* voice, painting a picture of their future life. Her world was so complete. The uncle of one *copine* was a Parti Québécois Member of National Assembly, the brother of another of her friends had become a rising junior minister in Ottawa. Her father served on the board of managers of *La Presse*, a neighbour was a columnist for *Le Devoir*. Her mother, who managed an art gallery, knew all of Quebec's painters, writers and film-makers, and invited them over for cocktails. When he and Maryse had met, he had been stunned that she spared him a glance. At the Université de Montréal the wealthy women in his classes, adjusting their scarves, would chat across the top of his head during the moments before lectures began. When Maryse consented to go out with him, his hands began to shake. After they made love for the first time he felt filled not with his usual sated sense of conquest, but with an uneasy awe.

Who would he have become had he married a woman from his own background? He imagined himself immured in an Abitbol-like remove from the city, his home an emotional museum: a territory apart from the streets where he was scrambling to earn a living. By marrying Maryse, he had locked himself into an unending tussle with Montreal. *Liberté*, the word of which Abitbol was so suspicious, revealed itself as an infinite round of overlapping lives.

Abitbol and Véronique claimed to have brought him up into a secure tradition—*les liens qu'on avait au Maroc!*—but when he thought back to their first Montreal apartment he could not remember a single Moroccan trait. Even their homes in Morocco, Abitbol would concede, had been vacant of furniture or art belonging to the country where they had lived for a thousand years. Religion had anchored them. The trappings of their day-to-day lives had consisted of bric-à-brac from the warehouse of international francophone culture: bottles of scent from the Côte d'Azur, Provençal red wine, bidets, Alsatian salad bowls, Swiss watches, *Maria Chapdelaine* and the novels of Anatole France and Saint-Exupéry. None of them would have displayed great interest in a Moroccan carpet. Abitbol, on a visit to his mother—still living in Fes, although all her relatives had left the country, or moved to drab, industrial Casablanca—had searched for keepsakes of the old life to decorate their apartment. He had returned empty-handed but for his father's skull-cap and shawl. He had pegged the garments to the wall for a few weeks, then taken them down and replaced them with his framed law diploma.

Their first apartment, just off Avenue du Parc, had consisted of three small rooms in a low building of gloomy corridors and dangling fire escapes. He lost his bedroom a year after his arrival, when Louis was born. Madeleine was born two years later. The babies, as he continued to think of them, had exiled him to the couch until he was sixteen. The infants kept him awake at night and left Véronique no time to speak to him. He lost his temper when Louis and Madeleine, now twenty-one and nineteen and both studying law at the Université de Montréal, feigned ignorance of the small apartments and constant moves of those early years. Abitbol's present stolid house in the heart of Outremont was the only home they recognized. To Marcel this house, which Abitbol had bought after he moved out, felt unreal; his sharpest memories were of their third apartment, a precarious perch on the edge of Outremont where for the first time he had slept in his own room.

—I can hardly wait to have a house big enough for my wardrobe, Maryse said, kissing him on the mouth. —*Mon beau juif,* with you life is never boring.—

Marcel slid his arm around her shoulder. Tomorrow he would have to deal with tenants, enter their apartments, gain their confidence. He conjured up the Victoria-Waterloo in his mind's eye. He found himself trying to imagine how many single women lived there.

ଔ ଔ ଔ

"I'm working in a little language school on Ste. Catherine. I wanted to say thanks. You were the one who told me to look for a job teaching English."

"I never said that. A guy like you should have a good job, Teddy."

"This is okay for now. Not everyone can teach literature at a Cégep."

"But I'll never get on full-time like those jerks who started in the seventies with half my qualifications. I'm still in a shitty apartment. Five years of university and I'm twenty minutes up the hill from where I started."

Teddy was on the brink of telling her that after their first long telephone conversation he had gone to visit Rue St-Jacques. It had taken him hours, via a series of infrequent bus connections, to reach the tinny low-rise buildings across the street from tawdry motels, the curled neon, gravel yards and rusted balconies. He had expected an inner-city slum; but the area where Janet had grown up felt far-flung and neglected, blemished by ugly tracts of bare earth and gravel, and separated from the city by barren industrial lots. Before he could speak, she said: "And don't make me sick with your fucking sympathy, Mr. Rockcliffe. You probably get more money from your investments in a month than I make from my teaching in a year."

"I don't know what I get from my investments."

"But your parents—"

"My parents are dead, remember?" A hot shiver shot up the backs of his legs. Janet's silence suggested a moment of genuine consideration. If he held off replying, she might even apologize. Deciding to spare her this indignity, he said in a soft voice: "Tell me about your childhood."

"My childhood was three big kids and two rowdy parents in an apartment where you could hear every car that passed on St. Jacques. The TV was in the middle of the apartment, it was on all the time and there was nowhere you could get away from it. My parents were always shouting in this weird Glaswegian dialect—we thought they were aliens. When my dad coached soccer I had to go with him to translate for the boys."

"What do your parents do?"

"Is this your way of slumming? My dad was a coal-miner in Scotland. When they came here he ended up working on the line in the Molson's bottling plant. My mum scrubs rich people's floors—in Westmount."

"Oh, man." In the silence, Teddy heard voices calling up through the floor from the basement. What had Janet been trying to do by going out with Graham Thornbridge? "Look, part of the reason I called was to let you know that I did get a job by networking with the one full-fledged working class girl at that party, but the other reason is that I'd like to see you. Can't we go to a movie?"

"Not now. I don't think I should get involved with anybody. In a few months' time I'm probably going to move back to Scotland."

"Scotland? But you told me you would never live anywhere but Mon—"

"I'd never go out west like my brother and sister. I'm the oldest, it's my job to stay here with my parents. But immigrating was a mistake for them. Their lives aren't any better here and this isn't our home. The only place I feel at home is in Scotland."

"Were you not born here in Canada?"

"I was three when we came over."

"So this is your home."

"You've been in the States too long, Teddy. You think everybody just slips into some American dream."

"Okay, so why don't we have dinner downtown and you can tell me how I'm wrong? I'll wear my black leather jacket and nobody will ever guess you're eating dinner with a guy from Rockcliffe."

"If you wear a black leather jacket, *everybody*'ll know you're from Rockcliffe." She giggled. "Teddy, sometimes you're a funny guy. But I just don't want to get involved. I'm moving to Scotland and that's it. Sometimes you have to make a decision and stick to it."

"This is the second time I've called you, this is the second time we've talked for over an hour then you've said no. You can't expect me—"

"Okay, so don't call me any more." Janet hung up.

Teddy undressed and flopped onto the mattress in his bedroom. He lay on his back and looked out the window at the shaft in the middle of the building. For days after the party he had been masturbating like a maniac to fantasies of furious sex with Janet . . . And those goddamn kids! Rollie and some buddies he had picked up were in their basement clubhouse every night. Rollie's incomprehensible patois came warbling through the floor. Teddy had begun to doze off when a triumphant shout stung him awake: "*Me pitch a brick through Beast Beauchamp's window!*"

He rolled over onto his stomach and pounded his fist on the floorboards. Voices, male and female, jeered in reply.

He woke late. When he knocked on the concierge's door, Joe's wife answered. A bulky, strangely nimble woman, she wore thick glasses. Her grey hair was still partly in curlers. She invited him in. The concierge sat at the kitchen table. The straps of his tank-topped T-shirt lay slack over the wide pads of flesh on his shoulders.

"Those kids woke me up again last night."

"You listen to me, Teddy," Joe said, rousing himself to light a Player's Plain. "I worked with cadets for twenty years—bad ones as well as good ones. And there's never one so bad you can't make him better. I gave those lads a place to live, I gave them work, they go to the washroom in the restaurant down the street. If I kick them out, the cops'll pick them up. Is that what you want?"

"I want a good night's sleep. The next time they wake me up I'm calling the police."

When he returned to the Waterloo side of the building, he noticed that two ceiling bulbs in the corridor had burned out. The marble pattern on the floor looked not only darker but dingier.

He took on more hours at the language school. The boss, a tense young man who wore funereal black suits, paced the corridor of the cramped suite of offices. He stuck his head in the door of Teddy's classroom at inopportune moments. "You're a good teacher, Teddy," he said, "but I prefer the attitude of teachers who don't talk back." Teddy wasn't aware that he had talked back; but that problem arose often here.

The school offered daytime classes for students with government subsidies and—far more lucrative for the teachers—early-morning and late-night private classes for bankers and business people. Teddy had hoped to be assigned the private classes, but the boss distrusted him. He taught the drones: unemployed francophones whose benefits were extended on the condition that they spend six hours a day doing English grammar exercises in notebooks, supplemented by an hour or two of conversation. Teddy was paid six dollars an hour for correcting the notebook entries and once a day asking the students to describe in English what they had done last night. "None of your business," some of them said, smirking.

Leaving the language school's blank office block every afternoon, he glanced at the balconied restaurants and frantic pick-up bars of Rue Crescent. Life—Canadian life, *his* life—cavorted beyond his grasp. He contemplated going to Ottawa for the weekend, but there was nothing left for him in Rockcliffe. A month went by and another began; he realized he would be spending Christmas and New Year's alone. Flying back to California for the holidays he ruled out as an admission of defeat. When he left, Zach and Marian had made him promise to stay in touch and crash at the house on his return visits. But every time he lifted the receiver to phone them he was stymied by the prospect of trying to explain his Montreal life. Even so, nothing would be easier than returning to Berkeley. He could sleep on the couch, go to parties with Zach and Marian, look up women he had liked. Yet if he was going to spend 1988 in Canada, part of him insisted, then he should be here for the first hours of the new year.

Every few days in December young black West Indian men wearing woolly hats knocked on his door. Brushing splayed fingers past their open mouths, they murmured: "Ganja, mon."

"I think there's somebody selling on the third floor."

He had gleaned this information from Mrs. McNulty. She had complained that the young Barbadian man who had moved in up there (why had Joe rented to him?) was selling drugs. There was traffic through his apartment at all hours; reggae music boomed from his stereo at four in the morning. Her son Paddy, a born-again Christian and, she said, a very moral boy, had threatened to call the police. Joe had warned him not to. Then the Bajan had come downstairs and yelled bad language in Paddy's face.

"I don't know what to do," Mrs. McNulty said. "For twenty-one years the Victoria-Waterloo was a decent place to live. I should phone Rubinsteins and tell them how Joe's running their building into the ground."

Teddy tried to tramp off his depression with long walks up snowpacked sidewalks. He had lost the resilience that used to let him exult at the Canadian winter. The wind swept through him as though he were immaterial, he opened his mouth too wide and felt an icy chill plunge to the bottom of his lungs. His flesh, receptive when it should be resistant, drew the cold inside him. Each time he stepped out of his apartment, Rollie, garbed in a black autumn jacket, was leaning against the mailboxes at the end of the hall. His face had grown skeletal, his cheekbones standing out like brands. The yellowish tint shining through his dark brown skin had become more pronounced. Teddy felt intimidated at having to walk past the youth in order to leave the building. Rollie was tall. But for his enervated, malnourished appearance, he would have been a commanding figure. He propped himself up against the mailboxes with a four-foot-long stake slightly thicker than a broomhandle. Sometimes, as Teddy walked past, he heard the stake crack against the heavy oak frame of the door. When he turned to stare the youth down, Rollie responded with a gaunt, canine smile. A cornered desperation surfaced in his eyes. He was standing there, Teddy realized, because he had nowhere else to go.

ભ ભ ભ

—Maman's very sorry for being late, Marie-Christine said, crouching down to kiss her daughter. —Maman met a friend who was lost, so she invited him home.—

Francine dealt André a pitying stare. Abandoning his impulse to try to earn the tot's affection, he examined the apartment. Originally one long crooked room of polished hardwood floors, it had been equipped with a bedroom by the insertion of two pressboard partitions and a curtain. The walls were decorated with posters of elephant-headed gods rearing their trunks against Taj Mahal-like backdrops. The air smelled of incense. Marie-Christine talked Francine into bed in a cot in the kitchen. She turned off the lights and motioned to André to follow her into the bedroom. Stepping around the curtain, he found that the queen-sized bed nearly filled the space enclosed by the partitions and the back wall. Marie-Christine switched on a pale lamp, kicked off her heavy-soled shoes and lay down. Bending over his gut to untie his shoelaces, André reflected that at eighteen rolling onto a bed with Marie-Christine, even fully clothed, would have made him gasp. He glanced at her eyes, uncertain how to read her sparkling, rueful welcome. It had been years since he had lain in bed with a woman. How would she react if he told her that?

Once he had pushed a pillow behind his head, he stared at their two pairs of feet spilling sideways shadows against the curtain. The chamber was hazy with lamp-glow. —Who's the girl's father?—

—Nobody important. A young guy with a wallet full of money who came into the store at closing time. I decided I couldn't go through with an abortion. I was terrified at the time, but now I'm so glad I had her. My grandmother in Gaspésie gave birth to twenty-one children and my mother gave birth to seven— —

—If our women were still like that, we wouldn't risk disappearing as a people.—

—*Franchement*, André! You wouldn't want to live with a woman like that.—

—No, I wouldn't want to live with a woman . . . like that.— He pushed himself up on his elbows. She was looking at the curtain. —So Raymond isn't Marie-Christine's father?—

—Is that what's bothering you?— She edged closer to him; he felt caressed and stung at the same time. —You can stop worrying: Raymond is infertile. That was one of the reasons our marriage ended. I wanted children and he couldn't give them to me.—

—Infertile?— He stared at the walls of the partition. How could Marie-Christine sleep in this tomb? —But neither of you said anything. I was there when your marriage was breaking up, I was there when you were learning to deal with each other socially again. I heard both sides of every argument, and neither of you— — He stopped, remembering Raymond's accusation that Marie-Christine refused to give up petit-bourgeois values. She wanted *children*, Raymond had groaned.

—I don't think we were as close as we liked to make out. We were our parents' children, after all. We had grown up in homes where many subjects weren't discussed.— Marie-Christine bit her lip. —André, what's happened to Lysiane?—

He tried to ignore the tremor in her voice. —You mean you're not in touch? When did you last—?—

—Two and a half years ago. Two weeks before Francine and I left for India. Even then she didn't want to talk to me. She told me I was part of her problems. Me! Her best friend! . . . When I got back from India she had moved and I couldn't find her in the phone book.—

—The last I heard, André said, she was working in the marketing division of Provigo . . . Tell me what you're doing.—

—I make seven dollars an hour in a poster shop.— She spread her hands in front of her; the boniness of age had begun to chisel at her veins. —I don't think I've organized my life very well. In the old days all I cared about was making love with Raymond and running around making a lot of noise at parties. Feminism arrived five years too late for me. The only thing I've succeeded at is having a daughter. Since Francine was born my life has had a shape.—

Her voice stopped. The refrigerator hummed. He squeezed her forearm, then withdrew his grip.

—You could stay the night, Marie-Christine said. —I mean just to sleep.—

—Thanks.— He studied her shaggy, unplucked eyebrows, remembering how exotic he had found her when they met. In fact, his upbringing in Ville Lasalle had differed little from hers in the Plateau Mont-Royal. But how different the Plateau had seemed! Papa and Maman had shaken their heads, baffled by his fascination with riding into the centre of Montreal to spend time in cafés on Rue St-Denis. In those days only the *intellos* hung out on St-Denis. The street was dilapidated and angry. Rallies erupted in the Carré St-Louis in fits of near-spontaneous combustion. He and Raymond, hunched over candle-studded tables, thrashed out the strengths, weaknesses and applicability to Quebec of every revolutionary doctrine tossed up by the Third World. Papa and Maman's disapproval heightened his absorption with the neighbourhood. In the end he had returned home: after marrying, he and Lysiane had moved into a duplex in Lasalle ten minutes' walk from his parents' cottage.

—Remember the rock concerts on the Mountain? Marie-Christine said. —Sitting on the grass getting high and falling in love with somebody?—

He remembered. As adolescent gawkiness yielded to a graceful self-assurance of movement, they assumed that this was their enduring adult state. They would always possess these slender bodies and smooth faces, this surging energy and moral certainty. They would always be in revolt, cheering Bourgault or Lévesque. They would always agree with each other.

Listening to himself and Marie-Christine, he realized that their thoughts were circulating in separate orbits. Half a dozen times he heard himself mention *le déclin post-référendaire*: he could not ignore how every aspect of life had grown smaller and meaner since the referendum. Marie-Christine's test phrase, *une grande ouverture d'esprit*, nagged at his brain. When he challenged her, she said: —You started me on this road, André. It was getting to know you that taught me that nice people existed outside my own neighbourhood, that in the end we're all human . . . —

—But our culture— —

—*Ma langue! Ma culture!* You sound like Raymond.—

—I'd rather sound like Raymond than like you.—

Francine began to cry.

—Idiot. Couldn't you keep your voice down?— She climbed out of bed, her long hair swaying. The lamp bled the lines in her forehead into black bands. He floundered around the curtain to find Marie-Christine kneeling over Francine's cot. She had turned on the light over the stove and was brushing her daughter's black hair off her forehead. Francine's eyes, seeking him out with an admonishing stare, looked even darker than her mother's.

Bending down to pull on his shoes, André broke into an ungainly hop.

—You're leaving?—

He tied his shoelaces.

—Your complexes can't handle this, can they? Me with a daughter and you with nothing but theories.—

I have more than theories, he thought. I have a whole world you know nothing about. He started to reply, but the unearthly darkness of the child's eyes reduced him to silence.

ભ ભ ભ

What a dive! Marcel thought. When Anglos ceased to be rich, they lived like animals. The peeling brown paint of the woodwork over the twin doors advertised an arrogant disregard for appearances. English-language community newspapers — *The Suburban, The Monitor*—sat stacked on the floor beneath the mailboxes; the crushed red-and-white Kentucky Fried Chicken container looked garishly alien by comparison with the brown-and-gold Poulet St-Hubert boxes he glimpsed in the districts of the city he usually frequented. He imagined Maryse's discomfort at such foreign crassness.

—What do you think? Abitbol said, flourishing his stubby arms. —Have I bought myself a *dar-el-hzar*?—

—Yes, Marcel said, with a hostile grunt, it's a real haunted house.—

—Your job is to exorcize it.— He laid a finger on Marcel's breastbone. A scrawny black youth slipped down the hall, regarding them with skittish eyes. —Drive out the spirits.—

They went downtown to the office Abitbol had rented for the numbered company. A sturdy 1930s block, the building stood on a crowded section of Rue Ste-Catherine. Long corridors of yellowing tiles led past doors whose detachable plaques announced the presence of passport photographers, private detectives, modelling agencies, fledgling labour unions and fly-by-night language schools. The office was on the fourth floor at the back. Tall buildings closed off the view. Looking down, Marcel saw a narrow alley opening onto a miniature parking lot dominated by a dumpster. The office contained two identical desks, one of them equipped with a monstrous second-hand manual typewriter. The imprints of vanished filing cabinets scored the grey wall-to-wall carpet. —It's not very luxurious.—

—You make money by holding down expenses, Abitbol said.

Marcel sat down on the desk, stretching his bluejeaned legs. What would Maryse say if he brought her here? Staring at his square-toed black shoes, he vowed to save every penny he earned until he was able to go into business for himself. They drove back to Outremont in Abitbol's BMW. The week after next, Abitbol told him, the engineer's report would be ready; he mentioned sources of cheap labour. Struggling to pay attention, Marcel tried to imagine what his life would be like once this conversion was over.

—Pierre, Sylvie said, as they came up the stairs into the outer office, the man you asked for an interview is on his way.—

Marcel glanced at Abitbol, who looked up from his folded pink message slips. —We're going to hire someone to help you clear the building, he said.

A moment later, as Marcel was making himself a coffee, they heard footsteps on the stairs. A broad-chested man wearing a tight-fitting, short-sleeved blue shirt entered the office.

—Marcel, this is Bruno, Abitbol said. —Bruno has applied for the job of helping us to clear the Victoria-Waterloo. Interview him, please.— He walked into the inner office and shut the door.

Marcel set aside his coffee and sat down behind his desk. He gestured to Bruno to pull up the low stool next to the wall. He saw Bruno appraising him from above the downturned black fork of a mustache that flared into waxed curls on his cheeks. His dark hair had receded at the temples. The grey plastic belt securing his bluejeans was disintegrating. Marcel asked him to describe his last job. Bruno shrugged his shoulders. Only two months had passed since his arrival in Canada from Calle Israel in Tetouan.

Marcel nodded, noting Bruno's Ladino accent—*Haketiya,* Abitbol called it. —What did you do at home?—

Bruno pulled a pack of Gauloises from his shirt pocket and lighted up. —I've spent the last two years in jail, he said. —But how can a Jew expect justice from Arabs?—

—What was the charge against you?—

—Receiving stolen property.— Bruno laughed. —All property is stolen if you think about it long enough, *no es así?*—

Sylvie's typewriter fell silent. Behind the house the Greek's truck whined out of the yard.

—The boss, Bruno continued, giving a Spanish roll to the *r* in *patron,* told me you're looking for a guy to strongarm some niggers. Believe me, I'm your man. I've spent half my life breaking nigger heads.—

Marcel leaned back in his chair, glad of the refuge afforded by the smoked lenses of his glasses. Sylvie glanced at him from behind Bruno's back.

—*Attendez un instant,* he said. He knocked on Abitbol's door, awaited permission to enter and slipped inside. —We can't hire that man. He's a criminal.—

Abitbol swore in Judeo-Arabic. —That snob wife of yours! Listen, Marcel: sometimes in order to live in Outremont it is necessary to employ people whom one would not choose to meet in a café on Avenue Bernard.—

—He's not like us . . . —

—Those *megorashim* can be tough customers. You don't like Bruno because he's what you would have become if we hadn't brought you to Canada. Cut yourself in half, Marcel, he said, chopping with the blunt cleaver of his outstretched hand. — You must be one kind of person with your family but you must be another kind of person to survive in the world.—

—I cut myself in half when I got married.— He collapsed into the hard chair facing Abitbol's desk. The tiny, packed office was suffocating him.

—Then you are ideally qualified to manage this conversion. Now go back out there and tell Bruno he's hired.—

Marcel got to his feet. In the outer office, he shook Bruno's hand and peeled off two brown hundred-dollar bills from his wallet as a retainer. Maryse dominated his thoughts for the rest of the day. He drove home through the Friday afternoon traffic dreaming of idyllic hours in her company. As soon as he stepped in the door they began to bicker. She wanted him to go to a party at her parents' house; he had told Véronique that he would celebrate *Chabat* with the family.

—Everyone thinks I married a rabbi, Maryse said, as they climbed into the Honda.

—I promised my sister . . . —

—Your sister! What about your wife? How am I supposed to explain to my uncle that you can't come and meet him because it's Friday night?—

She folded her long-fingered hands in her lap. He winced, remembering the clattering sound Ruthie had made as she rifled through his cassettes. He drove in silence to the fringes of Outremont. —It's the old litany: despise other people's customs. No wonder all the immigrants become anglophones.—

—Oh, so it's our fault they hate us?—

—Look at me, he said, turning the Honda onto a tree-lined street. Beneath the overhanging branches, bright streetlights illuminated the wavy grain of tightly mown grass. —Abitbol and Véronique tried to enroll me in a French school when I came here, but they weren't allowed to because I was Jewish.—

—The church controlled everything then. The system has changed.—

—The Québécois wouldn't accept us as francophones and the English-speaking Jews refused to admit we were Jewish. For them we were some kind of half-breed Arab . . . —

—Marcel, Maryse said, her fingers caressing his shoulder. —Is there anyone you're not angry at?—

He squeezed the Honda to a halt at a four-way stop. Hasidic boys pumped across the intersection on square, functional bicycles, the flopping pelts of their sidelocks lending their unformed faces a beaver-bright glossiness. As a boy he had hated the Hasidics for propagating an image of Jews as troll-like creatures possessed of bizarre customs. He had been horrified when they had pressured the mayor into banning sunbathing in Parc Outremont. He had blamed the Hasidics, as much as Véronique and Abitbol, for thwarting his efforts to fit in at high school. —I'm getting tense about this conversion. I want it to go right so I can get you out of Ville St-Laurent.—

—That's a pressure you've chosen to place upon yourself, she said, her twisted bun of hair grazing the headrest. —It's not my fault.—

I didn't say it was your fault. —I'd like you to come and look at the Victoria-Waterloo once we begin the renovations, he said. —I'd appreciate having your opinion on the interior decorating.— He stopped the Honda in front of her parents' house. —Will you do that for me?—

—Of course, Marcel. Can you come in for a few minutes? Just to greet my uncle?—

He unhitched his seatbelt. She slid her arm around his waist as they crossed the darkened lawn. When they stepped into the glare of the porch light her hand fell away and he was on his own, miraculously steering himself through a bourgeois Outremont home. The high-ceilinged living room, as spacious and wood-solid as a heritage barn, remained sparingly furnished; there were heavy bookshelves, their contents disordered by evident use, an austere high-backed couch and a long oak table sprouting bushy plants in earthenware jars. His early visits to Maryse's parents' house had left him envious of the confidence that enabled them to inhabit so much space yet leave it uncluttered. Véronique and Abitbol stuffed every cranny of their house with furniture, appliances and toys. At first Maryse's parents' house had struck him as neglected; then, during a difficult period when he feared she would not marry him, he had seen the long bare patches as symptomatic of the emotional hollowness that rendered even French-speaking Canadians incapable of valuing sentiment. Only later had he come to appreciate her family's restraint as the imprint of good taste. He thought about the large rooms and ugly parquet floors of the Victoria-Waterloo. He needed Maryse to help him flip the building.

He shook her father's hand, kissed her mother on both cheeks. In her parents' company Maryse became a demure girl who spoke in deftly trained phrases that admitted no doubts. She was recounting, as if their plans had been confirmed weeks ago, that at Christmas she and Marcel would host the family *réveillon* at their home in Outremont. Her combed bangs glowed. He stared at her, his consternation mellowing to confused pride as Maryse's mother soaked him in a look laden with moist approval. —Maryse was brought up to a certain level of comfort, she had told him when they had announced their plans to marry. —We're all proud of her painting, but she wasn't meant to live *la vie de bohème*, all on her own at thirty-two. She needs regularity.— Regularity meant marriage, but it also meant money. As long as he earned enough to live in Outremont, Maryse's mother would muffle her distrust of his background; and her ponderous, pontificating father would not dare to dent his wife's contentment.

—So when can we clear Maryse's paintings and wardrobe out of the upstairs room? her father said, ushering Maryse's uncle into the living room.

The uncle, an elderly man with a distracted manner who recalled the wardrobe from the days when it had graced the family home in Quebec City, elaborated on the heirloom's antiquity. He did not appear to remember Marcel.

—They can't get it through the door of that cottage they're living in, Maryse's father said. —They're camping up there.—

—We'll be moving back to Outremont in the fall, Marcel said.

—But you speak French well! the uncle said. —One would take you for a francophone.—

—He *is* a francophone, Maryse said. —Just like us.—

—Not just like us, her father said, the arm of his blazer describing a navy-blue sweep. —We don't leave parties early on Friday night. We go to church on Sunday, *nous autres*.—

—I'm walking Marcel to the door.— Maryse caught his elbow and guided him towards the porch. —I apologize for my father. Thank you for not responding.— She reached up to kiss him. Her full white face and warm mouth made him ask himself again how he had become the man she had chosen to marry. He loathed himself for having spent his passion on Ruthie, the Saguenay waitress, the Lebanese girl, the saleswoman. His memories of their bodies heaved before his mind's eye.

—Do you miss your wardrobe? he asked.

—I miss not having anything old in the house. I feel cut off from my heritage up there.— Her uncle's disjointed laughter staggered out into the night. —Listen, this may go on late. Maman's invited all her artist friends. I'll probably spend the night in my old bedroom.—

—All right, he said, perhaps I'll sleep at my sister's and we can drive back tomorrow morning.—

He slid into the Honda. Only three blocks separated Maryse's parents' house from that of Véronique and Abitbol. He couldn't transform himself that fast. He swung around the block, pulled to a halt and cranked up the car stereo. "Love is a drug," chanted Bryan Ferry. He should be craving the warmth of his family's *Chabat* celebrations. But part of him remained trapped around the block with Maryse, absorbed in Outremont repartee; part of him blamed Véronique's fussy traditionalism, Abitbol's nostalgia, for Maryse's father's rudeness.

He leaned away from Véronique's embrace as she answered the door. Her hands caught his shoulders, reeling him in. — How was your week? she said, giving him a determined stare from behind her glasses. Her long, grey-streaked hair brushed his face. —How is your work going? Is Maryse well?—

My sister asks about my wife, he thought, but my wife never asks about my sister. He remembered Véronique, twenty-one when their father had died, trying to rein in his terrified eight-year-old's hijinx. He had fled the *mellah* for the chaos of Fes el-Bali to escape her flustered efforts to discipline him. He suspected that Véronique had married Abitbol to secure him a stable family. He had never confided this to Maryse: it was family guilt; it stifled him, but he wasn't going to betray it to an outsider.

—Pierre's worried, Véronique said. —We had a phone call from Fes last night. His mother's ill again.—

—He didn't mention it at work.—

—Would you expect him to?—

Marcel sidled into the living room, picking his way around chairs and beanbags, three coffee tables, silk cushions spilling onto the floor in front of the wood-framed colour television. Abitbol did not believe in holding down expenses at home. Marcel had not put his finger on the contradiction until he had begun to work for Abitbol. Then he had begun to ask questions:

Why couldn't he have his own office when the house was stuffed with expensive toys? Abitbol had looked baffled. Work and home were separate: he was a different person in each place.

After his marriage, Marcel's criticisms had reversed. Rather than urging Abitbol to curb his tight-fistedness at work, he pleaded with him to demonstrate more restraint at home. Everyone will think you have no taste, he said, wounded by Maryse's assessment of his sister and brother-in-law's house as a nouveau-riche atrocity. Again Abitbol reacted with incomprehension. As his own marriage had developed, Marcel's censure of Abitbol had softened. He began to appreciate the inevitability of evolving into different people in different places. He avoided inviting Maryse to Véronque and Abitbol's house.

Véronique bent over the stereo, putting on a Selim Halali record to serenade them into the kitchen. Marcel hoisted himself onto a stool and watched Véronique preparing baked fish sprinkled with ground red peppers, chicken soup thick with *douida* noodles and a plate of tiny, spiced meatballs set among crisscrossed celery sticks. The baked-fish smell, Selim Halali's voice, the sight of Véronique moving around the kitchen—had he ever felt so at ease? The moment he detected his nerves unclenching, a bile-like access of guilt rolled through him: wasn't he betraying Maryse by feeling so much at home with his family?

They sat down to eat as soon as Abitbol, Louis and Madeleine returned from synagogue. Louis, plump and glossy-cheeked in a black suit, shook Marcel's hand with a resentful firmness. Madeleine accorded him a cursory flexing of her cheeks. Each time he visited, Marcel felt that he was disrupting the cloistered equilibrium of Louis and Madeleine's model family. All through childhood they had complained about him. Their friends asked if he was their big brother. If he was their uncle, why did he live with them? Why wasn't he old and married like other children's uncles? Marcel remembered Louis and Madeleine wailing in protest, in one of their early apartments, when Abitbol refused to let them watch television on Friday evening. All their friends were watching television! Abitbol brought them colouring books for the *Chabat,* then comic books; as they approached adolescence, he suggested chess competitions and tried to win them over to the music of Selim Halali.

—When are you going to take your accounting exams again, Marcel? Louis asked.

—Quiet! Abitbol said. He began to intone the opening of the *Chalom alehem.* —We are accompanied by angels . . . —

Marcel remembered his father, a very tall thin man, handing him the poem when he was six years old and telling him to read it three times. Holding it in front of his nose, he had sounded out the long words. When he stumbled, the whole family had prompted him.

He closed his eyes, murmuring the poem from memory. He prayed with a will, beseeching G-d to forge a universe where his spirit could be calm.

ive

Teddy-André-Marcel-Teddy

"WHEN A BUNCH OF GUYS ARE LAUGHING IN THE BASEMENT until four-thirty in the morning, I'm too tired to do my job." Teddy directed his glance upward, at the lard-packed canvas of Joe's neck.

"Those lads are just hell-raisers." Joe's hand clapped the door-post. "I bet you were a real hell-raiser a couple of years ago, Teddy. I sure was, until the Forces gave me a chance to straighten out. Those lads have a lot of disadvantages. You gotta give them time."

"Yeah, right—time. I get up early for work. And that means getting some sleep." He wasn't teaching the early-morning classes for businessmen yet, of course. But he hoped he would be soon. He was working on being polite to his boss.

"Those kids have rights, too."

"You're just afraid to kick them out because you'll have to start doing your job and clean up around here."

"I'm disappointed in you, Teddy. I never thought I'd hear you say something like that." Joe's long face subsided. His jaw tightened. "I gave those lads a good talking-to yesterday. Don't you worry, they're gonna start holding up their end of the bargain."

Teddy ducked out of the Victoria side of the building, stepping around a formally dressed fat man whose marmalade cat had got loose in the hall. He climbed the steps to the Waterloo entrance. Rollie lounged in the doorway in his flimsy black jacket. His wrists were trembling, drumming his wooden stake against the floor.

Teddy made spaghetti for supper and cranked up Elvis Costello to high volume on the tinny stereo that he could replace in an instant if he drew on his portfolio. He still had not given Zach and Marian his Montreal address; it was strange to think of the sheaf of pale windowed envelopes lying stacked on the kitchen shelves of the Victorian house up the hill from Shattuck. He remembered their all-night arguments about Plato, Hobbes, Rawls and justice, the place down the street where a slice of pizza and a soft drink cost ninety-four cents and all the customers were talking about Nicaragua, the mist on his face one evening when they piled out of the subway in San Francisco to eat in Chinatown. He had to phone them . . .

He bopped around the parquet floor, hoping the smack of his heels was giving Rollie a dose of his own medicine. But Elvis Costello proved to be poor dancing music. He was getting fed up with being a punk. He had submitted to the haircut only in the hope of getting the girl on the diving board into bed.

After supper he went out for a walk, turning the corner to take refuge from the wind rushing down the long channel of Sherbrooke Street. He slogged uphill into the mansions of Upper Westmount. Returning down the hill towards Sherbrooke Street forty-five minutes later, he cut along the side of the building and saw that the blinds were up in the concierge's apartment. Joe sat at the kitchen table, frowning at a sheet of paper. His glasses aged him, showing up the white points glinting at the tips of his crewcut.

In the middle of the night a familiar grinding moan awoke him. Jesus Christ, why did Rollie have to put him to the test?

He rolled over on his stomach on the mattress and pounded the heel of his hand against the floor.

"Fuck off, jake!" a voice shrieked.

He snapped on his bedside lamp. It was twenty to four. He thought about calling the police. One more chance, he decided. I'll give the bastards one more chance.

Creaky patois bored up through the floor. Teddy thumped his fist against the parquet until his hand throbbed. "Shut up! I want to sleep!" He burrowed under the covers.

He woke with his alarm, shaved, dressed in his office clothes, pulled on his parka and walked down the hall. He felt vulnerable and short-tempered; he longed to crawl back into bed. This was Rollie's final chance. Teddy was going to make clear to Joe that tonight, if he heard a peep from the basement, he would call the police.

He entered the Victoria side of the building and knocked on Joe's door.

No reply. He knocked again.

The door opened. A very tall, broad-shouldered young man with long blond hair appeared. His downcast expression focused on Teddy's midsection.

"I want to see Joe," Teddy said. "I'm fed up with his attitude—"

"My father has just passed away," the tall young man said.

It took Teddy a second to absorb the news. "Oh my God." He was too dazed to apologize. Announcements of sudden death had induced a mute panic in him ever since the night his grandmother had told him of his parents' accident. Her silver brooch had gleamed against her black sweater as she entered his bedroom. Her stride was firm with the assertion of her enlarged role in his life. The anger with which he had flailed against her during those early weeks, then again in adolescence, poured out of a longing to be encased in the unbudgeable snow. He wanted to be as sculpted and still as

Mum and Dad. His embarrassments, failures and awkward lusts disgraced the stroke of luck that had selected him to live.

"I'm sorry to hear that," he said.

"Who is it, Joey?" The door swung open. Joe's wife appeared. "What's the matter, Teddy? Can I help you?"

Joey laid his hand on his mother's shoulder. "Go back inside, Mum. Go have a seat."

"I'm sorry," Teddy murmured again, as Joey closed the door.

Joe's death changed the mood in the Victoria-Waterloo. The building drifted like a wayward log boom through the last lashing blizzards of February. A week after Joe's heart attack (Mrs. McNulty said he had been lighting up his first Player's Plain of the morning when the end came) a U-haul van pulled up in front of the Victoria entrance. Joey and two other young men jammed open the double front doors. With a barrage of beer-slurred four-letter words, they loaded up the concierge's furniture. Teddy wandered out to watch them. He heard a pained intake of breath. Rollie, looking as thin as his stake, stared at Joe's kitchen table as it disappeared into the van.

"He's dead," Teddy said. "Now there'll be a new concierge." When Rollie failed to reply, gazing at him with eyes sunken into almost fleshless sockets, Teddy said: "The new guy'll do the job himself. You better start looking for somewhere else to live."

"That man was me father," Rollie said. His skin was turning yellower. "It like me father die."

The young men forgot to lock the door of Joe's apartment. The detail coursed through the building like news of the plague. Mrs. McNulty, shuffling her heels against the grimy marble; Mrs. Austin, her two young children in tow; two preppie McGill students with whom he had never exchanged a word— they all stopped him in the hall to pass along the news. The open door became an omen. No one knew what would happen next. A mood of exultation rolled through the halls. The night after the U-haul came, the Bajan drug dealer threw a party.

Reggae music vibrated through the brickwork until five in the morning. "A 'ungry mon is a angry mon!" Bob Marley chanted.

In the days following the party the halls swarmed with young West Indian men. On weekends two or three youths a day knocked on Teddy's door in search of ganja. He gave them directions to the Bajan's apartment. Mrs. McNulty and Mrs. Austin, catching wind of his connivance with drug dealers, scowled when they passed him in the corridor. Mrs. McNulty claimed that Rollie had moved into Joe's apartment. "This building's going to the dogs!"

The party atmosphere withered on March 1st, when Mr. Crawford arrived to collect the rent.

A large man with quiet good manners and features of faded handsomeness, Mr. Crawford showed Teddy the rent book and a letter from the Rubinsteins authorizing him to collect the cheques. His deep-jawed crumbling façade of a face remained impassive as Teddy asked him whether he was the new concierge. "No, sir. They haven't hired a new concierge."

"They always get Crawford to collect the rent when they lose a concierge," Mrs. McNulty said. "What I want to know is how come they haven't told us about our rent increases. The leases expire on July 1st and they've got to tell us ninety days before. That's March 30th. But Rubinsteins always let you know a month early. They like to have lots of time to bargain."

At the end of the month, when Mr. Crawford knocked on the door again, Teddy handed over his cheque without a second thought. But Mrs. McNulty, who came downstairs fifteen minutes later, was distraught. "Did he give you a lease? He didn't give me one, either. Or Mrs. Austin. What are they tryin' to pull? This used to be a decent place to live. If they pull any funny business, with the shape Joe let this building get into—"

On Wednesday Teddy came home from work, his eyes hazed from hours of correcting the scrawls his students made in their exercise books, to see a crowd of people standing next to the mailboxes inside the Waterloo door. A moist breeze skimmed over the leftover scabs of snow. Through the glass panels he could make out Mrs. Austin and her children, the two McGill students, and stocky, red-haired Paddy McNulty. As he opened the door, Mrs. Austin turned towards him. "Look at this," she said, pulling a creased sheet of paper out of her woven hemp shopping bag. He glimpsed her stained-looking palms as she handed him the page. "You got one, too."

He opened his mailbox, unfolded the sheet and read both the French and English texts. The Rubinsteins had sold the Victoria-Waterloo.

Mrs. Austin's brightly patterned headscarf bobbed before his eyes as she pointed to the signature above the name of the numbered company that had bought the building. "That's the guy we s'posed to pay our rent to," she said. "Look at he name. Marcel Vir-condo-lett. What kinda name's that?"

෬ ෬ ෬

André woke up realizing that he had been dreaming of Marie-Christine. It was not a sexual dream, like those that had tormented him twenty years ago; he no longer had such dreams about women. As he rolled over on his side to face the early daylight his penis lolled limp. He slapped his belly to quicken his metabolism. Sluggishness held him in its thrall. In his dreams, Marie-Christine appeared before his mind's eye as he had seen her the other night, the gossamer grey hair overlaying the lustrous near-black locks like a veil.

He walked to the window and peeped between the curtains. The street was miraculously silent. The early light cupped the spiral staircases, grey stone façades and wooden cornices. The late-night boisterousness yielded to this silence each weekend morning in streets where no one, it seemed, was in a condition to get up before brunch time. He thought again of Marie-Christine, whose apartment lay a few blocks to the south. He was bound to run into her again—wasn't he? After eight years of silence their friendship should not end with a stupid

~ 108 ~

squabble. Her presence had left him physically unmoved, yet, without needing her, he felt incomplete without her.

He blinked into the sunlight. At last he and Marie-Christine were both inhabiting the Plateau Mont-Royal. He had chafed for years to escape Lasalle. Now that he had settled here the Plateau he had known was gone. No longer a cauldron in which the working class and the *intellos* swirled together in revolutionary ferment, it had become a neighbourhood of refaced stone, overpriced condominiums, guitar-building workshops, lesbian bars, street corner art galleries and tofu milkshakes. The grocery store delivery boys continued to dodge through the traffic on their three-wheeled pedal carts with the wooden boxes in front, the food in the bistros remained cheap and there were still plenty of apartments—such as this one—where the rents were low. But in other ways *le vrai Montréal* was fading—possibly because people such as him had not settled down into the kinds of families in which they had been raised.

He took a shower. Afterwards, as he was towelling himself, the telephone rang. —*Allô.*—

—So you're awake. I thought middle-aged men slept all morning.—

—Screw you.— It was Céline. His youngest sister was the only member of his family he could talk to, but since his return from France her chirpy nervousness had grated on him. Twenty-four years old and still living at home. No wonder she was edgy. She needed a man in her bed.

—Maman wants to know if you're coming to lunch.—

—What does she think? It takes over an hour to get out to Lasalle— —

—Now you're living in the Plateau Mont-Royal you're too conceited to come and see your family . . . ? Everyone'll be here, André!—

—So? Do I have to do everything my family wants? When Lysiane and I got married, we moved to Lasalle because of the family— —

—*Comment ça?*—

—You see. This is another favour you don't even know I've done you. At the time Lysiane and I got married, Papa was still dragging Maman out drinking in the evenings. You probably don't remember that— —

—I've got plenty of memories of Papa being drunk.—

—Yeah, at home. Back then they used to go to the bars. I don't know if Maman enjoyed it, but she used to go and she used to drink. When they came home they were incapable . . . Jacques was living in that low-rise down the block, so he would stop in and make sure you little ones got to bed. When I got married he told me it wasn't fair for me to move to the Plateau and leave him to look after *les petites* when he was about to start a family of his own. So Lysiane and I moved to Lasalle.—

—What did Lysiane think about that?—

—It wasn't a good start to our marriage.—

—You're blaming Papa's drinking for your divorce?—

A hardness had crept into her tone. He felt warned off. — That's not why my marriage ended, he murmured. This left open the question of why his marriage had ended. Before she could utter the question, he said: —It wasn't fair on Lysiane.—

—You know I remember this, André. I remember lying in that little back room where Chantal and I slept until I was eleven wondering when Papa and Maman would come home. And when they did, doing everything I could to please them, to make them happy because they were so unpredictable. I remember you and Jacques coming around to read us stories and tuck us in. You especially. You always did it better than Maman. You always gave us a hug. She's not a very maternal woman, our mother. Too much like her Iroquois mother. '*T'es correcte, là? Bon, je m'en vais.*' That was it. You knew that if you said everything wasn't all right, she would turn around and leave anyway. You never did that. You've done lots for me, André, right from the beginning. *Tu as changé mes couches.*—

They laughed. Their conversations often returned to the fact of his having learned to change her diapers when he was fifteen. Maman, smoking her Export A, would comment on his technique. She had spent too much of her life changing diapers, she said. One day she stubbed out her butt on the counter and said: —You have just seen me smoke my last cigarette.— She never smoked again, never mentioned any discomfort she might be experiencing weaning her body of its thirty-cigarette-a-day habit. Once he asked her about it. —I've given birth to eight children and seen two of them die. Pain means nothing.— She turned away.

—Won't you come? Céline asked, her voice quickening. — It's a bit pathetic, still trying to separate yourself like some adolescent boy at thirty-nine.—

—I'll come, but not every weekend. I can't take Papa sitting with a beer in one hand and the channel selector in the other, making sure the TV's always on an English station. It drives me crazy.—

—That's why he does it.—

—No, it isn't. He does it because he grew up working for Anglos and thinking English was better than French. It has nothing to do with me.—

—Except it gives you an excuse to stay away. Or do you have a girlfriend there in the Plateau?—

—No, I don't have a girlfriend.—

As he uttered the words he realized that the categorical tone of his denial nearly invited the opposite query: *Do you have a boyfriend?* Her long, frustrated-sounding silence made him wonder what he should say.

—André, you're useless! I tell you everything about my life and you don't tell me anything about yours. It's like Papa and Maman, except in reverse. You're cold like Maman, and I'm emotional like Papa, except since I'm a woman I don't need beer to deal with my feelings.—

Their conversation petered out. In a few moments he was standing on his hot, sun-barred carpet, his palm sticky from the receiver, thinking about his months in Paris. He had admitted to no one that he had left Montreal in part because the Plateau and the Gay Village had begun to feel too small. Then, as now, he walked the streets in apprehension of turning the corner and meeting François. He had craved anonymity—anonymity in French. Yet in Paris even gay men—sometimes especially gay men—chortled at his backwoods accent, desiring him, he felt, as an exotic specimen from the display case of sex tourism. Gay men in Paris seemed frenzied and uncaring, obsessed by *les boîtes,* as though only the tally of the number of nightclubs they had visited could confer on them the haughty status they all appeared to seek. He met men who carried porn videos in their chic leather satchels in the event of a chance encounter leading to an invitation to a man's apartment. He watched men hold their bodies between him and their doorpost keypads to ensure that he did not memorize the entrance codes to their buildings as they punched them in to admit him for a hurried blowjob or a brisk screw.

After a few weeks, uncertain what he was seeking, he withdrew. It was easy—easier than it had been in Montreal where a familiar face was sure to wink at him from the crowd on the Métro platform. He attended lectures at the Sorbonne, refreshed by occasional breezes of unfamiliar perspectives on history and literature, but mainly bored, uncertain of what he was doing here in a swirl of foreign students young enough to confuse their discoveries of Paris with their discoveries of one another. He grew restless; when he learned of the death of René Lévesque he wanted to go home. He lasted out the winter and spring and summer, feeling like a cipher. He could not contribute to this self-assured, totally formed country; once he dropped out of the gay scene he lacked a fleshly connection to the world. He felt that he was no one. At the beginning of August the death of Félix Leclerc spurred him to move up the date of his return flight by three weeks. Quebec was travelling on without him. Where was it going?

Where was he going? He dressed and pulled back the curtains. Two children trailed down the street. The sounds of the traffic grew louder. He longed to go out and walk through the Plateau for the sheer joy of moving and soaking up the sunlight that glanced off the top-hat-gables of the walkups, for the pleasure of watching the crowds and the couples and their clothes. Marie-Christine was out there, only a few blocks away; so, in all likelihood, was François. He wondered which of them he would meet first.

ଔ ଔ ଔ

Marcel woke in another man's bed to the sight of *Dungeons & Dragons*, discarded René Simard albums and dolls with chords dangling from their backs. Rolling out of bed, he picked up the nearest doll and pulled its chord. —*Bonjour,* the doll said. —*Je m'appelle Ken. Comment t'appelles-tu?*—

He dressed without taking a shower or shaving. Downstairs Abitbol was stirring his thick black coffee and scanning the economics section of *Le Devoir.*

—I'm leaving. Pass along my apologies to Véronique. I'll call you on Monday once I've spoken to the engineer.—

Outside, in the spring drizzle, the pink chipped gravel lay sprinkled around the flagstones. He gasped with relief as he slammed the door of the Honda. He was thinking about Maryse. One of her favourite verbs was *s'épanouir:* to bloom, to deepen one's vision; it was what she sought in her painting. Coasting the Honda along the streets of Outremont, winding nowhere in particular, he thanked her for the gift of *épanouissement.*

He rejoiced in the slurp of the windshield wipers as he crossed Avenue du Parc. He remembered the antique shop where he had bought her the spicebox. The address eluded him. He made a groping turn, found himself fenced in by one-way streets, then found the shop on what felt like the wrong corner. A bell over the door tinkled as he entered. The proprietress was patrolling the aisles, her grey pony-tail swishing along the length of her spine. In a twanging Acadian accent, the woman asked him what he wanted. —A lady's dresser, Marcel said. — But it must be small enough to fit through the door of a duplex.—

The woman led him to a compact oak dresser glinting with gold inlay. Three wide drawers sectioned the body; a box with a fold-up lid was mounted against the curlicue-edged backboard. —*Madame* keeps her clothes below and her jewellery above.—

It was perfect. He agreed to a price after only cursory haggling, opened his wallet and peeled off two hundred-dollar bills. The proprietress ordered a lanky middle-aged man in a sweater to help Marcel carry the dresser to his car, where they set it down on a plastic sheet on the back seat.

He ate breakfast at a Greek diner on Avenue du Parc, lingering over his coffee. An hour later, leading Maryse across the front lawn of her parents' home to the Honda, he held his breath.

She scrutinized the gold inlay. —It's beautiful.— She kissed him. —You have exquisite taste.—

—I wanted to get you a dresser that would fit through the front door.—

They drove back to Ville St-Laurent and paraded the dresser around the living room: trying it out in the corner behind Maryse's easel, pushing it snug against the wall. They carried it upstairs and set it down beneath the bedroom window, where it stood like an amplified reflection of the spicebox on the bedside table. Marcel sat down on the bed. She straddled his lap and rubbed her lips over his forehead. —But Marcel, you were so angry last night.—

—I'm sorry.— He kissed her mouth. —Thank you for saving me from marrying a Moroccan Jew.—

—What a compliment!— She giggled and ran her fingers down the back of his neck. Their lovemaking found its shape with an inevitability that left him stunned and grateful. Waking later, he became aware of the groaning of the Laurentian Autoroute. Why, of all the neighbourhoods in Montreal, had Abitbol exiled him to Ville St-Laurent? The video store in the nearest shopping mall boasted of its stock of *Films Anglais Français Arabes* and the adjoining café served baklava and *thé à la menthe.* Ten minutes' drive away a sleek mosque sprouted, incongruous as an onion, from a field of uniform suburban bungalows. Abitbol, with his sensitivity to such oddities, had known they would irritate him. His Arab neighbours were part of his punishment. He slipped his hands under Maryse's shoulder blades, kissing the space between her breasts. She murmured in complaint at his stubbly cheeks.

On Monday morning he met the engineer at the downtown office. They sat on opposite sides of his desk while Sylvie typed an arm's length away. Flexing his nicotine-stained fingers, the engineer delivered his report.

"This building's damn close to being a white elephant. The supporting beam isn't strong enough to hold up the weight of the two sides. You're going to have to lift the beam if you want to get these renovations approved. You'll also have to replace the plumbing and rewire the electricity. The wiring is substandard and most of the outlets aren't grounded. The roof needs a coat of tar. The rest is up to you. There's a lot of wood in there. I guess you can make it *look* pretty good . . . "

When the engineer had left, Marcel browsed through his report. The phone rang. Sylvie passed him the receiver. —I hope you enjoyed your day with Maryse, Abitbol said. —Please give our best to Maryse. We never see her.—

—She was busy. She hadn't seen her parents all week.—

—You hadn't spent *Chabat* with us in months. And then you run off on Saturday morning. Have you forgotten that *Chabat* goes from sunset to sunset?—

—Aren't you the one who told me to cut myself in half?—

—Did I tell you to betray your family? Why must you make your sister so unhappy?— Marcel refused to reply. He braced himself for an explosion, but Abitbol's next words were curt: —Have you spoken to the engineer?—

They discussed the contents of the report. —This beam worries me, Abitbol said. —We must keep our costs low. How can we know we will even find a buyer? Look: raise the beam if it is essential. But we'll have to cut costs elsewhere. There will be no unionized labour. I'll get a man to do the wiring who charges less than an electrician. Have you sent the tenants their evacuation forms?—

—I'm working on that.—

—Call me when you have a draft.—

Marcel hung up. Sylvie shot him an anxious glance. When Marcel had drafted the three-sentence letter instructing the tenants to pay their rents to the numbered company, Abitbol had denounced each word as misleading or legally perilous. —I went to English high school! Marcel had finally shouted at him. —I did not study at the *Alliance Israélite Universelle du Maroc. I* know how to write in English.—

—Give me one good reason why I should trust you, Abitbol said. A long, long silence. —I'm waiting: why should I trust you?—

Pulling a tablet of lined paper out of his desk drawer, Marcel began to write. *Dear Tenant, This is to advise you . . .* To be legally binding, the form must itemize the renovations he planned to carry out. He worked through the engineer's report, listing all the alterations they might end up making. When he read the draft to Abitbol over the phone, Abitbol hectored him into making two meaningless changes before grunting that the letter did not sound bad.

—*Enfin!* Marcel shouted as he hung up. He dropped the draft on Sylvie's desk, fled the office and stepped into the deep-sunken midday shadows of Rue Ste-Catherine. He felt the sunlight on the back of his neck as he crossed the street to Reuben's to eat a plate of smoked meat.

When he returned to the office, Sylvie had finished typing the letter.

Dear Tenant,

This is to advise you that your apartment will be the object of major renovations. The work will start the first (1st) day of May, 1988. The duration of the work will be of four months. During this period we would like you to evacuate your apartment.

The following is the work to be done:

A long, point-form list of renovations covered the next page and a half. At the bottom of the second page he had written:

Thank you for your cooperation and understanding.

Signed: Marcel Vircondelet

Conditions offered by the owner:

I accept to evacuate my apartment, #

Witness: *Signature.*

—Make a hundred copies, Marcel said, mail one to each tenant and leave the rest on my desk. Then get in touch with Bruno, Crawford and the architect and ask them to meet me in front of the building at four o'clock on Wednesday afternoon. I'm going to clear that place so fast it'll make Abitbol's head spin. *À demain,* Sylvie. I'm going home.—

—Marcel, she said, did you see the message on your desk?—

—What message?—

Sylvie passed him the folded pink message slip, where she had checked the *S.V.P. Rappeler* box. Below she had written the name of the person he was to call back. For an instant Marcel could not connect a face to the two scrawled words: *Ruth Rubinstein.*

ন ন ন

"We need to come in," Mr. Crawford said. "We've got to take some measurements." Teddy bristled at being caught in his fancy clothes. He had begun to wear grey dress pants and a white dress shirt to the office in the hope of persuading his boss that he could be relied on to teach the classes for business people. His haircut had grown out sleeker and less tufted than he had expected. His expensive appearance accentuated the humiliation of spending six hours a day correcting scrawled, semi-literate workbook entries. He felt duped. For most of his life he had perceived a choice between wearing dress pants to earn a professional salary and rebelling into minimum-wage bohemianism. He had ended up with dress pants, a minimum-wage income and no fun.

He shifted his weight to relieve the toe-pinching tightness of his polished black shoes. One of the three men standing behind Mr. Crawford slid to the front. Interpreting Teddy's pawing of the parquet as a sidestep admitting him to the apartment, he pushed into the entrance hall. "Thank you, sir," he said in a deep, clogged-sounding voice. Teddy tensed, preparing a retort, but the young man's tinted glasses rebuffed him. The young man roamed Teddy's four big rooms. Apparently oblivious to the cockroaches that scuttled for cover as he flipped on the kitchen light, he ran his long pale fingers down the cracked plaster. "High ceilings. We can do a lot with this, Mr. Crawford." His fingers slid to a halt. "But I don't like this bulge. I hope I haven't bought a white elephant."

The expression surprised Teddy. It sounded incongruous in the foreign, not-quite-French rhythm that Vircondelet's voice—he realized this must be the new owner—imposed on English.

"The bulge is nothing," Mr. Crawford said. "It just means a little moisture's gotten into the wall."

"I know what the bulge means," Vircondelet said. "You forget that I am an engineer."

Mr. Crawford walked into the living room, where the other two men were stretching a tape measure. The shorter, darker man was calling out figures in oddly accented French. The lanky young man took notes on a sheet of squared paper.

Vircondelet had tugged a Mars bar from the pocket of his acid-washed denim jacket and was peeling it like a banana. He made as if to pass Teddy the wrapper.

"The garbage is in the kitchen," Teddy said.

The irises of Vircondelet's dark brown eyes, obscured by his tinted lenses, had lodged low in his eyeballs, lending him a sedated appearance. "Thank you, sir." He crushed the candy bar wrapper in his palm, retreated to the kitchen and returned holding the form Teddy had received in the mail. "We're going to improve your apartment for you, sir. If you could sign, please . . . " He held out a ball-point pen.

"What am I signing?" Teddy said.

"It says that you agree to move out temporarily while we renovate."

"It says that I agree to move out permanently and give up all my rights."

"My apologies, sir. I was thinking of a different form." Vircondelet stared past him, his brown eyes unfathomable behind his murky glasses. "It's a good time to move, sir. There are lots of apartments available."

"I don't feel like moving."

Beyond Vircondelet's shoulders, he spied Mr. Crawford studying him with sullen gloominess. Vircondelet drew himself upright, his thick black hair brushing the top of his glasses. He stood three or four inches taller than Teddy. "When you are ready to move," he said, his voice dropping to a whisper, "sign this sheet and send it to me. I can give you money to help with your expenses—three hundred dollars."

Teddy stared at this loose-limbed, long-haired, denim-clad guy who was an immigrant, maybe five years older than him, and who bought and sold apartment buildings. He longed to puncture Vircondelet's complacent superiority. "You think I care about three hundred dollars?"

Mr. Crawford looked shocked. Vircondelet, who had been about to follow the two men who had taken the measurements out the door, stopped. "What do you do for a living, sir?"

"I teach English as a second language." A silence settled in, while Teddy realized that this did not sound very impressive. "I do it for fun. I don't need the money."

Vircondelet lifted his long, flat-bottomed nose to aim his dark glasses at Teddy. "We all need money. You can't get anything without money."

"Is that what we need?" Teddy said, nudging away Vircondelet and Mr. Crawford, as he stepped forward to close the door.

Later that evening, when he heard a knocking, he almost did not answer. He had no wish to see Vircondelet again; he was fed up with giving directions to young men in search of ganja. He opened the door a crack and saw a slight young woman dressed in a black polo-neck blouse that emphasized the narrowness of her shoulders. The end of her unusually wide mouth was walled in by acne. Her hair was cropped short in a style similar to Teddy's. "Hi, my name's Adriana. I live on the Victoria side of the building. We're having a tenants' meeting on Thursday night to talk about the situation with the new owner. A lawyer will be there to give us advice. Are you interested in coming?"

"You bet," Teddy said.

"Can I ask, have you signed the new owner's form? You haven't? Can I ask you not to sign before our meeting on Thursday?"

When Teddy said that he had no intention of signing the form before Thursday or at any other time, Adriana smiled. She wrote down Teddy's name and apartment number. "I hope to see you on Thursday."

That's the first woman in a long time to take down any number of mine, he thought later that evening, as he turned off his twelve-inch black-and-white television at the end of *The National* and *The Journal.*

The phone rang.

"Teddy? It's Janet. Why haven't you phoned me?"

Elated and maddened in the same instant, Teddy said: "You told me not to call you again!"

"I didn't mean forever!"

"Well what the fuck did you mean?"

"I meant give me a break. You were getting on my nerves. You upper-class guys—you're so logical you can't understand anything."

Teddy drew a long breath and sat down in the garage-sale armchair he had placed next to his phone. He thought about some of the things he could say, remembered his magical night skimming down the streets of Westmount with Janet's dark eyes and curls streaming alongside him, and decided he wanted this conversation to continue. "When are you moving to Scotland?" he asked.

"Oh, I'm moving to Scotland all right, but not right away. If I had a salary like the dead white males I work with, I could save the money in no time—but I'm just a woman, so all I get is courses on contract."

"So you think you'll be here for a while?"

"Why are you asking me that?" Janet spoke without her usual bravado.

"Is there something wrong with me asking you a question?"

"Don't play head-games with me, Teddy. It just shows you're one of those guys who's out of touch with his feelings."

"I'm not playing head-ga—"

"You are! If you're interested you should be up front and ask me out."

"I did that twice and you said no. I think it's your turn to ask me out."

"Fuck you, Teddy." Janet hung up.

I'm never going to talk to her again, he thought. Starting tomorrow, I am going to take a serious look at all the other women I know. He ran through them in his mind: there was Yvette, a French teacher at work who did not appear to have a boyfriend, there was the intriguing-looking woman he passed on the front steps, there was Adriana. And that was it. This was the frustration of Montreal: beautiful women flaunting themselves with Latin flamboyance on every street, yet so many barriers to meeting them: language, neighbourhood, the walls dividing cultures. And this wasn't just true of the women; it was true of communities, restaurants, bakeries, museums. Montreal simultaneously showcased its wares and kept them under wraps.

He slouched through the next two days at work and arrived at Adriana's apartment early on Thursday evening. The lawyer walked in and was offered an armchair. Adriana stood next to him like a nervous owner displaying a temperamental prize pet. A pair of old couches and a few stools had been arranged in a broken semi-circle facing the lawyer's chair. Mrs. Austin and Mrs. McNulty were sitting on one of the couches. Teddy pulled up a stool next to the russetly unshaven Paddy McNulty. The lawyer, a tall, lean-chested man of about thirty-five, waited until the gathering had swelled to fifteen or twenty people before he began to speak. As he talked his long, spade-shaped beard brushed against the front of a heavy blue sweater that looked as though it hailed from a Newfoundland outport. He wore black corduroy slacks and calf-high Wellington boots. His voice, self-consciously projected, seemed geared to a larger crowd.

"What this guy is trying to do is called a conversion. He wants to renovate, raise the value of the building and sell the building for a profit. In order to do this he wants to get you out of your apartment. He will try to intimidate you. But remember: you have rights. Don't let him enter your apartment! If he wants to bargain with you, let him stand on the doorstep. He'll feel at a disadvantage and you'll get a better deal.

"The Régie du logement has rules about conversions. Your job is to make sure this guy follows the rules. Learn your rights! If he wants to renovate he has to give you four months' notice, he has to pay to move you out, he has to pay for you to stay in equivalent temporary accommodation of your choosing, he has to pay to move you back in, then he has to let you rent your old apartment again for one year at your old rent. It doesn't matter how luxurious he's made the apartment: you have the right to return for one year. After that there'll be a huge rent increase and you'll probably have to move, but that's a long way down the road."

"But we don't have leases," Mrs. McNulty said. "They didn't give us new leases in March."

"If you have not been provided with new leases as a result of a landlord's negligence, your old lease is automatically renewed at your old rent." He gave them a hard, brown-eyed stare. "Make the law work for you. First, go to the Régie du logement office on Côte-des-Neiges Road and register your intention to contest. Don't let them intimidate you—just keep speaking English, even if they tell you they only speak French. I suggest you go as a group. That way nobody gets lost, nobody sleeps in and forgets to register. The Régie will give you a form to mail to Mr. Vircondelet. *Send it registered mail.* Otherwise he'll claim he didn't get it. The second thing you have to do is to pay your rent. Again, *send it registered mail.* Don't be dumb— don't hold back the rent because he came and shouted at you yesterday and you're mad at him: make the law work for you.

"Questions?" The lawyer's gaze raked the room. "Once you have registered, the Régie will set a date for your hearing. It will probably take two to four months. At the hearing the judge will establish conditions for a conversion. He'll probably rule that the four months' notice Mr. Vircondelet is required to give you must be calculated from the date of your hearing. It's nearly the middle of April now; if we get a hearing in July or August it's unlikely anybody will have to move out before the end of the year. The judge will require that Mr. Vircondelet inform you of how long the renovations will take. Before you move out, he has to give you a date when you can move back in." The lawyer's voice lost its parade-ground formality. His thin face cracked into a wolfish smile. "This is how you beat these guys. You tie them up in delays until they get desperate. If you get the law on your side, you can cost this guy a lot of money. You can make a little money yourselves. That way when winter comes you won't end up out on the street."

Six

André-Marcel-Teddy-André

ON WEEKENDS EVERY CORNER OF THE PLATEAU STREAMED with people. Insinuating himself into the crowds overflowing the eastern sidewalk of Rue St-Denis, where the afternoon sunlight fell, he felt warmed by the human current. When he paced the fringes of Parc Lafontaine, glancing down at the benches surrounding the sunken pond where he had met François, the feeling of inclusion thinned. Yet he could not live like an outsider in Montreal. This was his place; it would claim him, define him according to his will or against it.

Walking the streets of the Plateau on weekends was a kind of lighthearted Russian roulette where he tossed himself out before the multiple gazes of the city and waited to see which bullet of recognition struck him first. He had glimpsed a former university prof of his, looking suddenly decrepit, sitting at a café table with a woman who might have been his daughter. He thought he recognized a couple of men from the demonstration. But as yet, no François, no Marie-Christine, no Lysiane, no Raymond—or any one of half a dozen other people. Where had they gone? All of Montreal crammed into the Plateau on weekends, yet the faces of his formative years remained absent. He toyed with the idea of buying a car and visiting the Beauce, Quebec City, perhaps the Laurentians. He was back on salary at the Cégep. His rent was low, his tastes modest: he could afford a car if he wished (though, living in the Plateau, he would find nowhere to park it). But he preferred the perpetual visual flirtation of the sidewalks to solitary runs along the autoroutes. He could not imagine retreating to the backlands, as Marie-Christine said Raymond had done: the city was his place.

Darkness drove him to the Village. The bright colours of the afternoon, turning the faces and hair of the beautiful young men and women vivid as they bantered on the sidewalks, in the cafés, diners, bookstores of the Plateau, drained away in the evening. Night obscured the figures passing on the streets, ending his cost-free contemplation of the crowds: after dark, in order to look he must also touch. This was the barrier he had resisted crossing for months after Lysiane's departure. He had learned to break the downward tug of depression by walking. He walked for blocks and blocks, though in the end it did no good. The next morning he would wake with sore calves; it took him hours to get out of bed. As he was still living in Lasalle then, he went to the Plateau to do his walking. He drifted around the edges of Parc Lafontaine, squinting into the cores of the lights strung through the trees. The luminous ghosts imprinted on his retinas lingered when he closed his eyes. He ignored the fact that the men hunched on the benches beneath the lights were there for other men. He would sit down and talk to them, then walk away as though he did not understand what they expected of him. He had spoken to François twice before going home with him. On his early visits, his gaze snarled on the tall, almost obscenely thick ears that had earned François the nickname *Monsieur Spock*. The first time they spoke François baffled him with a barrage of offbeat opinions about health food, night-life in Tunisia (he had taken his vacation there three years in a row), the uniforms worn by Montreal bus drivers, the best neighbourhoods in which to find a truly superb apartment. —Which neighbourhood do you live in?—

—Ville Lasalle.—

—No wonder you come to the Plateau to look for men!—

Before André could stammer a denial, François complained that the categories used by supermarkets to display food were wrong. —Meat, vegetables, dairy products—who cares? What a man wants to know is whether a product is virtuous and good for the body, or whether it is pleasurable and sinful. Chocolate, pastries, bacon, cigarettes, beer, wine, sherry—especially sherry!—these should be on one side of the supermarket. On the other— —

Later that night, before they took off their clothes, François drank three glasses of sherry. André was overwhelmed, shocked by the buddy-like masculinity of their verbal then physical grappling. He had been looking for solace for unstaunchable wounds. François introduced him to a more intense, savage physicality. If this was tenderness, why did François, and most of the men who accompanied them into the Gay Village, drink so much before having sex? Why did the group, at least among François's *gang*, count for more than the couple? This had been the hardest part: understanding that he and François were not a couple in the same way that he and Lysiane had been. —I am not your loyal girlfriend! I am a *man*, François had told him, after André had responded with a whimper to his slavering pursuit of a young Algerian. As François grew drunker, he became more dismissive. In the early days André tried to stick with him when their group dispersed. François would lead them down the steep sidewalks that plunged from the spunky elegance of the Plateau to the grime of the Centre-Sud. They would fall silent as they passed cramped *dépanneurs* and quickie tattoo parlours where boil-faced young men in jeans jackets lounged in stark waiting rooms. The silence would break as they reached the refaced brick and new double-glazing of the sections of the Centre-Sud that had been gentrified and absorbed into the Gay Village. They would enter a bar on Rue Ste-Catherine and, by the end of the evening, go their separate ways. At first André couldn't stand it. Watching François talking to another man he would remember all the small, private ways they had sex: the casual reach from behind that brought him up hard against the front of his jeans, the thumb that pushed into his ass and languidly rotated, the late-night phone calls where François's voice made him writhe on his sofa. With François the boundaries of intercourse had melted; he had never thought, as he had when he had begun to sleep with Lysiane: we did it twice tonight, we did it three times. He would stumble down the wrought-iron spiral staircase out of François's apartment feeling that they had been together loving each other in a way they had invented for themselves. On the nights when François picked up an Algerian or a Moroccan or one of the mustached guys in leather jackets who squatted on the concrete blocks outside the Beaudry Métro station, André would drink himself into a stupor staring at the grainy screen behind the bar where the tongues of willowy naked boys perpetually licked impossibly thick penises. Why must his devotion be to François alone when François was obsessed with men rather than with *him?*

It felt strange to remember this anguish. In Paris, he saw, as he strolled the Plateau at dusk, he had evolved into someone like François. He had been pried away from the gay scene in Paris by the hesitations of a foreigner who fears his only value is exoticism. In Montreal, no matter how many different bodies his hands and mouth and penis probed, he would remain anchored. He could explore without losing himself. All at once he was ecstatic to be in Montreal, to be Québécois, to be gay. Vive Bourgault! Vive Michel Tremblay! Vive all the men who were like him, *souverainiste* and *gai,* and sure of themselves, and proud of their manhood. For the first time since his return he had no doubts about where he wanted to go.

He walked towards the Gay Village.

ଔ ଔ ଔ

"Start on the second floor," Crawford said. "Don't give them time to warn each other."

Marcel nodded, then regretted it. Unless he made clear that he was the boss, he would lose their respect. As they reached the top of the stairs, Crawford turned to the right. "No," Marcel said, veering to the left. "We're starting here, Mr. Crawford. Who is the tenant, please?"

"A couple of old krauts. The lady's a real bitch, but it's his name that's on the lease."

Marcel squared his shoulders. The gloomy hall was narrow—too narrow to attract quality tenants? They would have to install more powerful lights. His doubts about the building were growing. *A dar-el-hzar*, Abitbol had said. *Your job is to exorcize it.* But removing the tenants was only the first step; he would transform this building into a monument to the taste he had imbibed from Maryse. The Victoria-Waterloo would stand as a dashing incursion of francophone flare into the stodgy Englishness of Notre-Dame-de-Grâce.

A German, Marcel thought. A Jew-killer, a Nazi. He glanced at Crawford, Bruno and the lanky young architect's apprentice. If I can't handle her, they'll lose confidence in me. He was certain Crawford was spying on him for Abitbol.

His knocking resounded down the corridor. No answer. He knocked again. He heard a dragging sound, then a bump. The door opened. He stared down at an old man hunched over a walker.

"Good morning, sir," he said, gliding a copy of the release form into the old man's hand. "I've brought a sheet for you to sign. Everyone is going to move out of this building for a few weeks while we make improvements. If you sign now, I can give you a hundred dollars." Reclaiming the sheet, he pulled out a pen. In the blank for *Conditions offered by the owner* he wrote *$100.00.*

The German's head rolled up. Strands of white hair fanned across his gleaming skull. His bloodshot eyes wary, he said: "I must this paper sign?"

He wants orders, Marcel thought. He wants discipline. He pushed out his chest. His jeans jacket became a dress uniform, his forward step a parade-ground strut. "Yes, sir. I am the owner of this building and I am telling you that you must sign this sheet." The German pulled his glasses from the pocket of his ironed white shirt. He mouthed the words of the agreement under his breath. He accepted the pen Marcel offered him and twirled out a tangled Gothic inscription, pressing the release form against the bar at the front of his walker.

I can do this! Marcel thought, cautioning himself against showing emotion. —Let's go, he said, excitement rolling through him. —Let's get the next one.—

—The measurements, the architect whispered.

Marcel nodded. Bruno, Crawford and the architect pushed past the walker. As the other two stretched the tape measure, the architect recorded the size of the windows, the dimensions of the back rooms, the height and breadth of the doorways.

The old man was waving his hand. "You pay me one hundred dollars."

"You're absolutely right, sir. I'm the accountant. I'll pay you right away." He retrieved the architect's pen from the pocket of his jeans jacket, dated the first cheque in a fresh batch and copied out the man's name. Stupid Nazi, he thought. "There you go, sir."

The old man pinched the cheque between his fingers. A confused, crestfallen expression had gripped his face.

—Let's get out of here, Marcel said. He paced in the doorway, waiting for the others to leave. "Thank you very much, sir." He slammed the door. The hair falling over his forehead had turned damp with perspiration.

"All the apartments on this side of the hall are the same," Crawford said. "We don't have to take any more measurements until we get to the end."

"Who is the tenant in the next apartment, Mr. Crawford?"

"Old Jamaican ladies in the next two."

Marcel knocked hard on the door. A middle-aged woman in brown polyester slacks and a yellow top leaned out. "Good afternoon, *Madame* . . . "

"What you want?"

"I am the new owner, *Madame*. I'm very pleased to meet you."

The door of the next apartment opened. An older, bulkier woman stepped into the hall. Pink plastic barrettes shone in her black hair. "What he want, April?"

"Very pleased to meet you, *Madame*," Marcel said, turning towards the second woman. "I've brought a sheet for you to sign. Perhaps you've already received a copy . . . "

"I been in this apartment since I come to Canada," April said. "It gonna take more than a little renovation work to move me out."

Bruno edged forward. —You want me to take care of them?—

—Give me a moment!—

"I seen the sheet," the woman named April said. "You expect everybody to sign just 'cause you tell we to?"

Maisie said: "Who you to tell we what to do?"

"I'm a lawyer," Marcel said. "Do you want to go to court, *Madame?* Do you want to explain why you broke the law to a judge who speaks French? Do you speak French, *Madame?*" He thrust his head forward. He saw April's eyes blinking behind her glasses. "I will send you to jail, *Madame*. I've done it before!" April's face twisted. Maisie swayed forward. "Hey! Lay off, you."

Bruno shoved past the architect. Grabbing the woman from the side, he pulled her right arm behind her back in an armlock. Maisie gasped and stared at the ceiling. The white-tinted curls over her ears rolled up as Bruno tightened his grip. "Let go o' me!"

"Quiet!" Marcel said. "This man is a police officer. Do you want to go to jail for resisting arrest?" He stared into April's face. I *am* a lawyer, he thought. I can do this job as well as Abitbol. "The laws are in French, *Madame*. I've translated this into English for your benefit, even though I could get into trouble with Bill 101—"

Maisie cried out, struggling against Bruno's armlock.

—Let her go, Bruno.—

Bruno gave the woman's arm a parting upward yank. She gasped and stumbled against her friend. Marcel fought back an urge to scream at the women. This wasn't the moment to shout: Abitbol would know how to remain calm. He must not utter a word until they made him an offer.

No one spoke.

"You gonna have to pay us more than a hundred dollars before we leave," Maisie said.

Now they were getting somewhere. If Crawford can keep his mouth shut, Marcel thought, they'll make an offer.

"We want three hundred dollars," April said.

He pounced. Did they take him for a millionaire? He was a simple lawyer, with a family to support. Three hundred dollars to leave their apartments for the summer! He wasn't a charitable foundation; he wasn't the N.D.G. vacation fund. Their apartments would look stupendous when he finished with them. "One hundred and fifty dollars, *Mesdames*. That is my final offer."

They settled at two hundred dollars. The soft-voiced architect's apprentice adjusted his tie, avoiding Marcel's attempt at a shared smile. Crawford moved down the hall towards the next apartment.

"No, Mr. Crawford, we're going upstairs." They had made too much noise on the second floor; they must strike where they weren't expected. As they reached the third floor, he pointed to the apartment at the top of the stairs. "Who is the tenant, please?"

"One of them Rastafarian guys. He's a drug dealer."

Marcel knocked on the door.

"Yo!" a voice shouted. "What you want?"

"We want ganja, man," Crawford boomed, the carven slab of his features springing to life.

The door opened. A dark, shiny-black face topped by a red woollen hat poked out. "Good afternoon, sir," Marcel said. "I am the new—"

The door started to swing shut. Bruno met the rough wood with the toe of his boot. The door vibrated like a diving board.

—He wants to talk to you! Bruno shouted, hurling his weight forward to force the door open.

"I don't spreak French."

"Sir, I am—"

"What do you want—*sir*!" Gold medallions clanked against the dealer's chest beneath his black fishnet tanktop.

"I want to pay you money to move out of your apartment temporarily so we can improve it for you."

"What kinda hood are you?"

"We can do this two ways, sir," Marcel said. "If you sign the sheet, I will pay you to move out. If you make trouble, my boys will break your head."

The dealer's jittery dark eyes gave Bruno a quick look. "I got boys too. I bet you my boys are tougher than your boys."

—Bruno, he said.

Bruno's fist swung up and around, driving towards the black man's lean stomach. The dealer lifted his knee with a lazy fluidity. Bruno rammed his fist into the man's kneecap. His face clenched with pain. A squiggle of grey hair glinted at his temple. The dealer recovered in a second, rolling onto the balls of his feet. He kicked at Bruno's crotch and caught him high on the hip. Bruno grunted, then started forward with a slouching heaviness that told Marcel he was going to lose this fight.

—*Assez, Bruno!* Marcel shouted. —*Ça suffit!*—

The dealer, looking bewildered by the burst of French, reached into his gaudy dayglo belt and pulled out a knife.

—Close the door, Marcel said. —We'll take care of this one later.—

Bruno shut the door.

"Fuck off, fuckers!" the dealer shouted through the heavy, splintered wood.

Silence. Long, eddying breaths. He turned to Crawford and the architect, avoiding Bruno's eyes. In future Bruno must be used to threaten rather than to fight.

"Don't let it bother you, son," Crawford said, patting the goggle-eyed young architect on the shoulder. "You'll never find a building that doesn't have a few crazies."

—Some people come to this country, Marcel said, and they don't work to make anything of themselves.—

—*C'est sûr*, the architect said. —*Ils sont pas Québécois eux autres.* Not like *nous autres* with a country to build.—

—It's not a question of who's Québécois, Marcel said. — It's a question of who's willing to work.—

—*Oui, Monsieur Vircondelet.*—

Was the architect mocking his name? The suspicion poisoned his relief at slipping back into his own language after three difficult confrontations in English.

A door opened at the end of the hall. A young woman in jeans and a loose-fitting blouse appeared. Her dark brown hair was clipped short above earlobes fitted with discreet earrings; she carried a bulky leather satchel. Her Westernized outfit could not disguise her Middle Eastern origins.

He saw that Bruno had reached the same conclusion. He challenged the woman. —*Hal takalam Arabi?*—

She shook her head. No, she didn't speak Arabic. But she had understood the question. Blocking her path, Bruno asked her where she came from.

"I'm sorry, I don't speak French. I'm late for an appointment. Would you please let me past?"

Marcel offered her a copy of the evacuation form. "I'm the new—"

"You'll have to talk to my husband. Will we be allowed to move back into our apartments once the renovations are finished?"

"Of course, *Madame.* It is for your benefit that we are making these improvements."

"Then talk to my husband." She stepped around Bruno and started down the stairs.

—Arab whore, Bruno said, his gaze latched to the woman's retreating bluejeaned buttocks.

"Her husband!" Crawford said. "I've never seen no husband."

Marcel stared past him. Perhaps, he thought, I'll come and talk to her again when her husband is away. He was glad he had told her she would be allowed to move back into her apartment. The words had emerged without premeditation. It was easy to lie in a second language you spoke well. He could manipulate English words at will: they did not sink talon-like claims into him the way French words did.

—I need the measurements of the apartment at the bottom of the stairs, the architect said. —It's a different shape than the others.—

"All right," Marcel said, "let's go downstairs. Keep them guessing, right, Mr. Crawford?" He led the way down the staircase to the door tucked into a niche at the back of the ground floor. "Who is the tenant, Mr. Crawford?"

Who will I have to become this time?

"This one's just a regular guy," Crawford said. "A Canuck like me. He won't give you any trouble."

ʘ ʘ ʘ

The lawyer held up his hand. A large-boned German woman with an untidy bun of grey hair coming undone at the back asked her question more loudly than the rest. "What must I do? My husband has signed this sheet."

She showed the page to the lawyer. He read it. "I'm sorry, this is legally binding." He displayed the sheet to the crowd. "If you have signed this, there is nothing I can do. You'll have to abide by the conditions specified here."

"We must lose our home for one hundred dollars?" the woman said. "Vircondelet! What kind of name is this? This is a Hong Kong bastard or this is a Morocco bastard?"

Teddy saw Adriana, who was already looking uncomfortable in a velvety black skirt too short for the occasion, glance towards the lawyer. The wide line of her mouth compressed, reddening the knobs of her acne. "It's a Moroccan name," she murmured. "A Jewish Moroccan name."

"Before Canada was the English and the French," the woman said. "It was good. But today there are all these *breeds*."

She left the room. Two sobbing West Indian women picked their way through the crowd to show the lawyer their forms. He skimmed the sheets and shook his head.

"There is no shame in making a deal with this guy," he said, leaning forward in the tattered armchair. "Life will probably get pretty unpleasant around here. There is nothing wrong with deciding you don't want to put up with it. But settle for a fair price! At this stage you should be asking for at least a thousand dollars. And I promise you, as time goes on and he gets more desperate, the settlements will increase. So you may decide it's worth your while to hang in there. But it's your decision."

"He told me I go to jail if I don't sign," one of the two women who had signed said. "He be a lawyer."

"He's not a lawyer," Teddy said. "He's an engineer."

A stocky, bald man wearing a grey suit and a wide red tie said: "No, he isn't, he's an accountant. He knows what he's doing down to the last cent. He's going to screw us up the ass!"

"Teddy! Bob! Please." Adriana waved her thin arms.

"Is he really a lawyer?" Mrs. Austin asked.

"He's an accountant," Bob said. "He's gonna finish us off!"

"I'll check if he's registered with the Quebec Bar," the lawyer said.

"We have to stick together," Adriana said. "I suggest we all go to the Régie together on Monday morning."

Listening to the chaotic, intermittently inane discussion, Teddy wondered: is this the real world? Have I broken out of Rockcliffe Park? Then, with a thrust of despair: is this all my life is going to be? It was difficult to accept that this confusion was the ordinary life he had sought.

"Who's going to the Régie on Monday?" Adriana said. "Write your name and apartment number and we'll come and get you."

The lawyer nodded his approval. The crowd was a motley bunch: Mrs. McNulty and her son Paddy; Mrs. Austin and her children, and two other West Indian women with young children; a restrained, retired-looking white couple; a clutch of McGill preppies wearing moccasins and polo shirts; the man named Bob with his bright bald pate and shimmering scarlet tie. Teddy wrote his name and apartment number on the sheet Adriana was circulating. He turned around to hand on the clipboard and found himself staring into the round face of the dark woman he had passed on the front steps. His voice caught in his throat. She pressed the clipboard against her crisp bluejeans and signed. Her fingers were lithe, brown and bare of ornaments. He had thought she might be Québécoise, but the name she scrawled was long and indecipherable. Teddy, still twisted around in his seat, felt himself staring at her.

"Should I write my husband's name, too?" Her English, though accented, sounded fluent.

"Yes, write them both." Teddy watched her loop out a second lengthy chain of *k*'s, *l*'s and *m*'s, then turn away to pass on the clipboard.

"Is there anybody who isn't here who'd be interested in joining us?" Adriana said, her voice shrilling as she strained to project above the murmur of conversation.

"What about the Bajan guy?" Paddy McNulty said, as the McGill students snickered. "We should show him charity, even if he is a drug dealer."

"What about the guy who lives next to him?" Mrs. McNulty said. "The old bald guy?"

"We call he Family Man," Mrs. Austin said. "Back home when he was young he couldn't stop having families."

"I'll talk to them both," Adriana said.

"What about the guys in the basement?" a McGill student yelled.

"Oooh, I don't want to talk to them," Mrs. McNulty said.

Mrs. Austin said: "I don't even do my laundry down there."

Adriana explained Joe's bargain with Rollie to the lawyer. "If they're not tenants," the lawyer said, "don't include them."

"He'll clear them out," Bob said. "He'll clear us all out! He's gonna ream us! By winter we'll be freezing in the streets with no place to go."

"Don't you think that's a little paranoid?" Teddy said.

Furrows climbed Bob's smooth pate like invaders scaling a battlement. His bulging body slackened; he sat down on the couch.

"Quiet, please, Teddy!" Adriana said. "We have to stick together."

"Who are you to tell me to be quiet?" Teddy started to say more, but the room fell silent as the lawyer got to his feet.

"Look, I have to go, it's my daughter's bedtime. There are two points I cannot emphasize enough: get down to the Régie on Monday to register your intention to contest; and pay your rent!"

His Wellington boots squelched as he left. Teddy was about to follow him out of the room when he noticed that the woman behind him had stepped forward to greet a tall, fine-boned man who had just come in the door. Moving towards them, Teddy heard them speaking an unrecognizable language. He sidestepped to slip past them into the hall. Paddy McNulty nabbed him.

"Do you know Jesus Christ?" The red hair and pallid skin inherited from his mother had been intensified by pale blue eyes. His stubbly jaw resembled a crescent of suet embedded with rusting porcupine quills. "My friends are having a meeting—"

Paddy settled himself between Teddy and the door. Unable to skirt his bulk without disturbing the foreign couple, Teddy looked for another avenue of escape. Adriana was approaching him. "Could I talk to you for a moment?"

"As long as you don't tell me to shut up again."

"That's what I want to talk about."

They waited for the others to leave the apartment. Adriana closed the door and turned towards him with a lopsided smile.

Teddy felt ambushed by an unexpected sexual tension and at the same time by an ease that wiped out tension. He ran his gaze over the wall, where Ché Guevara floated redly aloft amid a ragtag collection of posters from exhibits at the Musée des Beaux-Arts and the McCord Museum. The wall behind Adriana's head radiated bright whites and blues from a photograph of ancient buildings perched above a pellucid seascape. "You live by yourself?"

"Yes! It makes me so happy!" Enthusiasm transformed her face. When he failed to respond, uncertain what to say, she went on: "Most Greek girls live at home until they get married—even if they don't get married until they're thirty-five."

"You're Greek?" He could see it now: the Levantine sharpness of her features, the copious crescents of her eyebrows; if her hair were longer, her wrists and fingers adorned with jewellery, he might have guessed.

"I'm as Greek as they come—brought up on Park Avenue. My parents just didn't get why I wanted to move out. They thought I wanted to do you-know-what. It took me six months to explain I just wanted to be independent. Then it became: why do you want to move down to N.D.G. with all those English people? Why can't you get your own apartment here on Park Avenue?" She met his eyes. "If I get kicked out of this place, they're going to reclaim me. For them, it's a scandal that I'm here. My grandfather refuses to talk to me."

Oh Montreal, Teddy thought: all the little islands jostling each other on the big island with the extinct volcano in the middle; the flamboyance, at first so enticing, that turned out to be each group's way of holding others at a distance. He had been foolish to feel excited at being alone with Adriana. Her reference to "you-know-what" gave him pause. She's had kind of an uptight upbringing, he thought. But then so had he.

"I'm sorry I told you to be quiet," she said. "But you shouldn't have attacked Bob."

"He was demoralizing everyone. If one person in a group starts talking like that—"

"Why did you have to use the word 'paranoid'?" She stepped forward with a jut of her chin. "Bob is a paranoid schizophrenic. That's an illness, you know. He can't help it. His only friend is his cat. He puts on a suit every day because he hopes an employer will notice how well he dresses and offer him a job."

"I didn't know that."

"Well now you do. The next time we have a meeting you'll ignore him."

"I'll try."

"You'd better."

He thought she was joking, but her expression was remorseless.

"I have to ask those West Indian guys about going to the Régie," Adriana said. "They live on your side of the building. Will you come with me?"

She was avoiding his eyes. Was this Adriana's idea of a date? "Sure," he said. "I'd like to see what happens."

"Will you wait for me a second?"

He nodded, surprised by her probing expression. Adriana disappeared down a hall. He heard a door close and a bolt slide shut. When she returned her black skirt had been replaced by bluejeans that emphasized the spindly length of her legs and the cups of her hips. He found his eyes lingering on her. She bowed her head, blushing.

"Let's go," he said, turning towards the door.

◌ॐ ◌ॐ ◌ॐ

There was more double-glazing on the Village's sidestreets than there had been a year earlier, but Rue Ste-Catherine had not changed. Men whose faces had been poached by alcohol into crusted pink-purple masks stumbled down the sidewalks. Hollow-cheeked, fetchingly slender boys wearing tight faded bluejeans and gaunt teenage beggars whining in rural accents flitted in and out of the pairs of stocky middle-aged men strutting along hand in hand. Neon branded the night; whiffs of urine and vomit pierced the prevailing aroma of French fries. Men were everywhere. That was what had intoxicated François the first time they had come down here together; André, barely familiar with this eastern stretch of Ste-Catherine, had seen only the poverty, the imposed unevenness of tasteless, jammed-together logos that denied any Québécois heritage. Their worst argument had started on the corner across the street from a garish hotel that offered rooms by the hour. André had demanded that François recognize that the men on this street were oppressed as gays *and* as Québécois, and François had incensed him by murmuring: —*Y a rien de plus platte que la politique.*—

The memory consoled him. He would never dismiss politics as boring, but today he would be less extreme. He dug his fists into the pockets of his jacket and looked the men walking towards him in the eye. Bursts of dance music and mincing English voices broke in upon his hearing. He stepped into a bar. On the screen behind the petite blond barman in the laundered white T-shirt that moulded his pecs, a small pert mouth was opening to suck a totem-pole penis. André ordered a Coca-Cola. The barman's smile was cruel. —You're hitting the hard stuff, he said over the jolting beat of the music.

—The hard stuff, André said, is below my belt.—

He was through with getting drunk in order to get laid. Getting drunk was being like Papa: it was Papa forcing Maman to go out to the bars with him because she was afraid that if he went alone he might not return. Maman had soaked herself in alcohol to hold onto her husband. Her hard warrior face had grown puffy around the jaw. Her looks had never recovered. During the months that he and François had been together he had felt that he was ruining her life all over again by drinking like Papa.

Or had he been drinking like Maman, desperate to hold onto his lover?

He was past that misery; he was past tormenting himself in the search for love. Passion was his goal. Men could be wonderfully passionate, but they were not made for devotion. That much had become clear in Paris. The unblinking cynicism of Parisian men had disarmed him, but in the last few weeks he had grown grateful to have experienced it. Parisian gay men drank less. They suffered less from self-hatred. If one wanted to screw men, one screwed men—*bof*, as the Parisians said, who cared? Any man who needed to drink away his scruples was *arriéré*. Liberation was being able to enjoy fucking another man stone cold sober.

The man at the next stool glanced at his drink. André liked his avid face, which made him look younger than his likely age. His skin was light brown, his body, dangling over the stool, excitingly long-legged and tapered. A North African, though his skin was lighter and his features squarer than those of most North Africans. —You come here often?—

—I like to drink.— The man studied André's glass. —You don't?—

—I'm a Muslim, André said.

The other man laughed. His teeth lacked the white polish André had been hoping to see. They were incongruously small and splashed with ochre-coloured stains. —I remember you. *Tu étais avec Monsieur Spock.*—

He's slept with François, André thought. He was one of the boys François chased while I tried to cling to him. —I used to drink then.—

—And now you don't? Allah will smile upon you.— The young man's face was solemn. —I have degenerated. When I came to Montreal I obeyed the mandates of Islam. But later I spent too long in bars . . . —

—It's a small sin.— André bought the boy another drink. Süleyman was not North African but Turkish, and he was no longer a boy. The pleats in the corners of his eyes made him look closer to thirty than twenty. His hair was straight and glossy, parted on the side, his skin, of a honey-and-olives softness, was only two shades darker than André's complexion. They had been talking for less than ten minutes when André got an erection. This was another advantage of not drinking. In a few months he would turn forty: his erections were no longer as reliable as they had once been, and under the influence of alcohol they became even less trustworthy. He preferred to screw like the cynical Parisians, sober and with open eyes.

—Do you want to go to a hotel? I'll pay.— Only as he asked this question did André spot the safety pin clipped to Süleyman's collar. He wanted safe sex. So much the better.

—Are you sure you want to go to a hotel with me?—

—I'm sure.—

The nearest hotel that rented rooms by the hour—the one he had stared at as he and François began their argument—was only two blocks away. Süleyman smiled all the way. His smile bulged with self-centred greediness. André did not care. He felt the same. They knew what they wanted: they were both men.

A fat man with an earring sat in a small, locked booth in the hotel doorway. André paid him, took the key and climbed the stairs. In the upstairs hall two seared tinfoil trays, the size of his palms, lay on the orange wall-to-wall carpet that was coming unstuck at the edges. Süleyman gambolled ahead of him. He was living his own intoxication. One intoxication or another was essential to sustaining the illusion of ecstacy. A moment's faltering and the momentum would be gone.

He opened the door, turned around and pulled Süleyman inside as though he were a long-lost brother. Wrestling Süleyman to the bed with just enough force that a moment's fear might course through the boy and quicken his arousal, he did not glance at the room. Laughing, kissing, grappling like mismatched twins, they did not bother to turn on the light. Süleyman was taller than him, but André was stronger. The washboard glass in the window fused the dissonant shades of neon in the street into a crossbred glow. In a few minutes they were naked. My first glimpse of a brown ass, André thought. There was no denying that Süleyman's brownness made André's cock stiffer. It was time to let someone else be the outsider: he had served his expatriate sentence, done his stint as an exotic. He might feel as though Quebec were being invaded, but he wasn't going to refuse a round brown ass in bed. Fuck, I'm appalling! he thought. More reactionary than Papa! Except he wasn't, he knew he wasn't—he was a goddamn *tapette*, inhaling the whiff of Süleyman's thighs, crazy to suck the boy's unbelievably elastic cock, he was left-wing and granola, he was *souverainiste*. Did that mean all the pieces had to click together?

He pushed his torso between the boy's legs, opened the boy's ass with his hands. The boy shuddered, looking up at him with held breath and a weak smile. He creaked like an old house as André tilted him back, found the channel, then pushed harder than he had ever pushed. The boy screamed. The pressure on André's cock, even through the condom, was incredible. He would not be able to keep this up. These days the first orgasm came too quickly, the second one took forever or didn't happen. The boy stretched his long legs. His scaly heels rasped against the sides of André's back. André revelled in each impossible thrust, his mind fogged.

Süleyman came before he did, with a whimpering desperation that seemed to be bidding André to stop. André refused to relent. His groan sheered into a high-pitched yelp that made the boy laugh. For a second André felt indignant. Then, laughing with Süleyman, he fell alongside him and stroked his hair.

In the hall, a door slammed. Rhythmic music filtered up through the floor. In the absence of a bedside table, a plastic-covered Bible had been propped up on the window ledge. André heard his breath heaving. —Have you seen Monsieur Spock lately?—

—I sometimes see him in the bars. I don't think he remembers me. He was the first man to fuck me when I came to Montreal.—

—He was my first, too, André said, in spite of himself. — Where did you learn such good French? I thought Turks learned English.—

—Most learn German. But I went to a school where we learned French. I spent six months in Paris. When we came here, it was easy. French is easy for us—a lot of the words are the same. Your word for bathing suit, *maillot*—in Turkish it's *mayo*. It's easy.—

André was no longer listening. —Why did you say 'we came here'?—

—I moved to Montreal with my wife.—

Relief cut through André so sharply that he laughed. —A wife! *I* had a wife . . . —

—She lives down in Notre-Dame-de-Grâce. She doesn't speak French. I visit her once a week. Most of the time I stay in the Village. I know lots of guys here. There's always somewhere I can sleep.—

How did this vagabond maintain his impeccable grooming? —From now on, you're welcome at my place.— Behind Süleyman's smile André discerned a bleak lunar surface; he worried that he had made a mistake. He hadn't intended to gamble again with emotions: Süleyman was almost certainly the wrong person on whom to bet. Had he sounded pathetic? He had no choice but to make the invitation explicit. —You're welcome at my place any time you don't want to stay with your wife in Notre-Dame-de-Grâce.—

Uma Vida Nova (2)

IN THE FRONT ROOM OF THE BOARDING HOUSE JOÃO MET AN OLD man named Agostinho who introduced him in the bars. Agostinho was so tiny that he made João feel tall. His mouse-like face, with its clover-leaf cheekbones and cunning eyes, was mobile and animated. Plans, hopes, schemes slipped from between his lips. He had come to Montreal from Ponta Delgada twenty years earlier, six months after his wife's death, because his son had been working here. Five years ago, having saved enough money to buy a house and a fishing boat, his son had taken his family back to the Azores.

—My son has a closed mentality. He is one type of islander. I am the other type. I am a navigator!— He laid his hand on João's elbow. —Montreal is like the ocean. The whole world swims these streets.—

Agostinho had no job and was vague about his finances. In twenty years in Montreal the old man hadn't learned more than ten words of French or English. Every morning at dawn he bought *Le Journal de Montréal* to consult his horoscope. They had been acquainted for only a week when Agostinho began to steal into João's room at six AM, shaking him awake and waving the newspaper before his face. —*Faz favor*, tell me what it says!—

João struggled to translate the roundabout phrases into Portuguese: *The presence of Leo and Sagittarius persons could make today a propitious date to conduct business. Love-life is highlighted—*

—Love! Agostinho breathed. —Perhaps I have time to fall in love again?—

João went back to sleep. Later in the morning he would flip through the job listings in *Le Journal de Montréal* and *La Presse*. In the afternoons he and Agostinho tramped the rectangle of sloping streets between Boulevard St-Laurent and Rue St-Denis, visiting the bars. João asked the men whether they knew of a garage that needed a large-engine mechanic. The men shook their heads. There was no one from his village: no one who had a duty to help him.

—Do you never feel any *saudade* for your village? Agostinho asked, as they walked down Avenue du Mont-Royal, the crooked tower of the stadium leaning against the clouds in the distance.

—I left there a long time ago.— Mother had been dead for years, Father had gone blind. His sisters had married, produced children; one had died. The facts, reaching him in brief scrawled notes, had not changed his imaginative picture of home. In the restless nights, when he thought of the Beiras, he was always a child: tile floors, bland mealy suppers, cold fish except for the *tripas* they ate on certain Sundays, hills dripping with mist, his horde of prying sisters . . . Everything came back to his sisters. The only one he wished to see again was Gabriela. The eldest, she had married when he was an infant and gone to live in her husband's house. Never presuming to handle him as the others did, she treated him with courtly reserve. — My little man! What has *o senhor* been doing today?— He remembered her wearing her dark hair piled on top of her head to show off her neck and ears. He thought of Gabriela more than he thought of Mother. Time had whittled away his visual memory of Mother to a shadow; all that remained was the sound of her infirm voice rasping prayers: —*Louvores ao Pai, ao Filho e ao Espírito Santo por nos haverem concedido a graça de mais um ano de vida* . . . — Incredible to think that pretty Gabriela would be sixty-three now.

—My rent's due in two weeks, he told Agostinho. —How can I think about my village?—

Agostinho said: —We need a drink. Let's go to Le Padrão.—

In the rectangle of streets west of Boulevard St-Laurent the park unfurling from the side of the Mountain spread silence over the deep-set sidewalks. Le Padrão, where sombre English-speaking students drank among the mainly Lusophone crowd, was the bar preferred by speakers of Portuguese who did not come from the immigrant cradles of the Azores, the Minho or Trás-Os-Montes. It was a place for outsiders—for navigators, Agostinho said. Maps of the territory of the old Portuguese Empire were painted on the walls. Intricately stitched shorelines projected from bloated continents; curves of latitude and longitude crossed land and ocean like wayward voyagers. The mouth of the Amazon, the squiggled outline of Cape Verde, the wavy coast of Timor, the pimple of Goa, the plains of Angola and the sinuosity of the Mozambique Channel—

—All the discoveries of the navigators! Agostinho said. In each place where they had come ashore, the Portuguese had set up *um padrão*, a stone signalling overlordship and discovery.

The Angolan owner shook their hands and treated them to a round of Sagres beer. A corpulent, pallid man, his face was drawn into a sag by the weight of his mustache. His conversation was tidal, waves of syllables mixing African slang with standard Portuguese rushing forward then receding before tense, sucking silences until the next wave broke. João remembered Father, leaning close to the hull of his radio, cheering on Professor Salazar's vow to defend the African provinces against the insidious designs of the twin anti-Portuguese titans, Kennedy and Khrushchev.

—I hid rebels in my house, the Angolan said. —I even grew a beard in the last days of the Empire: if you had a beard it meant you supported the revolution. But all the risks I'd taken meant nothing once we got our independence. The South African tanks were advancing on Benguela, Neto was calling the Cubans for help and having a beard didn't protect you anymore. I ceased to be Angolan the moment Angola became a country; suddenly I was Portuguese . . . Portuguese! I'd never been to Portugal in my life. Even my father could hardly remember the place. They say Angola's hell now, but I wish I could have stayed. My wife was a *mestiça*. History ended our marriage. She has two children with a black man now. The day they rounded up all the taxi drivers in Luanda and slaughtered them as an example to other whites, I knew I had to leave. But I felt like a fraud in Lisbon. It's better here in Montreal. In this city everybody's a foreigner.—

—Foreigners don't get jobs, João said.

The Angolan reached for *The Gazette*. There were no advertisements for mechanics, but the Angolan scribbled a list of promising jobs: factory labourer, light assembly worker, shipper in a warehouse.

—But I don't speak English, João said.

—They'll answer the phone in French. Businesses in Montreal work in French but English is better for business so they advertise in the English newspaper even though they expect you to reply in French. It's logical, *certo?*—

That night he had barely closed his eyes before the room filled with light. Daubs of sweat budded from his flesh where Agostinho's fingers had latched to his shoulder. —My fate, the old man said. —I must know my fate.—

Le Journal de Montréal flopped before his face. He could not move. His paralysis had returned, pinning his arms to the mattress while his head swarmed with darkness.

Agostinho shook his shoulder. His arms came back to life. He took the newspaper, mumbled a curt translation of the old man's prospects for the day, then let his head fall back onto the pillow.

—What about love? Agostinho said. —Doesn't it say anything about love?—

João looked again and found a phrase he had missed: *Informal encounter could set the scene for long-term romance.* He translated the sentence and Agostinho left the room looking radiant. João's body felt sticky beneath the sheets.

Remembering the Angolan's list of jobs and telephone numbers, he stumbled down the hall to the bathroom. At one minute past seven he lifted the receiver of his landlady's telephone and responded to the advertisement for a steel-cutter's assistant.

A man speaking French with a strong English accent asked him about his work experience. —You obviously wake up early, the voice said. —It shows you understand why we're in business. Why don't you come up to the factory for a trial?—

രു രു രു

The August heat clinging to his skin at seven o'clock in the morning, he walked into the steel-cutting plant and punched his card in the time-clock. The unshaven faces of the men on the night shift lolled up as the day-shift workers ambled in. The grinding and clanking of steel, drumming against the gloom, made him hunch his shoulders. A trailer truck stood in the middle of the plant floor, its motor idling. João could have dismantled and cleaned that motor, but here that was not his job. He breathed the sluggish, oil-tasting air while the crane operators loaded the last pallets of stacked steel strips onto the trailer and the driver strapped down the cargo. Once he had changed into his dark blue worksuit and pulled his yellow hardhat out of the top of his locker, João would sit on the bench and stare at the concrete floor, waiting for the howl of the siren. He concentrated on his memories of Rivière-des-Prairies. At six-thirty each morning, on the bus, he looked out at the wide blue channel of water, the bright green banks, the stone convent on the Montreal side facing a condominium block of Mediterranean whiteness on the Laval shore. He carried the vision with him all day. Once he had set up his own garage, he would buy a condominium overlooking Rivière-des-Prairies.

At seven-twenty-five the scream of the siren sent the day shift slouching onto the plant floor. The night-shift men remained at their stations for five minutes until the siren screamed again. Then, the transition completed, the night shift turned away.

The plant was so different from the Renault factory in Lyon that his initial impulse was to denounce it. He had the same reaction to his fellow workers' instructions. All of the men in the plant spoke Québécois, though a few trailed Irish or Italian surnames. Their careless slang left him uncertain of what was expected of him. The Renault factory had been no less bleak, but his position had been defined: he had stood on the assembly line wearing his mask and soldered the same three parts over and over; he had been allowed three tickets a day to the toilet. In Canada a man could wander off to the toilet at whim, all activity around him shuddering to a halt. The supervisors would tolerate the shirking for a while, then a muscular, T-shirted ogre would charge down the metal stairs from the office overlooking the plant floor and swear at everyone in sight until work resumed. João grasped that his job allowed no place for dignity. He suppressed his frustrations, as he had suppressed his needs during his first months in France. He squelched his complaints, straining to make sense of the *joual* in which he was bossed around. He fought against the heat and his aching muscles. He spoke less and less.

He had expected the plant, like the Renault factory, to be organized around an assembly line. But nearly half the floor space was given over to storage: immense rolls of steel, each one twice a man's height in diameter, towered into the gloom in stacked pyramids. The line, which was compact enough to be supervised by two men, unrolled these coils, cutting them with tremendous stamping thuds into huge sheets that were piled on boards on the floor. Then the sheets had to be cut. The plant's true centres of activity were the two shears.

—Yuh ever seen one of these? big Gilles asked him the first morning, chewing on the blond mustache that obscured his upper lip.

Marco, the operator, showed him how the shear worked. Built of green-painted steel, the machine stretched as high as João could reach above his head. On the side where Marco and Gilles stood was a waist-high platform; reinforced iron spars enabled the two men to hold long sheets of steel rock-steady as they slid them into the shear. An adjustable frame beneath the cowling on the back of the machine caught the steel sheets and clamped them in place to be cut. The control panel above the platform allowed Marco to extend or retract the frame to cut the sheets to the dimensions required.

Marco led him around the back of the shear. —You work here.—

He stared into the shadow beneath the cowling. Marco, a blubbery phlegmatic man who scorned the regulation worksuit, preferring track pants and a black T-shirt with a gouged-looking hole in the belly, pushed a padded saddle towards João. The saddle was mounted on ball-bearings and tilted back to cup the sitter in steeply reclined posture. —Sit, Marco said. He sat, and Marco shoved him under the back of the shear.

He worked in the long narrow cavity where the steel fell when it was cut. His job was to stack it. Before they began each order he slid a wooden pallet flush against the wall of the machine. Gilles would hammer together a skid. They would mount the skid on the pallet. João, tilted back in his saddle, would grab the slices of steel as they flashed down through the gloom, trying to place each strip on the skid before the next one could smash his knuckles. After each order had been completed Gilles would remove the pallet and the skid with a pallet truck. The steel had to be piled on the skids in even, symmetrical rows. Once he and Gilles had straightened the piles, they would fold small flaps of pliable steel over the corners, anchoring the flaps with wooden blocks, then bind the pile with steel straps. They ratcheted the straps taut, hammering flat the metal thimbles the straps passed through to ensure that nothing slipped. The package was carted away on a forklift and a new order began.

Packaging gave him his only chance to get out from under the shear. He spent most of the day curled on his back on the saddle, slapping steel sheets into place as they clanged down next to his elbow. His world shrank, excluding all that was not visible through the slot-like opening, three metres long by ten centimetres high, into which Marco and Gilles advanced the steel sheets. Each time they stopped to smoke a cigarette he glimpsed Marco's torn black T-shirt and Gilles's huge hand nonchalantly scratching his crotch. Quaffing their last draughts of smoke, they would push the sheet forward again, blotting out his view. The drone of the shear's engine rose to a vibrating pitch and the severed sheet slammed down close enough to shave the hair on his forearm. During his first few days in the nook he felt constricted. He learned to propel the saddle across the cavity with a kick of his heel. The shear's innards dripped oil: it accumulated in small slicks on the concrete floor; two or three times a day he sprinkled sawdust on it, then swept the sawdust away. He cared for the filthy nook as he would tune a cherished Renault. When Marco adjusted the frame between orders he stared transfixed at the spiralling hydraulic screws a hand's breadth above his eyes. He cracked his head against the underside of the cowling twenty times a day. His helmet saved him. As the summer heat pushed up past thirty-five degrees Celsius, drenched in ninety per cent humidity, the plant grew hellish. By eight-thirty in the morning his sweat-saturated worksuit clung to his skin. He fled to the water cooler. In August the twelve men on the plant floor emptied an eighteen-litre water drum every three hours.

It was impossible to work under the shear without getting cut. One piece of steel plunged straight down while the next piece leapt out in a spouting arc. Marco shoved the final section of each sheet through the slot without warning. João's forearms were scored with red gashes and deep blue scars. Looking at the slash-marks as he soaped himself in the shower in the evening, he felt detached from his flesh. The hum of the shear, the crashing of the assembly line and the moan of the cranes bored into his mind, accompanying him onto Boulevard St-Laurent in the evening.

He grew less aware of the people surrounding him in the boarding house and on the street. He developed a honed sensitivity to steel.

There was heavy grey steel that looked like iron, and shiny white steel that he could bend in his hands; there was the glossy twenty-three-gauge steel that tore like tissue paper as the assembly line unspooled it from the coils. Steel could be hundreds of tiny wafers, no longer than a bolt or a screw, that cracked down onto his knuckles as fast as Marco could cut them. It could be comfortably sized sheets, one or two metres square, that slapped down onto the skid so raptly that the pile barely needed straightening. Steel could bite him, cut him, caress him. It chewed up his work gloves. He was allowed a fresh pair of gloves every two days; lubricated to facilitate cutting, the steel turned the palm and fingers black within two hours. By the second day rents appeared in the soft felt. Each time his gloves flashed out in front of him, he glimpsed his skin through the rips.

Some of steel's moods frightened him. One afternoon they were cutting square sheets of medium-heavy density steel. Each sheet clacked down onto its predecessor with a sharp smack. As the second sheet struck home, a point of pain shot deep inside his skull. Sheet after sheet slammed down with the same piercing report. Washing his hands in the toilet during the next break, he watched the other men's mouths moving as they exchanged inaudible jokes. He realized he had gone deaf. His deafness passed by evening. After that, he wore earmuffs when they cut the medium-heavy steel. Unable to force his helmet on over the earmuff-strap, he rolled into the nook bareheaded, choosing bruises over deafness.

Steel showed its most forbidding face when they cut the eleven-gauge sheets. The eleven-gauge was the densest material the plant handled: a short strip could weigh a man down. The crane operators brought it to the shear in sheets twenty feet long by eight feet wide. They had to slice these sheets into strips eight feet long by two feet wide. João dreaded these days, praying each week that the eleven-gauge order would come up during the evening or the night shift. The news that one of the shears was about to cut eleven-gauge steel stirred the plant floor into a state of wariness. Men stood clear of the load as the crane operator and his assistant guided the sheets towards the oil drums João and Gilles set out to receive them. The supervisors would wave men off other jobs to help with the eleven-gauge cutting. The sheets were so heavy that five men, straining until sweat rolled down their necks, could barely budge them from the drums. Some days they had to use the crane to slide the sheets into the shear. Curled in his nook, João waited for the first slice to fall. He installed the longest, heaviest pallet to withstand the impact of the eight-foot eleven-gauge slabs. As slowly as the men on the other side of the shear pushed the steel towards the blade, he had to screech at Marco each time to wait, not to cut yet. At this length, sheets invariably fell crooked. He scooted from one end of the nook to the other, wrestling the sheet until it dropped flat. As each subsequent sheet bore down on those below it, his only way of aligning the ends and edges was to seize the underside of the cowling and swing himself feet-first at the piled steel. His boots did the job. But driving the topmost sheet flush with the others at one end could swing it out of line at the opposite end. It took three feet-first lunges to straighten the pile after each eight-foot sheet fell. One sheet left askew would carry out of line those that followed, making the pile impossible to bind or haul away.

The eleven-gauge sessions left him wrung out and staggering. He was too old to fling his body around like a boy of seventeen. Half the men in the plant were his age or older;

but they were not working under the shear. They had not committed the crime of changing countries. The immigrant had to repay his foreignness with sweat.

He thought of his hours under the shear as a form of purgatory. This neglected concept from Mother's religious vocabulary helped him to explain his presence in a plant where he did not belong. Qualified to do specialized work, he was putting in time while he established himself—again—in a new country. Did the other men think the same way? Was the plant purgatory to them, or was it hell? He spied on them through the slot in the shear. The union representative, a taciturn young man named Denis, had secured himself the best job on the floor, manning the controls on the line. None of the men liked Denis, but they were all proud of their union. The two crane operators, stubby strongly built men, were both named Normand. The louder Normand wore a blue T-shirt with a pack of cigarettes lodged up the sleeve. As he crossed the plant floor, holding the controls of the crane in one hand and steadying his load with the other, he yelled into the face of every man he passed: —As-tu fourré hier?— Did ya fuck yesterday?

He sauntered up to João during breaks and hurled the question in his face. João looked at his feet.

Most of the other men treated him well. Magloire, the big Haitian who did the dirty work on the line, breaking open the rolls, swabbing away the excess oil and feeding in the ends of the steel coils for flattening and cutting (while Denis operated the controls), told him: —I spent three years under that machine. If you stick with it they'll let you into the union. After three years down there, working on the line is paradise.— João couldn't think in terms of some jobs being better or worse than others. It was all purgatory; he remained locked in a plant that did not put to use the skills that had gained him entry to this country.

It was impossible to assimilate into a full Québécois life. Portuguese shops, restaurants, cafés, radio stations and banks kept him shrouded in the old world; the English blaring from radios and televisions punctured holes in the Québécois mask he was struggling to fit to his face. He settled for making his French sound sufficiently Québécois to earn acceptance at work. There seemed to be little point in going further. His ignorance of English left him no alternative but to make peace with Portugal. French became a tool. Steel sheet smashed down on steel sheet, pulverizing the European French self he had cultivated in Lyon. Huddled in the overheated incubator of his nook, he practised his Québécois pronunciation of *tasser*, "to push," and *de même*, "like that"—the two phrases around which all instructions seemed to revolve. —*Tu le tasses de même*, Gilles told him each time he asked for assistance. The vagueness drove him mad. Yet he didn't dare challenge Gilles. His eagerness to show off his intelligence had cost him a couple of teeth as a youth in the Renault plant. At home precocious observations had knitted his sisters into a daunting wall of authority, deflecting him towards Father to be beaten. Immigrants, like children, were expected to be diligent and unquestioning.

His curiosity, dammed up against the dangers of conversation, seeped into other channels. He thought about who he was. In Lyon all the Portuguese-speaking people had been from Portugal. When he drank with those men, the wooded hills through which Father strolled with his dogs took form in the cigarette smoke drifting over the tables of the *brasseries*. After a couple of beers he was a boy in the Beiras again. Lyon had suspended time, delaying his recognition that adulthood had begun.

In Montreal he didn't need to be persuaded that his village belonged to the past. He moved among a mixture of Portuguese, Azoreans, Madeirans, Angolans and Brazilians. Quebec newspapers spoke of *la francophonie*, the community of French-speaking nations. Just as the Québécois beat back their isolation through cultural dalliances with West Africans,

Belgians and Haitians, so João started to see himself as a man of the Portuguese-speaking world. Every afternoon he came home through the heat, his fingers stiff, layers of drying sweat wrapping his forehead in throbbing bands. After he had taken his shower, scrubbing what smeared oil he could from the fresh wounds in his forearms, he would collapse onto his bed in time to hear Radio Centre-Ville broadcast the evening news in Portuguese. If he finished his shower early he would catch the last minutes of the Spanish-language broadcast run by the Chileans. The Chileans were commemorating the fifteenth year of their exile by reading from the works of Chile's greatest poet. —*En las calles de invierno . . .* , João heard, knowing, without having studied Spanish, that in Portuguese this meant: *Nas ruas de inverno*, in the streets of winter. *Inverno* made him think of *inferno*, forcing him to promise himself that the job in the steel plant would not become his hell, only his purgatory.

The Portuguese broadcast came on. His language, sluicing through his mind, revived him as sharply as his shower. Portugal, the Azores, Angola, Brazil, Guinea Bissau, Mozambique, Cape Verde, Madeira, East Timor: the newsreader's tour brought him the world—his world, a Portuguese-speaking man's vision of the planet. Before, being Portuguese had meant poverty, guilt, crippling formality and introversion; in Montreal his culture was one of the reasons he was better informed than his workmates. *His* radio station, *his* community newspapers instructed him about events unmentioned by Radio-Canada, *La Presse* or Agostinho's discarded copies of *Le Journal de Montréal.*

He never saw Agostinho in the evenings. Since he had started working the old man waited for him at the bottom of the escalator of the Mont-Royal Métro station at ten past six every morning. They would retreat from the workboot-clad early-morning commuters. Standing next to the photograph booth, Agostinho unfolded the newspaper to the astrology section. —Love, he would murmur. —What does it say about love?—

The old man kept his head down, listening as João translated. Once he had assimilated the day's portents, he would turn away towards the up-escalator, leaving João the newspaper to read on the trip to work. The crowd engulfed the old man's frail body.

One morning, arriving at the bottom of the escalator, he did not see Agostinho. He stared up and down the bare passage, ducked his head into the tiny *dépanneur* next to the photo booth. He let a northbound train pass. He waited, staring at the tired faces descending on the escalator. The next train rushed into the station. He had to get this one, or he would miss his bus across Rivière-des-Prairies to Laval. All the way north his hands ached for the weight of the newspaper.

As soon as he returned to the boarding house that afternoon he knocked on the door of Agostinho's room. There was no reply. João gripped the doorhandle and pushed.

—*Não 'stá, senhor.*— The landlady looked at him from beneath her brows. —*Não veio para casa ontem à noite.*—

—*Obrigado.*— Agostinho hadn't come home last night? He tried to absorb the thought as warm water spattered over him in the shower. In his room he lay on his back on the bed, listening to the Radio Centre-Ville newsreader describing the famine in Mozambique. What did he care about a crazy old man?

Next morning Agostinho failed to appear. During the long afternoon, João imagined all the fates that could have overtaken him. He realized that he did not know Agostinho's surname or his son's address in Ponta Delgada.

That evening, his shoulders sore from stacking steel, he roamed from the stark, overbright interior of the Café Portugal to the lugubrious gloom of the Bar Açoreano. No one had seen Agostinho. João retreated to Le Padrão, where he drank a bottle of Sagres beer with the Angolan. —Has the old man been in here?—

—The little fellow? I only see him when he's with you.—

That night he was awoken by a cry. He stared at the ceiling, realizing that the squawk was a child's yell, not the braying of an old man. When he tried to roll out of bed, his arms, lying leaden against the mattress, refused to budge. His vision swirled and receded. In the morning he felt fine. He bought himself a copy of *Le Journal de Montréal* to read on the Métro. He checked Agostinho's horoscope. *This time you may have found true love . . .*

João tossed the newspaper away. When he arrived at the plant the men were milling around the time-clock at the bottom of the metal stairs. One of the supervisors was talking to the boss. The boss had pulled on a dark blue smock over his white dress shirt and narrow tie; he wore a white hardhat. —*Ça va?* he asked João, his English accent growing stronger as he raised his voice to make himself heard over the thud of the line. —*Vous aimez travailler ici?*—

João nodded. —*Oui, Monsieur.*—

—Good. I think you understand why we're in business. Marco's ill today, so Denis will take over on the shear.— Denis, his blue worksuit ironed to sharp creases, stationed himself behind the boss's shoulder. —We have a union here, we can't hire just anybody. But Marco and Gilles like you, I don't think there'd be a big problem if you wanted to become permanent. Right, Denis?—

Denis unbuttoned his chest pocket, pulled out a felt marker and wrote DENIS in block letters across the back of a pair of workgloves.

—Think about it, the boss said. —Tell the supervisors tomorrow if you're interested and we'll see what we can do.—

—*Oui, Monsieur. Merci, Monsieur.*— Joining the union! The offer was a joke. He was a large-engine mechanic: in a few months he would be earning more money than these men could hope to see in five years.

Their first task of the day was to complete an order left unfinished by the night shift. Denis and Gilles eased long medium-gauge sheets into the shear and cut them into strips a couple of feet in length. João worked in sweaty discomfort. Deprived of the sight of the hole in the belly of Marco's black T-shirt, he couldn't relax into the memory-obliterating fog of exertion that usually enveloped him a few minutes after the morning siren sounded. Peeping up through the slot, he confronted twin uniformed bodies. Gilles's long fingers looped down to scratch his crotch; Denis's hands hung at his sides. Time dragged past with gruelling slowness. João fidgeted on the saddle, changing his position to relieve his sore back. He wondered what he should do if Agostinho did not return.

Denis relayed his orders to João via Gilles. He cut more slowly than Marco and took more breaks. He lapsed into long moments of stillness where he appeared to do nothing. He did not smoke and rarely went to the water cooler.

They finished their first, endless order at the height of the afternoon heat. Waiting for one of the Normands to bring over the next load of steel, João spread sawdust over the oil-spotted concrete beneath the cowling. He was sweeping the sawdust away as he saw the sheets approach, emanating the unmistakable grey glower of eleven-gauge steel. Normand's assistant was straining to hold the sheets steady. Standing clear of the load, Normand lowered the steel onto the waiting oil drums. The assistant unhooked the crane's grapples from the four corners of the eleven-gauge pile. Normand thumped Denis on the shoulder, barked a few words that were lost in the crash of the line and the whir of the shear's motor, and pumped his pelvis. Gilles laughed; Denis, looking bored, studied the order paper. After a moment Denis called Gilles over and gave him his instructions. And my instructions, João thought. He longed to step between the two men and insist that Denis speak to him directly.

Gilles came towards him. —Denis says you gotta break the fall with your hands.— He held out his hands palm-up. —They're real wide so if you don't slow them down they'll fall off the skid.—

João rolled into his nook. As Gilles and Denis fed the first sheet through the slot he perched on the lip of the saddle, his hands held palm-up in front of him. Denis cut. The sheet drove down onto his work gloves, turning his arms into a lever: his head rocketed upward into the underside of the cowling. He felt his hardhat, absorbing the impact, rebounding him down into the saddle. The ball-bearings shrieked as he sped backwards out of the shear. One of the ball-bearings snagged in a crack in the concrete, spilling him onto the floor. The concrete felt cool. It took him a moment to realize what had happened.

He picked himself up and rushed around the side of the shear. Denis was pulling a tape measure across a rectangle of steel.

—Who do you think you are? João shouted. —What kind of fool do you take me for? Are you crazy?—

Denis looked up. —*Hostie d'tabarnac d'importé*—

João saw his gloved right hand swing around in front of him. His oily felt palm and fingers cuffed Denis's cheek, leaving black streak marks. Behind Denis's shoulder, Gilles's long form stiffened with surprise. João let his hands fall in front of him, resting on the edge of the shear. Denis looked away. He shrugged his shoulders, reaching under the shear.

Straightening up, he hauled a polished hammer shoulder-high and smashed it down on the outspread fingers of João's left hand.

Pain lashed up the inside of his arm. He hugged his fingers to his chest. A howl ripped from the bottom of his lungs, clamouring against the barrage of the machinery. His body spun through the murk of pain; he fell on his back behind the shear, his saddle standing near his head. He saw the hydraulic bars from which the cranes hung crawling across the ceiling.

When he opened his eyes worksuited bodies were bending over him, obscuring his view of the ceiling.

—We warned him not to hold his hands too high, Denis was saying to a white-shirted supervisor.

—Did you get down and show him? the supervisor asked. —Did you tell him to keep his fingers out of the shear?—

—Sure, I told him he'd hurt his hands unless he was careful.—

—It's a goddamn shame, the supervisor said. —The boss wanted to bring him into the union.—

Gilles stared down from an immense height, frowning. The two Normands spread a scratchy blanket over João's chest like a shroud. He thought of Mother's death: *Louvores ao Pai, ao Filho e ao Espírito Santo . . .* He wanted to tell the supervisor what had happened, but he was shivering too hard to speak.

Seven

Marcel-Teddy-André-Marcel

MARYSE DOZED BESIDE HIM. SHE STRETCHED AND BLINKED. He stroked her shoulder and they rolled onto their backs, lapsing into the early-morning murmuring that eased them into the day. —I'll get the groceries when I go to the art store, she said. —What about the rent?—

—There are so few of them left. By October I won't be collecting rent . . . —

—I mean our rent. Have you paid Abitbol?—

He swung out of bed, reaching for his glasses. The filigreed arabesques of the spicebox on the bedside table gleamed in the damp heat. The hair in his armpits felt musty with humidity. It was August; the lawyer had been pestering him since just after Passover. When he closed his eyes the faces of the tenants who refused to leave swarmed through his mind. He longed to slap the madman in the suit across his fat jowls; he lay awake thinking of tricks to drive out the drug dealer and get his revenge on the Anglo on the ground floor who had treated him with decency at first but now refused to negotiate. He kept thinking about the woman on the third floor. They were all his, but like everything that was his—everything except Maryse and his other women—they really belonged to Abitbol.

Maryse was sitting up in bed when he returned from the bathroom. With his glasses on he could pick out the fold of discontent below the corner of her mouth. Her silence was wearing him down. Even the shape of his marriage was Abitbol's creation. Yet if he had married within his community, it would have been much worse. He envisaged himself and his wife dining with Véronique and Abitbol every weekend, interminable phone conversations with cousins in Casablanca . . . He would suffocate. With Maryse he had a chance. She encouraged him to find himself, her despondent silences and rich girl's demands urged him to make their lives better. She did not understand all he was struggling against; he loved and resented her for her certainties.

He drew a deep breath as he stepped into the bedroom. He dressed, kissed Maryse on the mouth and left without eating breakfast. Sylvie was working downtown; he had promised to be at the office by nine. But as he wheeled the Honda out of the suburb, he found himself turning towards Notre-Dame-de-Grâce. He drove to Sherbrooke Street and parked outside the Victoria-Waterloo. He heard the work crew swearing as he entered the Waterloo side of the building. The ground floor apartments were all vacant except for the Anglo's den at the back. Doors propped open revealed Kentucky Fried Chicken boxes strewn over heaps of plaster. The corridor was steeped in gritty gloom. During the first weeks he had increased the pressure on the holdouts by cutting off their mail delivery. In a moment of frustration he had smashed the lights in the entrance hall. The next day he had waylaid the mailman. Slipping him a pair of hundred-dollar bills, he reminded the man that Canada Post did not have to provide service to buildings whose entrances were inadequately lighted. Mail delivery had halted two days later. The tenants had protested, but before the end of the week three more apartments were vacant. His spur-of-the-moment rage had paid off. The same roving fury was firing through him today.

—How's it going, guys? he said, leaning into an apartment where two workers were shovelling broken plaster into bags.

—Real good, sir.— They leapt into action, swaying pony-tails baring boil-pocked necks. In their eyes he was the boss; they were unaware of Abitbol. Lacking union cards, they knew he could fire them at his pleasure. He had underlined the point by sending two workers home at the end of the first week.

He scanned the room. A lot of work remained to be done before he could invite Maryse to advise him on interior decoration. He watched the men shovel for a moment, then slipped away. Climbing the stairs to the third floor, he knocked on the door of the dark woman whose husband, according to Bruno's surveillance, almost never spent the night with her.

"Yes?" The door opened a crack. The plucked arches of her eyebrows, their delicacy incongruous beneath the dense helmet of her hair, steepled into feathery half-hoops. "My husband isn't here."

"I'm looking forward to meeting your husband, *Madame*. I will tell him how wrong he is to ignore you."

She shrugged her shoulders. "I've got work to do."

"He shouldn't treat you like this. You are his wife."

The door slid open a few degrees. "Why do you care?"

"I shouldn't care, should I? It's funny, *Madame*, I know it's a weakness, but for me it's impossible to work on a building without caring for the people who live there."

Her dark eyes stared at him almost harder than he could bear. "You didn't care for the people you forced out of their apartments." Determined not to reply, he waited for her to continue. "I wish I'd left then. It's horrible here now. When I come home at night I have to walk past empty apartments in the dark—anybody could be in there. And during the day there's so much noise I can't concentrate."

"All you have to do is sign the sheet."

"My husband has to sign. His name is on the lease."

"I'm very sorry," he said, leaning around the edge of the door. He expected her to retreat, but she held her ground. "I'd like to help you. It's so unfair that you're trapped here. You're not like the other tenants, I realized that the first time I saw you. When I think of this building it's always you who comes into my mind . . . "

"Would you like a cup of coffee?" The door opened. The apartment was a broken K of shadowy, high-ceilinged rooms. The variety of the units baffled him. He struggled to understand the thinking of the architect who had designed the Victoria-Waterloo and the builder who had paid for such intricate plans to be realized. What kind of businessman would accept a design that revelled in differences, knowing how much the differences would cost?

As the woman made coffee, he observed the lilting hitch of her bluejeaned buttocks. He found her poised but resentful, a little frightening in her intelligence. It occurred to him she must feel a lot of anger towards her husband.

"My name is Hetty," she said, bringing him a demi-tasse of dark, sludge-like coffee. "That's who I decided to become when I arrived here from Istanbul. You couldn't pronounce my real name."

He let her defiance pass. "I'm Marcel." In her educated, lightly accented English she told him she was writing a doctoral thesis at McGill. Her refinement surprised him; he had imagined Turks to be coarse, brutal, anti-semitic. He felt his palms growing damp—and not just from the morning heat or the warmth of the coffee mug. Hetty's self-possession was more difficult to unravel than Ruthie's gabby confidence. What did she want? "When is your husband coming back?"

"I don't know. My husband leads a very strange life. Would you like to see the rest of the apartment?"

She got to her feet. From now on, he thought, I'm only going to choose women who speak French. It had been hard enough dealing with Ruthie on the uncertain ground of his second language. Now, pulled farther out of himself than before, he was trying to seduce a woman in English that was native to neither of them. Who knew what they were really saying to each other? As she led him into her bedroom, he still didn't know whether she felt the remotest sexual attraction to him.

Her desk was piled high with books, scrawled-over sheets of foolscap, a stack of neatly typed pages. She had taped a postcard of the Bosphorous to the wall. For the first time he thought to ask her what she was studying. Critical social theory, she said. The words dissolved into the August heat. He felt his glance lingering on Hetty's unmade double bed. Noticing his scrutiny, she blushed. Her loose-fitting purple blouse shirt invested the flush in her cheeks with an air of demure restraint. She murmured that in her husband's absence she slept odd hours, waking early in the morning with her head buzzing with ideas that clamoured to be pinned down on paper lest they vanish. "My housekeeping has suffered. I don't know why I'm talking to you about this. I have so few people to talk to. Do you understand what it's like for me living alone?"

He reached for her hips. They stood clasped together in the centre of the shadowy room. Traffic thundered past on Sherbrooke Street; the keening of the drilling on the second floor vibrated through the parquet floor. He began to undress her. They did not kiss. Her pubic hair was a luxuriant, tangled net, more profuse than Maryse's or Ruthie's or any woman's he could remember. He cupped his hand between her thighs, nudging her towards the unmade bed. He did not touch her lean breasts. She uttered a stifled moan as he entered her, pushing closer and closer until his pubic hair meshed with hers. He held still, hoping to pin her like that, but she began to squirm, desiring to be run through at precisely the angle that pleased her. She writhed against him until her body shook. The realization that she was having an orgasm gorged him with excitement. He felt himself plunging and plunging. He finished only a second after she did. He laid his hands on her shoulders, waiting for his breath to return. It seemed as though barely fifteen seconds had passed since his fingers had brushed her bluejeans.

"Could you roll over?" she said. "I can't breathe."

He slithered onto his back and stared at the ceiling. The sound of the drill rose to a piercing shriek. He smelled the unfamiliar tang of the slick of sweat on his chest—his and her perspiration mingled. Hetty returned from the bathroom carrying a roll of toilet paper; her legs were trembling. She prodded the toilet paper at him, sat down on the bed and watched him with a fixed stare as he wiped himself. When he handed her the roll, her wrist quivered.

He gripped her forearm. "What's the matter?"

"Nothing's the matter. It's just been a long time—"

Feeling a flash of anger, he said: "What about your husband?"

She fished her panties off the floor, slid them on and lay down on her back on the rumpled sheets. He watched a dark, curled hair on her breast rise and fall. "My husband and I live in different Montreals. He speaks French, I speak English. We're always at opposite ends of town."

"Why did you come here?"

"I had a letter of acceptance from McGill. He had money and he wanted to leave Turkey. So we made an agreement and got married."

Marcel lifted his head. "If he had money why did he want to leave Turkey?"

"To escape his father and to be sodomized by old perverts."

Se faire sodomiser. Marcel translated in his mind, never before having heard the word used in English. It sounded distant and clinical, accentuating the intimidating chill of Hetty's insight. The buzzing of a motorcycle scaled above the grinding rumble of the traffic. It was time to get going. Hyped-up uncertainty seized him, clouding the sense of release that had dissolved his tension. "When can I talk to your husband about signing the sheet?"

"He visits me two or three times a week. We do care for each other . . . "

"The next time he visits you, please give him my phone number."

She sat up, tugging at the sheets. "Do you only think about your job?"

"I have to—"

"Don't say it," she said, tightening her jaw as though biting off an unwanted lump of emotion. "I don't think I can stand to hear you say another word."

He sat up, pulling his eyes level with hers. His nakedness exhausted him; his limp, lolling penis was an embarrassment. "Hetty . . . "

"I can't even tell you to leave," she said. "We rented this apartment semi-furnished; even my bed belongs to you."

"Not to me," he said, his voice shrivelled. "To Abitbol."

"Who's Abitbol?"

But he had already got to his feet. He tugged on his clothes and headed for the door.

ଙ ଙ ଙ

The door opened. "What you want?"

"We'd like to speak to you about standing up for our rights," Adriana said.

Teddy felt himself grow tense. Where had she come up with a phrase like that? But the Bajan didn't seem to mind. He glanced up and down the hall, then beckoned them into his apartment. It was one of the smaller apartments on the Waterloo side: two medium-sized rooms and a bathroom. The front room was dominated by a powerful stereo system; a water mattress and a pair of chairs with orange plastic seats were the only furniture. Climbing the back wall of the kitchen to above the height of the Bajan's head was a phalanx of empty eighteen-litre water bottles. The bottles had been stacked on their sides, their flat bottoms pushed flush against the wall and their blue plastic caps pointing out into the room. The wall of symmetrically patterned blue dots created a dancing, surreal effect.

The Bajan waved at a pair of grease-splotched pizza boxes lying on the table. "The girl she go back to Barbados to see her family. I got to wash and cook. The only good thing about it is at night I can go out and see the girls. When she's home that's—" He drew his index finger across his throat and laughed.

Teddy looked at Adriana, searching for her reaction. Holding herself upright, she said: "Have you signed the sheet the new landlord sent?" Her poise drew his attention to her face, handsome in profile. Her acne was concealed from this angle. If she could just loosen up, maybe let her hair grow . . .

"No way," the Bajan said. "He try to make me sign, he tell me he got his boys. I tell him my boys's tougher than his boys."

He began to pace. The litheness of his movements made Teddy realize how young he must be. His flamboyant garb—red woollen cap, black slacks, black shoes, thin belt winking a rainbow of dayglo colours, fishnet black tanktop corralling a herd of medallions against his chest—had blinded Teddy to the fact that this was a nervous, edgy kid of about nineteen. Insignia rings bloomed from his fingers when he clenched his fist.

"On Monday morning," Adriana said, "we're going down to the Régie to protest the conversion. Would you like to come with us?"

"No, mon." Continuing to pace, the young man addressed his reply to Teddy. "This be my last month in Canada. I got to go home, become minister for my district. It's a family thing, you know, mon. They kill my uncle, he was minister. He was thirty years old. As soon as I go back to my country three-four guys tryin' to kill me because of my Rastafarian religion."

"If you stay here," Teddy said, "we can get the owner to pay compensation money. It could be a couple of thousand dollars."

The Bajan came to a halt, the water-bottle collage twinkling over his shoulder. "No, mon. I hope you get your money, mon. But that is not my way. In my country the Americans get everybody all technologized, more and more Americanized. By the time you start fighting back they put the squeeze on you: no, you can't have no more credit, no more food. Here in Canada you got so technologized you can't drink the water from the tap no more. Water is *life*, mon. A land without good water is dying. You watch what happens when you ship your water to the U.S.A. You watch Canada die, mon. No way. I can't help you, mon."

They found themselves back in the narrow, gloomy hall. "I don't think you knew how to relate to that guy," Teddy said.

"And you did?" Adriana said. "If you're such a genius at dealing with culture gap, you talk to the next one."

"I didn't mean—"

He struggled for words. The defiance in her face spread into a haughty smile. "Go ahead," she said. "Show me how to do it."

Teddy knocked on the door. It opened a slit. "Yeah?" Family Man said.

"Hello," Teddy said. "Could we talk to you for a few minutes?"

"You Jehovah's Witnesses?"

"No, we're tenants here, like you. I live downstairs, at the end of the hall." He delved for a memory of an experience they shared. All he could recall was the day Family Man had asked him for a birthday present. "You know that the new owner is trying to kick us out?"

"Maybe."

"Have you signed the sheet that says you have to leave?"

The door opened wider. Family Man's ears stood out from his varnished mahogany skull. "I not here when he come."

Teddy started to explain the tenants' plans to contest the conversion. "If you come down to the Régie with us . . . "

"Don't know no Régie."

"It's on Côte-des-Neiges Road. You catch the 165 bus from Guy station."

"Don't know no 165 bus."

"It leaves right from the station."

"You go there, get the paper for me, okay, mon?"

"A group of us are going together on Monday morning. Would you like to join us? Mrs. Austin is coming, Mrs. McNulty—"

"You go for me, mon."

"If you don't go down to register he'll kick you out."

"You do it for me, mon."

The door closed. They stared at the white paint flaking away from the bevelled grooves of the woodwork

"Another culture gap," Adriana murmured.

"Will you shut up?" Teddy caught himself. "I'm sorry."

He saw her dark gaze raking him with a furious scrutiny. Their eyes met. She lowered her glance, her intensity subsiding. "I told you to shut up and you told me to shut up. I guess we're even."

"Yeah, now we never have to talk to each other again."

He had hoped for a laugh, but she turned away and started down the stairs. He followed her. Studying the span of her shoulder blades and the feathery black chimney of down joining the collar of her polo neck to the burnish of her thick, cropped hair, he was overwhelmed by her femaleness. He wondered how she would look naked from behind. He ached to fondle her shoulder blades, absorb the textured heat of the flesh covering those small wings waiting to unfold. He wondered whether Adriana had slept with a man and guessed that she had not. She was all roiling potential, passion and determination with no outlet. What willpower she must have shown to argue with her parents until they agreed to let her move out!

When she turned around to face him at the bottom of the stairs, she was smiling again. "That was fun. I'll see you on

Monday." She offered him her cheek. Taken by surprise, he leaned forward and gave her a peck. She laid her hand on his shoulder and with disarming self-confidence pulled him back towards her. "It's both cheeks," she said. "You haven't been in Montreal very long."

Offended by the thought that in her eyes he was the virginal one, he lavished a smooch on her neglected cheek. He had thought that only French people kissed each other's cheeks. He wondered whether Adriana's warmth simply reflected the way people treated each other in the Greek community. Having little experience outside that community, she might be sending signals that were stronger than she realized. He was still trying to untangle the contradictions when she murmured: "I'll see you on Monday morning."

He stepped into his apartment. As he closed the door, the sound of Adriana's footsteps receded down the corridor.

On Friday evening, two hours after he returned from work, the heat went off. Cooking supper he became aware of a damp chill seeping into the stuffy air of the kitchen; beads of moisture were condensing on the pipes in the corner. His bedroom felt even colder than the kitchen. A grumbling complaint eddied up through the floor from the basement. He was finishing his ravioli when Mrs. McNulty knocked on his door.

"He's trying to freeze us to death." She was wearing a blue toque. "I phoned his office but he didn't answer."

"In a couple of weeks it'll be May," Teddy said. "He won't be able to get us like this."

"He'll find other ways." She looked down the stairwell in the direction of the basement and motioned that she wanted to come in. She stepped inside and looked him in the eye, not bothering to appraise his housekeeping. "He's letting them stay in that clubhouse Joe built them," she whispered. "That Ayrab Jew's letting those boys do his dirty work. You be careful, Teddy. That Jamaican boy tried to hit my son Paddy with that pole he totes around."

The heat stayed off all weekend. On Sunday morning Teddy woke up sniffling. He felt the building wheeze and contract. When he went out into the streets the feeble spring sunlight almost warmed him, but the moment he returned home he shivered again with the dungeon-like cold.

By Monday morning he was sneezing. He rolled out of bed and, without bathing, dressed in a heavy sweater. He met Adriana at the Victoria entrance. The glint of her dark hair in the morning sunlight made him want to kiss her again, but this morning she was all business. Following her list, they went to each of the twelve apartments whose tenants had signed up to contest the conversion. Allowing for the Bajan, Family Man and two apartments full of McGill students—none of whom could be roused to contest—Vircondelet had cleared thirty-four apartments out of fifty. The halls thudded and whined with the sounds of renovations; with each apartment that fell empty the din grew louder. Ground-in sawdust dulled the marble tiles, bags of garbage were piling up at the bottom of the basement stairs. The Bajan, succumbing to the mood of disintegration, had begun to toss garbage and bottles out of his window into the shaft in the centre of the building. He flung pizza boxes out into space as though he were hurling frisbees. The pile of garbage in the shaft had almost reached Teddy's window. Even with the window closed, he could smell the stench in his bedroom.

Sneezing bitterness brought out the tenants in gusts of early-morning anger. Most were ready to go when he and Adriana knocked on their doors; nobody stayed home. As they boarded the 165 bus at Guy Métro station he looked around at spruce, hyped-up Bob, dressed in a brown suit and a pumpkin-coloured tie, Mrs. Austin in her gaudy headscarf, grim-faced Mrs. McNulty accompanied by pudgy young Paddy, the dark woman with the unpronounceable name leaning into her slender husband. It was odd to think that he had longed to talk to this woman. Observing her looking so sensual next to her husband made his longings feel juvenile. Today it was Adriana who opened up a pit in his stomach. She stood near the front of the bus, speaking with a West Indian woman who had brought her children. Admiring her unforced friendliness, he felt a pang that she had not sat next to him.

The Régie occupied a large second-floor suite of offices. Teddy stood in line behind Bob, explained his situation to a counsellor, signed a form. Their group dispersed as they were directed from line-up to line-up. He lost sight of the others in the crowd and was relieved when, arriving at the bottom of the stairs, he found Adriana bantering with the foreign couple. The woman paused to greet him. The tall young man shot him a smile. Adriana, taking advantage of the lull in their conversation, said: "I've gotta go." Clasping Teddy's arm with a familiarity that surprised him, she guided him towards the door. The husband, to whom he still had not introduced himself, offered Teddy a curious little farewell wave.

"Hey, why don't we go back with them?" Teddy said, as they passed through the swinging doors.

"I'm not going anywhere with them." Releasing his arm as they approached the bus stop, she hissed: "They're *Turks*."

"Is that where they're from?"

"Yes, and they should stay there. Do you know how long those people occupied my country?"

"I thought your country was Canada."

"I'll never forgive the Turks for what they did to my people."

They boarded the bus in silence. When the door opened at the first stop cool morning air washed Adriana's odour, at once harsher and more delicate than Janet's smell, across his face. In five years in the United States he had not heard anyone, with the exception of an aging white southerner interviewed on television about black people, express this kind of venom towards another culture. He wanted to ask Adriana how, in light of her political science studies at Concordia University, her volunteer work in the impoverished Little Burgundy neighbourhood, she could cling to this sort of outmoded intolerance. But he knew that asking this question would close down their friendship. The bus moaned as it began the haul over the Mountain towards the downtown core. They entered a zone of raw rock. One of the boulders had been splashed with painted white letters: *La Loi 101*! In paint of a creamier shade, another hand had added an equals sign and a swastika. Teddy glanced down at his and Adriana's legs fitted alongside each other. He had been waiting all morning to talk to her and now he had nothing to say. On the way downhill past the Montreal General Hospital, only a few moments away from the Guy Métro station, he said: "I have to go to work from here. I got permission from my boss to come in an hour late. Are you going to be around . . . ?" He heard his voice trail off.

"I'll be around all summer. I'm taking a course and I'm working at the Posh Imports store in Westmount." She laughed. "I'll be here until we get kicked out."

Teddy tried to echo her laugh. "See you," he said, dragging his hand over her arm in a perfunctory way. This time she did not invite him to kiss her cheeks.

As soon as his feet hit the sidewalk he wished he *had* kissed her; it would have stalled their drifting apart. All day he wondered when he would see her again. His boss, drenched in aftershave and corsetted into a three-piece blue suit too grandiose for the owner of a small language school, stalked the hall. Yvette, the French teacher Teddy had been cultivating during coffee breaks, told him about her new boyfriend—*Un gars ben smatte*, she said, as they chatted in French—and the gossipy yet prim young Italian secretary informed him for the third time that the boss was considering him for the early-morning private classes for bankers; he need only demonstrate an improved attitude. He wasn't going to demonstrate that today. He brooded over Adriana. When he returned home he walked in the Victoria side of the building and ambled up and down the vacant corridors on the pretext of examining the renovations. He lingered outside Adriana's door, where a trickle of music filtered out like a taunt. Had he been in a more upbeat mood he might have knocked and pretended he had dropped by to discuss some aspect of the conversion. Yet he felt too gloomy to pull it off. He walked out onto the street and back in the Waterloo entrance.

The phone was ringing as he came in the door.

"Teddy, it's Janet. I—"

"I don—"

"—know there's no reason for you to even listen to me say this, but I'd like to ask you out."

Out on Sherbrooke Street a large truck drove past.

"Ask me to what?" Teddy said.

"A party. It's a reunion party for the people from my M.A. theory seminar at McGill. Some of them are out in the real world now like me, others are doing Ph.D's . . . You don't mind that it's going to be such a hardcore academic crowd?"

"I've got an M.A. from Berkeley." Teddy heard his voice roll out like the stutter of a rusty machine. He was barely focusing on this conversation. Drawing a breath, he realized that the heat had come back on. He suppressed his irritation that Janet was taking for granted his acceptance. "When is this?"

"Of course you would have to remind me of your bourgeois privileges. Not all of us got the chance to go to Berkeley."

"You got the chance to go to McGill—and after that, you still think you're part of the working class."

"Sometimes you're not a very nice person, Teddy." He refused to apologize; her voice turned meek. She said: "It's on Friday."

"I'd like to go," he said. "But Janet, I feel like I hardly know you. We haven't seen each other in months. You've just become this voice on the phone."

"This crazy voice on the phone, right? I'm sorry about that, Teddy. There's been a lot of weird shit happening in my life and you're a strange guy—I don't know what to make of you. It's hard. Look, why don't we have dinner before the party? I'll meet you at the Vendôme Métro at six-thirty on Friday and we can go eat downtown, then go to the party."

Teddy gazed at the receiver as he hung up. Before he could think he had begun counting the hours until his date with Janet. It was Monday night. How would he survive until Friday? Friday, when he would stare into Janet's dark brown eyes; Friday, when they would talk, staunching his loneliness; Friday, when he might finally have sex with her energetic peasant girl's body powered by half-demented passions. He stepped out into the street for a brisk walk up the hill.

On Friday he came home from work and took a bath in the free-standing metal tub dominating his slot of a bathroom. He selected a burgundy dress shirt from his cupboard, hung his black leather jacket on the back of a chair and was blow-drying his hair—creeping over his earlobes now—when the telephone rang.

"Teddy, this is Janet." A pause. "Look, I've been thinking . . . I don't think you're going to be very comfortable at this party. It's all going to be people who know each other talking about the old days and telling stupid academic in-jokes . . . "

Teddy sat down in the armchair. His chest was seizing up. He could not believe this was happening. At the same time, he had known it would happen. He gasped for air.

"Teddy? Are you there?"

"What does this mean?" he said, struggling to keep his voice level. "Are you afraid of me? Do you think I'll embarrass you in front of your friends? Have you just found out the guy in the seminar you always wanted to sleep with is going to be there . . . ?"

"Teddy, there is no such thing as a guy I wanted and didn't sleep with." Her laughter volleyed down the line. "You don't know me very well . . . Look, I just think this isn't the right party for us to get to know each other. I'll call you next week."

And her voice was gone.

Never again, he thought. Never, ever again would he speak to Janet. He felt his limbs disintegrating as he crossed the floor to his bedroom. He fell onto the mattress, gulping sobs that would be heard all over the building if the building weren't three-quarters empty. He got up, took off his shirt and hung it in the cupboard. He drank the only bottle of beer in the fridge, then went into the bathroom and washed his face over the sink. He looked at himself in the mirror. Why had he been chosen to survive? Spotting his pretentious black leather jacket, he grabbed it off the back of the chair. As though dressing like a punk could change anything! He shoved open his bedroom window. In the darkness the mounds of garbage resembled bloated bodies. He took a step back, picked up the jacket and slung it onto the stinking pile in the shaft. He slammed the window shut.

He lay down on his bed. He tried to masturbate, but felt disgusted with himself. He wondered whether Adriana was home and realized he had no idea what she did on Friday and Saturday nights. A couple of hours later, aware that he was drifting into a headachey, feverish sleep, he undressed and turned off the light.

A shriek cut through his coma. He had never slept so deeply or been so abruptly awoken. He sat up.

The phone was ringing. He groped for the clock: four-seventeen AM. An emergency. But what emergency? Who had died?

No one could have died because everyone was already dead.

"Hello," he murmured into the receiver.

"I'm here at this stupid party and I'm missing you so much." Teddy was too dazed to speak. "I just know I'm going to fall in love with you. That's why I'm afraid to see you . . . I want to see you so much."

"Every time you say that," Teddy said, "there's some reason why you can't see me. I can't take this any more, Janet."

"All right," she said, her voice clearing like bad reception turning crystalline, "I'm coming over."

ଓ ଓ ଓ

He woke to the sound of Süleyman leaving. The half-remembered click of the front door lingered in his mind as he ambled to the bathroom. The roof of his mouth was arid from last night's sherry. *Sacrifice*! he murmured under his breath as he peered into the mirror at the stiff sag of his cheeks, the lone banner of hair flipped the wrong way completing the picture of pouchy decay. I'm glad he left before he could see me with Papa's face!

He had envisaged himself cooking a cheese omelette for the boy (who was not a boy), inveigling him back into bed for delicious morning sex that would seal their companionship. Last night, naked with Süleyman, rubbing oil into one another's backs and drinking sherry after sex, he had felt luxuriantly *together*. But Süleyman was a cynical tramp: he bartered his ass for a night's lease on a good mattress and with sunrise he was gone. André felt a pulse of excitement at the image of Süleyman being penetrated by a different man every night.

Entering the living room, he saw that his cassettes lay in disarray.

A sob of anger: not because Süleyman had robbed him, but because the robbery meant he was not coming back. He regarded André as a bourgeois bed. His passionate arching, the sweat that had soaked the pillow into which he had ground his proud head, had meant nothing.

André pawed through his favourite LPs: Beau Dommage, Robert Charlebois, Félix Leclerc. They were intact; Süleyman's taste was predictable. He had stolen recent music from France, which André had bought on cassette: Renaud, Jean-Jacques Goldman, Francis Cabrel . . . What was Süleyman planning to do with a handful of cassettes? Sell them on St-Denis to buy his breakfast? André would have cooked him breakfast! He would have cooked Süleyman a different breakfast every day of the week.

Sometimes a man needed his family.

He had asked Céline to tell Maman to expect him this weekend. He lifted the receiver and dialled to ensure the message had been passed on. —*C'est beau*, Maman said. —*La vie est belle quand les enfants sont à la maison.*—

She hung up. Never time to talk, never any pleasure in conversation. Céline was right: it was Papa who harboured all the sentiment. As he made toast and coffee, André thought of Maman leaving school at eleven to work in a milk-bottling plant. The departure of the men for the Second World War—a war only the Anglos wanted to fight—had driven young girls into the factories, as it had driven into the bush Québécois men who refused to die for an English king. At that time workers in Lasalle had ridden to the factories in horse-drawn carts. He had asked Maman once whether she had been frightened— envisaging a tiny slim girl with part-Iroquois features climbing into the cart for the first time with men and women who had been working for decades. —I was never frightened, Maman said. —I always knew you had to work.—

He never got beyond that level. None of them did. Oh, Maman, he thought, how I would talk to you if you confided in me! Did Papa feel the same? But he could have done better: Papa could have helped Maman unlock her feelings . . . Why was he going to visit his family? He felt uncomfortable already. He walked down Avenue du Mont-Royal towards the Métro and loitered outside the station, finishing the first of his ration of three daily cigarettes. The Plateau, empty as always early on weekend mornings, offered long clear sight-lines, the whitish sunlight haloing the smooth grey stone of Notre-Dame-du-Très-Saint-Sacrement. Süleyman was nowhere to be seen.

In the Métro he barely noticed the stations passing. Stepping onto the platform to change lines at Lionel-Groulx station, he wondered how many of the young black men, brown

Latin American women, blond Anglos knew who the Abbé Lionel Groulx had been, knew that he had written the first modern history of Quebec. When he taught his students about Lionel Groulx they were amazed that the Métro station had begun its career as a man. He delighted in the students who began to put the pieces together: to see that names were not arbitrary, that each street or building grew out of the past, as all people grew out of the past. The crowd carried him along. He wondered whether any of them had read Lionel Groulx.

In the subterranean light each male body advertised its potential for pleasure. There was something about sex with Süleyman . . . It made him feel *queerer* than before, providing a new layer in the perpetual reaffirmation of the self that everything around him refuted. It made him carry his body with a jaunty disregard, moving like a proud boat on rough seas, confident his bobbing motion was recognizable to other men of his fleet. (What would the Abbé Groulx, whose Quebec nationalism had been inseparable from his Catholicism, say about *that?*) André sat down in the train. None of the men in the carriage was as beautiful as Süleyman.

Sunlight shone down onto the platform as the train entered Angrignon station. André rode the bus home along the high banks of the St. Lawrence River, getting off a block from the former janitor's cottage for the local primary school, where they had all grown up. It was a low white clapboard cottage with a dwarf second floor. If Papa and Maman had spaced their children less carefully, if the older children had not married by the time the younger ones were growing too big to share beds, the family never would have fit into the house. Now they all squeezed in for a few hours each Saturday, grandchildren clambering over children, Maman stirring a huge pot of spaghetti in the kitchen, Papa urging his sons and sons-in-law to drink more beer. Papa's shoes dominated the room; the hurricane of children swirled around the point where he sat down.

André knocked on the door. Papa answered. He hadn't been ready for this. He stared at Papa's double chin and bony snout. Never let me get that fat and bald and weasel-faced, he thought. For a second he longed to come clean and confess that last night he had been naked with a Turk.

—Why are you standing there? Papa said. —Have you got a hangover?—

—No, I've stopped drinking, André said, coming in the door, while a flock of Jacques's and Anne's and Nicole's children capered around him. Papa's belly drooped over his narrow belt.

—I want to change the channel! Jacques's youngest girl said.

—This is my house, Papa said. —In my house I change the channel.— He looked at André. —In my house a man can drink like a man.—

—*Gran'papa!*—

—*Non.*— Papa sat down and punched the channel selector, snapping the television to an English-Canadian channel where two men in suits were arguing about free trade. André turned to leave the room and found himself chest-to-chest with his brother Jacques. A dispatcher for a delivery company, Jacques was wirier than André and had lost less hair, though he was two years older. He read the national and international sections of *La Presse*, not content with the *sports, sexe et sang* of *Le Journal de Montréal*. If more working guys were as aware as Jacques, André often thought, Quebec would be a lot closer to independence.

—What do you make of this? Jacques said, nodding towards the television.

—Free trade? Who cares? All this opposition's just a way for the Anglos to get rid of a Québécois Prime Minister and replace him with a Wasp. I'm voting for Mulroney. Those other two guys can't even speak French. *Le père non plus il ne parle pas français. I' se prend pour un Anglais.*—

He slipped past Jacques, hearing his nieces pick up on his words in a bantering chorus: —*Gran'papa's* an Anglo, *Gran'papa's* an Anglo . . . !— Nothing in the world made him as angry as Papa's obsession with the goddamned English. On the last federal census Papa, Onésime Deschênes of Ville Lasalle, Quebec, had listed his ethnicity as "English-Canadian" and claimed that the first language he had learned in childhood was English. Attacked by his children for these fabrications, he had concocted a story about playing with English neighbours when he was a child in Verdun. —I learned English before I learned French! he said, while his family shook their heads.

André laid his hand on the banister leading to the second floor, struck by the cottage's doll's-house dimensions. In the kitchen he found Maman and Anne and Nicole and Anne's husband, a sleepy grocer who ran two overgrown *dépanneurs* in Laval. Children rushed everywhere, abandoning crayons and paper and matchbox cars in their wake. Peril lurked underfoot. There was hardly room to breathe. As a teenager, when any house would have felt too small, he used to burst out the back door and draw huge draughts of river-chilled air into his lungs to flush out his suffocated rage. He would walk to the grassy bluffs overlooking the St. Lawrence and watch the Iroquois teenagers, gauging the gaps between trains, pick their ways along the ties of the railway bridge that spanned the river at the Caughnawaga reservation. A few times he had shared cigarettes or joints with Iroquois boys, even though you had to speak English with them. When he was furious with Papa and did not want to return to the cottage, he would push out to the point at Lachine, where the canal of the St. Lawrence Seaway enabled him to see ocean-going tankers, mounting the channel beyond the opposite bank of the vast river, appearing to sail through the earth.

Could he make Süleyman see this?

He stepped forward to kiss Maman. —*Ah, des becs!* she said, laughing briskly as he held her a moment too long. —*J'aime ça, des becs.*— She squirmed free and continued stirring the vat of spaghetti. The others clapped André on the shoulders. For a moment he felt wonderfully welcomed by this group that made him: the group that *was* him, and without which he did not exist. Then his isolated, seeking self drove him to question whether a single one of these cheerful people would accept the acts he performed with such joy. His spirit was at home, yet his body felt misshapen. When they asked him the expected questions about how it felt to be teaching Québécois teenagers again after a year of freedom in Paris, he struggled to formulate the answers which by now he should have had down pat.

—*Et la française, elle est où?* Anne's husband asked. —We expected you to bring back a Frenchwoman to visit the little Quebec cousins.—

Süleyman's smile, enigmatic as snow, taunted his mind's eye. In spite of his fluid French, Süleyman had not spoken much. Not enough. If André had made more of an effort to talk to him, would he have stolen the cassettes? —Oh, Frenchwomen . . . , he said, and felt stymied again. His eyes fixed on the deep pink robes of the enamel Virgin Mary who presided over the white kitchen walls—though Papa and Maman attended church only intermittently. The eruption of three children disputing a scrabble box gave him a pretext to catch his breath. —The French . . . They're not like us, you know— —

The others nodded. —They have wonderful things to buy, Anne's husband said. —My brother spent three thousand dollars in two weeks in France.—

—Your brother could spend three thousand dollars for lunch at McDonald's.— Nicole, whose husband was a bricklayer, was the family member most disdainful of Anne's nouveau-riche extravagance.

The conversation shifted. André withdrew. In the front room, Jacques had brought out the dog-eared songbooks they had all chanted from as children. The grandchildren were piled onto the couch and the floor, but Papa, his polished black shoes soldered to the rug in front of his chair, continued to cradle the channel selector. He edged up the volume on the English station, where a large figure in a suit had appeared. "Look at this guy," Papa said. "This guy's a sonofabitch."

—*Franchement, Papa!* Jacques said. —Speak French! There's nobody English here! Okay, *les enfants,* I know which song we're going to sing.— He got them started on the Saguenay folk song whose every verse concluded with the words " . . . *Un Anglais tête-carrée!*" —Sing, *les enfants,* sing! It's *Gran'papa* who's the English square-head!—

—Will you stop that goddamn groaning? Papa said. —I'm in my own goddamn home and I want to watch TV.— He gestured at Anne's oldest son, who was twelve. —Go get your *Gran'papa* a beer. That's what you should be doing instead of sitting there howling like a crazy beast.—

Jacques got to his feet. —Okay, *les enfants,* no fun today. *Gran'papa est en maudit.*— He walked out of the room. André laid his hand on his brother's sleeve. They retreated to the bottom of the stairs. —Onésime Deschênes! Jacques said, with a furious scowl. —*Tabernac,* I'm glad I'm not related to him!—

André laughed. —Does that worry you, too? Figuring we're going to end up like that bastard?—

—It's not my fault he wanted to be a lawyer and he had to leave school at fourteen, Jacques said. —I don't see why we all have to keep suffering for that fifty-two years later. My job's not always fun, either . . . Hey, he said, lifting his sharp chin, how's it going, anyway? You got a new woman yet?—

André shook his head. —No time for that.—

—Come on, there must be some nice single women teachers at that Cégep of yours.—

—I haven't met them.— André didn't think he could take this much longer. —Where's Céline? I finally make the trip out here and she's not around.—

—She's upstairs working on something. She's got this new job. Why don't you go see if she'll come downstairs? Maybe she can calm down Papa.—

He climbed the tiny stairs, taking them two at a time. A hip-high bookshelf on the upstairs landing contained the only books in the house other than those in Céline's bedroom: half a dozen volumes of *Reader's Digest* condensed books, all translations from English, in shiny pseudo-leather covers, three French-English dictionaries and Léandre Bergeron's *Dictionnaire de la langue québécoise.* That was it: the culture we grew up with, André thought; no culture at all; an index of colonization, except for Bergeron's dictionary. —Céline! he called.

She hurried out of her room. —You came!— As he leaned forward to kiss her cheeks, nearly obliged to stoop in any event by the low ceiling, he noticed that her glossy brush of dark hair had pushed nearly to her shoulders. The black bars of her eyebrows heightened the vividness of her slender, snouty face: Papa's face, in a softer female incarnation. She guided him into her room. Anyone taller than five foot two would have felt suffocated by the low ceiling. Céline had a well-stocked bookshelf—her urban planning texts, books of sociology in English, and Québécois and French novels in French—a small ghetto blaster, a pile of cassettes, a miniature cupboard so stuffed with clothes that the door would not shut. Beneath the window, a large, official-looking map lay across Céline's child's desk, rescued in some past time from the primary school. English television voices grumbled through the floor. A child shrieked. Motioning André to sit down in her wicker chair, Céline said: —I wish Papa would turn down the TV.— She clicked a cassette into her ghetto blaster and sat down on the bed with one leg folded beneath her. The music rose in a gale: André recognized the swift, clever vocals of Jean-Jacques Goldman.

—You're working hard, he said, glancing at her desk. Céline was the only sibling with whom he slipped into serious conversations without preamble. The family had made them that way:

they were *les deux méchants bols*, the two wicked brains, the only children who had gone to university. Conversation that was ridiculed as pretentious if it involved anyone else was expected between Céline and André: they had come to expect it of one another. At times André found their seriousness a burden. As Céline was the only member of his family in whom he could confide, he did not always want to speak to her as an intellectual.

Céline's degree in urban planning had led her into the post office. She was working on the conversion of the postal system from home delivery to neighbourhood supermailboxes. —It goes against everything I learned about community, she said. —The streets will look empty without mailmen.— Her job was to plot the points of the new urban network of brown boxes. André, feeling sidetracked, stared out the window, where the grey rim of the St. Lawrence was discernible in the distance. Céline followed his gaze to her desk. —Pretty, isn't it? she said, lifting the map for his scrutiny. —It's the Quebec Ministry of Natural Resources map of two streets in Laval. At work we have maps of the neighbourhoods on the wall. Each street that's going to have a supermailbox is yellow; we put green sticky dots to show where the supermailbox will be.—

—How do you decide? André asked, embarrassed by his wavering attention.

—*À quoi tu sers?* Jean-Jacques Goldman sang over the mumble of the television.

—The Canada Post maps don't always tell us enough. That's when we use the Ministry maps. They show every tree. I have to follow the rules: no one has to walk more than six hundred feet to pick up mail, no supermailbox can lower property values or be placed outside the window of a residence or at the edge of a park. When there's no other solution the municipality will landscape. But we can't ask them to do that too often because it gets expensive and they have the right to reject our plans . . . André, is something bothering you? Don't you like the music?—

—I had a Jean-Jacques Goldman cassette stolen this morning.— He looked back at her surprised gaze. His head throbbed. There was no doubt: the sherry had given him a hangover. Neither of them spoke. Céline frowned—wondering, he supposed, what he was going to say next.

ଓ ଓ ଓ

Abitbol sat on the desk in the Ste. Catherine Street office, cradling his mint tea in Arabic fashion: four fingers stretched across the bottom of his glass, his thumb pinched over the rim. —You're more than an hour late.—

—I was at the Victoria-Waterloo. Working.—

—I want to know what you're going to say at the hearing.—

Marcel glanced at Sylvie sitting behind her typewriter. A worried expression had turned her face long and knobbly. — You told me this was my job, Marcel said. He tried to say more but came up empty.

Abitbol's unshaven face absorbed the muggy heat. He set down his glass and stared at Marcel through veined eyes. — How can I trust you when you don't come to work on time?— He slapped at a pile of unopened registered letters from Victoria-Waterloo tenants. —You must deny everything. The judge will side with the tenants unless you can show him that they are fanatics. They will complain about the lack of mail delivery, the construction work, the smell when we were tarring the roof; they will exaggerate Bruno's role in clearing the building. You must tell the judge that they are still receiving their mail, we did not tar the roof, work never starts before nine or continues after five, and you have never heard of Bruno.—

—Do we have to talk about this now? The hearing's not for another week.—

—We do have to talk about this now.— Abitbol slid off the desk and stood up. —I'm booked on a flight to Casablanca this evening.—

That could only mean one thing. Marcel embraced his brother-in-law. He clung to Abitbol, overwhelmed by sympathy for Abitbol's grief. He must conclude the conversion; he must comfort Abitbol. A stream of misery sent the pain of his own childhood bereavement pouring through him—not as a distraction from Abitbol's pain, but as an amplification of it, part of their pool of shared family suffering. —Don't worry about the hearing. I'll take care of it. I'll take care of everything.—

—She stayed in Fes until the end. I always felt guilty about leaving her there.—

—She wanted to stay there, Pierre, Sylvie said. —She wouldn't have felt comfortable anywhere else.—

—Who did she talk to? I always think about how lonely she must have been. Everyone she knew was dead or had left the country.— He picked up his glass of tea. —I know nothing about the last fifteen years of my mother's life. I was working so hard that I ignored my duty to her.—

He looked out the window, staring into a mid-distance foreshortened by tall buildings. That's why he's always harassing me, Marcel thought. The thrust and heft of the Turkish woman's body made him sit down behind his desk. He wished the others would leave so that he could phone Maryse. —I'm very close to clearing the building, he said. —Of the twelve apartments that contested in April, only eight still haven't signed.—

—You won't get rid of them all before the hearing.— Abitbol turned around. —Tell me what you're going to say to the judge.—

—I'm not going to say anything. I'll phone at the last minute, when the tenants are at the Régie, and announce I can't make it. The judge will postpone the hearing, the tenants' preparations will be frustrated. They'll be so demoralized that some of them will give up and sign. The few who are left will be even more isolated. I should be able to eliminate them before the judge can set a date for a new hearing.—

Abitbol jammed his wide hands into the pockets of his jacket. —I think you're starting to learn, Marcel. But your strategy contains risks. It may make the fanatics even more obsessed with ruining our lives.—

—If the renovations were at a more advanced stage I would agree with you. But we don't *need* to get into those apartments yet; we've got plenty of other work to do. If Bruno and I visit the tenants right after the hearing's postponed, we'll get rid of most of them.—

—Bruno should pay more attention to the fanatics. Encourage him to be himself.—

—And if he goes too far?—

—He's in this country illegally. Let them deport him.— Abitbol picked up his glass and stared at the crumpled tea leaves. —I'm meeting my cousins in Casa. We'll travel together to Fes. I may be away three or four weeks—perhaps till October. My heart will rest much easier, Marcel, if I know that my business concerns are in good hands.—

When Abitbol had left Marcel closed his eyes, removed his glasses and thought about the day his parents had died. No images came, only voices wailing in the Judeo-Arabic he no longer spoke. He had been a myopic, hyperactive boy who crashed into walls and dark alleys and the hardwood stalls of the *mellah*. The day of his parents' death he had felt himself sucked down by the deepest shadows of Fes el-Bali. The maelstrom of pain and loss and silence had never left him; it lurked in his chest, waiting to overwhelm him whenever he felt alone.

—Sylvie, would you like to take a coffee break?—

She picked up her handbag. Marcel lifted the receiver and called Maryse.

—I'm intoxicated, Maryse said, when she answered. —I'm lost in my painting.—

He felt himself relaxing. What a relief to speak to a woman in French again! —When you get so obsessed with your painting I worry about you losing touch. When I'm not worrying about the things Abitbol pays me to worry about.—

—He doesn't pay you enough. When are you going to find a real job?—

—I failed my accounting exams, remember?—

—Three-quarters of the accounting students in Quebec fail their exams. That's just proof you're a real Québécois . . . —

Her laughter took him off guard. A squib of defiance flared up in him. He didn't want to be Québécois. He wanted to be in Morocco with Abitbol, mourning their dead.

— . . . you may not be a chartered accountant, but you've still got your degree. You could get another job. Your family isn't— —

—Don't criticize my family. You don't know what it feels like to be an immigrant here.—

—Marcel! *Assez!* You have no right to speak to me like that.—

I do have a right, he thought. There is so much you don't understand . . . And there is so much you do understand that I can never explain to my family. He felt winded by the unsuspected force of his loyalty to Abitbol. Steadying himself, he told her that Abitbol's mother had died. As he listened to her silence, he sensed her resentment that, today, his devotion to his family was beyond reproach.

After a moment's awkwardness she told him that she was trying to paint an image from her dreams: a vision of trees and a stream, grazing sheep and leaping fish, all blending together into a harmonious landscape.

—What about wolves? he said. —Have you got wolves to feed on the sheep?—

—Marcel! she said with a laugh. —I would never think of such a thing!—

Sylvie returned to the office. He said goodbye to Maryse and shovelled the pile of registered letters onto Sylvie's desk. —Cash the rent cheques, he said, make a note of who's paid, file the formal complaints and if there are vulgar personal attacks open a file for those, too.—

—I'm worried about Pierre, Sylvie said.

—He'll be fine once he meets his cousins in Casa. Our job is to finish this before he comes back.—

—I've never seen him— —

The phone rang. Marcel interrupted his pacing to grab the receiver. —*Allô.*—

"Is that you? Hi, how *are* you? It's Ruthie."

—*Sacré fils.*— Fine points of sweat broke out across his chest. He carried the telephone to his desk and sat down before a curled blueprint of the model apartment the work crew was completing. "I'm fine. How are your uncles?"

"I quit! I'm taking the one-way ticket down the 401. I'm going to law school in Toronto. I went down last week and got an apartment . . . Aren't you going to congratulate me?"

"Congratulations."

"Look, relax. I'm not asking for a rerun of our little trip up north. I mean, like it was fun, eh. But after all, you *are* married."

"That's true," he said, swivelling around in his chair to elude Sylvie's scrutiny.

"Don't get me wrong, I had a great time. And one teeny-weeny night with me isn't going to sink your marriage. But . . . well, I don't want to be a homewrecker." She paused, as though awaiting his response, then continued: "The reason I'm calling is I'm having a going-away party and I'd really like you to come. Even if you can just drop in for a few minutes—"

"I'm working hard, Ruthie." Her name popped out before he could suppress it. He glanced over his shoulder at Sylvie, thankful for the limitations of her English.

"Spoilsport. All work and no play makes Marcel a dull boy. Besides, it starts at seven this Friday. You can drop in after work. Your wife will never know."

"My wife—"

Sylvie's chair creaked.

"Please say you'll come. My rogues' gallery won't be complete without you. I'm inviting every man I've slept with. And you were my first married man."

Were? And what was a rogues' gallery? He felt penned in by her offhand articulateness. No one else he knew made him so conscious of the fact that English was a language he had not started to learn until the age of eight.

"I'm giving you plenty of warning so you won't have any excuse for wimping out. It's at my girlfriend's apartment downtown. I'll give you the address, okay?" He scrawled the street and apartment numbers in his agenda. "Don't have an anxiety attack over it," she said. "I know your office is downtown. It's not like I'm asking you to schlep out to Hampstead . . . So you're going to come, right?"

"I'll try."

"*Great!* See you then!"

He hung up to find that Sylvie had opened only one registered letter. Her long, thick hair lent her dark eyes a tragic expression. —Oh, Marcel.—

—Please get to work, Sylvie. I need to know which tenants have stopped paying. It's time to throw them out into the street.—

*e*ight

Teddy-André-Marcel-Teddy

WHEN THE KNOCK CAME HE WAS WEARING UNDERPANTS and a garish yellow T-shirt never seen outside his bedroom. His hair was rumpled, his face stiff with the salt-pans of dried tears. All the lights in the apartment were out except for the lamp next to his mattress. He glanced towards the illuminated slit beneath the door. Could Janet really be out there? He turned the doorhandle in a trance. She came through the doorway in a rush. She in her high-heeled party shoes was taller than he in his bare feet; the rapids of her hair poured down the left side of her face. As she kissed him with her whole weight he tasted booze and cigarettes and the familiar sharp pelt-like smell. He had just time to see that her face was not as he remembered it—thicker through the chin, the eyes smaller and darker— before their mouths met. This time she welcomed his tongue. Beneath his fingers he felt the heat of her back throbbing through the silky fabric of her blouse. They were staggering towards his bedroom, where he had fantasized so many times about women. In the small room Janet's body felt huge, her presence an almost frightening intrusion. Her fingers fumbled with his underpants, then yanked them down with an impatient tug that left him rampant and exposed. She slid his T-shirt over his head. "What is this?" he murmured between kisses. "Am I the only one who gets to be naked?"

She stepped out of her shoes, her face dropping down to the level of his throat. His anxieties about standing naked in front of this taller, well-dressed woman he had met only once who was caressing his penis with a long-fingered gusto that tugged moans out of the bottom of his lungs dissolved. He squeezed her in his arms, reached for the back of her blouse but found no button or zipper. She stepped back from him and undressed in an effortless dance. Her sports bra, a hefty, almost rigid contraption, came off last. Silence fell; in the upwash of lamplight he thought he detected a shimmer of fear crossing her face. The shadows of her body paralysed him with too much gorgeousness to ever fondle and taste. Without either of them speaking, they ducked beneath the sheets of his bed and turned off the light. For a moment they lay still, holding each other, neither of them daring to breathe. A second before Janet hurled herself on him, ravaging him with her mouth and hands, he thought he heard Rollie's voice murmuring through the floorboards. His hearing evaporated as Janet enclosed the crown of his penis in a soft, toothy bite that joined them in a trembling pivot of flesh. They writhed together. Before he could explore her—*his* woman: the one he had been waiting forever to meet—she was straddling him, riding him with a seething, whimpering energy. His naked penis, hard as a pestle, pounded out his shape inside her. She shuddered above him, discernible in the darkness like an enormous aquatic growth sprouting from his midriff. She contracted, then stretched again. Her body grew so heavy it seemed to be all bone but for a light sheath of sweating flesh. Her weight pinned his hips to the mattress as she took her pleasure and screamed, then relinquished her smothering, momentarily terrifying hold just long enough for him to lodge himself one millimetre deeper inside her where he was certain he had come home.

"I never sleep with a man on the first date," Janet said, a long time after his whimpering had ended.

"You call this our first date? If you count the phone calls it's about our tenth date."

"I'm sorry about the phone calls." He sensed her looking at him. "Tell me you care about me."

"Janet, I feel like I came to Montreal because I had to meet you. That's the only way things make sense."

They rolled together, kissing, his limp, elongated penis plastered against her stomach. No condom. They were beyond that. He had met the woman of his dreams.

"I'm so alone I could die and no one would notice," he said. "My family has two hundred years of history in this country. Now we're almost extinct. I have no parents, no brothers or sisters, no aunts or uncles. A few second cousins I hardly know. I mean it: I could die and not one single person would wonder where I was. My classmates in Ottawa would figure I'd stayed in the States and my friends in Berkeley would figure I'd gone back to Canada."

"We've only been here since I was three," Janet said, "but I've got family all over the country. My brother and sister and their families out west and my parents here. My brother's wife's family in the Maritimes. Your family is everything . . . "

They drifted towards sleep. It was almost six AM. Teddy told her about Rollie and his gang. "They usually keep me awake but since you got here they haven't made a sound."

She laughed. "I bet we showed them! They're still getting over their shock!"

When he woke it was noon. The day's heat had baked the stench of the garbage in the shaft outside his window into a choking mustiness. He returned from the toilet to find Janet dozing on her back. This time he paid the beauty of her body the attention it demanded. His fingers and tongue ran over her from stem to stern. He embraced her, body to aroused body, as he kissed her mouth. —*Tu es ma montréalaise.*—

—*Je s'rai ta femme, mais je ne s'rai jamais ton pays.*— Her spicy working-class Québécois accent startled him. "Don't confuse a woman with a country. It's not fair to either of us."

They made love with a grinding, full-fleshed bodiness that crushed his previous experiences of love and sex. Was that the clue? Was this the first time that sex and love had coincided?

Hours later, she said: "I still haven't heard a peep from that guy in the basement. We must have put the fear of God into him."

"Where did you learn such good French? I was brought up almost bilingual—"

"But your French doesn't sound like anything a French Canadian would ever say. I don't really speak it—I wouldn't want to—I just got the accent from fighting with the kids from the French school."

"You used to fight with them?"

"You really are from Ottawa, aren't you? You think Canada is Switzerland and we're all born bilingual. When I was in school we fought the French kids with bottles and stones. If I go down the East End I still get the shivers because I know they've got me surrounded."

"So you just talk to English people?"

"Why would I talk to French people? They're not my kind of people." She rolled over and looked him in the face. "How many French people do you talk to, Mr. Bilingual?"

"I haven't been here long. So far, I haven't met many—"

"You think that's going to change? Forget it. That's the way it is: English with English and French with French. I've never even been out with a French guy . . . " She settled an appraising look on his face. " . . . And believe me, I've been involved with a lot of men."

The distance between the two ends of his pillow seemed to lengthen. He saw her pushing him to ask the question she wished to answer. "How many men have you slept with?"

"I guesstimate forty-five to fifty." The heel of a hand pressed against the bottom of Teddy's heart. His expression—was it awed? appalled?—must have shown on his face, because Janet said: "Don't look shocked, dear. Once you get started, it's easy. Something goes wrong, you get depressed, you go to parties and drink too much and suddenly you've gone through ten guys in six months."

"It was never that easy for me. But I was in a different country."

"I could do it in any country. Put me down in some hard-line Muslim place and I'd find a way!" Her bravado plummetted into meek-voiced introversion. "I wasn't always like this. I had the same boyfriend from fourteen to twenty. I wanted to marry him. That's how it is when you're a working-class person: you marry the first person you go out with and have kids with him. That's what my parents did and that's what my brother and sister did, too. I would have done the same, except when I was twenty my boyfriend turned into a self-centred *jerk*. I went off the rails for eight years."

He hugged her, more embarrassed by the flimsiness of his life-experience than he had been by standing naked before her in her party clothes. What could he say? What was the right response? His childhood spent alone bored a hollow inside him as he reached for the resources to comfort her. He kissed her mouth, wishing his life had been half as dramatic as hers sounded. He wanted to *be* Janet. "I know I can give you the relationship you need."

Her face broke into a startled smile. She seemed to be regarding him with sympathy. He kissed her mouth, feeling the sting of incipient tears punching at the surface of his eyes. He mauled the ridge of her collarbone. Realizing he was erect, she guided him inside her. They made love with a lunging languidness, grinding long moans from one another's bodies. Teddy heard their groans echoing in the shaft outside his bedroom window, imagined them filtering into the corridor where, he was certain, he heard a response: a thud, running feet, desultory shouts. The uproar faded from his ears as Janet's body became the world. They collapsed together into a sleep he would have believed them to be sharing had the knocking not begun.

A hard knocking on the door. He had been asleep barely five minutes. The knocking continued. "Teddy? Are you are in there? Come quickly!"

He could hardly hold his eyes open. The knocking continued. He stood up, aware of the stench from the shaft and the residual tremors running down the backs of his legs from their lovemaking.

"Teddy! It's Adriana. Vircondelet's kicking the old man out of the building."

He glanced around in search of clothes and could find only the ugly yellow T-shirt. He wrapped it around his waist, pinning the ends together over his hip with his left hand. He stepped out of the bedroom and opened the door with his right hand. "What old man?" he asked.

Adriana shrank back, her face lean and censorious. "Put some clothes on, Teddy! I don't want to see you like that."

"I'm sorry, Adriana. I just woke up . . . What old man?"

"Family Man—the old guy on the third—"

"What's going on out there, Teddy?"

Adriana's eyes swelled beneath her sloping Levantine lids.

"You got no right!" a voice shouted from upstairs. "I got no place to go!"

"I'm coming," Teddy said. "Did you call the lawyer?"

"Who are you talking to?" He could hear Janet getting out of bed.

"Wayne's out campaigning." Adriana shrank back. Her voice became a squeak. "I'm sorry if I bothered you, Teddy. I didn't know—"

"I'll be right there," Teddy said. He closed the door, dropped the yellow T-shirt to the floor and hugged Janet, who had stumbled out of the bedroom.

She pushed him away. "How many women are you seeing, Teddy?"

"Only you. Adriana—"

"Oh, *Adriana!*" Her hands hanging next to her naked hips, her face broke into a wince that made her eyes look smaller. "Nothing like those hot Latin chicks, is there?"

"Janet, she's very young, very conservative, she's probably a virgin. We've been working together on this—"

"She sure came to you in a hurry. As soon as she has a problem, it's, '*Oh, Teddy, Teddy! Come quickly.*'"

"What's the matter with you?" he said, staring down the resentment anchored between her dark eyes. Her mouth was ridged with pain. "Look, I'm not responsible for the fact that your boyfriend acted like a jerk. I want to be with you but at the moment there is a crisis in this building—"

He ran out of breath and flailed in despair. How could they be so unhappy standing naked together?

"You can't have a clue what I've been through."

Was that an apology? In the shadow of the foyer her body looked heavy; his felt spindly and inconsequential. He pulled her towards him and kissed her on the lips without dislodging her fixed stare. A barrage of shouting erupted upstairs. "I have to go," he murmured. "I'll be right back."

"I'll wash up," she said.

"When I come back we can go out for breakfast, lunch—" He turned away, found a pair of jeans and a plain white T-shirt. He pulled on his Adidas over his bare feet, tied them and went out the door and up the stairs. The odour of spilt plaster killed the rising hunger in his stomach. The marble steps were coated with a paste of powdery plaster dust and smeared oil; there were nicks in the banisters, stray lengths of lathe on the landings, torn sacks and crushed cigarette packs everywhere. As he reached the third floor he found Adriana backed up against a wall. Vircondelet's sleek head swung around, his gaze shuttered by his glasses.

"Go back to your apartments," Mr. Crawford said, his broad-shouldered body paunchy in repose. "We're just getting rid of a troublemaker."

Family Man, his body shaken by sobs, was stuffing clothes into a green plastic garbage bag. Two full bags sat in the hall. The man with the heavy mustache, whom Bob referred to as Zorro, prodded him. —Anything that's not in the bag in five minutes stays here.—

"You got no right!" the old man said. He leaned forward, the Expos baseball cap slipping to the floor. "Tell me what give you the right."

"I have an expulsion order from the Régie du logement, sir!" Vircondelet's sleepy voice grew abrasive. "You are in violation of the law. If you don't leave, I will send you to jail!" He waved a sheet before the man's eyes. The distance separating them had shrunk to a few centimetres. "You'll have to speak French in court. Do you speak French, sir? If you don't speak French, the judge will send you to jail. You better believe me, sir. I'm a lawyer."

"Why aren't you registered with the Quebec Bar?" Adriana said.

Vircondelet spun around with a speed that made Adriana stumble back a step. "I know who I am! I am who I say I am!"

"Go back to your apartment and mind your own business," Mr. Crawford said.

Speaking past Vircondelet to the old man, Adriana said: "Sir, our lawyer checked this man's name. He's not a lawyer. What he's telling you isn't true."

Family Man stared down at the plastic bag at his feet.

"Your lawyer is a liar!" Vircondelet said. "You're all criminals. I'm going to put you all in jail!"

Zorro slapped Family Man across the elbow. The old man resumed stuffing his clothes into the plastic bag.

A door opened at the end of the hall. As he recognized the dark woman with the long name, Teddy felt panicked. Were all the women he had been attracted to converging? The woman saw Vircondelet: her face crumpled into a sickly expression. Vircondelet took a step towards her. She retreated into her apartment, slamming the door.

Teddy looked at Vircondelet. "Can I see that expulsion order?"

"It be in French," Family Man said.

Vircondelet slid the order into the breast pocket of his jeans jacket. Zorro, wax flaking off the ends of his mustache, blocked Teddy's way. —*Fous le camp cet instant ou je te casse la gueule.*—

Mr. Crawford said: "If you know what's good for you—"

"You are obstructing justice!" Vircondelet said. "Go away, or I'll call the police."

Teddy, more worried by Zorro than the others, started to back up. Adriana stepped forward. Her chin raised, she said: "You can't get an expulsion order without a hearing at the Régie. There hasn't been any hearing. It's obvious your order is a fake. What kind of idiots do you think we are?"

Family Man dropped his garbage bag on the floor.

"You keep packing," Mr. Crawford said. "These are just troublemakers talking a load of bullshit."

Zorro pushed forward. His raised elbow knocked Teddy back against the wall. Adriana laid her hand on Teddy's arm. They walked to the end of the hall and stood in bristling insubordination on the top stair while Vircondelet and Mr. Crawford shouted at Family Man to get moving. The three of them disappeared into the apartment and returned a few moments later, the tenant in front, the other two flanking him. Family Man was dragging his plastic garbage bags. His baseball cap had been yanked askew. In the shadow of the cap's long bill, his tears made black blotches on the roundness of his brown cheeks.

"You should've paid your rent like these guys," Mr. Crawford said. "They're real good payers."

"Where I go?" Family Man said. "Winter's coming. You can't sleep on the streets in winter."

He shook his head, his jaw squirming. He stumbled past Teddy and Adriana without looking at them.

As the three men walked past them and started down the stairs, Teddy hissed at the janitor: "How can you sleep at night?"

Mr. Crawford's handsome features clouded. "Just wait till you see what we're gonna do to you."

Zorro grabbed Teddy's elbow. —You two wait here.— He held them at the head of the stairs until the three men had disappeared. When Teddy made a move to descend, Zorro blocked him again. —Not yet.—

—But my girlfriend— — A sharp look from Adriana curtailed his protest. They stood and waited, and waited.

At last Zorro let them go. Teddy had thought of dozens of things to say to Adriana, but on the way downstairs they dried up in his throat. A hideous tension set in. She refused to meet his eyes, though she jabbed him with surreptitious glances. When they reached the ground floor the corridor was empty.

"I'm going to look for Family Man," Adriana said.

"I'll be there in a second. I just have to—"

"I know what you have to do."

As soon as he opened the door he knew the apartment was empty. It took him a moment to find the note next to the telephone. Janet's writing was an angry black twirl like the clubs on his grandmother's deck of cards. *I hope you get to ball your Exotic Other Virgin. Call me! Smooches, Janet.*

ೞೞೞ

—So I have a brother who's a *tapette*! *C'est le fun!*— André felt he had given Céline a new toy to play with. She had responded with neither discomfort nor a gush of supportive emotion. She continued to sit on the bed with one leg folded beneath her; her smile widened; the contrast between the glow of her white skin and the gloss of her dark hair and brows grew sharper. He could not work out what she was feeling. Sometimes, for all her passionate open-mindedness, Céline was more like Maman than she realized.

—You're still going to talk to me?—

—Of course!— This time she bent forward, her fingers closing around his sleeve. —I'm going to talk to you more than before. It's something different, isn't it? Having someone in the family who has a different experience of intimacy makes everything richer.—

He felt a gruff resistance rising in him. He reminded himself of how young she was. —You can't tell the others.—

The din downstairs had subsided. For a paranoid instant he imagined the whole cottage was listening to their conversation. —André, I don't think they'd react as badly as you think. Papa would be unbearable . . . — She drew out the syllables of the last word: *in-sup-por-table*. — . . . Especially after a couple of drinks. But the others would be on your side, I'm sure of it. They'd shut him up if he treated you badly.—

—You don't think they'd be worried about their children?—

Her eyes widened while her mouth grew still. —I hadn't thought of that. Maybe. But they'd get used to the idea. I think you should tell them when you're ready. We can't have the family based on ignoring how things are.—

—We already base the family on ignoring Papa's drinking.—

His words sounded harsher than he had intended. Her poise unnerved him. What right had his little sister to render such judgments? As the Goldman tape ended he watched her get to her feet and rustle among her cassettes—searching, he imagined, for a recording by a singer who was known to be gay. But she chose Gilles Vigneault, voice of a traditional Quebec where being gay was inconceivable. Vigneault's hoarse voice brought back the rallies and concerts of André's youth: the hot summer afternoons when he and Lysiane had persuaded themselves that they were in love. He rarely felt nostalgia for married life, yet the firm boundaries which so much from that time took for granted, from the inevitability of heterosexuality to the ethnic certainty of a French Quebec, still exerted a pull on him.

Céline smiled. —Tell me about your love life. Do you have a boyfriend or do you go to bars?—

He could feel heat igniting below his ears and spreading beneath his beard. He was *blushing*. He opened his mouth but could not speak.

—You must go to bars, Céline said. —Discovering a new way of having sex isn't something that happens every day. If that happened to me, I'd want to try it out every whichway.—

She let a silence elapse, continuing to prod him with her insistent dark gaze. From the ages of seventeen to twenty-one Céline had gone out with a strangely passive boy named Claude. They had all expected her to marry him, as every other member of the family had married his first love; then she had dropped him. There had been no man in her life since then.

—At first I had a boyfriend . . . a man older than me. I see now I was trying to make a gay relationship like a straight relationship. But François, my boyfriend, he didn't see it that way . . . Now I am more like him. I go to bars. But you can still fall in love . . . You can meet someone in a bar and decide you like him a lot and want to stay with him.—

He inhaled, subduing his blush. Céline's maps curled over the ends of her desk. He realized how badly he needed to talk about Süleyman: it was the only way to bring him back. —The one who stole my Jean-Jacques Goldman cassette— —

—Spaghetti's ready!— Anne's oldest daughter flung open the door and looked from Céline to André. —What are you guys talking about?—

—People who steal cassettes, Céline said. She got to her feet and hugged the little girl. —And people who open doors without knocking!—

Before André could catch his breath, Céline followed their niece out of the room and downstairs to the kitchen.

He had to get out of the cottage. There was no space in the kitchen. The regular kitchen table and the spare folding table were lined with children digging into their lunches. Between every second or third child sat a mother retrieving runaway spaghetti squiggles that looped around the salt shaker, snaked over the edges of the plastic tablecloth and fell to the floor. The fathers, along with Papa, Maman, André and Céline, stood along the counter, holding their plates in their hands. Jacques had hoisted himself onto the counter below the enamelled Virgin Mary, swinging his legs as he ate. Wedged in next to Papa, André was struck by the bareness of the kitchen walls. The crush of people underlined the absence of calendars, paintings, books, records, cassettes. In the past he had blamed the spareness of his parents' cottage on poverty—were they still so badly off? The children supported themselves. Papa's last job prior to retirement had included a pension plan, and he continued to work on the side for a local real estate agent. They were empty people, he thought. Colonization had gutted them of all interests beyond filling their stomachs and watching television. As in adolescence, he felt he would die in this stale air. The shouted conversations bombarded his ears. He longed to walk out to the bluffs overlooking the St. Lawrence, inhale the cool breeze off the river and find an Iroquois boy willing to share a joint.

He observed the others watching the tumult at the tables. None of them saw this room as he did. The row of men leaning back against the counter, their hips set so close together that Papa's belly weighed into André as the old man reached for another Labatt's Blue, struck him as a nearly erotic spectacle. What would Jacques see? Wives looking after children and husbands taking a break? André watched as Céline put down her plate and went over to the folding table to help Nicole with her temperamental younger daughter. Maman was dishing out the last of the spaghetti from the huge grey vat. Jacques's youngest son shoved back his chair and squashed a crooked white strand against the linoleum. The men bunched closer together along the counter, torpid before the swarming activity of women and children. The rift between the sexes told André that he would have no further opportunity to tell Céline about Süleyman. If he wished to mourn Süleyman's disappearance— and he had to mourn it; it was drilling a hole in him—he must find someone capable of appreciating a lithe, brown boy.

He could think of only one person.

He finished his spaghetti, then circled the room at a deliberate pace, speaking to the family members he had neglected earlier. In twenty minutes he was ready to leave. He shook his brother's hand, waved at Papa and his sisters and kissed Maman on both cheeks. As he stepped out of the cottage and glanced across the paved yard to the redbrick primary school, he felt his tension beginning to uncoil. He walked to the bus stop to wait for the bus that would carry him back along the banks of the St. Lawrence to the Angrignon Métro station. The buffeting air liberated him, yet a low hum of tension had set in between his ears. He felt more distrustful than ever of the foreigners on the Métro platforms. Let them into your life and they run away; let them into your house and they steal your songs.

He changed trains at Berri station. Amid the crowd emerging from the dingy depths of the line that crossed the river to Longueuil—the petite office girls and Chinese immigrants dwarfed by guys in black leather with smeared green tattoos on their forearms, short bangs and long spears of dark hair behind—André noticed an introverted-looking man with unfocused eyes, curly brown hair and a mustache. He wore a short brown leather jacket and carried a fat paperback under his arm. The man entered the same platform, then the same car of the train as André. As the train departed, he opened his rumpled paperback copy of Balzac's *Illusions perdues* and read with an absorption that appeared to blot out the surrounding crowd. André could not remember where he had seen this man, who was still reading when André got out at Laurier station and began walking east. A tomcat scooted out of an alley. He was only ten minutes north of his own apartment, yet the streets felt strange; he had not ventured into this neighbourhood since his return from Paris. Perhaps his apprehension had been misplaced; perhaps François had joined the half of the Plateau's population that moved apartments every July 1st.

When he reached the low brick apartment building, set back from the narrow street with stone walk-ups on either side, he hesitated. The creepers clinging to the brick looked more luxuriant than they had the year before. François's name was still on the buzzer; the foyer felt smaller than he remembered. When he rang the buzzer, François came downstairs, opened the door and said: —You've been away somewhere, haven't you?—

—France, André said, brought up short by the size of François's body. The thought that he had submitted himself to this man's embrace rooted him in place. He remembered one of their early nights together when François had stepped naked out of the washroom and walked towards him with deliberate steps, his torso upright, the saddle of his hips funnelling the spill of his paunch into his long, dandling cock. His skin retaining the yellowish tint of a fading sunburn, his thighs blazing white, he had resembled some half-tamed animal tipped up on its hind legs for a ceremonial occasion. Today, with his sunburn refreshed and his receding hair tangled, he looked distracted.

—I've just come back from Tunisia.— The tops of his Vulcan ears flushed red. —My fourth visit.—

They went upstairs. The beach boy posters on the walls had changed since André's last visit: the boys were getting darker. The living room with the hardwood floor and the small balcony over the alley, embellished in his memory as the scene of his first experience of gay sex, seemed small and ordinary. As they began to talk, André felt rankled by aspects of François's personality which, in the old days, he had been unable to perceive clearly enough to protest them: his refusal to pay attention to his friends' words unless he was trying to seduce them; his self-centredness; his domineering manner . . . How had he put up with this bullshit?

François poured them each a finger of sherry and sat down on the couch facing out over the balcony. —Tell me about Parisian men.—

His avid smile washed away André's complaints. No one was more fun to be with than this man. You could fail to see him for months and pick up a conversation where you had left off; he could be interrupted at any hour of the day and respond with equal attention (or inattention). He was always himself.

The balcony doors stood ajar; creepers twined around the railing fluttered their leaves against the breeze. André spoke of Paris for a few minutes before bringing the conversation back to Montreal. —I met a Turk in a bar. A very handsome Turk. Just before we checked into a hotel he told me that *Monsieur Spock* was the first man in Montreal to fuck him.—

—Did that make you more excited? François asked.

—Yes, André said, his breath growing short as he admitted this. —Do you remember this boy? Tall, slender, a really handsome face . . . ?—

—I remember hundreds of boys like that.—

—Last night he came to my place, but he ran out this morning and stole my cassettes . . . I'm crushed, François. I really wanted him to like me.—

—He likes you, François said. —He likes you so much he wanted something of yours to keep. Or he wanted to make sure you noticed him.—

—I'm terrified I'll never see him again.—

—André, you will see him so often you will become bored with him . . . — François shrugged himself to his feet, prowling over the bare hardwood floor in his red socks.

—You really think so?— The quaver in his voice would have been humiliating had he believed that François would notice it.

—He's probably knocking on your door right now, François called from the kitchen.

—You're right. I'm going home to wait for him.—

—André! You can't go now. Your second sherry awaits you . . . That boy won't come by in the afternoon; he'll show up at night, when he needs a bed. Sometimes it's better not to be home. If he can't find you it will fuel his desire . . . —

André settled back into the couch. —I don't drink any more, he said, as François edged closer to him, peddling the long finger of sherry like a banner of an antique faith.

—Take a drink, François said. —Then you'll feel better about that boy.—

ભ ભ ભ

"What are you doing to my uncles' building?" Ruthie's voice strained over the Melissa Etheridge cassette cranked up to high volume. "I drove past yesterday and there were all these humungous ropes hanging down the front."

"We're sandblasting. Next week we'll start showing the model apartment." Marcel pinched the plastic stem of his wine glass. Beyond the padded shoulders of Ruthie's turquoise blouse, young men and women flailed and shook on the polished hardwood. BON VOYAGE, RUTHIE! read a banner draped across a boarded-up fireplace.

"It's up to me to modernize my dad's garment factory . . . " the tall youth next to Marcel was saying.

Ruthie introduced them. "Josh," the young man said with an intimidating handshake. He rolled Marcel's name around his palate as though it were wine that had turned to vinegar. Recognizing the Ashkenazi sneer, Marcel looked away.

Ruthie caught his elbow. "What did you think?" she whispered, as Josh restored his attention to a woman with a dark tan and gold bangles on her wrists. "Josh was *my first.*"

Marcel felt tired. When he had arrived he had leaned forward to kiss Ruthie on the cheeks. She had responded with a smack on the lips. Now she was tugging his arm, pushing her mouth close to his ear. "I've slept with seven of the men in this room. And before tonight's over, for old time's sake . . . " As he straightened up, pulling away, she said: "What's the matter? I didn't mean *you.*"

"I'm sorry, Ruthie. This building—"

"How's your brother-in-law? The religious one?" Her saucy expression dissolved: they could have been cousins trading family news.

"He's in Morocco. His mother died. I have to get rid of all the tenants before he comes back."

"There are still tenants in there? No way! What's their problem?"

"Some of them stay because they want money and some of them stay because they hate me."

"Come on. Dance with me; make somebody jealous."

"I want to expel two more tomorrow . . . Even when they haven't paid their rent the law's slanted against the entrepreneur."

"Why don't they pay their rent?" The music sent her long-legged body into a spasm. Writhing close to him, she sang along with Melissa Etheridge's throaty voice: Marcel caught something about lust and fire. She bobbed forward, pecking him on the mouth. "Remember?"

She spun away in self-absorbed pirouettes, her arms arched over her shoulders. Her posture threw her breasts into relief. He began to dance in the restrained way that seemed least likely to subject his gangly form to ridicule. Ruthie's frayed curls thrashed from side to side like an animal's tail with a prehensile life of its own. She chucked a bright-faced young man under the chin and spun back towards Marcel. "The jealousy index is on the rise." Her body buckled, her legs and arms slithering before him in sensual invitation. As the music rose to a crescendo, she moaned into his face: "I wa-a-ant *you!*"

The song ended. Bursting into laughter, she fell full-length against him with the leggy plunge he remembered from Rue St-Denis. Before he could embrace her, she had slipped away. She smiled at the boy she had chucked under the chin. As the music resumed Marcel saw her come weaving back in his direction. He twisted his hips and kicked his legs a little higher. He was starting to enjoy himself. Maryse would be astonished if she could see him. He must get home to her; he couldn't stay much longer. Not having betrayed her since Hetty, he had decided that he was turning over a new leaf. He and Maryse grew closer when Abitbol was away. Tracking the rise and fall of Ruthie's breasts, he imagined Maryse's smile.

Ruthie reached for his shoulder and pulled him towards her. No, he thought. I don't want to be her last-night's stand, her one-for-the-road. I want to eat supper at home with my wife. In an effort to defuse his attraction to her, he let his gaze meander around the apartment. He took in the twelve-foot ceilings, the creamy thickness of the paint. Someone had invested a lot of money in this place. A building of this standing enabled an entrepreneur to earn a respectable profit: located right downtown, yet constructed with the solid, early twentieth century care that permitted two dozen people to dance on the floor without provoking complaints from the apartment below. When he had his own company, he would manage buildings like this one.

The music slashed to a halt. Ruthie, her forehead shiny with sweat, said in an out-of-breath voice: "I hope Toronto is this much fun. It's really different, eh. People in Toronto don't look at each other on the street. My cousins down there hardly speak any Hebrew. But at least everybody's a potential friend—not like here."

"What do you mean?"

"I mean everybody in Toronto speaks English . . . Don't look at me like that with your dark glasses—it's true! Montreal's so *stupid.* We're getting free trade but we've lost the freedom to put up an English sign. The French Canadians have ruined this city. They're anti-semitic, they've wrecked the economy. They're just stupid, okay?"

"My wife is French Canadian."

Ruthie's voice caught. "She's not Jewish?"

"My wife is Québécoise!" he shouted. —*Ma femme est Québécoise, comprends-tu?*— The anger that he thought he had danced out of his system beat through his chest and temples. Distracted faces turned and stared. He didn't care. These Ashkenazis would regard him as a wild beast no matter how suavely he behaved. Let them have their prejudices confirmed! Let them tremble in indignation!

"How come you never told me?" Ruthie said.

"Did you expect me to be married to an anglophone?"

"But you're Jewish!"

Their voices dropped; around them, other conversations resumed. The girl with the gold bangles snapped a fresh cassette into the stereo. As the music rose they stood staring at one another, their arms hanging at their sides. Around them couples were slipping into soft clasps to dance to the slow ballad swelling from the speakers. Ruthie shook her head. "I'm glad I'm leaving. I don't even understand my own tribe any more."

He caught her elbows, holding her with the lightest possible touch. They shuffled around the floor. Reaching out to brush away a streaked tear from the corner of Ruthie's eye, he felt like more of a traitor to Maryse than he had when they were naked together in the chalet.

"Ruthie," he said when the song ended. "I have to go."

"Thanks a million for coming, Marcel. Good luck with everything." She wrapped a turquoise arm around his shoulder and kissed him on both cheeks with Québécois fervour.

He stumbled down the staircase to the street. Manoeuvring the Honda through heavy traffic, he played cassettes by Québécois singers—first Pierre Flynn, then Richard Séguin. What would his life have been like if, choosing religion and ethnicity over language, he had married an English-speaking Jewish woman? He would have lived in English, loved and argued in English. The thought made him feel exhilarated that he lived in Quebec; he was ecstatic to be returning to Maryse.

She was untying the strings of her smock when he came in the door. She told him in a distant voice that her painting was nearly finished. A blue river bubbled across the middle of the canvas, dividing dark forest from bright pasture. He could see the shafts of light between the tufts and felt the sun push the grass towards him. Fish cavorted in the current, sheep and cattle grazed on the grass.

—I still think it needs a wolf.— The sound of the traffic on the Laurentian Autoroute began to irritate him. He curled his arm around Maryse's waist and kissed her mouth. —Is there anything for supper?—

—Oh Marcel, I'm sorry.—

—It's okay, we'll order out.—

Later, as they sat in front of a *téléroman* eating fried chicken and coleslaw, she asked him about the building. —When can I visit?—

—Soon. It won't be long now. I'm worried about our electrician. I don't know if he's up to rewiring the building. But the wiring's the last big job. Once it's done I'll need your advice.—

She smiled at him. That night they made love three times. Maryse, though distracted, seemed appreciative. She lolled on the green grass of her painting: he could not fix himself in that landscape and she could not leave it. The last time he entered her, near dawn and from behind, the paler, firmer curve of Ruthie's ass intruded on his senses and hardened his erection. He pushed the shadow away, murmuring: —Maryse, Maryse . . . —

He arrived at the Sherbrooke Street office at nine AM with his hair still damp from the shower. Sylvie and Crawford, neither of them capable of speaking the other's language, sat nodding politely to one another over mint tea. Bruno entered the room a moment after Marcel. He was unshaven, white glints peeking out from the bluish mass of his stubble. He looked as though he had barely slept.

"Yesterday," Crawford said, "I visited all the tenants. Two of them are behind on their rent. The one we really gotta get out of there is that drug dealer. He's tossed a pile of shit about yay high into the shaft. If we don't get that cleaned up, we're gonna have rats. The stuff's gonna keep pilin' up as long as the guy's living there. Then there's the other nig—, I mean black guy— the old guy who never pays his rent. I say we get Bruno here to kick him out. He's too soft to put up a fight."

"What about the drug dealer?" Marcel said.

"That guy'll put up a fight. But he hasn't paid so now's the time to get rid of him. The two ladies on the second floor, Mrs. McNulty and Mrs. Austin, they'll probably go for about fifteen hundred each. The others are gonna be stubborn. It's like it's some kind of mission in life for them to screw us. Bob's the worst of them. You can't bargain with him because he's crazy. Then there's that Turkish bitch. She calls one room of her apartment her *study*. Well la-dee-dah, I guess I know how come her husband left her—"

"Get to the point, Mr. Crawford."

"Well, sir, like I say, we can deal with the two ladies and we can throw out the niggers, but those other four are gonna need a swift kick in the rear."

Marcel looked at Bruno. —We may have some heads for you to break.—

Behind her desk, Sylvie winced. Marcel slapped Bruno on the shoulder, hoping to thump fresh malice into the older man's physique. His doubts about Bruno's fitness for this sort of work were increasing. Bruno was forty years old. It was becoming clear that two years in a Moroccan jail had harmed him more than they had realized. Though Marcel had ordered Bruno to report on the tenants' habits, on his visits to the building he found the Ladino thug crouched on the plaster-splattered floor of a vacant apartment, smoking Gauloise cigarettes and playing solitaire. The information Bruno passed on was eccentric and largely useless.

—I'm ready, Bruno murmured.

"Good," Marcel said, looking at Crawford. "We'll meet at the Waterloo door at noon. First we kick out the old guy. Then we will kick out the dealer." Turning to Bruno, he said: —Are you ready to kick out the drug dealer?—

—*Oui, Monsieur.*—

Crawford shook his head. "The old guy, yes. But the dealer's too risky. We're talking about a violent criminal. I've got a better idea."

☔ ☔ ☔

Family Man had disappeared. "It's no good," Adriana said in a breathless voice as she returned from the sidestreet leading to the Vendôme Métro station. Her flushed face accentuated her Mediterranean features, a glossy strand of hair brushed her right eyebrow. "I lost him." She sat down on the steps. Teddy seated himself beside her; she edged away from him. "That's the last time that man will have a home. The next time anybody sees him he'll be out on the streets in Montreal West or in some shelter in Little Burgundy."

"You hardly see anybody living on the streets here. It's a much bigger problem in the States."

"When we get free trade it'll be our problem. And once they're out there, they don't go back. They get skin diseases, they get AIDS . . . AIDS is really dangerous." She gave him a long, furious look.

"I know that."

"Some people do really stupid things."

"Lots of people do stupid things."

"Even people who are supposed to be smart. People who went to really good universities in the States."

Jesus Christ, she *couldn't* know that he and Janet hadn't used a condom! When he looked at her she turned her head away. A small tremor ran up her left cheek.

Teddy stared at his feet. His night with Janet had expended so much feeling that he had none left over for Adriana, who was fighting battles he only half understood. She wanted him, perhaps, but remained terrified of sex before marriage. She was competing with Janet deprived of the weapon of her sexuality. Teddy could see all this—at least this was what he thought he saw—but, afraid of the outpouring that might follow, he did not dare verbalize it. Janet's disappearance had left him breathless with suppressed panic; he was in no shape to comfort anyone else.

The traffic roared past. Adriana laid her head on her arms. He stared at her straight, glossy hair, remembering how last week its sheen had fascinated him; then he remembered the controlled madness of Janet's body. He felt the nudge of a fresh erection and was uncertain which woman was the object of his desire. He closed his eyes. It was Janet. He would make love with Adriana this instant if he had the chance, but it was Janet he missed.

In the muted midday light a shadow fell across them. Teddy turned around.

"Wh'appen to Fam'ly Man?" Rollie said. His cheeks looked hollow, his hand was shaking on his stick.

"They took him away because he didn't pay his rent," Teddy said, as Adriana looked up with reddened eyes. "They're clearing the building. Have you got somewhere to go? You need to think about—"

"Me stay here. This be my father's building. Me only father live here."

"You have to think about—"

"What you know? You know nothin'. You're ignorant. You fuck some girl ten times last night." He gave a short giggle.

Adriana stood up.

"She yo' matey?" Rollie said. "She the girl you fuck?"

"Don't you dare talk to me like that." Adriana's expression was more desolate than menacing. Teddy jumped to his feet. Rollie, small wings of fear rising in his eyes, retreated into the Waterloo. Adriana said: "I don't go out with—"

But Rollie was gone. In the doorway he nearly collided with two workers carrying a huge sack. They dropped the sack on the top step.

—*Hostie! Ça pèse en maudit!* one of the young men said. — *Assez. On va prendre not' break.*—

The two young men sat down on the steps. They wore dusty jeans, T-shirts and workboots. Their hair was pulled back in pony-tails. The man with the shaggy mustache tugged a pack of cigarettes out of the shoulder of his T-shirt, planted a cigarette between his teeth and offered the pack to his partner.

Adriana, who had begun to walk away, stopped. —How's it going? she said to the two young men. —What's in the bag?—

—Lathe. Debris, the man with the mustache said. —We got about fifty more sacks like that one.—

—Hard work, Adriana said. Teddy was intrigued by the way she held herself, upright and proud yet a little rigid: she was engaging, assertive, friendly, sexy even, yet all these qualities were muted by a formality that could not have survived in an English conversation. Feeling he was glimpsing the secret codes of a Latin city, Teddy watched in fascination. Adriana spoke perfect Québécois; her tinge of an accent sounded Greek, not English. —What do you guys get for working on Saturday? Time and half? Or is it double time?— —

—We don't get none o' that stuff, the non-mustached but stubblier young man said. —We get our pay, we better shut up and be happy with it.—

—But union regulations— —

—Those unionized guys get good money, the mustached man said, drawing the smoke from his cigarette deep into his lungs. —*Nous autres, c'est pas la mer à boire.*—

Teddy glimpsed the surge of triumph in Adriana's eyes. Her offhand stance with her hips tilted, her slender legs spread a few centimetres wider than her posture demanded, was calculated to hold the men's attention. The coexistence of such calculation with her agonized, principled morality made him stare even harder at her. Adriana tossed her head. —So you guys don't belong to a union like the other guys working here?—

—Are you kidding? the guy with stubble said. —Nobody here belongs to a fucking union. Not even old Gratien who's doing the wiring. That's how come they pay us such shitty wages.—

—You take work where you find it, the man with the mustache said. We're all guys who never got into unions. You gotta be grateful to have a job.—

The conversation continued, but Teddy could sense Adriana's intensity dwindling. She had learned what she needed to know. When he glanced at her, she avoided his eyes.

As the men stubbed out their cigarettes, hauled the sack to a truck parked next to the sidewalk, then returned to the building, two police cars pulled in against the curb.

Four male officers got out. They hurried up the steps into the Waterloo entrance. Teddy stood at Adriana's side. He touched her arm. She retreated a step but continued to hold his eyes. "They're non-union! All of them!"

"Is that important?"

"Don't you know anything, Teddy? You can't use non-union labour on a job like this. It's illegal." She glanced towards the Waterloo entrance. "Let's go see what's happening."

They walked into the building and followed the corridor to the back of the ground floor. Standing in front of Teddy's apartment, they heard boots pounding up the stairs above them. As they followed in silence, the thud of boot-steps ceased. A fist knocked on a door. A deep, French-accented voice said: "Police. Please open the door."

A voice shouted back as Teddy and Adriana came to a halt on the stairs just below the third-floor corridor. "The drug dealer," Adriana whispered.

The police knocked again. "Please open the door, sir." Another angry shout. "We must come in, sir. If you do not open the door—"

Another shout. A crash shook the third floor. Dust fluttered above their heads. They edged up the stairs, craning for a glance into the corridor. The police stood in tensed pairs on either side of the Bajan's door; two of them had drawn their guns. In spite of their menacing, swat-team crouches, their expressions were sheepish.

A faraway clunking sound began to echo through the building. The sound repeated and repeated . . .

"The water bottles," Adriana hissed. "He's throwing them out the window."

More garbage outside my bedroom, Teddy thought. He did not have time to pursue the thought because the policeman began to speak again in an almost pleading voice. "Please open the door, sir. If you do not open the door . . . "

The clunking of falling bottles continued. One cop nodded to another cop. The biggest and beefiest of them took two steps back and threw his shoulder into the door. He hit the door a second time, and a third. The hinges whined. The bottles stopped falling. The only sound audible was the officer's body-grunt as he slammed into the door.

Teddy and Adriana moved up one step and inched around the corner into the corridor. She was leaning over his shoulder, her hand balanced on his arm, her breath emerging from behind his ear. As the cop hit the door, they breathed as one person. Arousal scrolled through Teddy's body. Adriana's impassioned contradictions, her mere difference from Janet— her slenderness, her darkness, her Mediterraneanness, her repression—made him dizzy. He struggled to keep his eyes focused on the cop.

With a wrenching shriek, the door yielded. The policemen pushed through the narrow doorway, two of them with their guns drawn, the other two shouting. Teddy heard four-letter words in French and English. The Bajan screamed at the men. There was a scuffle and a thudding sound.

A gunshot exploded.

Adriana hugged him. She held on for a moment, prolonging their terrified clutch. Teddy, shaking, was glad of the contact. They stared at each other, their faces so close they were almost touching. "Oh my God," Adriana said. "They killed him!"

A moment passed in silence.

—*Tabernac!* a voice shouted. —*C'est un sacré lit d'eau.*—

"They didn't shoot him, they shot his waterbed," Teddy said. Adriana's hands dropped away from his shoulder.

A rivulet of water spurted out of the Bajan's door. The dull tiles shone as the water rolled along the corridor. It lapped at the next door down the hall, where Family Man had lived, and spread into a dull pool that grew steadily wider.

In the Bajan's apartment thuds and shouts collided.

—Plug that thing, I'm getting soaked.—

"On your feet. You're under arrest."

—How do you want me to plug it?—

"Fuck you, beast."

—I don't care, just plug it! Use your jersey if you have to.—

"Get off the mattress! You're making it worse."

"Don't touch me, beast. Leave me alone."

A ripple combed across the pool in the corridor, extending its boundaries. More grunting and swearing. The Bajan swayed out the door, his arms handcuffed behind his back. His woolen-capped head bowed, he sloshed through the water. Two police officers walked behind him. The jersey of the officer on the right was sodden. The officer on the left was naked above the waist. When he caught sight of Teddy and Adriana—especially Adriana—he sucked in his beer gut. "Get out of here, please," he said, scowling over his black mustache. "Move along. Mind your own business."

They started down the stairs in front of the Bajan and the officers. On the second floor the door opened and Mrs. McNulty came out of her apartment, followed by Paddy. "What in heck's going on here?" Mrs. McNulty said. "We got a flood coming through the ceiling."

Paddy pushed forward, his pale blue eyes gleaming. "Yeah, what's going on?"

"Move along!" the shirtless police officer said, his face seized up with misery. "Go back to your apartments." He gave the Bajan a shove.

"Don't touch me, you fucking beast!" the Bajan said, wheeling around to glare into the officer's eyes.

"My apartment's flooded!" Mrs. McNulty said.

The Bajan stumbled forward. Paddy blocked his path. "You must learn to know and love Jesus Christ—"

"You don't know nothin' about Ras Tafari," the Bajan said. "Your god is an illusion."

"You are going to your punishment. Divine justice is done on earth!"

"Divine justice," Teddy said, "is soaking your apartment."

"If you guys don't move along," the officer with the drenched jersey said, "somebody's going to get arrested for obstruction of justice." His partner sneezed.

Mrs. McNulty shook her head. "I've lived in this building for twenty-one years. Now it's time to leave."

Teddy and Adriana spent the afternoon helping Mrs. McNulty and Paddy mop up and move their furniture away from the dripping coming through the ceiling. The first drops to fall had splattered the black-and-white photograph of the late Captain McNulty in his military uniform that presided over the dresser in the living room. A trickle of water had infiltrated a cupboard whose dusty boxes of old books and letters had not been touched in years. They opened the boxes and spread their contents over the carpet in the dry section of the apartment while Mrs. McNulty shook her head and sobbed and sometimes blushed at the sight of a curled letter or card. Twice Teddy slipped away to phone Janet. Both times the phone rang and rang, and both times Adriana regarded him with dark disapproval on his return. "Don't go, Mrs. McNulty," Adriana said. "You're through the worst of it. From now on it'll get better and you'll get more money when you leave."

"That Ayrab Jew'll find some way to make it worse. He always does." Mrs. McNulty shook her head and looked down at the lace-screened covers of old Christmas cards. "The fight went out of me after that hearing. That's when I realized the law doesn't mean nothing to his kind. You can't rely on the law any more. You just have to look out for yourself and keep out of the way of rich people."

Teddy struggled to think of a combative reply. Like Mrs. McNulty, he had felt his morale plummet after the hearing this summer. Adriana and the lawyer had planned for the hearing for days; the tenants had dressed up in their Sunday clothes and ridden the 165 bus over the Mountain to the Régie du logement. Then Vircondelet had failed to appear. The judge had scheduled a new hearing for December, at which he would set conditions for the conversion: he would order Vircondelet to pay for equivalent temporary accommodation for the duration of the renovations, he would set the date on which the tenants could move back into their renovated apartments for one year at their old rents. Yet it seemed increasingly unlikely that any of this would occur. The delay in rescheduling the hearing had given Vircondelet time to wear down people like Mrs. McNulty. With the onset of the federal election campaign, their lawyer had become almost impossible to reach. They all felt increasingly alone.

"I don't know how much longer I can stand it," Mrs. Austin said, as she came in to see how Mrs. McNulty was holding up.

"You have to fight!" Adriana said. "Unless you fight people like this, only rich people will have rights—"

Teddy left. He phoned Janet again. There was no reply. Where could he go? He had no family left in Ottawa, he still resisted calling Zach and Marian in Berkeley. No friendships were blossoming for him in Montreal. Janet had been his hope, the impassioned answer to his search for meaning. He kept calling her, though it seemed futile; he did his job, though he knew his boss would never judge him subservient enough, *Canadian* enough, to teach the business clients; he tried to remember the integrated Canadian world his parents and grandmother had stood for. One day after work he walked up Rue Crescent, where the balconies of the pick-up bars had closed for the autumn and distant music resounded from indoors. He reached the top of the street and wandered along Sherbrooke Street. At the corner, as he waited for the light to change, he smelled a sharp burning odour. He turned around. A short, dumpy man with long thick hair swept back from a face in which bulldog aggressiveness collapsed into hound-dog moroseness walked past Teddy as the light turned green.

Prodding his smouldering cigar in front of him, the man disappeared into the Ritz-Carlton Hotel. Teddy thought: a man without a land is nothing. A shiver ran through him.

That night there was a knock on his door. He rushed to open it. "Adriana!" he said, feeling alert to all her contradictions as she stood before him. In tight bluejeans and her black polo neck sweater she radiated the self-confidence she had displayed talking to the workers; the acne in the corner of her mouth was shrinking. He sensed it would not be long before she established a solid, passionate relationship with a man. "Come in. Please. Sit down. I'll make you a coffee."

"I don't have time." She remained outside the door. "I just thought you should know: the Bajan's been charged with trafficking and Mrs. McNulty's settled for fifteen hundred dollars plus moving expenses. That leaves you, Mrs. Austin and the Turkish woman in the Waterloo, and Bob and me in the Victoria."

He tried to think of something he could say that would emphasize their solidarity. All he could think of was: "What about Family Man?"

"Nobody's seen Family Man. I don't think we'll see him again."

A wall went up between them. Adriana gave him a farewell nod and walked away down the empty corridor. Teddy watched her until she reached the front door. He closed his door. Adriana would not come in and Janet appeared unlikely to return. The only human sound in his apartment was Rollie's nocturnal maundering. Teddy sat down in his armchair and stared at the floor.

ℕine

André-Marcel-Teddy-André

HIS SECOND SHERRY SMOOTHING HIS PATH, he marvelled at how dark the streets of the Plateau became at nightfall. The dwarf trees skeletal without their leaves, the wrought-iron staircases, outbreaks of shrubbery and mats of ivy shielded the gloom against the glow of the low streetlights. The grey stone bulges of the walls looked soft enough to cup with his palm. As his numbness faded, the touch of François's fingers returned. — Not now, André had said. —If the boy's there when I get back— —

—You still haven't learned not to save yourself for the impossible dream?—

No, he had not. One impossible dream had succeeded another: idealization of Raymond, worship of Marie-Christine, his perfect partnership with Lysiane, all contained within the grander dream of a sovereign Quebec; then thralldom to François's hedonism, a passing surrender to Paris, and now bewitchment by this boy, who was in fact a married man.

He opened the door of his apartment, hesitating before turning on the light. He avoided looking at the scattered cassettes.

Walking into his bedroom, he thought about all the mistakes he had made today. It had been a mistake not to wake up in time to prevent Süleyman's departure, it had been a mistake to come out to Céline (how could he expect her to keep his secret?) and, given that Süleyman was unlikely to return, it had been a mistake to reject François's advances. His life had veered off course somewhere along the line. He lived among the ruins of his miscalculations, his only outlet to the youth he had wasted glistening in a deceitful young man's smile. He was pathetic. If François were here, he would accept a third sherry.

The telephone rang. He picked up the receiver on the first ring.

—André? *C'est vraiment toi?*—

The words she had uttered on Rue Duluth sounded querelous over the phone. —How did you find me?—

—There are lots of A. Deschênes in the phone book, but not so many in the Plateau.— As he struggled to think of a phrase to apologize for their argument, Marie-Christine said: —André, I'm calling because Raymond is here. He's at my place. He's only in Montreal for one night. I thought you might like to see each other— —

Raymond? What would he say to Raymond—especially if Raymond had changed as much as Marie-Christine had said?

He glanced around his apartment. —I'm coming over.—

When he stepped back out into the street the November chill had made the darkness crisper; the globes of the street-lights clipped black edges on the wooden gingerbread of the gables. The walk-ups stood like mourning cards. As he approached Marie-Christine's street of close-set wrought-iron staircases, he felt a childish pulse throbbing below his heart. He was going to see Raymond!

His heels clanged on the black metal of the spiral staircase. His body was surprised for the thousandth time in his life at the steepness of the steps of a Montreal walk-up. Standing on the balcony pressing the buzzer, he felt as though he were perched on the side of a pyramid.

The door buzzed and he went up the narrow indoor staircase. Marie-Christine had already opened the door at the top. He kissed her on both cheeks and stepped past her, more hastily than he had intended, to find himself confronting the little girl.

—Did you and *Maman* play together when you were kids? Francine asked, regarding him with her deep-set eyes of almost Spanish darkness.

—No, your *Maman* played more with Raymond, André said. Surprised at his own nervousness, he was gratified by Raymond's snort of laughter as they shook hands.

Raymond's body had slackened into a fullness that emphasized his solidity. Fly-away greyness turned his long beard lank. His paunch stretched his flannel shirt, his rambling stride lilted over the clods of an imaginary field, the square black frames of his glasses announced their durability. A spear of grey hair poked out from between the top buttons of his shirt.

When André murmured a perfunctory query about how Raymond found Montreal now that he lived in the Beauce, Raymond replied: —There are some things I always enjoy in Montreal . . . *Les Montréalaises sont toujours les plus belles femmes au monde!*—

André shot a look in the direction of Marie-Christine, who was motioning for him to sit down in her tartan armchair: she seemed unperturbed by Raymond's remark. At his Cégep proclaiming Montreal women the most beautiful in the world would have had a sexist ring; it sounded exoticizing, colonialist—*Parisian.* Uttering such a remark in class would provoke complaints from his alert seventeen-year-old female students. Worse, it sounded dated. It was the kind of thing Montreal men had said in the 1970s—which, when he thought about it, was close to being the last time Raymond had lived in the city.

Marie-Christine poured him a glass of *dépanneur* red wine. Raymond drank a bottle of Belle Gueule, Marie-Christine juice and Francine Pepsi Cola. The three of them sat facing him on a couch, Raymond and Marie-Christine at opposite ends and Francine between them. Ambushed by jealousy, André had to remind himself that Francine was not Raymond's daughter. For an instant he wished that he and Lysiane could lounge on a couch together—though perhaps the fact that they could not indicated that, against all odds, their relationship had turned out to be the deeper and more emotional of the two failed marriages.

Bending over the ghetto blaster on the shelf beneath the posters of elephant-headed gods, Marie-Christine slipped in a cassette. André heard the tinkle of the opening chords of "*Tous les palmiers.*" Beau Dommage's first album. He thought he was going to burst into tears.

—Who would think that we would all be here together so many years later? Raymond said.

You would never know he grew up in Montreal, André thought, hearing the almost too-deep twang of Raymond's rural accent. —That surprises me now, he heard himself say, but at the time I expected us to be friends all our lives.—

—We're not all here, Marie-Christine said. —None of us knows where Lysiane is.—

—I think she's in Montreal, André said. —She's probably living in some boring suburb like Brossard.—

—With some boring businessman, Raymond said.

André felt himself hunch forward in his chair. He despised me for marrying her, he thought. He knew I would always be jealous because he was able to marry Marie-Christine.

Before he could think of a retort, Marie-Christine said: —I miss Lysiane. I'd love to see her again.—

Francine stared at her mother. André wondered whether Francine knew that Raymond and Marie-Christine had been married; at the least, she must sense the bond between them. What sort of questions would Francine ask her mother tomorrow?

They were all looking at Marie-Christine, allowing her space to continue speaking; a remark from either of the men would increase the tension. Aware that he had lost every argument he had ever started with Raymond, André preferred to hold his peace. He had expected Raymond to launch into one of his torrential disquisitions, but Raymond simply leaned back on the couch and sighed. Francine started to speak. Marie-Christine, cutting her off with a quick hug, said: —I hope she is with somebody. That she isn't alone like the rest of us. For me that's the surprising part: not that we're still in touch, but that we're alone and we haven't had children. Among the four of us Francine is the only child we've produced.—

—It's goddamn awful for Quebec, Raymond said. — Nowadays even the rural Québécois aren't having that third child that makes our population grow.— He glanced at André. —You didn't remarry after Lysiane? No woman in your life?—

André shook his head. He had failed Raymond's expectations again. And he had failed himself. If these were his two closest friends, why couldn't he share with them the most fundamental fact of his recent life? Raymond and Marie-Christine stared at him. Exhaustion dragged him down. He refused to put himself through the ordeal of coming out twice in one day. —I'm going home, he said, shifting in his chair.

He expected Marie-Christine to detain him, but it was Raymond who leapt up from the couch. —You can't, he said, gripping André's wrist with a muscular claw. For the first time André spotted the glitter of the old passion in his eyes. —We've hardly started to talk.—

ର ର ର

—I can't hear you.— The line was scratchy with static. Marcel had caught only scraps of Abitbol's description of his mother's funeral, his visit to Marcel's parents' graves, the unearthly whiteness of the cemetery clinging to the eroded hillside outside the *mellah,* now empty of Jews. —When are you coming home?—

—I'm going to the Sahara . . . my mother's village . . . —

—We're down to five tenants. We've tarred the roof, we've lifted the beam, the sandblasting is almost finished. Gratien is working on the wiring.—

Abitbol was listing the relatives who sent Marcel their love, who added special love for Maryse. Certain that he had not met most of these people, Marcel said: —When are you coming home?—

— . . . My spiritual— —

A click slashed through the static. Silence.

Marcel glanced around the empty office. Since Abitbol's departure, Sylvie had spent most of her time running the office in Outremont. He missed her company. In her absence he brooded over irrelevant details of the conversion rather than concentrating on the big problems. His two most urgent tasks were removing the last five tenants and deciding on the refurbishment and decoration for the model apartment. In recent days he had begun phoning Maryse to ask her advice. The last time he had called, to sound her out on the choice of a varnish, she had said: —I'd have to see the apartment to be sure.— He would have to make good soon on his promise to show her the building. If only he could get rid of the madman in the suit and the Greek girl and the Anglo . . . and Hetty.

He hated opening the mail. Last week he had received a registered letter, signed BOB in scarlet block letters, consisting of three pages of anti-semitic bile. The world was full of vulgar nobodies. His father had bequeathed him no wide estates, but together he and Maryse would create a life of refinement. He only wished that the zone of refinement could include his working life.

Today the first letter he opened was a form from the Régie du logement announcing that Hetty had filed for a retroactive rent reduction to compensate for the decline in her quality of life caused by noise, dust, garbage in the corridor, irregular waste collection, loss of mail delivery and arbitrary cuts in heat and electricity. The other envelopes, one from each of the remaining tenants, contained identical claims. The Régie would set a date for hearing these claims. He would have to stand before a judge and refute the stupid allegations of these horrible people. If he failed to appear a second time, the judge would interpret his absence as an admission of guilt. He had to wrap up the conversion before the Régie could interfere; otherwise this struggle would continue into the depths of winter. The trapped thumping in his chest returned. He removed his glasses.

He had to put an end to this.

He drove out to Notre-Dame-de-Grâce, along the elegant curve of Sherbrooke Street, past the heavy English façades of the apartment buildings. The red and yellow leaves trampled along the sidewalks looked outlandish beneath the grey sky. The frozen smiles of federal election candidates grimaced from windows and lawns. Michel Rivard's voice swirled from his speaker system.

What would he do if he saw Hetty? The disdain in her eyes the day they had removed the old West Indian had paralysed him. He had thought their sex, however unexpected, would create an understanding between them. How could Hetty hate him when it had been she who had downplayed their coupling as the product of her frustration? Her reaction made no sense, he thought, remembering his conversation with Abitbol about women. His mind was invaded by an image of Abitbol rocking through the hard reddish desert south of Marrakech in a bus, the television blaring in Arabic. The three sandblasted storeys of the Victoria-Waterloo reared up with the force of a mirage. Workers sat on the front steps of the dual entrances, smoking cigarettes and swigging from thermos flasks. Getting out of the Honda, Marcel addressed the foreman: —Taking a vacation?—

—It's their break.— Gratien, a hardbitten man of fifty whose close-cropped mustache was flaked with white, squinted at his wristwatch. —They got four minutes left.—

—How's the wiring going?—

—Slow. I been down in that basement all morning. Fuck, it stinks!—

The men snickered. Marcel stepped around them without speaking. He entered the cool, dusty gloom of the Waterloo corridor. The noise of the traffic receded. The open doorways of the apartments loomed like black sheets that acquired a third dimension as he approached them, telescoping back into eerie holding tanks for whitish slag heaps of plaster. Passing apartments where the renovation work had advanced, he could smell the resin-like varnish. The echo of his footsteps pursued him across the smeared marble. When this was over he and Maryse would take a vacation somewhere warm where Maryse could find great art to engage her eye. He would stop having affairs; his fluttering heart would grow calm.

The Waterloo side of the building felt as empty as an abandoned cathedral. —Bruno! he shouted. —Bruno, where are you?—

On the second floor he leaned into an apartment and saw Bruno hunched in the dark. He snapped on the light. Bruno stood up, blinking as he rubbed his greying stubble. Lines of cards made a grid on the floor. —I can't get used to the light, he murmured. —My cell was so dark— —

—We're not paying you to play solitaire.— Marcel grabbed the fringes of Bruno's padded sleeveless vest and shoved him back against the wall. Bruno was heavier than he, but Marcel was taller. —I want you to terrify these shits. Unless I see some action, you're going to be back in Tetouan fencing stolen jewellery.— Blood thumped through his temples.

Bruno whispered: —You don't care what happens?—

—Not any more.—

—Then give me a pass key. I can really scare them if you let me get into their apartments.—

—*Fini le break*! Gratien shouted in the downstairs hall. —*Au travail!*—

Marcel released Bruno. He pulled the key ring out of his pocket and slipped off the spare pass key. —Don't lose this. And I want to see results!—

Leaving the room before Bruno could reply, he followed the staircase past the ground floor into the basement.

As he entered the darkness, he thought he was going to vomit. The stench of shit, seasoned with the sting of stale piss, made him gasp as he crossed the rough concrete floor in almost total blackness. His stomach clenched; he reached out for a purchase. Waving his arms, he piped air into his lungs. He edged forward, his nausea receding. His hand collided with wood. He patted with his palms, realizing that he was standing next to the plywood cubicle Crawford had told him about.

He called out to Gratien.

—Over here, boss.—

A flashlight beam punctured the darkness. Marcel picked his way towards its source. Gratien was peering up at a multicoloured spaghetti of wires, their rubber casings peeled back to reveal silvery metal tips. The wires hung in an opening in the low roof. Thick, insulated cables crossed above his head. His hand traced a cable to its intersection with the wires.

—Where did you learn about wiring?—

—Used to be an electrician's apprentice.— Gratien stared up through the steel-rimmed bifocals he had put on. —That was thirty years ago. I ended up in carpentry.— He splashed the flashlight beam on the wooden cubicle. —You gonna demolish that shitbox?—

—Of course, Marcel said, though he had decided to leave the black boy's refuge intact until the tenants were gone. Crawford, whose information was often better than Bruno's, had reported that the boy intimidated the tenants, especially the women. Remembering the twist of Hetty's signature on this morning's letter from the Régie, Marcel hoped she felt terrified. —I want you to choose a reliable man and send him to the hardware store to buy new numbers for the doors of the five apartments that are still occupied. Take off the old numbers, change them, and send me a list of the new numbers.— If he did have to go before a judge, he would use the discrepancy between the numbers on the doors and the numbers on the forms to get the rent reduction claim dismissed.

—I'll get it done right away, Gratien said. In the glow of the flashlight he twined the silver point of a blue-jacketed wire around the point of a wire encased in red. The smell became suffocating. Marcel took two steps towards the wooden cubicle and kicked it.

"Yo!" A cigarette lighter flared. In the yellowish updraft Marcel glimpsed a woebegone sickly brown face, grizzled black hair, the huge distended whites of a pair of cornered eyes. As the flame was snuffed out, a heavy wooden staff cracked against the cubicle above Marcel's ear.

—What's going on?— Gratien shined his flashlight beam on the boy. The boy ducked away into the darkness.

—Where did he go? Marcel asked.

—Through the tunnel to the Victoria basement. It's like the goddamn Métro down here. You never know who's around.—

—I'll get rid of him, Marcel said as he left. On reaching the top of the stairs, he stopped in front of the Anglo's door. His stomach was churning. He steadied himself for an instant before going upstairs in search of Bruno. The second floor was empty. He climbed to the third floor. Arriving on the landing, he paused to look in the direction of Hetty's door. A thumping sound was coming from the apartment that had been occupied by the drug dealer. He stepped inside to find Bruno manhandling a spar of wood taller than he was towards the jacked-open window. —What are you doing?—

Bruno balanced the spar on the window ledge, more than half its length extending into the well-like shaft in the centre of the building. Sweat had broken out on the tender skin high on his forehead, where his hair had receded. Puffing and sweating, he pointed with his finger to a darkened ground-floor window on the opposite side of the shaft. —The Anglo's bedroom. He changes there every day after work.— He smiled with the sour pleasure that Marcel recalled from their first interview. —I'll be waiting for him.—

CR CR CR

An unexpected glint caught his eye. The paint-flecked metal "5" on his door had been replaced with a shiny "7." He fingered the fresh hook of brass. What was going on? Less and less of what happened in the building made sense. Mrs. McNulty, who had supplied him with gossip, had left. Adriana had stopped speaking to him. Every time he phoned Janet he was greeted by an answering machine. Refusing on principle to speak to these alienating gadgets, he kept calling, then hanging up as soon as he heard her over-emphatic voice saying, "You've reached *Janet* at . . . "

Today at work, when a new evening course for business people had been announced, Teddy had been excluded again from the teachers participating. He went to see Pia, the boss's secretary. "You've got to change your attitude, Teddy." He did not know how to change his attitude; he thought he was being friendly and polite. "What should I do?" he said. She stared at him from beneath her dark blue eyeshadow, her wrists and throat shimmering with gold ornaments. Her expression condemned him as a ruffian or a fool. Before he could ask again the phone rang and she was chatting in Italian, sewn up in another of the communities where he would never belong.

He stepped into his bedroom. The pile of garbage outside the window had stopped growing since the Bajan's arrest. Beneath the sunken cardboard boxes, empty mineral water bottles and green-bearded pizza crusts, he glimpsed the flattened arm of his leather jacket. He ran his hand through his collar-length hair, trying not to inhale too deeply.

He turned away from the window, shrugging himself out of his jacket.

A titanic splintering crash. The initial compressed smack exploded into a metallic clinking sound. He was thrown forward by the fractured glass flung against the back of his jacket. Glass nicked the plaster in front of him. He fell to his knees, his head bent. Running his hand through his hair, he felt a sliver of glass prick his palm. When he stood up, a bar of shadow had dimmed the room.

A spar of wood had smashed through the double panes of glass. The front end protruded over his bed; the back end was wedged against the opposite wall of the shaft. Wafers of broken glass and chewed-off morsels of dark wood littered the bedcover and the carpet. If he had been facing the window, the flying glass would have cut him.

He stood breathing, feeling his emotional balance shifting in the sickly ripe odour from the shaft. His depression threatened to smother him; then, for the first time in days, it dispersed, leaving him alone with an uncontainable anger.

He walked into the hall and started up the stairs. Vircondelet stood on the second-floor landing, his hands hanging at his sides. Jesus, he looked guilty! "You fucking asshole! You tried to kill me. I'm going to get you charged—"

"This is a construction site, sir," Vircondelet said in his hoarse whisper. "Speaking as an engineer, I can assure you we take all reasonable precautions—"

"*You tried to kill me.*"

"I would never kill you, sir. You pay on time. I want you as a tenant in my next building."

He wrapped a long arm around Teddy's back. Teddy felt a charged warmth flowing between them. His desire to punch Vircondelet in the face ebbed into a mire of confused feelings as they rocked back and forth like the best of buddies. He wished Vircondelet would take off his shaded glasses. He broke out of their awkward embrace. "I don't want to be a tenant in your building. The only place I want to see you is in jail."

"I repeat, *Monsieur*, we take every reasonable precaution." Turning to a young guy with a pony-tail who had come downstairs from the third floor, Vircondelet ordered the man in his round-vowelled North African French to repair Teddy's window. "Telephone me when you are ready to negotiate your departure," he said, turning away up the stairs.

Two young men followed Teddy into his apartment. They rammed the head of the spar out the window. The spar remained wedged across the shaft, its diagonal shadow continuing to darken the bedroom. Smoking as they worked, the men spread a sheet of transparent plastic across the window. The pony-tailed one held the sheet taut, while the taller man took a crooked grey staple gun and stapled the edges to the frame. —*Ça y est. C'est beau!* he said as they left. Teddy stared at the scattered glass and macerated specks of wood. The smells from the shaft mingled with cigarette smoke. The room was cold, and would get colder overnight. He moved his sleeping bag into the living room, threw some clothes into cardboard boxes and carried those into the living room as well. He closed the bedroom door behind him. As he huddled on the cot that he used as a couch, his body slowly unwound. In the open spaces of his almost unfurnished living room he felt able to breathe, to stretch his arms and legs, and move about free of surveillance. Within an hour his mood plummeted. He was isolated and alone, there was no one he could call to talk about the attack, he did not feel up to phoning the police or trying to track down the lawyer. Zach and Marian would have written him off by now. He imagined them tipping into the garbage the windowed envelopes delivered to the house above Shattuck. To his friends from Rockcliffe—had they been friends?—he would be one more Canuck who had drifted away to the States.

No one knew he was here, except for Janet and Adriana, who despised him for mutually contradictory reasons. It was Canada he had returned to meet, through the incarnation of Montreal, the emblematic Canadian city. The bitter election campaign being waged on the streets outside threatened the end of that self-sufficient Canada: the death of even the memory of Canadian lives such as those his parents and grandmother had led.

He lay down on the cot and tried to sleep. He paced the floor until after midnight. When he woke in the morning restlessness brought him to his feet again. With Janet's face fixed in his mind, he lifted the receiver and phoned Pia to tell her he would not be coming in today. "The developers broke my bedroom window to try to get me to move," he said.

"Where do you *live*, Teddy?" Pia sighed. "Okay, I'll tell the boss."

Another strike against him. His days at the language school were numbered. People with positive attitudes did not live in buildings where developers broke their windows. He hated the school's false ceremony, Pia dressing like a receptionist for a major corporation and the boss attired like an investment banker in the cramped, dingy suite. He lifted the receiver again, dialled Janet's number and listened to her energetic taped voice. He *must* talk to her.

Discovering it was ten o'clock, he redirected his pacing in a straight line that carried him across the living room, out the door and down the corridor through the whine of drills and the shouts of the workers. He turned west on Sherbrooke Street, glancing towards the Victoria entrance, overhung with ropes and scaffolding. Was Adriana in there? It didn't matter. Only Janet could become his world.

Too impatient to wait for the bus, he walked farther into Notre-Dame-de-Grâce. On the west side of the rift-valley of the Décarie Expressway, Sherbrooke Street turned placid, the neighbourhood shops open for business but little patronized, the streets of redbrick family homes dozing in silence. Time moved so slowly that Teddy felt he had stepped back three decades into a sleepy Montreal of unquestioned Anglo superiority. French signs were sparse. The English signs still contained apostrophes, eradicated elsewhere in the city. The street's long, low horizon heightened Teddy's sense of disorientation. Both time and space had stretched to almost infinite lengths. He walked long blocks for minutes on end without advancing. He began to distrust his perceptions. He could see the shapes around buildings but squinted to be sure whether this building was a confectionary, that one a delicatessen or an apartment block. He knew Janet's address by heart, though he had never visited her. For block after block he remained certain he was about to come upon it; the street numbers played tricks on him. He imagined his father, who had studied at McGill, walking through this neighbourhood during his years in Montreal. He became his father, looking forward to a job in the civil service and a role in building up the country.

This must be it. The number on the brown brick matched the number he had memorized from the telephone book. Janet's building was similar to the Victoria-Waterloo, the main differences being that it had a single entrance and that the foyer was equipped with a locked main door and a buzzer system. The wooden panelling of the foyer was fitted with mirrors. As Teddy opened the front door he heard the bus stopping outside. The mirrors threw his own elongated body back at him, disclosing a glimpse of the street behind him and the bus pulling away. He found Janet's surname and buzzed. No answer. He buzzed again. When he looked up he saw her, magnified to twice his height, slouching alongside him. He reached towards her: his hands clutched air.

She was coming in the door behind him.

She looked tired, her hair was unbrushed. Stepping past him, she pulled her keys out of her pocket. Her plump cheeks, upturned nose and, he saw, rather small eyes, grew still as she recognized him. "What are you doing here?"

"I came to talk to you."

"There's nothing to talk about. We could have had a really great relationship, we could have had everything and got married, but you betrayed me."

"I did not betray you, Janet."

"You were about to. You expect me to stick around while you treat me like that?"

"I never even—"

"Teddy," she said, clutching her keys next to her hip, "I am a very moral person. You rich guys never get that, do you? Where I come from you meet a person and you stick with them, okay? I'm very traditional like that. Nobody treats me—"

"Is there nothing I can say . . . ?" He stepped forward to hug her. The stiffness of her posture brought him up short. He struggled to pull her face into focus.

She turned away, a heaviness in her cheeks, and unlocked the front door. "I'm tired, Teddy. I went to visit a friend last night and I stayed the night."

"So you didn't get any sleep on the couch?" he said, surprised by the scorn in his voice.

She stopped, then peeped around the glass door at him with the defiant, disgusted, lusty smile he remembered from the night at the party. "Teddy, you should know I never sleep on the couch."

The door closed. He watched her walk upstairs to the apartment he would never enter. He found he did not feel as bad as he had expected. Walking home he was barely conscious of his own movements until he reached the door of his apartment.

A yellow piece of paper pulled him out of his reverie. It had been slid under his door. His stomach bracing against the stench that ebbed from his bedroom, he bent down to unfold the sheet. *Dear Teddy,* a flamboyant hand had written, *I was very sorry to hear that they broke your window. Don't worry, I know how to get them back. Just wait and see. Yours sincerely, Adriana.*

ᘓ ᘓ ᘓ

He inhaled the odour of incense. Francine's head was nodding. Marie-Christine picked up her daughter and carried her through the curtain to the bed behind the partition. —Go to sleep, he heard her murmuring, *Maman* will come to bed soon.— He held Raymond's eyes, maintaining a desultory conversation about whether Michel Rivard's new solo album was as good as his work with Beau Dommage. If Francine was sleeping with Marie-Christine, Raymond would be out here on the couch. He was not sure why he should have imagined otherwise, given that Raymond and Marie-Christine were divorced and had not seen each other in two years. Yet this afternoon he had very nearly had sex with François. Of course this was different. He was imagining Raymond and Marie-Christine's interactions in terms of how gay men—or at least François—might act in similar circumstances.

He had not realized how estranged he had become from heterosexual dynamics.

Raymond noticed his distraction. —Did you prefer the music you heard in France? he asked, with a grate of hostility.

—No, André said, French popular music is insipid by comparison with our Québécois singers.—

—Québécois singers have been getting better lately, Marie-Christine said. She turned off the kitchen lights, sitting down at the opposite end of the couch from Raymond. —Our culture is exciting again. After the referendum it was so boring . . . If the Supreme Court in Ottawa says our language laws are unconstitutional, everything could start again . . . —

—It could be like before, André said, surprised and gratified to hear Marie-Christine raise this possibility. —This time we might get our independence.—

Marie-Christine glanced at Raymond. —Would you come back to Montreal?—

Raymond studied his baggy grey pants. —When you have cows it's hard to go away. They have to be milked. The boy from the next farm is milking them tomorrow morning, but I can't stay in the city much longer.—

—But, Raymond, this is what you always wanted!— You're the one who made me believe, he almost added; but, recalling François's gibe about impossible dreams, he said no more.

Raymond got to his feet. Shaking off his lethargy, he began to pace with the light-hipped impatience that carried André's mind back to cafés on St-Denis. —The independence I wanted, Raymond said, was the independence of a *people*. A history teacher should know what that means. I wanted a society where love could be love of a collectivity, of something beyond the egotism of sex or self-love. I wanted to give life a texture where acts would have resonance beyond the individual— —

My God, André thought, so much of who I am comes from him.

Raymond turned around, the incense hanging in the candle-light wreathing him like a dusky halo. —You can still feel that in the Beauce, he said. —Maybe you can feel it in Quebec City. But in Montreal the thread is unravelling. And it's Montreal that will set the tone for a sovereign Quebec. What kind of sovereignty will we get ten years from now? A multicultural granola where the Chinese or the Tamil is as Québécois as I am? A place where we all talk about respecting each other's differences instead of respecting the nation we build out of our common history? That's not what I spent fifteen years fighting for. What we were trying to build was deeper than that, more *spiritual.*—

He sat down. The image of his pacing hung in André's brain. An outrageous thought possessed him: had Raymond been his first gay crush? Over the years his image of that light, nervous stride—almost a gay man's gait—had refused to fade. As Raymond finished speaking, his step changed: he stood like a farmer again, heavy-footed and hunched. André remembered

Raymond's long hair gummed with blood the day they had hurled the Pepsi bottles at Trudeau. He barely heard Marie-Christine say that the walls between Montreal's neighbourhoods were beginning to break down. Already there were young Anglos moving into spiral-staircased walk-ups in the Plateau, bourgeois Québécois buying redbrick English houses in Notre-Dame-de-Grâce.

Raymond scoffed. —That's as *flyé* as meditation.—

André sensed an old fight brewing between them. He saw Raymond's tie lapping over his shoulder as the police dragged him down. How strange to think they had all worn ties back then. How constrained they had been! If he had had a crush on Raymond, he never would have known it.

—A real Québécoise doesn't meditate, Raymond said.

—How can you say that to me? You're not going to move back to Montreal even if Quebec becomes a nation!—

—*I* know where I belong. Besides, I'm too old to march in demonstrations. At my age I'd look ridiculous.—

—André still marches . . . —

—You told me I looked sad, André said.

—Anyway, you should keep your voices down. You'll wake Francine.—

—I am awake! Francine called from behind the partition.

Marie-Christine and Raymond looked sheepish. Marie-Christine disappeared behind the curtain. When she returned the three of them sat close together and spoke in murmurs. André looked at his watch. —I have to teach tomorrow.—

This time no one detained him. Why should they? They did not know the most basic fact about his existence. Raymond and Marie-Christine, and especially Lysiane, had been agreeable Métro stations he had whooshed through on his way to a destination far beyond them. Süleyman's lean body buckled before his face as the night air bit him. The spiral of Marie-Christine's staircase felt infinite.

No, he thought, as his feet struck the sidewalk. He could not separate himself from Raymond and Marie-Christine. So what if his friendship with Raymond had been enveloped in homoerotic yearning? Raymond had lent him Frantz Fanon's *Peau noire, masques blancs* and Michel Tremblay's *Les belles soeurs.* (Neither of them had realized then that Tremblay was gay.) Raymond had urged him to read Lionel Groulx, and had taken him to hear Pierre Bourgault speak. Raymond had introduced him to Lysiane. Neither his obsession with Süleyman nor his awe of François could change the fact that his first serious, adult-sized longing had been for Marie-Christine. He could not belittle this period of his life and still tell his students that history was important.

He shook his head at the thought of Raymond allowing a herd of cattle to control his life. While he ran for the Métro each morning, Raymond was hauling on distended udders!

For the rest of the week there were tests to mark in the evenings and books he should have read years ago that called out to him. He read a new history of the 1837 Patriotes' rebellion and a book on the Kennedy family that had just been translated into French. His hours with Raymond and Marie-Christine felt more and more unreal. He considered breaking the endless silence of the evenings by phoning someone—but whom? He had known, while he and Raymond were exchanging phone numbers, that neither of them would call the other. The thought of talking to Céline or Marie-Christine made him uncomfortable. Süleyman was his dream, but François remained his temptation. It would be so easy to call him. François was certain to make time for him and the odds that they would have sex were high. Yet calling François felt like going backwards; it meant a return to acquiescence with someone else's fantasies. He no longer wished to be with François: he wanted to be like him.

The November nights grew colder. He read and marked. He was afraid to go out to the bars in the Gay Village. What if

Süleyman came while he was away? What if he went into a bar and found Süleyman with another man?

How François would laugh at his paralysis!

One night the buzzer rang. As the building was not equipped with an intercom, he could only lean on the button marked *Porte.* He opened the door and reached the landing as the boy started up the stairs. As always, he carried nothing. His hair was precisely combed, his slacks immaculately pressed; his safety pin had been transferred to the collar of a black leather jacket. His smile widened the mouth that was too broad for such precise, handsome features. He evinced no doubts, no hesitation—no *shame.* The luscious bastard knew that André would take him back.

André had to stop himself from hugging the boy on the landing. Once they had stepped into his apartment he felt a wariness set in. The boy showed no sign of noticing the scattered cassettes on the counter that André had left exactly as they had tumbled. The gesture—part memorial, part accusation—was fruitless. Could anything he did make an impact on Süleyman's blithe face?

—Can I offer you a sherry?—

—Yes, the boy said. —It's been a heavy day. A bunch of scheming Jews are taking over my wife's building. They won't give her the money to move—money she has a legal right to. They broke into her apartment while she was out today and shit on her bed.—

—Shit on her bed?—

—These are Jews from Morocco. I know the type. *Séphardim.* We used to have Jews like that in Istanbul. They don't do business like normal people.—

—It's nice you care about your wife, André said.

Süleyman, catching the irony in André's voice, smiled. It did not take them long to move into the bedroom. André cast away his misgivings with his clothes. His lovemaking with Süleyman was driven by the conviction that it would be wrong to die without experiencing this passion. He received the thought as evidence that he was getting older. The taste of Süleyman's cock became the taste of life. He dozed and woke and reached for Süleyman. When he realized that day was breaking, he shook Süleyman awake. —This time you're not leaving. We're staying here today.—

Süleyman looked amused. He burrowed his head into the pillow. —All right. I don't do much during the day anyway.—

André woke again; it was eight-thirty. To his relief, Süleyman remained asleep at his side. André swung his legs out of bed, lifted the telephone receiver and called in sick. The lecture on the Quebec Act whose ringing lines he had rehearsed in his mind hardly seemed worth delivering. He lay back under the covers and stared at Süleyman's shoulder.

At noon he cooked Süleyman a cheese omelette. Süleyman observed him moving around the stove with a smile. André revelled in the smile's warmth, telling himself all the while that Süleyman's smile did not mean a fucking thing. Tomorrow or the next day, if André let the boy slip through his fingers, he would be smiling at some other man cooking him a cheese omelette. But why not enjoy this pleasure while it lasted?

As they sat down to eat, a lance of pain went through him. —Why did you steal my cassettes?—

—What cassettes?— The boy's face looked beatific.

—Jean-Jacques Goldman, Renaud, Francis Cabrel . . . I woke up in the morning and you'd walked off with them.—

—Do you care about your little cassettes more than you care about me?—

—No. But you shouldn't— —

—You should be pleased to give me a gift. Don't you think I deserve it?—

—You deserve the gifts I give you. This omelette, for example— —

—An *omelette?* That's all I'm worth?— Süleyman pushed back his chair.

—That's a start, André said, laying his hand on Süleyman's elbow, then tightening his grip. He did not let go even after Süleyman shuffled his chair back towards the table. He wanted to dominate the boy, punish him: rough treatment might be the only language he understood. Releasing the boy's arm and digging into his omelette again, André muttered: —You think that because we've fucked you have the right to steal. Who do you think you are? Jean Genet?—

—Was he another of your Québécois nationalists?—

André felt his tension break. It was hopeless. His relationship with Süleyman was wonderful because it was hopeless. That afternoon they fooled around and watched television in bed. As darkness fell, Süleyman's long limbs stirred. —I am worried about my wife, he said. —I must go and see if she is all right.—

—I'm coming with you.—

—You want to meet my wife? Süleyman said with an amused expression. —She doesn't speak French.—

—It doesn't matter.—

Süleyman shrugged his shoulders and allowed André to call a taxi. When the driver rang the buzzer, they went downstairs and sat together in the back seat of the car. The black driver spoke to them in French while listening to a radio program in what must be Haitian Creole. As the cab reached Sherbrooke Street and turned west for the long trip across the centre of the city, André looked around in discomfort. He rarely travelled to the western part of downtown; it was foreign land, occupied territory. Along the south side of Sherbrooke Street ancient light-brown apartment buildings of Anglo-Saxon stolidity asserted their dominance. Here a British colonial eye had allocated the rectangular lawns separating building from street, sketched the slumberous arches of windows, disdained walk-ups and spiral staircases in favour of tunnel-like awnings and heavy double doors designed to insulate from their francophone subjects those who commanded an empire on which the sun never set. André laid his hand on Süleyman's thigh. Süleyman interrupted his conversation with the driver to return the gesture. He felt comforted by the company of these two dark men who shared his foreignness to this part of the city, who spoke to him, and even to each other, in French. In his classroom he caught glimpses of a dawning multi-racial French Montrealness, but did not trust it to last. The warmth of these two men's bodies lent the vision a new certitude. As Süleyman leaned forward over the back of the front seat, his hand nearly brushed the Haitian's shoulder. —Why are you slowing down?—

—On the radio they just said there's trouble on Sherbrooke Street West.—

They had passed through Westmount and were entering Notre-Dame-de-Grâce. The driver gestured with his chin. —Look, there's a roadblock and police. This is as far as we can go.— He peered over the steering wheel. —There are fire engines up there.—

Süleyman's voice turned flat. —That's my wife's building.—

Uma Vida Nova (3)

HE SPENT THE NIGHT IN THE HÔPITAL ST-LUC and returned to the boarding house on foot in the morning. Pain plucked at the second and third fingers of his left hand, held rigid by splints. But when he knocked with his right hand on Agostinho's door, his knuckles tingled with numbness.

—*Há quatro dias que não 'stá*, the landlady said.

Four days! João went upstairs, lay on his back under the sloped ceiling and dreamed about beating Denis's head with a hammer. At this moment the men were cutting, stacking and securing sheets of steel. Who lay curled in his nook? Another immigrant? He turned up the volume on his transistor radio.

—If he's not back by the end of the week, the landlady said, when João got up to shave, I'm sending his clothes to the Salvation Army.—

—We should call the police.—

—No.— The landlady shook her head. —No police.—

João left the house and walked south on Boulevard St-Laurent in search of food. He kept walking until he reached Chinatown. Stepping around crates piled high with silvery fish and women bargaining in abrupt, singing voices, he noticed a restaurant whose French-language sign, below the clumped Chinese characters, read: *RESTAURANT DAME DE CHINE. Repas légers et abordables.* The interior was stark: round tables topped with orange formica, drizzle-like lighting, the decor restricted to a garish pagoda mobile suspended above the cash register. The waitress who approached him was young and very thin, her long black hair pulled back in a pony-tail. She addressed him in English. When he replied in French she did not understand.

He slid around on his chair, preparing to leave. Urgency streaming up in her eyes, she said: —*O senhor fala português?*—

His chest contracted. —*Onde aprendeu falar português?*—

—I grew up in Mozambique.— Her accent was elusive, but there was no doubting her fluency.

—You left after the Revolution? You came here in 1975?—

—*Não, senhor.* I've only been here a year.— Her slender legs stretched for an almost inconceivable length beneath the pleated hem of her uniform skirt. Her flat-soled black shoes were scuffed. —Are you ready to order, sir?—

He ordered the most expensive of the three specials. The waitress departed, exchanged a few words with the older woman seated behind the cash register and disappeared through a swinging door. When she returned with his tea, he said: —Are you all from Mozambique?— It was too good to be true: a Chinese restaurant where everyone spoke Portuguese!

—No, sir, this is my uncle's restaurant. His family comes from Malaysia; only my father moved to Mozambique.—

She spoke with lowered eyes as she arranged his cutlery and paper place mat. She was concealing their conversation from the woman at the counter.

When she brought him his food, his questions failed him. He mixed the vegetables and sweet-and-sour pork with his rice, impatient to learn more about her. She returned with his bill. He said: —Did you move to Canada with your parents?—

—*Não, senhor.* I came alone after my father died. *Estou sozinha no Canada.*—

—I'm all alone in Canada, too. Might we know each other's names?—

—*Boa tarde, senhor. Obrigada.*— She collected his modest tip and sped away towards the counter.

Feeling he had made a fool of himself, João followed Boulevard St-Laurent back up the hill onto the Plateau and turned west towards Le Padrão. He had barely set foot in the bar since he had begun working. The Angolan started up from the table beneath the maps to greet him. João showed off his plastered splints. Soothed by the sketches of the coastlines where the explorers had gone ashore, he said: —I'll get workmen's compensation until my hand has healed. I'm going to take the time to find a job repairing big trucks. I'll make more money in a day than those guys in the plant make in a week.—

Over their first bottle of Sagres, they talked about Agostinho. Midway through his second bottle, João heard himself confessing: —I met a Chinese girl from Mozambique.—

The Angolan stared at him with a boozy leer. João wished he had said nothing.

ॡ ॡ ॡ

The boarding house was silent when he returned. His neck seeped sweat as he stepped in the door. In the darkened front room, he noticed a new wing of shadow.

Agostinho's door stood ajar.

He crept into the room. Agostinho's belongings were gone. His bed had been stripped to the mattress.

The bitch! What had she done with the old man's fishing sweater, his photograph of his son? He tried to clench his fists: his splints sent a dart of pain flying up his left arm. Behind the pain, cushioning it, lay a numbness. He went upstairs, opened his window in a hopeless attempt to escape the heat and fell into a heavy sleep. The thundering of machinery and the clap of falling strips of steel, which in recent weeks had drowned out all other chords in his dream-repertoire, receded before the onset of more precisely etched phantoms. He ran into the street to find it paved with cold tile, his sisters encircling him. Each sister held swaddled babies: three, four, five, six babies each. The babies spilled from their arms, thumped onto the tile and crawled towards him.

When he went downstairs in the morning the landlady sat at the kitchen table. —The old crook finally paid up. He came back yesterday, took his things and left.— She reached for her black coffee. —He said he was in love.—

—In love?—

—Yes! Can you imagine any woman falling in love with that old snake?— She shook her head. —He left his address on the table in the hall.—

João borrowed a pen, copied the information—Agostinho's new address lay about fifteen blocks north—and set off on foot. Two blocks south of Agostinho's street, he stopped in a Lebanese *dépanneur* and bought a copy of *Le Journal de Montréal.*

The address led him to an antique shop. A bronze bell tinkled as he opened the door. The shop was air conditioned. The floor, packed with wooden trunks, high-backed couches, dressing tables and hinged mirrors, was presided over by a tall woman. A thick braid of greying hair bobbing almost to her waist, she was showing a small clock housed in varnished red wood to a woman in her thirties who was wearing a diaphonous blue scarf.

Wrong address, João thought, turning to leave. The air conditioning detained him. Feeling his sweat cool, he watched the woman and her customer bargaining, the owner speaking in a rustic twang, the customer serene and insistent as she whittled down the price.

—I'll have to consult the owner before I can reduce the price, the woman said.

She knocked on a door at the back of the shop. The owner stumped out. He was a tiny man in a sombre black suit and a dark waistcoat with polished brass buttons. He was bad tempered and miserly looking and full of spite.

He was Agostinho.

The woman gabbled the price of the box at Agostinho in her backwoods French, which João was certain the old man could not understand. Agostinho stretched his elfin face into an expression of arrogant appraisal. He scrutinized the box, curled his lower lip, then nodded.

—You're lucky, the woman said. —Most days he'd put his foot down at a price that low.— She set the clock on the table and began to wrap it. —Is this a gift, *Madame?*—

—Yes, for my husband.— The customer stepped forward. —He's renovating an old building. I want to give him something beautiful when he finishes.—

—There's nothing more beautiful than this clock, the woman said. Her braid swinging as she turned to João, she asked: —Can I help you, sir?—

—*Queria falar com Agostinho.*—

—*Quoi?*—

She did not speak Portuguese. He repeated his explanation in French.

The customer slipped her gift into a large floppy bag. As she left, Agostinho stepped forward to shake João's hand. —What do you think of my new clothes?— His voice dropped. —I'm in love!—

—But how do you talk?—

—We work together. We understand each other. Words are not always necessary.—

Showing the old man his wounded hand, João started to tell him about his accident. —Fall in love, Agostinho said, interrupting him. —When you are in love everything makes sense . . . I have discovered that I am still a man. You may not believe it, but I am.— Agostinho's stare blossomed into a curling smile. —We live upstairs in Thérèse's apartment. I varnish furniture, I put up signs and when it is necessary I pretend I'm the boss . . . I came in here, sat down in that rocking chair and decided I was not going to leave. My horoscope had mentioned a propitious encounter.—

João unrolled *Le Journal de Montréal*. —Would you like to hear your horoscope?—

—No—take it away!— Agostinho's hand swatted the newspaper. —I'm happy. It can only bring bad news.—

He walked away. Thérèse ordered him to rearrange the display where the clock had sat. Agostinho, misinterpreting her commands, headed in the wrong direction. Seeing Thérèse's mouth clench, João translated her request into Portuguese. The other two stared at him as though he had intruded on their lovemaking.

—We'll have a drink, João said. —Saturday night at Le Padrão . . . —

Agostinho shrugged his shoulders. They shook hands. João folded *Le Journal de Montréal* under his arm and left the shop.

ের ের ের

—One sweet-and-sour pork special.—

—*Sim, senhor.*— The waitress scratched at her notepad. — Your hand is better, *senhor.*—

—Yes, I start work next week.—

—What work do you do? she asked, keeping her back to the counter, where her aunt perched like a dowdy dowager on a high, padded chair.

—I'm a large-engine mechanic. I fix big trucks.—

She brought him his tea, setting the pot on the table a trifle too hard. Tea spilled onto the orange formica. —*Desculpe, senhor,* she said, wiping with a paper towel. —I'm not really a waitress. In Maputo I managed a shop. My father was in poor health, so I ran the business. But here I must obey my uncle.—

João watched her. She was inviting him to see her as a woman who shared his professional competence. He felt confused, challenged and greeted in equal parts. Uncertain how to respond, he hesitated too long. Her gaze dropped. She turned towards another table.

When she brought him his bill, he met her eyes and told her his name.

She writhed on her long legs. —*Meu nome é Vitória Wong.*—

—*Boa tarde, Vitória.*— He got to his feet, leaving her a more generous tip than the last time.

He could afford to be bountiful. A friend of the Angolan's had put him in touch with a trucking depot on the South Shore. The physiotherapist had assured him that with regular exercise his fingers would regain most of their dexterity. It would be a relief to earn wages again. He ambled into the tatterdemalion humanity of the red-light district where Ste-Catherine crossed St-Laurent, delighted by the ramshackle tolerance of this city that left him alone to become whomever he wished. His realization that he would never be accepted as Québécois had liberated him. Once he had recovered from the physical wounds he had suffered in making that discovery, he would be content. His years in Lyon began to feel like a grinding pretense of trying, fruitlessly, to become French. In Montreal he could celebrate being part of the flotsam of the Portuguese-speaking world. This, among other things, he shared with Vitória . . .

He crushed the thought. During his first days at the trucking depot, it returned. The other men, all Québécois, were shadows whose names he barely bothered to learn. The boss guided him into the garage and showed him the pit. Wider and deeper than his nook in the plant, it filled him with the security of his own increased importance. The first truck which they put him to work on had a faulty transmission. It was an articulated six-wheeler: a short-wheelbased tractor unit designed to tow a two-wheeled trailer. Peering up at the unit's underside, he hesitated. Where was the worm shaft? And the intermediate shaft, with its two universal joints and sliding joint, that coupled the worm shaft to the rear axle? He ran his gloved index finger around the casing, probing the angled bars and riveted joints. The tractor's unit casing was fixed to the frame. He tried to make sense of the design. A train of gears relayed the drive down to the bottom shaft, whose ends were coupled via universal joints to the bevel pinion shafts of the axles. The bevel pinion shafts were mounted with short torque thrust tubes. That was why there was no sliding joint: the tubes rendered it unnecessary.

He flew to work, fascinated by the difference between European and North American design. North American trucks were more powerful, but European trucks, like European people, had greater adaptability. The pleasure of mastering a new design invigorated him. The first week he worked from seven to four. By the second week the boss was asking him to work overtime. Other men grumbled about wives and families and hockey games on TV. João was happy to come in on the weekend. He earned time and a half and double time, piling stacks of extra dollars onto his handsome wage. Taxes bit into his pay cheque, but the figures he punched into the banking machine when he deposited his cheque late every second Thursday night continued to amaze him. One evening he looked at the balance printed on his transaction slip and thought: what do I want? He decided to move out of the boarding house. In Montreal, he learned, a tiny financial margin divided privation from prosperity. For three hundred fifty dollars a month he rented a bright, airy furnished three-room apartment. He could take showers both before and after work. He no longer had to endure the landlady's Beira voice shivering Mother's moaned prayers through his bones. He could invite workmates home for a drink, entice women back to his bed. In reality, though, he did not make friends at work and restricted his drinking to infrequent visits to Le Padrão. A month after moving into the apartment, he glanced at the relentlessly rising total on his transaction slip and again asked himself: what do I want?

He realized that more than two months had passed since he had eaten at the Dame de Chine Restaurant.

൪ ൪ ൪

He rocked in a café chair on Boulevard St-Laurent. Vitória was half an hour late. She was not coming. He closed his eyes, straining to recall the expression that had lighted up her face as she had agreed to meet him. He had entered the Dame de Chine tired but content and ordered straight off the menu, forsaking the specials. A moment passed in tensed recognition, neither of them daring to speak. She had broken the silence.

—*Há muito tempo que o senhor não janta aqui.*—

—I've been working hard at my new job.— He rolled his hand over the curve of his paunch, trimmed and hardened by hours in the pit. —I've moved into a bigger apartment. And you, *senhora?*—

—Still working for my uncle and aunt. Never working for myself.— Her thin face glowed. —In Maputo my father slept in the back of the shop and raised vegetables in the *machamba* and I took the decisions.—

He stared after her as she disappeared through the swinging door into the kitchen. She returned with his tea. Pouring his first mug, she spilled it, then reached around him to mop it up. The odour of her body grazed his nostrils: a dense, undefinable smell. All through his meal he thought about Agostinho and his antique shop owner. *Fall in love!* If the old Azorean could find a woman, then he, a man in his prime earning handsome wages . . .

When she brought him his bill, he fumbled in his wallet. —Will you meet me for coffee? he asked, staring at the dull orange formica. —When are you free?—

For an instant, he was certain, her face had glowed. She had accepted with a nod, taut cheeks flushed. Then the line of her mouth had grown firm. She shot a furtive glance over her shoulder at the dowager on her padded throne. They whispered times and places, settling on a café on Boulevard St-Laurent on Sunday evening.

He had been sitting here for over an hour. She had been supposed to arrive forty minutes ago. The waitress circled, asking him if he wanted a second coffee.

—No, he said, climbing to his feet. He left her the skimpiest of tips. No more women, he thought. At least when he had been living in the boarding house, that temptation had been off limits.

Out on the sidewalk a slender woman raised her hand, waving at someone behind him. He lowered his head.

—*Senhor!*—

Vitória's thin legs appeared to trail in the wake of her angular torso. She was wearing bluejeans and a narrow-shouldered sweater. During their previous conversations he had been sitting and she standing. Free of her uniform, she radiated threatening female complication.

—Thank you . . . for waiting . . . — Her breath came in gasps. She was a few centimetres taller than he, but her height was in her legs. If he opened his arms, he could envelop her.
—My uncle and aunt . . . they always try to keep me at home . . . never go out on my own . . . in Maputo . . . —

—My sisters in Portugal never let me out of their sight. I had no freedom until I went to France.—

A cluster of young people rolled past, laughing in loud English. He had never talked to Flore about his sisters.

—I had my freedom when I was young, Vitória said, and now I've lost it.—

They returned to the café and found a table at the back. According to her uncle and aunt's plan, Vitória said, only marriage would liberate her from waitressing. They brought home young Chinese men who were afraid of her because she had been raised in Africa. Her would-be suitors insinuated that she might be infected with the AIDS virus. And, to a man, they were dull and bossy. They were seeking wives who would greet their every murmur with compliance.

She met his eyes. He managed not to look away.

—If only I'd moved to Lisbon!— Africans so poor they wore strips of cardboard on their feet instead of shoes arrived at Lisbon airport to be welcomed by the Portuguese authorities.

If she had disembarked with the money she had made selling the stock in her father's shop on the black market—money that duty had obliged her to turn over to her aunt and uncle upon arriving in Montreal—she could have established herself in comfort. She had accepted her uncle's invitation to Montreal because she had been told that Canada was modern. She had never expected to find herself shackled by tradition.

—Didn't your parents observe Chinese traditions?—

—It wasn't the same. I grew up African. In Montreal my family has remained Chinese. By the time I was in my teens the Chinese community in Maputo had dispersed. We were among the few to remain. We had friends in the government; we became Mozambican . . . — Portuguese-speaking Indians from Goa and English-speaking Indians from Tanzania, Portuguese from Portugal and Portuguese born in Africa, Chinese from Indonesia and Chinese from Malaysia, English and Greek merchants from Zimbabwe, blue-black Africans from the interior and fine-boned coastal Africans whose ancestors had been the children of Arabs or Malays: as he listened, she ticked off on her long fingers the types of people found in her country.

The African provinces, João thought, remembering Father leaning close to the hull of the radio. —It's not like that here—

—But it may become that way. Not for my aunt and uncle, but for me and you.— She blushed. —I mean for people of our generation.—

João was too charmed to speak.

—There was too much suffering in Mozambique, Vitória said. —By the time I left people were starving, the South African attacks never stopped, the luxury hotels along the beach where we used to sell fruit and meat to the restaurants had been taken over by squatters. My parents were dead and I was lonely. I thought it would be good to have a family again. I forgot that you have to give up your freedom to have a family.—

—It's been so long since I had a family . . . —

They left the café at ten o'clock. He had to be at work on the South Shore at seven the next morning. He was putting in eighty-hour weeks in the pit. The totals the banking machine printed on his transaction slips staggered him. He was making as much money as a doctor or a lawyer. As the weather grew colder, it became more difficult to rouse himself from his bed in the morning. He hobbled through the day on the crutch of thoughts of Vitória. They met every Sunday night in the back of the café. Vitória's hair gleamed black. Her anger towards her family grew less pungent with regular airing. She longed to scandalize her uncle and aunt by leaving the restaurant and going into business for herself. By the fifth or sixth time they met she was making mordant jokes about her captivity. One evening João persuaded her, on her way back down Boulevard St-Laurent, to visit his apartment. He waved at the small rooms. —It's bright during the day.—

—It's larger than I expected, she said. —Thank you for showing me your apartment.— Stuttering goodbyes, she walked towards the door.

He began to invite her in each time they met. By mid-winter they had dispensed with the café and were meeting in his living room. He dreamed about Vitória in unexpected moments. One evening, as he thought about her, he was surprised by an erection. The next night he burrowed into his pillow. He must safeguard his freedom. But when Sunday night arrived he was pacing the floor an hour before she rang the buzzer.

One night in January he held his breath and kissed her on the cheek. Blushing, she turned away. His heart thumped. She cut a circle around the room, sat down on a stool and asked him to fetch her a Sprite from the refrigerator. He blundered into the kitchen feeling devastated. When he returned to the living room, she greeted him with a smile, reaching out to accept the glass. Yet the smile, trembling with chaste affection, stopped short of an invitation.

CR CR CR

In March he woke to feel a shift in the weather. He lumbered out of bed, the pit wavering before his eyes like a phantasm. Not until he reached the bathroom did he become aware of the numbness that had taken over his limbs. His arms dangled at his sides like lengths of limp rope. He reached for his shaving cream. His right hand brushed his thigh, setting off a small tickle of sensation in his leg but no corresponding feeling in his fingers. The shaving cream lay untouched on the ledge of the sink. He reached for it again; a soft object tapped his leg.

He could not raise his hands.

He watched his face contorting in the mirror, fear compressing his bristly cheeks into inert grey pouches. The desperation in his pupils, flickering at him from the mirror, pumped hot panic through his body. His frightened whimper escalated into a scream.

He careered into the living room. The touch-tone phone lay on a low table. He fumbled and jabbed with inert digits that refused to do his bidding. 9.1.1. He crouched on his knees and bellowed his illness into the overturned receiver.

CR CR CR

—Stress, the doctor said, leaning over his hospital bed. —You've got to stop working eighty-hour weeks. Relax a bit. Learn to enjoy life and you'll feel fine.—

By the time they sent him home, four days later, he could dress, flush the toilet, prepare simple food. But any activity that required working above the level of his shoulders was impossible. He could not shave or replace the light bulb that had burned out in his bedroom. He felt a deep-seated sickness inside him. Three days later his arms were once again dangling limp. This time the doctor X-rayed his spine. By the end of the week he had reached a diagnosis. Syringomelia. João's spinal chord had ruptured, opening up a long, asymmetrical cavity which had filled with fluid. The initial symptoms varied, the doctor said, but he could expect his hands to shrivel; the disease was nearly always progressive. Contrary to what João had at first understood, "progressive" meant that his symptoms would inexorably worsen. It meant he was going to die.

He rejected the diagnosis. His ailment was not overwork but the fact that he no longer cared what happened during the remaining minutes, hours, days, years of his life. It was indifference that enabled him to work eighty-hour weeks. Moments passed during which he believed that his growing, wary devotion to Vitória would fill him with a sense of purpose.

Vitória stopped in three evenings a week to shave him. The touch of her fingers on his cheeks was the most soothing, sensual experience of his life. He loved watching her pile her hair on the top of her head before she set to work with her warm lather. Sometimes she did his shopping or cooked him a meal. He paid for the ingredients: generous unemployment cheques, the ghost of his lofty wages, had begun to arrive. Her thin body moved about his kitchen, her slender limbs filling his apartment with affection. Presenting him with a plate of *xima*, she would say: —My mother always said this was one African food Chinese girls should not eat because it makes our stomachs stick out. You can imagine what I thought it would do to me!— She bent over him. —Get better, João. We'll open a garage. I can keep the books and speak to the English customers and you can do the rest.—

—And your family?—

Her despairing blush defeated her. She shrugged her shoulders.

He turned the idea of running a garage with Vitória over and over in his mind.

On each visit she brought his mail. The shoulder-high lock on the mailbox downstairs defied his efforts to open it. Most of the time he received only commercial flyers and utilities bills. One day there was a letter from his sister Gabriela. After ploughing through two pages of indigestible family news—his sisters' children, whom he had never met, were starting to marry and have children—he read a line that filled him with leaden dread: a neighbour who had been working in Lyon had returned for Christmas carrying a letter for João from a Frenchwoman. He pulled the smaller, sealed envelope out of the larger one and turned it over in his numb hands. When he opened it, his fingers collided with a photograph: a black-haired little girl smiled out at him from beneath the coal-smudges of her eyebrows. She had Flore's lean face, his sisters' round cheeks, a resilient wave in her hair that might have been his. The letter, written in Flore's scrawl, was a plea for money. *Ta fille a besoin de toi, Jean. It's your duty to support her.* His daughter's name, he learned, was Béatrice. A senseless name. He would have called her Gabriela.

He stuffed the letter under his mattress. His days dragged by. Some evenings he woke to the trill of the buzzer. He struggled to his feet and leaned his shoulder into the button next to his door to let Vitória into the building. Each week it became more difficult to pretend that he was regaining his strength. One evening, feeling entombed by loneliness and panicked despair, he asked her to accompany him to Le Padrão.

As they set out beneath the gaslight-style streetlights of Avenue Duluth, the sight of Vitória's rangy profile loping at his side invigorated him. His short legs carried him forward. He could do it! He could walk to Le Padrão on his own two feet.

His face grew sweaty as he struggled for breath.

Vitória walked more slowly. —You're very ill, João. *Você está muito doente.*—

—*Não tem importância.*—

She kept walking, glancing up at the glaring cross on top of the Mountain. —How much farther? she asked, as they reached Boulevard St-Laurent.

—Not far.— He struggled towards the crooked, wanly lighted door halfway up the sidestreet. The sign above the door brought him to a halt: *Le Monument.*

—Is that it? Vitória asked.

He pushed her aside. The doorhandle felt clammy against his palm. Inside, the Angolan slouched behind the counter. His unkempt mustache, longer than João remembered, spread across a face drained to pale haggardness. His usual post beneath the navigators' charts stood empty. The maps had disappeared: the delicate lacework coastlines of Brazil, Angola, Timor, Macao, Goa, São Tomé, Cape Verde, Guinea Bissau and Mozambique had been paved over with beige wallpaper.

João staggered. The Angolan rushed around the end of the bar, but it was Vitória who caught him. Together they lowered him into a chair.

His vision blurred. The Angolan leaned over him. —I threw out a drunken Québécois customer and he complained to the language police that none of the writing on the maps was in French. I got a phone call . . . —

—They ordered you to change the name? João said.

—No, the Angolan said. —I didn't hear from the inspectors again. But I was afraid. After what I went through in Angola, I don't take chances. So I papered over the maps and changed the name so that if they came to inspect my business . . . —

—But it's not the same! João said. —*Um padrão* is much more than a monument. There's no French equivalent.—

The Angolan shrugged his shoulders. —I don't know French. I learned English when I came here.—

—You could have fought!—

—Sometimes you can't fight. Sometimes you realize history is going to change you. That's what happened to us in Angola.—

—And to us in Mozambique, Vitória said.

So I'm really going to die, João thought. This shard of a culture he had been inhabiting was destined to disintegrate.

Every individual, and every cultural variation that brought the individual to life, disappeared in time. I thought that my life would begin when Vitória and I got our garage. But all the rest, all that chaos—that was my life.

—João . . . ! Vitória said.

—I want to go home. I have to make a decision.—

—Drink a Sagres, the Angolan said. —You'll feel better . . . —

—*Faz favor, senhor*, he heard Vitória saying to the Angolan. —Call him a taxi.—

He regained consciousness as they helped him into the back of the cab. He let his head droop on Vitória's shoulder. She caressed his hair. Family, in spite of the straightjacket it imposed, was the most important consideration . . .

—You've got to get better, João. When we open our garage we'll be happy. A garage or a shop . . . I could manage the business . . . —

She helped him up the stairs and out of his clothes and rolled him into bed.

—I have to go. My uncle and aunt . . . Promise me you'll call the doctor . . . João! Answer me!—

—I'm thinking, he said.

She kissed him on the cheek, then on the mouth. Her long black hair drew a pepper-like odour across his eyes and nostrils. —I'll come and see you as soon as I can. Please call the doctor, João. You should be in hospital.—

After she left the blackness thickened, plunging him into a cavern filled by the terrifying brevity of his own existence. When he woke it was late afternoon. He gathered the strength to struggle to the toilet. He returned to bed and slept. That evening, groping beneath his mattress with hands that obeyed his wishes as slowly as salamanders, he dragged out Flore's letter. The springs had cut white wrinkles in the snapshot, rearranging the girl's smile into a truncated grimace. Vitória had left his wallet on his bedside table. He turned it upside down. His most recent deposit slip fluttered out. Printed across the *solde mis à jour/updated balance* box was the figure: $**96414.62.

I have to make a decision.

The next time he woke he rolled out of bed, then fell flat on his face on the threadbare wall-to-wall carpeting. His daughter's photograph stared at him from a spot an arm's length beyond his reach. A long time later he dragged himself to his feet and collected a pen and a notepad from the living room. As he returned to the bedroom, his strength deserted him.

He woke at dusk, his nose pressed into the notepad. He sneezed, wrenching a crick in his neck. The pen remained clutched between his fingers. His hands would never again repair the engine of a large truck. In a month, maybe sooner, he would lose the power to write. He let his head slump onto his arm. The impulse to burst into tears swept through him, evaporating before a ray of determination. He must start to write; there would be time later to telephone the Angolan to witness the document.

Imagining each pained stroke of the pen as a step in the reassemblage of a dismantled engine, he called up his best Lyon French. The sun was setting over the Plateau, turning the wooden combs of the walk-ups across the street into black heralds rimmed with fire. In the streets outside he dreamed that he could hear the sound of parades.

João wrote:

24 June 1989

I, João Gonçalves, declare my wish to bequeath my worldly possessions, including the contents of my savings account, CIBC448998291003692, to Mlle. Vitória Wong of the Dame de Chine Restaurant, 7B Boulevard St-Laurent, Montreal, Quebec, Canada . . .

ten

Marcel-Teddy-André-Marcel-Teddy-André

—THE BASTARD FLEW IN LAST NIGHT WITHOUT TELLING ANYONE.—
His hand brushed the spicebox as he replaced the receiver and
burrowed towards Maryse beneath the covers. He pushed his
arm around her shoulder. —He found his mother's village.
There was nothing there. The people he met refused to believe
that Jews had ever lived there.—

Maryse cuddled against him, her limbs drowsy with sleep.
He envied her ability not to snap awake at first light. —Do you
want me to come and see your renovations?—

—Definitely. We should do it while Abitbol's too jetlagged
to cause trouble.— He stared at the ceiling. —I've got to clear
the building . . . The black woman is close to settling. The
Turkish woman wants to leave, but her husband is never there
to sign. The other three are fanatics. I don't know what to do
about them.—

—Come on, *mon beau juif,* I can't believe you don't have a
plan up your sleeve.—

She rolled her seal-sleek weight against him and gave him
a long, musty morning kiss on the mouth. Clambering atop
him, she traced the lines of his neck and shoulders while her
short legs gripped his trunk. —This is nice, she whispered. —
You tell me everything now.—

—Yes, you're the person I tell everything to.— The grit behind his eyes dissolved into a stinging sensation. His throat clogged with feeling as his penis prodded erect. The conversation begun by their voices was taken up by their bodies; Maryse's fingers eased him inside her. He heard himself crying out as their flesh slapped together. He felt dizzy with gratitude at this rediscovery of the woman who shared his home. Tensed urgency concentrated their latent, everyday knowledge of one another, transforming familiar baggage into toeholds for understanding. I'll never do this with another woman, he thought, as the core of his body surged into hers. They collapsed alongside one another, still entwined. Her pummelled-looking face settled on his shoulder. Infidelity was a stage, a bad habit he had outgrown. He might always need outlets for parts of his life Maryse was unable to share, but the outlets would no longer be other women's bodies. Was this what happened when you turned thirty? He had not expected to be engulfed by contentment.

They woke an hour later, showered and dressed and went downstairs. The welcoming green spaces of Maryse's painting, now framed and hanging on the wall, greeted him as he entered the living room. On the drive downtown they discussed the renovation plans. *Our* plans, he thought. Leading Maryse down the yellow-tiled corridors of the building on Ste-Catherine, he begged her not to judge his office too harshly.

—You'll have other offices, she said.

He pointed out his desk and resupplied himself with tenant release forms. As they were sauntering towards the door with their arms around each other, the telephone rang. He hesitated a moment before answering.

"Marcel?" a rough-edged voice said. "Marcel, this is Bob. I just want to wish you a nice day."

He laughed and hung up.

—You see the kind of people I'm dealing with, Maryse? Lunatics and sadists.— Marcel slammed down the receiver.

—Shhh.— She laid her hand on his arm. The telephone rang again. —Let's go, Maryse said.

They stepped into the hall, locking the door on the squealing phone. Nervous agitation bubbled through him all the way out to N.D.G. He watched Maryse's manicured nails caressing the navy-blue silk of her scarf. The thumping pressure in his chest returned, wringing out sweat on his forehead.

As he parked next to the curb in front of the Victoria-Waterloo, Crawford approached. "Am I glad to see you! We just had all hell break loose here."

The building loomed up over his shoulder, a silent, battered relic amid the roar of the Sherbrooke Street traffic. A discarded hammer lay on the Waterloo steps. The platform for the sandblasting crew, three planks sagging across metal scaffolding, stood abandoned. "Why aren't the men working?"

"The inspectors came. One of the tenants found out the guys were non-union and reported us. It was like a goddamn drug bust. The car pulls in and out come these mean-looking sons of bitches with clipboards. They block off the stairs and the guys have to jump."

"What do you mean 'jump'?" Marcel asked, glancing at Maryse.

"They jumped from the back of the second floor. Landed on the lawn of the house up the hill. Fucking Korean family didn't know what hit them. The guys just downed tools and high-tailed it. Everybody made it except Gratien. He jumped like the rest, but the guy's my age. You can't blame him for breaking his leg."

"Have you called an ambulance?" The sweat plastering his hair to his forehead began to tickle the space between his eyebrows. The cool imperturbability of Crawford's face was irritating him. He wanted to be alone with Maryse. He could feel her tensing up beside him, looking straight ahead through the windshield.

"The really bad news," Crawford said, "is the fine. Five hundred bucks per working day, retroactive to the beginning of the conversion. With an additional fine per worker per day to be assessed later."

"We can't pay that!" He caught Crawford's arm through the window of the car. "Send Bruno to see me." As Crawford nodded, Marcel leaned towards Maryse. —Please be patient, *chérie*. I swear this is not how I wanted it to be.—

—Take your time, Marcel. *Ça ne me dérange pas de patienter un peu.*—

—*Merci! Merci!*— He kissed her. She continued to stare through the windshield. Once he had taken two steps towards the building, his rage came coursing back. Six months he had been planning Maryse's tour . . . ! He thought about the fine. It would run into tens of thousands of dollars. He wouldn't pay, of course. He would delay and prevaricate and contest the charge; he would be as tenacious as his tenants. But Abitbol would be furious.

Bruno met him on the Waterloo steps. The bags beneath his eyes had grown deeper. Brought to attention by Marcel's haste, he said: —I trashed an apartment yesterday.—

—Which apartment?—

—That goddamned Turkish bitch's place. She drives me crazy.—

—Forget about the women! Marcel said, as they crossed to the Victoria side of the building and climbed the gloomy, sawdust-powdered staircase. —The women are going to leave. Focus on the men. They are our enemies. And this is the worst of them, he said, knocking on Bob's door.

The door jumped open. Bob stood in a grey suit and a wide red tie. His black mustache broke down around his mouth. He withdrew a hand from the doorpost to nestle his marmalade cat in his arms.

"Good morning, Bob," Marcel said. "I'm here to wish you a nice day."

"We're gonna ream you, Marcel. You're gonna have to pay me ten thousand bucks to get me out of here."

Marcel slapped Bob's face. He hadn't realized he was going to do this. The sudden satisfying winching of his shoulder muscles, completed by the stinging in his palm as he made contact with a meaty report, yielded to a feeling of revulsion as his hand lingered on Bob's greasy cheek. How could he offer to Maryse a hand that had touched this scum? Cut yourself in half, Abitbol had said. But the two halves must come together again.

Bob's cat curled its head forward and buffed its ears with a moistened paw.

"I will pay you two thousand dollars and you will leave tomorrow. Do you understand?" He pulled his hand back again.

Bob shook his head. "I didn't call the inspectors, Marcel, I swear. It was Adriana. But you won't get her. She took off. Her parents are packing up her stuff."

"If she vacates her apartment without signing a release form she forfeits her rights."

He peeled off a release form, filled in Bob's new apartment number and the figure $2000.00 and handed him the sheet. As Bob lifted his arm to receive the form, the cat took refuge on his shoulder.

"Sign the sheet and give it to Bruno. I'll come back and write you a cheque. If you don't sign, I'll tell Bruno to kill your cat."

He walked around the building to burn off his anger. Adriana's door hung ajar. Inside the walls were bare. Two middle-aged men were rolling up posters. Open cardboard boxes stood around them on the floor. Knocking, Marcel said: "Is Adriana here?"

"Adriana go home. This is no place for a girl. A good girl she live at home."

"Of course, sir," Marcel said. "You are absolutely right, sir." He paused, watching the two men work. "Do you think you will finish moving today?"

"We finish today," the man who had spoken before said. He smiled. "We finish in time for supper."

"Very good, sir. You can leave the key on the window ledge. Have a good day."

A lightness piping through his veins, he crossed to the Waterloo side of the building. Two down; only one difficult tenant remained. He followed the corridor to the back of the ground floor and knocked on the Anglo's door. No reply. He shrugged his shoulders and walked out to the pay phone on the corner. —Sylvie, he said, when the office phone was answered, promise me you will not tell Abitbol what has happened. It's going to be all right. I've almost finished clearing the building. If Abitbol calls in, tell him to get some rest. I'll talk to him this even— —

—But what's happened? I didn't understand, *Monsieur* Crawford was speaking English— —

—Just tell Abitbol the situation is under control. He'll ruin everything if he interferes.—

—I can't hide things from him, Marcel.—

—*Sylvie! Je t'en prie.*—

—Just do your job, Marcel.—

He put down the receiver in anguished silence.

The workers were beginning to return to the front steps. Bruno was loitering in the Victoria entrance. —He wants till this afternoon to sign.—

—If he doesn't sign, Marcel said, you will kill his stupid cat.—

—It'll be a pleasure.—

Marcel gestured towards the young men smoking on the steps. —Write down their names. Find out where they were working before the inspectors came and send them back to their jobs. We're going to have to figure out a way to keep the renovations going without Gratien.—

Exhausted, he turned towards the car. —Can I see the model apartment now? Maryse asked.

—*Bien sûr, ma chérie.* Your patience is marvellous.—

He ushered her through the crouching workers, revelling in their envy at his possession of a woman too fine for their nicotine-stained nails and callused palms. They climbed to the model apartment that had been prepared on the top floor of the Victoria side of the building. At last he was alone with Maryse, showing her the monument he was building to her good taste. When the sandblasting resumed, it sounded far away.

Maryse examined the model apartment. —It's got superb potential, she said. —If only we could put in another window.—

—Maryse! he said, more delighted than exasperated. —We have a budget to respect.—

She wanted turrets at the corners of the top floor. Her other suggestions, such as a sloping hood covering the back of the building as a storage and garbage area, delighted him with their blending of elegance and practicality. When she spoke of dual arches framing the front doors and of installing skylights in the top-floor apartments to elevate them to luxury status, he tried to calculate how much these innovations would cost.

Before he could notice the time passing, it was one-thirty. —Let's have lunch downtown, he said. On his way out of the building he checked with Bruno, who told him that all but four of the workers had returned. That solved the labour problem. There was still the question of the rewiring job that had been left incomplete by Gratien's injury. —Fire the men who haven't come back, he said. —And I want you to make sure Bob signs the release form.—

Bruno met his eyes. —I'll make sure.—

He drove downtown with Maryse. They ate at an Italian restaurant on Rue Crescent. Lunch spun itself out to two hours. When the plates had been cleared away they held hands across the dark green table cloth, waiting for their cappuccino.

—It's going to be a very beautiful building, Marcel. You should be proud.—

His eyes stung. He couldn't reply.

—Our house in Outremont will also be a beautiful building, she said.

She was off again, plans and visions percolating up in her high, perfectly trained voice. They returned to the Honda and drove back out to N.D.G. The clustered election posters in front of the old English apartment blocks resembled shiny hoardings presaging the completion of an enigmatic building project. The sight of the workers sandblasting above the Waterloo door made him realize it was time to drive Maryse back to Ville St-Laurent.. —Let me see how things are going, then I'll take you home.—

He had expected her to remain in the car, but she followed him up the steps of the Victoria side of the building. As they entered the corridor the ceiling lights flickered and went out. A moment later they came back on. They began to shudder like guttering candles.

—The foreman hasn't finished the wiring, Marcel said. —I need to find Bruno.—

He led her outside, then up the steps and in the Waterloo door. The clocks having been turned back, chill November dusk was already flooding the street. Asking Maryse to remain in the entrance, he hurried upstairs to the room where he had found Bruno playing solitaire. The room was empty. The lights kept flickering. He could feel his achievement eroding by the minute in Maryse's eyes. He rushed back downstairs, hooked his arm in hers and said: —We'll take one more look in the Victoria. If I can't find him, I'll drive you home then come back later to get rid of the Anglo and make sure Bob signs . . . —

—*Fais-toi-en-pas, Marcel,* she said, shuffling her pronouns into the colloquial order she permitted herself only when among friends. —Please don't worry.—

As they entered the Victoria corridor the lights went out again. A voice broke through the darkness in ranting, barely comprehensible English. Marcel felt himself shudder. He took

Maryse's arm, leading her into the gloom. Sliding his fingers down her forearm to hold her hand, he felt her pulse press his thumb. Or was it his pulse? It was impossible to tell.

The lights came on. Bruno stood with his hands planted on his hips, watching Bob, who had edged into the hall, confronting a familiar thick-set figure. "Three thousand dollar I give you," Abitbol said. "You sign now!"

—*Non!* Marcel shouted.

Abitbol turned. He had cropped his dark curls short, giving them a grizzled appearance. His seamed face had soaked up a harsh-grained desert darkness. The baggy black jacket he wore over his white shirt and cotton T-shirt looked as wrinkled as a garment worn on a day-long bus journey. He gave a furious hop and swore at Marcel in Judeo-Arabic. Marcel felt himself gobbled up and annihilated by Abitbol's rage. —I told you to have this building cleared by the time I got back!—

—It would be cleared if you didn't interfere. This man is settling for two thousand.—

—I am giving him three thousand. The important thing is to get him out, not to squabble over small change.— He turned to Bob. "Three thousand dollar, yes?"

Maryse, her presence unnoticed by Abitbol, retreated. Her profile had turned pale and brittle.

"Okay," Bob said. "Three thou and I'll get out of here in a week." He pulled on the knot of his tie.

—*Très bien*, Abitbol said. —Pass me a release form, Marcel.—

—I am not your delivery boy.—

—Give me the form!—

Marcel pushed the sheets towards him. He could not look at Maryse.

"Hey, Marcel," Bob said. "Three thousand smackeroos! I reamed you."

Marcel broke forward. Bruno's hand seized his wrist, holding him back.

—Let me go or you're fired, Marcel said. —*Lâche-moi.* I'm your boss.—

Bruno turned towards Abitbol. Signing the release form with lowered eyes, Abitbol murmured: —You can let him go, Bruno.—

Marcel shook himself free. —You have no right . . . —

—As of now, Abitbol said, I am running this conversion.— He passed the release form to Bob. "Sign please, sir."

—The building's almost empty, Marcel said. —You're not giving me a chance.—

—I've given you months. I gave you a job when you failed your exams. I gave you a house to live in. When will I stop having to give you things?—

Marcel could feel Maryse, standing behind him, staring at the floor. He longed to soothe her, to feel the touch of her hand.

Abitbol slid Bob's form into the inside pocket of his jacket. He withdrew the drooping tongue of his cheque book, wrote out a cheque and handed it to Bob. He and Bruno growled at each other in throaty Judeo-Arabic phrases. Their burly, low-slung bodies propelled their words past him half a head below the level of his ears. Marcel, though he understood, was unable to join in the conversation. —Bruno says all the Waterloo tenants are in, Abitbol said. —The black woman who has agreed to leave, and the two recalcitrants. Let's finish this job together.—

That was as close to an apology as he was going to get, Marcel thought, as they moved in a cumbersome convoy down the hall. Outside, isolated figures picked their ways along the street through the first chill of winter. Marcel slid his arm around Maryse. Her hips felt stiff. —Do you always let him treat you that badly? she whispered.

Unable to think of a reply that would not make him sound pathetic, he remained silent as they entered the Waterloo side of the building.

His first glimpse of Hetty reassured him. Another touchstone of his experience, another instant of shared pleasure: her dark brows and close-cut black hair made him feel less alone. She was walking with furious haste. As the swinging door hissed shut behind them, he realized something was wrong.

She seized the sleeve of his denim jacket. "Are you happy now that you have shit in my bed? It is not enough to come on my sheets, you must also shit on them!"

He was too bewildered to speak. Abitbol's baffled look reflected his confusion back at him. Hetty's grip prevented him from turning around to see Maryse.

The line of Hetty's mouth trembled as she drew his face closer to hers.

"Is your husband here?" he asked, unable to throw off the paralysis that was creeping over him. Why could he not summon up one of Abitbol's tirades to dismiss this accusation? The sound of the sandblasting, even the sound of the traffic on Sherbrooke Street, had faded away.

"If my husband were a man he would kill you." She pushed him in the chest with the flat of both hands. "Is that why you never came back after we made love? Because you think I am shit?"

—Bruno! he said, whirling around. —What did you do to this woman's apartment?—

His voice was a stifled creak. He knew, before he turned around, the drained, papery look he would see on Maryse's face. She was retreating with hesitant steps, watching him from beneath lowered lids that hung like shields protecting her from the pain of full sight. He could not work out whether she was seeing him from some hideous new angle or whether she did not want to see him at all. He crawled after her, his limbs too feeble to match the inexorable pace at which she was stumbling through the swinging door. Her earrings glinted from the other side of the glass panel as the door closed behind her.

He had humiliated her. He had not felt so frightened since the day his parents died. The blackness of Fes el-Bali obscured the lenses of his glasses. He felt dizzy with the odour of effluent, the coursing of putrid gutters, the sight of gaunt men working naked to the waist in mud-floored factories, brown men whose hands were white from repeated dipping in vats of tanning fluid.

He followed her as she headed down Sherbrooke Street. Abitbol shouted at him twice, then fell silent. He saw a taxi stand at the corner of a pharmacy. Maryse crossed the street and entered the taxi. *Non*, he thought. Only when it was too late did he start running.

He sprinted across the street, the cold air catching in the bottom of his lungs. The taxi pulled into the Sherbrooke Street traffic and drove away.

Bruno was touching his shoulder. —The boss says you have to come back.—

—She'll never come back.—

Bruno slid his arm through Marcel's elbow. —It's important.—

—I'm coming.—

They walked back to the Victoria-Waterloo in silence. He saw that the reason the sound of the sandblasting had stopped was that the workers were packing up to leave for the day.

As Bruno opened the front door of the building, Abitbol, looking strangely hunched, was commiserating with Hetty in broken English. "We have boy to work . . . Sometimes very bad boy . . . I am very sorry, *Madame . . .* "

Hetty, looking oddly touched, ignored Marcel's return. The lights began to flicker. It's less than fifteen minutes by taxi to her parents' house, Marcel thought. In fifteen minutes I can call her.

—I am going upstairs to inspect the damage to this poor lady's apartment, Abitbol said, his pugnacious face leaping in and out of the darkness. —Could you please do something about the lights?—

Marcel took a glance into the street. The lights went out. He longed for them to stay out. He did not want to open his eyes again until he saw Maryse in front of him.

—The lights! Abitbol said.

Marcel walked to the end of the corridor. The dampness rose through him as he made his way down the stairs. He ducked under the lintel. Blackness swamped him. The smell of shit nearly knocked him off his feet. He bumped into the boy's cubicle. Where had Gratien been working? He opened his eyes as wide as he could. Silence—not even the muted sound of traffic he would hear living alone in the house in Ville St-Laurent. It took a long time for his eyes to adjust. Finally he saw that the darkness was not absolute. He could move forward. As he began to walk, his stomach flipped over. For a moment he was certain he was going to vomit. A beehive bundle in the darkness caused him to raise his hands. Next to the first bunch of wires he found a second cluster dripping through the opening in the ceiling. Gratien had peeled back the rubber casings from the two sets of wires—in preparation for splicing them? Had the operation been interrupted by the arrival of the inspectors? Was that why the light was flickering? Because the red and blue wires were hanging in separate clusters?

Reaching up, he drew the wires with the red casings close to the wires with the blue casings. Opposites must come together: that was how people cut in half became whole. He jammed the heads of the red wires against the heads of the blue wires.

A shudder of magnesium-bright sparks jostled in front of his face. He was no longer afraid. Nothing could be more frightening than Maryse walking towards a taxi. The blackness of Fes el-Bali had deserted him, chased away by a gust of laughter. The flopping powerlessness of his arms was hilarious. Sparks cascaded over him in an oceanic gush and still he could not release his lifeline of humour. He heard his laughter echoing around the basement. Above him the sparks haloed a rotting beam. The overlap of blue and red acquired substance as the beams began to glow. Flickering teeth of light ate into the basement darkness.

Marcel laughed and laughed.

"Yo!" a voice shouted. "What you *doin'*, mon? Are you crazy?"

A long stick hit him in the ribs. The second blow, catching him on the elbow, made his forearm go numb. He had lost his grip on the line of laughter. As he fell to the ground he saw that the light continued to glow as the red and blue wires fell apart. The stick came down on his shoulder. It came down on his head. He tried to push himself towards the light. The stick came down on his head again.

ଓ ଓ ଓ

"She's gone, Teddy!" Bob said. "She called the inspectors, then she split."

"Where did she go?" His half-closed fist lingering above the shiny "12" on Adriana's door, Teddy wished Bob would go away. He did not want to talk to anyone. He was not even certain he would be able to talk to Adriana. His mind had become a vast pit where events dwindled to tiny incomprehensible echoes.

"Back to Park Avenue with Mama and Papa and all the Greek cousins. You better forget about her, Teddy. You ain't gonna see little Adriana again."

"I just wanted to thank her for calling the inspectors."

"Yeah, are them Ayrab Jews ever pissed. We sure reamed them, eh Teddy?"

Bob turned away, patrolling the empty corridor like a chesty little coastguard boat smacking against high seas. The silence had begun to crack as the workers returned from their hiding places. By the time Teddy stepped out of the Victoria entrance, the sandblasting was resuming. On the Waterloo steps Zorro was directing two men to return to the apartment where they had been removing paint. He did not look up as Teddy walked past. The shape of the corridor enveloped Teddy; he saw the long walls reeling past but could not perceive the gloom between the walls. The frame of the door rose up in front of him, yet when he reached for the handle his knuckles grazed the wood. What would he say when Vircondelet came to persuade him to leave? Was there any point in holding out for money merely to torment Vircondelet? Yet after all this effort— his time, the lawyer's work, Adriana's organizing, his neighbours' endurance—giving up felt like a betrayal. *You will always be provided for,* his grandmother had said. Too much pressure. He reached for his key.

He ran his fingers over the shiny new "7" on his door. Lucky seven. A movement at the bottom of the stairs caught his eye. Glancing down into the basement, he saw Rollie ducking out of sight. A moment later Rollie's head returned. "Yo!" he said.

"How're you doing?" Teddy said.

Rollie climbed the stairs, his wooden stick striking the marble. Stooped forward in a black autumn jacket far too thin to withstand the coming winter, he looked like a conflation of a blind beggar, a back-country shepherd and the grim reaper. He stopped on the top step, his breath coming in short stabs. His light brown face looked yellower than before. "Wh'appen blood? What's the bangarang?"

"My friend called the inspectors and got them into trouble. But it's no good. It's almost over." His voice flowed in a grumble from deep in his chest. He was surprised to find that he wanted to talk to Rollie. He wished they had spoken more often. "You're going to have to find somewhere else to live. Everything's almost finished."

"Ain't got no place to live. That old man he built me the only yard me have."

"They're going to tear down your clubhouse. The renovations are almost finished."

"Cho! They naa tear down me yard. They no soke wi' me. They come down here, me jook them."

"You need to think about somewhere else to live."

"You too, mon."

"That's different. I've got . . . a job," Teddy said, averting himself from uttering the word "money."

"Don't make no difference. We're all gonna need someplace else to live." Rollie glanced down the corridor. The sound of the sandblasting keened higher. Rollie lowered his head. He returned to the basement without saying goodbye.

Teddy's mood dived as he closed his apartment door behind him. His conversation with Rollie felt unfinished. Adriana's disappearance chipped away at him. Like Janet, she had left without saying goodbye. He lay down on his cot. The sounds of the sandblasting faded. The workers' boots marched down the corridor to the street. Later the sound of raised voices in the corridor roused him from his doze. He waited for Vircondelet. The young developer was probably the only person in the world who wanted to talk to him. Tomorrow he could return to work, talk to his students in artificial textbook English, deflect the disapproval of Pia and the boss and hope that he held onto his job. Unable to summon the energy to get up and turn on the lights, he stared into the advancing darkness.

When he woke again, someone was knocking on the door. An unfamiliar, French-accented voice shouted a single alarming word. He must have heard wrong. But as he sank back into the gloom, the word returned: "Fire!"

ೞ ೞ ೞ

They got out of the taxi, skirted the police line and passed behind the crowd on the south sidewalk of Sherbrooke Street. André watched Süleyman jog ahead of him, looking for his wife. Cold air encircled his collar and streamed down his spine. He had only set foot in Notre-Dame-de-Grâce twice in his life.

English voices shouted everywhere, their cries battering him. He saw Süleyman's head bobbing above the crowd. It struck him, as though for the first time, that Süleyman was a *husband*. Even if he did not make love with this woman, they remained man and wife.

So many voices he only half understood. Was this still his Montreal? Three fire trucks were lodged across the middle of the street, an *Urgences Santé* ambulance parked behind them. Hoses wound across the tarmac like fat black arteries. The revolving light of a police cruiser swabbed the faces of the crowd and the glimmering pools of water. In the cruiser's headlights the shiny black tires of the nearest fire engine looked as though they had been coated with lacquer. The apartment building was a typical redbrick Anglo block. Two dwarf balconies projecting from the upper floors had caught fire. Hooded firefighters barraged the front of the building with water, sending up hissing rings of smoke. The musty pungency of doused ash, mingling with the sour smell of sodden, scorched brick, permeated the air.

Süleyman returned, his face twisted. —I've found her, she's lost everything. Her thesis. She's lost two years' work.— His breath came in hoarse gasps. —I need some time with her.—

He left without waiting for André's reply. André spotted an empty bench and sat down. In front of him a Québécois police officer was waving his arm and ordering the crowd to move out of the street; working in English, just like Papa.

A black woman wearing a scarf on her head herded two small children out of the crowd. The children looked entranced by the sight of fire engines and police cars; their mother was gulping down tears. She seated herself on the bench. Bundling the children against her, she settled herself closer to André. She hauled the youngest child onto her lap. She was pushing against André's hips, nudging him towards the end of the bench. Let them into your country and they want to take over, he thought, refusing to budge.

"Come on, mon, I've got children here. Move over a little, you can accommodate! You go to some black-people country, they treat you like a goddamn king!"

He stiffened his muscles. He was not going to speak English in Montreal. That was how it had begun with Papa: he had spoken English to his foreman at work and soon he had been trying to speak English to his sons over the dinner table. This was his place: he would talk to immigrants who learned his language. As the woman leaned into him again, he said: —*S'il vous plaît, Madame,* I have the right to sit here too.—

"You French people. Can't you learn English?"

Before André could reply, a fat man with a shiny pate rushed up. "Mrs. Austin, are you okay?"

"We lost everything," the woman said.

"I lost my cat. I don't know where he is. My stuff's all gone, but I got my cheque. Three thousand dollars—"

André got to his feet. Where was Süleyman? The Québécois police officer continued to gesture towards the sidewalk. A small crowd had surrounded him. Motioning to her children to remain on the bench, the woman with the scarf went to join the argument.

"No! That boy go away. He no here." A man in a funereal suit scythed his arms in front of the officer. Two francophones speaking to each other in English! André stared at the gathering. As he watched, the conversation switched into French. Speaking with native fluency in a North African accent, the man in the poorly tailored suit said: —He moved out last week. My brother-in-law was the last person in the building.—

—Rollie? the police constable said. —Rollie put a brick through my window.—

—He's lying, a young Anglo said, in fluent but artificial-sounding French. —I spoke to him an hour ago. He is still living in the basement.—

He kept walking, peering through the moving mass of people, until he saw Süleyman standing with his arms wrapped around a dark, slight woman whose crumpled face squirmed with tears. They clung to each other beneath a streetlight, oblivious of the crowd. He backed off, uncertain where to look. A tremendous heaving crack struck the crowd silent. The smoke had thinned. Sheets of flame polished the window panes a vivid orange. A vertical fault-line cleft the sooty brick between the two front doors. The fissure widened: a brick jarred loose and fell to the sidewalk. As it hit with a smack, the police raised their arms to contain the pedestrians. A window burst in the heat. The building's interior was being consumed. André did not move for five minutes, perhaps ten, as he watched the building teeter towards destruction. The interior melted away. He became aware that only the walls remained intact, thrusting up into the cold night like the gristly exoskeleton of a rearing, eroded insect. More bricks dropped away, striking the sidewalk with a hail of splintering reports. The two halves of the building heaved apart, contracting in the heat. A deafening rain of bricks came down. The firemen scattered. The two husks, the moment they split from one another, lost all recognizable form. He watched them crumble into piles of rubble.

୯୫ ୯୫ ୯୫

Can you hear me, Marcel? Words in his father's language: the language he understood but could not speak. *Father,* he said, always so tall I never knew whether he noticed me. Then he was gone as though he did not see I was there to be brought up like any other boy.

The face was not his father's. It belonged to Abitbol.

—Maryse, Marcel said.

—Maryse is fine.—

—Let's go, one of the men behind Abitbol said.

Marcel began to cough. The light suturing the blackness had been driven out by acrid-tasting heat. The men behind Abitbol came forward to crouch on either side of him. They caught him under his armpits so that his arms fell across their shoulders. He felt himself being hoisted towards the low ceiling. Charcoal filled his throat. The milling blackness stung his eyes. He searched in vain for the bunches of red and blue wires. The more he searched the sharper the pain in his eyes became and the more difficult it was to breathe. His feet fumbling the floor as the men hustled him forward, he thought: my glasses. When he swung his head back to look for them, blackness rushed over him.

He woke as he was being dropped onto a stretcher in the corridor.

—Somebody sure gave him a wallop. Is there anybody else down there?—

—No, Abitbol's voice said, the tenants have moved out.—

—Who hit him?—

—A crazy boy who was squatting down there. He ran away.—

—We need to be sure . . . —

One of the orderlies fell to his knees next to Marcel's stretcher, coughing and coughing.

—We *need* to get out of here, Abitbol said.

They picked him up and ran. Through the blur of his sight, he watched the ceiling of the corridor unfurl above him. Here he had been a boss, an accountant, an engineer, a decorator, a lover, a husband. Had he been Maryse's husband for the last time? If only she realized he would not betray her again. It was simply impossible: they were settled now. All he wanted was Maryse . . .

The shock of the edge-of-winter night air made him sob as they burst into the street. He was surrounded by voices and lights. The cold impaled him. He could not see properly. The red strobe of a police cruiser squandered its gaudy glow as it passed across the side of a fire engine. Broad streaks of colour, shadowed figures stumbling back as the orderlies shouted at them to get out of the way. His face was frigid with tears. He could see the yellow rectangle of the *Urgences Santé* ambulance approaching. With a breath-scooping lift, they swung him inside. Sound dimmed, the voices growing more distant. Long, cool fingers probed his skull. They found a tender patch, making him cry out.

—How many fingers?—

—Three? I'm not sure. I've lost my glasses.— He sat up on the stretcher. A firm hand pressed on his shoulder. —No, I'm fine. I just need some air.—

—I think you're in shock, sir.—

—I'll stay in the ambulance. I want to sit closer to the door.—

—If you need air, we'll give you oxygen . . . —

—I need to hear the voices.— He edged forward until he was sitting on the end of the stretcher, looking out into the fuzzy-edged confusion. An orderly's hand touched his arm, then desisted.

"Move back, please. Get well away from the building."

—It is my building, Abitbol said. —I am the owner.—

"Constable Beauchamp!" a West Indian woman's voice said. "There's a boy still inside."

"What boy?"

"The boy in the basement. You know that boy!"

"No!" Abitbol said. "That boy go away. He no here." —He moved out last week. My brother-in-law was the last person in the building.—

—Rollie?— the officer said. —Rollie put a brick through my window.—

—He's lying, the Anglo said. —I spoke to him an hour ago. He is still living in the basement.—

—He's the one who's lying! Abitbol shouted.

"What are you all talking about?" the woman said. "That boy's still in there."

—I'm sorry, sir, you must lie down on the stretcher. We're taking you to the hospital for observation.—

—No, he heard himself creak. Why was he crying? The doors closed and he began to cry harder. They gave him an injection. A sharp prick, then a horrible false calm carried him away.

It was nearly eleven o'clock when Abitbol picked him up at the hospital.

—How much do you remember? Abitbol asked, as they climbed into the BMW.

—I went downstairs to check the wiring . . . —

—No, Abitbol said, turning his key in the ignition. —How much do you remember about Morocco?—

—Morocco is not my life. My life is here with Maryse.—

—Tonight you almost lost your life. I sent Bruno downstairs to see how you were doing with the lights. He found that boy hitting you. If Bruno hadn't stopped him— —

—Did Bruno kill him?—

—Bruno stopped him from killing you. The fire will do the rest.—

—He may not even have been dead! How could you tell the police . . . ?— He gasped down pebbly tears as Abitbol stopped at the traffic light at the summit of Avenue du Parc. On the left the wide-winged angel statue ascended into the black bulk of the Mountain. *We are accompanied by angels . . .* He knew what his father would have said in this situation. —It's wrong to lie to prevent a body from being discovered.—

Abitbol, hunched over the steering wheel, regarded him with fury. —We would have lost everything, Marcel. I have not worked for twenty-five years to have my family destroyed. Our place in this city is worth more than that. Would you inflict poverty on your sister and Louis and Madeleine?— He shook his head as the parks on either side of the avenue gave way to closed souvlaki houses and pizza parlours. —Bruno will leave the country. That will be the end of it.—

The end, Marcel thought. Too many sources of anguish: the tree-lined streets of Outremont muffled his vision. Maryse would be only a few blocks away, drinking coffee with her mother. As soon as they reached Abitbol and Véronique's house, he would phone. *Mon beau juif,* she had called him. Maryse, let me continue to be your handsome Jew. We're on the brink of success: the money is getting better, I'll never need another woman. We'll be back in Outremont by Christmas, I'll go to *réveillon* with your family, I won't make you suffer through my observances on the *Chabat.* For you I will be a ghetto Jew and dance, for you I will be a banker Jew and contribute to your proud old line, for you I will conceal my bloated pain no mind can understand. Just lend me your elegance, don't take away your wonderful Latin warmth: so few people value sentiment in this cold country. As soon as we get in the door, I'll phone.

Abitbol pulled the BMW into the driveway. As his feet crunched over the chipped pink rock, the door opened. Véronique came out and hugged him. —I'm so glad you're safe. Marcel, we can't afford to lose anyone else in this family!—

He embraced her. In the end, there was only family. But his family should include his wife.

When they entered the house Véronique paused in the foyer. Observing him with an uncertain look that pulled wrinkles in the high forehead rising above the rims of her glasses, she said: —A package came for you, Marcel.—

—When?— Hope flared, brighter than any flame, amid the crushed ashes of his heart.

—A couple of hours ago. A very elegant woman in a black car . . . —

—Maryse's mother?— His breath caught. Among Maryse's relatives, her mother was his constant ally.

—Yes, I think it might have been. Of course I only met her at the wedding . . . Just a moment, I'll get you the package.—

The package was wrapped in plain brown paper. He tore it open and reached inside. There was no letter, no note. There was nothing but the spicebox.

He held the box at arm's length. It contained no message. The compartments behind the tiny wooden doors remained as empty as they had been when the box stood guard on their bedside table. His unfocused eyes smeared the carven, painted arabesques and delicate filigree into an uneven glow.

She must have taken the taxi straight home to Ville St-Laurent, then carried the spicebox back to her parents' house in Outremont. There could be no retreat from such a calculated gesture. Not with Maryse. Other women might return gifts as a call for attention, but Maryse did not demand attention: she demanded respect.

His arm shook.

—What is it? Véronique said.

—It means she's not coming back.—

—But what's happened?—

—You tell her, Marcel said to Abitbol. He carried the spicebox past Véronique. The walls of the upstairs hall felt too narrow. He shut himself into the guest room and set down the spicebox next to Madeleine's discarded Ken doll. He waited for the enormous tearing to rip him in two.

The drugs in his system suppressed his emotions. Sitting on the bed, he imagined he was watching his body pitching down the Lachine Rapids. Feeling foamed through him without making an impact. As long as he stayed in this room, this house, he would be insulated from his pain. He dreaded the moment when he must return to the chilly streets as a man who had been married to a marvellous *Montréalaise* only to lose her. Any glimpse of elegance would be a source of agony. He had never set out to deceive Maryse, but there was no single life that fit him. No matter whom he was speaking to, the core of his being defied articulation; in any situation part of him remained alien, hungering for other perspectives.

The door opened. Abitbol came into the room. —Your sister thinks you are a fool.—

—Yes, I'm a fool! But it's more complicated than she realizes.—

—I know that, Abitbol said. He lowered his weight into an armchair covered with a teddy-bear pattern. —When I was in

Casa I met a prostitute. *Elle m'a abordé* . . . I wouldn't have tried to pick her up. 'Do you want to make love?' she asked. Now no man can say no to this question . . . —

—I don't want to hear this, Marcel said.

—But you're always trying to get me to talk about women!—

—Not tonight. Tonight I want you to stop talking to me in French. I need to hear Judeo-Arabic.— He faltered, tried to formulate a sentence in the language his father had spoken and realized he could not do it. Frustrated by his inability to feel or express his anguish, he said: —I have reached a decision. When I marry again, *if* I marry again, my wife will be a Sephardic Jew.—

ଔ ଔ ଔ

—He *is* in there! Teddy said, hearing English tones slicing through his French as he strained to make the policeman believe him.

—This boy is a troublemaker, the man in the baggy suit said, in an accent stronger than Vircondelet's. —I can't even tell you all the trouble this boy has caused. He just wants to make problems for people.—

—Me, a troublemaker! Teddy said. —My family has been in Canada— —

—I'll talk to the firemen about it, the constable said. —Now you all have to move back from the building. Please. Everybody on the sidewalk. Get off the street, please.— He waved his hand, motioning to Mrs. Austin. "Move along, *Madame*. On the sidewalk, please."

Teddy pushed himself in front of the police officer, his knuckles brushing the hard paraphernalia of the cop's equipment-laden hip. —You have to go look for that boy, he said. —He could disappear and nobody would notice.—

"Move along, sir."

"Nobody cares about that boy."

"I will alert the *pompiers*. Please move back, sir."

Teddy shuffled backwards. A shout went up as one of the tiny third-floor balconies plunged flaming into the street, hitting the north sidewalk with a two-tone crack half metallic and half stoney. The railing keeled over onto the balcony's burning wooden floor.

"Come on," Mrs. Austin said, tugging Teddy's sleeve as she walked towards the south sidewalk.

Teddy watched the yellow *Urgences Santé* ambulance ease around the end of a fire engine. A policewoman opened the cordon crossing Sherbrooke Street to let the ambulance depart. On the north sidewalk firemen with hoses were surrounding the burning balcony. Teddy sloshed through a puddle banked against the south sidewalk that elongated the flames into molten light.

He slid his jacket off his shoulders and dropped it into the shimmering light.

"Why'd you do that?" Mrs. Austin. "Now you're gonna be all wet and cold."

"I'm an idiot," Teddy said. He picked up his sodden jacket. "I'm going to see a friend."

"That's right," Mrs. Austin said. "You do that. We all need our friends at a time like this."

Holding his dripping jacket in front of him, Teddy stepped onto the sidewalk. His pace quickened as his conviction grew firmer. He ducked behind the file of rubber-necking pedestrians, passing through the shadows between their backs and the red brick low-rise buildings on the south side of the street. As he had suspected, the police cordon ended at the corner. He crossed to the north side of Sherbrooke Street and started up the slope. A marmalade cat was miaowing miserably in the middle of the street. The back of the Victoria-Waterloo was deserted.

The fire looked less severe here. Only the total absence of light in the building suggested that something was wrong. The lawn of the two-storey brick house behind the Victoria-Waterloo rolled down nearly to the ledge of Teddy's window. A narrow concrete path, barely as wide as Teddy's shoulders and closed off by a wiremesh fence, divided the lawn from the apartment building.

The quickest route was through his own apartment.

The wiremesh pressed into his shoulder. As he reached his window, his foot kicked against a pile of bricks. He heard Rollie's voice: *Me pitch a brick through Beast Beauchamp's window.* He picked up a brick and, turning his head away from the window, heaved it through the pane. The glass shattered with a more brittle, jangling report than the sound the wooden spar had made. Smoke poured out of the hole in shockingly enormous, foul-tasting clouds. Teddy backed off, waiting for the smoke to pass. It kept coming and coming. He threw another brick through the window to enlarge the opening, then a third brick. Smoke was everywhere. He crouched down on his knees and let it roil over his head. The lights were on in the house up the hill, he was seeing more clearly than he had in days, but there was no sign the residents had noticed the release of smoke. Breathing in sparing gasps from the cavity formed by his arms and chest, he ground his eyes shut. When he opened them for an instant, the stinging felt less painful. Was the smoke thinning? If he was going to do this, he would have to withstand a little smoke. He wrapped his soaking jacket around his head and threw his leg over the window ledge. The parquet floor creaked under his feet just as it had when he was living here. Guiding himself by memory, he walked through the apartment, suppressing thoughts of belongings he wanted to save, and opened the front door.

The doorhandle was so hot he had to pull his hand back inside his sleeve to open the door. Smoke enveloped him. He fell to his knees, coughing and coughing. To his surprise, he began to shiver. He sneezed, shaking loose the shawl of his jacket. Smoke gouged his eyes with unbelievable pain. He jammed his eyes shut, wrapped the jacket tighter around his head. He bowed his head close to his chest, clamping his mouth closed and willing himself not to breathe. Smoke forced its way up his nostrils. Trapped in absolute darkness, he hoped that enough moisture remained behind his eyelids to salve the pain of his seared eyeballs. Entering the corridor felt like stepping inside a wood stove. Heat spread under the collar of his shirt, radiated over his shoulders and back. He must hide in the basement. It was cool down there. He reached out with a leg and found the top step. He was breathing from an air pocket wrapped inside his jacket. The jacket was no longer soaked, yet his urge to sneeze returned. He could feel dampness inside his ears offsetting the baking in his eyeballs. He entered the basement. The smoke felt thicker. The rasp of cinders paved the inside of his throat. The fabric of his shirt felt like hot ash. His ankles itched. In the blackness, panic nearly overcame him. There were moments you couldn't pull back from; moments when you could only go forward. He fought through the smoke. Memories of women crowded in on him: was this his life passing before his eyes? Behind these images lay the promise of a cool funnel of snow. Then, realizing he was on his knees, he thought: no death. Terror caught him. He whimpered into his jacket. He thrashed to his feet and felt his breath polluted with hot specks that scorched his throat. He fell over, struggling to hold his eyes and mouth closed while he coughed. His body hit a wooden plank and he realized he had bumped into Rollie's clubhouse.

"Ahh!" a voice said. Perhaps it was merely the creaking of timbers, the sound of the Victoria-Waterloo devouring itself with heaves that broke through the roar of the burning. The groan came again. Teddy peeped between the folds of his jacket, which had turned as hot and dry as a bedouin's turban. The flaming ceiling beam provided a wavering, menacing light. For a second the flames lighted up the door of Rollie's clubhouse. Teddy pulled the door open. His eyes jammed shut, he reached out and felt a warmth that was comforting rather than aggressive, the texture of Rollie's boney face taking shape beneath his hands. His fingers slipped on a pad of blood. More moans. Coughing and coughing, he moved his hands down Rollie's body. The wooden stake lay broken in two against Rollie's side. His body contorted into a paroxysm of coughing and panic—he might die here, he might really die—Teddy shook Rollie until the groaning grew louder. He dragged the boy's face against his. Coughing until he thought the bottom of his lungs would shear into slivers, he gasped: "*Go out through my window.*"

Rollie give him a kick as he scrambled to his feet. Teddy heard him spitting, then hacking. He wrapped the useless jacket around his face and, wretching from the bottom of lungs too dry to perform the acrobatics of a cough, he started after Rollie towards the stairs. He fell on his side, his body twisting. His mind ceased to rage, growing as cool as snow. The jacket dropped away from his face. Smoke tortured his eyes as he squinted at the ceiling. Flames sabred through the smoke, eating up the beam with a roar. He heard the beam moan and saw it sag towards him.

ভ ভ ভ

Long after the fire had burned low and the crowd had dispersed, Süleyman and his wife clung to each other beneath a streetlight. "Go home!" the Québécois police officer shouted to the few remaining spectators. "Move along! If you didn't live here, please go home."

André looked in the direction of Süleyman as the officer approached him.

"Hey," the cop said, "do you live here?"

—*Non*, André said, *je r'ntre chez moi, moi.* As for me, I'm going home.—

The Basement (2)
Uma Vida Nova (4)

VITÓRIA HAD BEEN MANAGING THE REAL ESTATE OFFICE for almost three years when she won the contract to represent the Montreal interests of Commercial Properties, Inc., (Hong Kong), with offices in Tokyo, Singapore, Vancouver, Sydney, Los Angeles, New York, São Paulo, London and Berlin. The company's first Montreal project, a pagoda-roofed apartment building in Chinatown, made a profit. Commercial Properties increased its investment in Montreal, giving Vitória more work than she could handle. She could barely spare a moment for her French lessons, workouts at her club, or weekend visits to her aunt and uncle. Her loft condominium overlooking the cobbled streets of Old Montreal was a place where she slept but spent little time.

The most modest of the company's projects, which she neglected in favour of buildings where more money was at stake, involved the construction of a new condominium block on a vacant lot on Sherbrooke Street. The original building on the property had been destroyed by fire. The rubble had been bulldozed and the lot fenced off with high, blank boards.

She parked her Volkswagen Passat against the curb and got out, her waved hair curling against her collar, her black leather boots and black jacket elongating her body in a way that she knew made her more intimidating to the men she did business with.

She met the foreman at the corner. "The day we came in with the bulldozer," he said, "there was a kid squatting here. We had to kick him out before we cleared the rubble. But now there's something else I have to show you."

He handed her a yellow hardhat. She slid it on and followed him to the spot where the backhoe had been excavating the basement. "They took out the first few loads and then we hit this."

He pointed at a charred, splay-limbed outline which drew an off-kilter black star on the light dirt. It reminded Vitória of the cave paintings she had visited during her vacation in France last summer. She stepped closer. Flesh and features had been annihilated. All that remained was the powdery, blackened sediment of bones sketching a charcoal diagram of a man.

"Looks like somebody got caught in that fire." The foreman lowered his voice. "Look, ma'am, we've got a choice. We can report this and have cops and journalists crawling all over the place and get a year behind schedule. Or I can tell them to start up the backhoe again and we can pretend we never saw this guy."

Vitória cast a glance at the form etched into the dirt like the shadow of a man in a pit. "Tell them to start the backhoe."

ACKNOWLEDGEMENTS

For their close readings of earlier incarnations of this novel—some of them twice its present length—I am grateful to Nino Ricci, Tom Henighan and Michael Carroll. I thank Elisabetta Cassese for provocative commentary at a time when the novel was stuck, Kalowatie Deonandan for making it possible to submit the manuscript while the author was out of the country and Al Forrie at Thistledown for his support. Many friends and family members helped with suggestions or logistical assistance. The Ontario Arts Council provided financial backing.

This is the third of my books to be edited by Seán Virgo. Seán's role in helping me polish my work has never been greater than it was here. I owe a huge debt to his marvellous engagement with this novel's characters and language.

—*Fulham, Suffolk, Whitechapel: 1988-1989. Montreal: 1990-1992. Oxford: 1993. Guelph: 2000- 2002. Antigua Guatemala: 2003.*

Nominated for the Governor General's Literary Award for *When Words Deny the World*, **STEPHEN HENIGHAN** is also the author of two previous novels, two short story collections and a widely praised travel memoir. He is a frequent contributor to magazines such as *Geist* (Vancouver), *Matrix* (Montreal), *The Times Literary Supplement* (London) and the *Bulletin of Spanish Studies* (Glasgow). His work has been published in eight countries. Henighan teaches Spanish American literature in the School of Languages and Literatures, University of Guelph.

ACKNOWLEDGEMENTS

For their close readings of earlier incarnations of this novel—some of them twice its present length—I am grateful to Nino Ricci, Tom Henighan and Michael Carroll. I thank Elizabeth Crosby for provocative commentary at a time when the novel was still in its infancy; Kathleen Donaldson for making it possible to submit the manuscript while the author was out of the country; and Al Forrie at Thistledown for his support. I am also thankful that, in these days of shrinking legislation and commitment to the Ottawa arts Council, provincial funding is strong.

This is the third of my books to be edited by Seán Virgo. Seán's role in helping me polish my work has never been greater than it was here; I owe a huge debt to his marvellous engagement with this novel's characters and language.

—*Fulham, Suffolk; White Eagle: 1988/1989. Montreal: 1990/1992.*
Oxford: 1993. Guelph: 2000–2002. Antigua, Guatemala: 2003.